THE PENGUIN CLASSICS

FOUNDER EDITOR (1944–64) : E. V. RIEU

Editor: Betty Radice

MAGNUS MAGNUSSON is an Icelander who has been resident in Scotland for most of his life. After a career in newspaper journalism in Scotland, he now works as a freelance in television, specializing in history and archaeology on the BBC 2 programme 'Chronicle'. He studied English and Old Icelandic at Oxford University, and his hobby is translating from Icelandic, both old and new. With Hermann Pálsson he has translated four Saga volumes for Penguin Classics: *Njal's Saga*, *The Vinland Sagas*, *King Harald's Saga*, and *Laxdaela Saga*; in preparation is *Gisli's Saga*, and future plans include *Grettin's Saga*.

HERMANN PÁLSSON studied Icelandic at the University of Iceland and Celtic at University College, Dublin. He is now Reader in Icelandic at the University of Edinburgh, where he has been teaching since 1950. He is the author of several books on the history and literature of medieval Iceland; his most recent publications include *Legendary Fiction in Medieval Iceland* (with P. Edwards) and *Art and Ethics in Hrafnkel's Saga*. Hermann Pálsson has also translated *Hrafnkel's Saga*, *Laxdaela Saga*, *The Vinland Sagas* and *Egil's Saga* for the Penguin Classics.

NJAL'S SAGA

TRANSLATED WITH AN INTRODUCTION BY

MAGNUS MAGNUSSON

AND

HERMANN PÁLSSON

PENGUIN BOOKS

Penguin Books Ltd, Harmondsworth, Middlesex, England
Penguin Books, 625 Madison Avenue, New York, New York 10022, U.S.A.
Penguin Books Australia Ltd, Ringwood, Victoria, Australia
Penguin Books Canada Ltd, 2801 John Street, Markham, Ontario, Canada L3R 1B4
Penguin Books (N.Z.) Ltd, 182–190 Wairau Road, Auckland 10, New Zealand

—

This translation first published 1960
Reprinted 1964, 1966, 1967, 1970, 1971, 1972, 1974, 1975, 1976, 1977, 1979

—

—

Made and printed in Great Britain
by Hazell Watson & Viney Ltd,
Aylesbury, Bucks
Set in Linotype Pilgrim

CONTENTS

INTRODUCTION

Njal's Saga is the mightiest of all the classical Icelandic sagas. It was written in Iceland by an unknown author in the last quarter of the thirteenth century – somewhere around the year 1280, as nearly as can be deduced; and, from the outset, it has always been regarded as the greatest of the vast, uneven, and (to the English-speaking world, alas) largely unfamiliar prose literature of Iceland in the Middle Ages. Its early popularity can be seen from the fact that more vellum manuscripts of *Njal's Saga* have survived than of any other saga (twenty-four, some of them very fragmentary). Succeeding generations of Icelanders have endorsed this immediate affection, and the reputation of the saga has emerged enhanced from 150 years of rigorous scholarly examination.

Njal's Saga is an epic prose narrative about people – people who lived in Iceland, intensely and often violently, some 300 years before this saga was written. It would be as misleading to call it a history as to call it an historical novel. The saga is broadly based on authenticated historical event, its material is drawn from oral traditions and occasional written records, but it is given life and force and significant artistic shape by the creative genius of its anonymous author. The original manuscript of the saga has not survived; the earliest extant MS. is from *c.* 1300, that is to say approximately twenty years later. Our text of *Njal's Saga* is, according to latest scholarly opinion, two or perhaps three removes from the original.

Readers unfamiliar with Old Icelandic literature may find it helpful to be shown *Njal's Saga* in its historical perspective; for it was written at a crucial period of Iceland's early history, both literary and political, which had an important effect on its composition.

Iceland was discovered and settled by land-hungry Norsemen late in the ninth century A.D. – some 400 years before *Njal's Saga* was written. It was the last convulsive movement of peoples in the great Scandinavian migrations that had already sent Viking ships to Russia, to the British Isles, to France, even

9

to North Africa. But Iceland, let it be said, was never a Viking nation, in the popular conception. This new nation, a composite of settlers from Scandinavia and the Norse colonies in Ireland and the Hebrides, numbering at most perhaps 60,000, quickly established a unique parliamentary commonwealth (in 930), which finally broke down only a few years before *Njal's Saga* was born. It is difficult to believe that the author was not affected by the events of his lifetime – the years of savage internal strife, murderous intrigues, and ruthless self-seeking power-politics that led, in 1262, to the loss of the independence that her pioneers had created. It had been an independence based on law and the rights of the individual – 'With laws shall our land be built up but with lawlessness laid waste,' as Njal says in Chapter 70. In an age where his land had indeed been laid waste by lawlessness, the author could look back to an age which must have seemed truly heroic in comparison, when a man's pride and honour were more dearly prized possessions than wealth or even life itself. There was strife enough between men, yes; but it was strife over human principles, not politics.

Alongside the progressive deterioration of civil order and integrity in Iceland there had been a compensatory development of literary awareness. Vernacular prose-writing in Iceland started in the early years of the twelfth century, functional and fragmentary at first, but growing steadily in output, in craftsmanship and stature and artistry. The written language was exercised strenuously and extensively on all the familiar subjects of medieval literature – saints' lives, historical chronicling, treatises, translations of foreign books on religion, philosophy, poetry, education, astronomy, travel. . . . But as well as this mass of 'applied' learned and literary activity, of what one might call 'official' literature, there was evolving a unique type of literary entertainment called saga. By the end of the twelfth century, sagas were being written about life in Iceland from the earliest stages of her history down to contemporary times, as well as biographies of the past and present kings of Norway. Saga-writing grew apace throughout the thirteenth century, with such great achievements as *Heimskringla*, *Egil's Saga*, *Laxdæla Saga*, and *Gisli's Saga* as well as a host of others; and at the apex (but not the end) of saga development came *Njal's*

Saga. It was an age of writing with no disengagement between literature and life; Snorri Sturluson (1179–1241) was the leading political figure of his day as well as a great historian, poet, and saga-writer. The author of *Njal's Saga*, too, seems, on the internal evidence of the saga, to have been urgently aware of the larger events of his own day.

This awareness of his times is constantly reflected in the saga, superficially in the numerous echoes of contemporary persons and events, but more significantly in the capacity of his experience. And when he came to apply his own personal experience to the major tragic issues of the tenth century, the essential craftsman's tools were already to hand – a literary form sufficiently developed to contain this tragedy, and a literary language sufficiently sophisticated to express his own complexity, his irony, his vivid observation, his dark and brooding intelligence of fate.

*

It is impossible to summarize briefly the 'plot' of *Njal's Saga*. At its core is the tragedy of the influential farmer and sage, Njal Thorgeirsson of Bergthorsknoll, who with his family is burned alive in his home by a confederacy of enemies. The long tale of events that lead up to this, and the consequences of it that spill over into many of the countries of Europe, form the central theme; but it is a theme with innumerable ramifications.

It starts on a quiet note with a group of people, neither particularly good nor particularly bad, who, because they are the way they are, clash with each other; not violently, but sufficiently hard to cause ill-feeling. This casual ill-feeling is transmitted to kinsmen and descendants, to friends and to allies. More and more people become involved, with fatal results – first Njal's great friend, the heroic Gunnar of Hlidarend, and then Njal himself and his four sons. The early actors of the drama fade out, but the troubles they have started now seem to have a life of their own, until the action is galloping headlong, with brief tantalizing pauses where control seems to have been momentarily asserted, from minor mishap to major tragedy, until finally its inevitable impulse is exhausted in the last elegiac chapter.

The saga opens with the betrothal between Hrut and Unn (c. 960). We are also briefly introduced to Hrut's niece, Hallgerd, with an ominous reference to her 'thief's eyes'. Hrut delays his marriage in order to visit Norway to collect a fortune he has been left there; and this attempt to improve his position is, in a way, the spark that lights the powder-trail to the burning of Njal, fifty years later. For Hrut's marriage to Unn is blighted by the witchcraft of the nymphomaniac Queen Mother of Norway; and when Unn later divorces Hrut, his pride is so affronted that he refuses to return her dowry. Now Hallgerd reappears, strikingly beautiful, arrogant, volatile, passionate, and ruthless. She marries twice (956 and 959); both her husbands have occasion to slap her face, and promptly die for it at the hands of her jealous and unruly foster-father, Thjostolf.

Once again we meet Unn, a woman curiously demoralized by the failure of her marriage. She squanders her inheritance from her father, and, desperate for money, persuades her cousin Gunnar of Hlidarend to try to get her dowry back from Hrut. Gunnar goes to his friend Njal for advice, and eventually succeeds in forcing Hrut to pay up. With her money in her hands, Unn makes a sudden and rash marriage to an unpleasant man called Valgard; gratitude to Gunnar turns sour, as it does so often, and their son, Mord Valgardsson, grows up to hate Gunnar with a blazing malevolence. Mord is the only deliberately evil agent in the saga, as plausible and malignant as Iago, racked with envy and coldly dedicated to destroying others. First Gunnar is overwhelmed by the forces of evil released by Mord; by then the sons of Njal have become involved, and soon they, too, with agonizing credulity, are ensnared and doomed.

But to return to the story: after defeating Hrut, Gunnar goes abroad to win fame and fortune. He returns in a blaze of glory and falls in love with Hallgerd at the Althing, the annual national assembly (974). He marries her, to the dismay of the prescient Njal, who foresees nothing but trouble from the match. Hallgerd and Bergthora, Njal's large-tempered wife, quarrel and start a killing match; seven men die before their feud is stopped, and one of them is the man who acted as foster-father to the sons of Njal. Present at his killing was Thrain Sigfusson, Gunnar's vain and ambitious kinsman and Hallgerd's son-in-law; it was something the Njalssons were never to forgive.

However, the deep friendship between Njal and Gunnar remains unimpaired, and for a time violence is contained, until Hallgerd contrives to create more trouble for Gunnar, this time by stealing food from a churlish farmer, Otkel, who, prompted by his malicious, lying friend Skamkel, refuses Gunnar's handsome offers of compensation. Violence erupts again, and once more is appeased. But by now, Gunnar's prowess and fame are a provocation to all men of turbulence, and Gunnar is soon once more fighting for his life. Njal is continually trying to avert the tragedy he foresees, planning desperately to outwit fate. But Mord, scheming in the background, ruthlessly using other men's lives to bring about Gunnar's downfall, succeeds in the end. Gunnar, weary perhaps of the constant harassing, defies a sentence of outlawry passed on him in order to allow passions to cool, and is attacked and destroyed in his home after a heroic lone defence (990).

Here the saga pauses, to tidy up the loose ends of the 'Gunnar episode'. Summary vengeance is dealt out by Njal's eldest son, the formidable Skarp-Hedin. Njal's two younger sons, Helgi and Grim, go abroad, but find themselves in trouble in Norway as a result of Thrain Sigfusson's actions. The smouldering hostilities flare up anew. Accompanied by their brother-in-law Kari, a Hebridean Norseman who had rescued them from Vikings, the Njalssons kill Thrain; their long grudge against him is repaid (995).

Once again Njal tries to avert fate – but only with even more disastrous results. He tries to control and contain the lurking violence by adopting as his foster-son Thrain's young son, the saintly Hoskuld. This, he hopes, will ligature a potentially dangerous blood-feud against his sons. He does everything in his power to advance the young man, and even manipulates the Constitution to provide him with a chieftaincy in order that he can marry Hildigunn, the fierce, proud niece of the chieftain Flosi (1005).

At this point the author introduces a few chapters to describe the conversion of Iceland to Christianity, by parliamentary decree, in the year 1000.

To be forgiven by a man you have wronged can impose an intolerable strain. The feverishly intense friendship between the Njalssons and Hoskuld is grossly artificial, and their father's obvious predilection for his foster-son only adds to the tension. Now Mord steps in again. His own wealth and authority are being undermined by the popularity of the new chieftain, and now he plots to destroy them all. He finds the Njalssons all too ready to believe ill of Hoskuld, and on a fine spring morning they slaughter him in his cornfield (1011).

Even now, Njal still struggles. Helped by his many friends, he persuades Flosi to agree to a financial settlement over the killing (*wergild*). Flosi is himself under vicious pressure from Hildigunn to exact a blood-revenge, but is still prepared to accept honourable terms. At the Althing, where the case is being arbitrated, tempers snap in the tension; a well-meaning gesture by Njal is interpreted as an insult by the overwrought Flosi, and hopes of a peaceful settlement are brutally smashed.

It is Njal's last attempt to avert doom. When Flosi comes to attack Bergthorsknoll with a hundred men, Njal insists that his sons try to defend the house from inside. It is suicidal advice, and Skarp-Hedin realizes it; but at the old man's entreaties, they all go inside, and are burned to death. Only their brother-in-law, the 'lucky' Kari, escapes (1011).

Both Kari and Flosi gather allies from all over the country for a trial of strength at the legal proceedings at the Althing. After a lengthy and dramatic court battle, a fatal legal blunder by Mord gives rise to a pitched battle with weapons between the opposing sides. When peace is eventually restored, Kari refuses to be party to a settlement and sets out on a lone vengeance, helped first by Njal's kinsman Thorgeir Skorar-Geir and then by the rabbit-hearted, comic Bjorn of Mork. Flosi makes no attempt to retaliate as the Burners, his supporters, are killed off one after another. Eventually Kari's revenge-lust is sated, and the two men are reconciled (1016). All passion is spent; the evil forces aroused by greed and envy and brutality have exhausted themselves. 'And there I end the saga of the Burning of Njal.'

*

Modern readers may find the saga-technique, with its impersonal economy of style and consistent lack of explanation of motive, a little strange at first, before they are acclimatized to it. It certainly has difficulties for us that never existed for the

14

contemporary audience, and a few comments about the more obvious saga characteristics may help the reader to overcome this initial awkwardness.

First of all, there are certain narrative conventions that the thirteenth-century audience was fully conditioned to expect and to appreciate. Newcomers to the saga are formally introduced ('There was a man called . . .') and given a brief character-sketch and genealogy. The character-sketch is both perfunctory and final; from then on, the reader is expected to draw his own conclusions about the personality as it becomes revealed in action, speech, or silence – never by interior analysis. The genealogies tend to be much longer. To us they may seem tedious and intrusive at times, but they were in fact much the more significant source of information, because the contemporary audience could not only recognize the family characteristics of a person and deduce character from the quality of pedigree, but could fit him or her into a known historical context, through familiarity with other sagas. For instance, the early characters of *Njal's Saga* had already figured more largely early in the 980s which seems to have had considerable effect in *Laxdæla Saga*. In this translation, the genealogies have been relegated to the footnotes, where they can be read if desired; we were reluctant to omit them altogether, for they can be a source of much interest to the lively reader. To take only one example: the drum-rolling genealogy of Mord Valgardsson (Chapter 25) is one of the best in the whole saga – the catalogue of picturesquely-named Viking heroes in his pedigree is impeccable; yet Mord is a rogue. The forceful family characteristics of heroic rivalry and tough self-reliance have degenerated into foxy cunning and plausibility; but at the same time Mord's ancestry helps to explain both his urge for revenge (to regain a dwindled authority) and his importance to the other characters in the saga.

From these genealogies, the reader is expected to untangle the intricate relationships by blood and marriage which dictated loyalties and actions. The author was able to take for granted a detailed knowledge of historical and social background, and did not require to stress the aspects which prove significant – such as, for instance, the crucial, pervading conceptions of honour, of luck, of fate, of nobility of character. Behaviour which may seem to us inexplicable, and which is given no explanation by the author, was often the peremptory response to these conventions.

'Honour' is a word that occurs with great frequency in the Icelandic sagas, but in none more so than in *Njal's Saga*. Any slight, real or imagined, to one's honour or to the honour of one's family had to be revenged, with either blood or money. It is a little pathetic, now, to read how vulnerable these men were to calls on their honour; it was fatally easy to goad them into action to avenge some suspicion of an insult. Without realizing this, it is impossible to feel the apalling pressure which Hildigunn put on her uncle Flosi with her elaborate, almost formal, taunts in Chapter 116; but it is essential to recognize it to be able to visualize Flosi's stiff-legged, suspicious, bristling approach to the abortive peace-meeting with Njal and his sons at the Althing (Chapter 123).

The legal system in Iceland was at best an uneasy substitute for revenge. Too often legal actions brought by a dead man's kinsmen against the killer were thwarted by the intricacy of court procedure, and then the only alternative to further violence was mutually-agreed arbitration. Even when a verdict of guilty was brought, it was still the plaintiff's duty to execute the sentence; the state had no power to enforce outlawry.

'Luck' is another word which has wider connotations in *Njal's Saga* than is usual in our day. Good luck or ill luck was inherent in every individual, and ultra-sensitive men, like Njal or Hrut, could detect it in others, like an aura. Skarp-Hedin is 'ill-starred', but Kari is 'lucky'. Some men were doomed to bring ill luck to all they touched – Hrapp, for instance. One's luck was an inescapable part of the complex pattern of fate.

The concept of Fate plays an important part in *Njal's Saga*. The action is swept along by a powerful under-current of fate, and Njal's fierce struggle to alter its course heightens the conflict of personalities. Njal was prescient; he could see aspects of the future, blurred glimpses illuminated by sudden ambiguous shafts of knowledge. He was not a fatalist in the heathen sense – a man content to accept what fate had in store, but careful to meet it like a man. It is only when Christianity and its effects begin to filter into the saga that Njal achieves peace with his own fate.

In addition to fate, the saga has constant recourse to the supernatural. Some have complained that this in some way 'spoils' the bleak realism of the saga. But it is important to remember that in the thirteenth century and earlier, these manifestations of the supernatural were wholeheartedly believed in – ghosts, prophecies, dreams, hallucinations, fetches, portents. The audience believed in them, and the story-teller believed in them. In the second place, this supplied the author with an accepted and valuable literary device. By means of prophecy and visions, he could adumbrate future events without compromising his suspense effect or the conventional chronological presentation of the narrative. And later, by underlining the eventual truth of these prophecies, the author could tighten the strand of narrative.

In effect, the supernatural elements are used as the tissues that knit the sprawling material of the saga into firm structural units; they provide interior tension within the solid tripartite construction of the saga (Chapters 1–81; 82–132; 133–end).

The author could also use the known social fabric to create subtleties of behaviour which we might overlook. Formal hospitality was an integral part of this social structure, and the occasional breaches of the etiquette of giving and accepting hospitality had enormous significance. It is fitting that *Njal's Saga* should end with the formal test of Flosi's character through his capacity for hospitality, when his enemy, Kari, deliberately goes to his house for shelter.

It is tempting to multiply these examples of submerged subtleties, in desperate concern lest they be missed. But this Introduction is intended only as a hand-rail to a fuller enjoyment of the saga for those reading it for the first time, not as a critical analysis nor a scholarly thesis. There are very few notes in this volume, for without doubt the saga, read as a whole, is practically self-explanatory. It paints a vivid and unforgettable picture of a living society – men and women at work and at leisure, a quiet self-reliant rural community through which occasional violence erupts brutally. Hoskuld Hvitaness-Priest is killed on a brilliant spring morning as he sows seed in his cornfield. No one, not even the least significant characters, exists without relation to this society; men die making charcoal, or trading, or carting dried fish, or herding livestock. The land itself, mountain, river, and pasture, is constantly before our eyes, the land that sustained and conditioned this people, the land that held Gunnar's heart in thrall. The land has not changed; today one can go by car from Reykjavik to the 'Njal country' and back in a single day, and recognize with a shock of pleasure the places described by the author.

Within this busy and active society, conceptions that are alien to us nowadays fit naturally and without strain. The formalities of betrothal and divorce, of lawsuits and challenges, of horse-fights and religious life, of manners and morals – all these emerge gently and clearly. The tenth-century farmhouse takes shape through the slow accumulation of incidental description, the pattern of clothing and weapons, wealth and poverty, power and subservience, unfolds before our eyes.

There is no need to say much about the system of laws. There are strong indications that the author of *Njal's Saga* used some written law code as his model for the extensive legal matter in the saga – and not always accurately, at that. This is a rather specialized subject, and it would be unnecessary to annotate the occasional discrepancies. The picture of the law system at work is in general a true one.

But perhaps a few words on the social and political context may be useful.

Some sixty years after the settlement of Iceland began, the Icelandic state was established with the institution of the 'Althing' (General Assembly). Previously there had only been local assemblies, as in other Scandinavian communities, under local chieftains; they were judicial rather than legislative. But in 930 the leading chieftains of Iceland founded the Althing, having commissioned a legal expert to prepare a special code of laws for the new state, based on Norwegian law.

The Althing was held annually in the open air for two weeks late in June at Thingvellir ('Assembly Plains'), and was the main judicial, legislative, and social event of the year. Those who attended it were accommodated in semi-permanent 'booths' – stone-and-turf enclosures which were temporarily furnished (often most lavishly) and roofed with cloth for occupation. Constitutional and judicial authority was in the hands of the chieftains, who combined religious and secular power and had the title of '*goði*' – priest-chieftain. There were thirty-nine of them in Iceland at this time, and their status was largely hereditary, depending on the wealth and influence of their ancestors who had settled in Iceland; but the office could be bought, sold, divided, and even temporarily borrowed, as well as inherited (cf. Chapters 109 and 141).

Their function as heathen priests seems for the most part to have been rather perfunctory; their real power lay in wealth, in kinship, and in the personal allegiance of their followers. Paganism in Iceland seems to have been rather a diffuse religion. Belief in the existence of spirits was widespread, and the careful pagan took pains not to offend them; these spirits were thought to live in stones or groves or waterfalls and were sometimes propitiated by gifts of food – they were the 'natural geniuses' of the place. In addition to this, Icelanders believed in gods – a loose hierarchy of supra-mortals whom they liked to make friends with, rather than worship. In Iceland, Thor seems to have been the staple god. The gods were not all-powerful themselves; they were subject to impersonal, indifferent Fate, and to the same vices and virtues as mankind is.

The priest-chieftains were responsible for the upkeep of temples, which were used for sacrifices; but the degree of devotion shown varied very much according to the individual. It is clear that belief in the gods was weakening right from the earliest settlement of Iceland, although men continued to believe in the *idea* of a god. Many of the original settlers had come into contact with Christianity in Ireland; some of them were already baptized Christians, others were to a greater or lesser degree familiar with it. One of the first settlers, Helgi the Lean, half Norse and half Irish, 'believed in Christ but invoked Thor for sea-journeys and times of crisis'; he named his farm Kristness. Throughout the tenth century formal paganism was on the decline, and contact with Christianity abroad increased; which partly, at least, explains how the conversion of Iceland to Christianity in the year 1000 was achieved without bloodshed (cf. Chapters 100–5). There was a Christian mission to Iceland early in the 980s which seems to have had considerable effect on men's minds, although it ended rather abruptly after blood had been spilt.

Christianity, once accepted by Althing decree, did not seem to make much immediate difference to Iceland. If anything, violence increased for a time. The pagan standards of conduct were based not so much on religion as on the old Germanic social code of self-reliance, personal loyalty to one's leader, and obligations to one's kin . . . a code of ethics best expounded in the tenth-century *Hávamál* poems ('The Words of the High One'). Immortality was conceived of in terms not of another life, but of fame; and the conception of Valhalla, where slain warriors feasted with Odin and prepared for the last great battle, was purely a literary one that never seems to have had any great effect on popular belief. Under Christianity, the moral code in Iceland did not change at once; but its tensions may well have been increased.

Nor did the social structure of Iceland change immediately. The priest-chieftains retained their titles and authority, which many of them reinforced by becoming leaders of the Church. But it did have one effect that seems to have been far-reaching: it hastened the decline of the individual freeholding farmer.

All the original settlers who came to Iceland during the period of the settlements became land-owning farmers. They brought with them some dependants and followers, but most of the farm-work was done for them by slaves, who were plentiful – mainly captives taken during Viking raids.

Slaves were owned body and soul by their masters; but in Iceland they had rather more sympathetic treatment – even certain legal privileges – than was common elsewhere. The sagas record many instances in the early days of slaves being given their freedom and even some land of their own as well. Slavery gradually decreased in Iceland during the tenth century, for whereas in the early days there had been land for all and no need to work, now freemen could no longer get themselves land cheaply or for nothing, and had to take jobs to keep themselves. Furthermore, the market in slaves diminished and it became as cheap to employ labour as to own it. Slaves could buy their freedom for half their market value, the rest to be paid later on the instalment system. Slavery continued in Iceland on a rapidly diminishing scale until early in the twelfth century, but continued elsewhere in Scandinavia for another two centuries. Probably the ultimately telling factor was the ban, under Christianity, on the practice of exposing children at birth (cf. Chapter 105); this robbed the slave-owner of his favourite means of controlling the slave birth-rate and thus easing his household costs (there is only one recorded instance of a slave being castrated).

Throughout the tenth century the free-holding farmer was the core of the community. Iceland was an aristocratic state, certainly, even though it was not considered an indignity to do farm-work (*Njal's Saga* is full of examples of this). The chieftains administered the country through the political authority and laws that they had themselves created and which they could easily frustrate when it served their purpose to do so.

But the power of the chieftains rested ultimately on the free-holding farmer. Each chieftain had a varying number of supporters; householders of a certain standard of wealth were bound by law to adhere to a chieftain, but they could freely choose to which chieftain in their Quarter they gave their allegiance. They paid him temple-dues and were committed to attend the Althing to support him or, in lieu of that, pay him a tax to defray the expenses of the Althing visit; in return, the chieftain was committed to give his followers protection and help. The chieftain was no less dependent on his followers than they on him (cf. Chapter 107, where Mord Valgardsson is seen to be losing authority and wealth because his followers are transferring their allegiance to Hoskuld Hvitaness-Priest).

With the advent of the Church in Iceland, the social structure changed to the extent that landlordism on a large scale came into being (there is no evidence of it in the tenth century, but that is not necessarily conclusive). The Church quickly began to amass ownership of land which was let to tenant farmers, and a new dimension was added to the conception of power. Previously, chieftains had derived power from a mutual relationship with their followers; now their power began to grow independent of goodwill. Furthermore, once the system of power through temple-allegiance broke down under Christianity, the potential bounds of power were extended; for previously a chieftain's followers were drawn from those who lived within a reasonable distance, at least, of the temple to which they subscribed.

The Church, thrustful and demanding, added a new factor to the ceaseless jockeying for power and influence that goes on in any community. In addition to arousing savage internal disputes in Iceland, it opened the way for external interference, for the Church connected Iceland with the outside world far more than it had been before. It brought Iceland within the power-range of Scandinavia; for instance, Bishop Gudmund, during his long struggles with chieftains at the beginning of the thirteenth century, invoked the assistance and authority of the archbishop of Norway.

Gradually the chieftains became more and more ambitious, more and more arrogant in their attitude to the law and their dealings with each other. By the beginning of the thirteenth century effective power throughout the land had been gathered into the grasp of some half dozen families. The violent disputes that arose in Iceland gave the rulers of Norway, who for centuries had wanted to get their hands on Iceland, the opportunity to intervene. Chieftains who tried to extend their power over the whole of Iceland used the Norwegian throne as an ally – only to find themselves fatally mortgaged to it. Finally, in 1262, came the inevitable end of the republic; the Althing, under heavy pressure, agreed to pay tax and allegiance to the crown of Norway. It has taken Iceland nearly seven centuries to regain that independence.

These comments refer, of course, only to social and political changes caused by the Church. They ignore the many beneficial effects of the early Church in Iceland, particularly the part it played in developing Icelandic literature, not only through the introduction of writing but by the early exercise of literary ability.

*

One of the questions about *Njal's Saga* most frequently argued is – 'How true is it?' Some have thought it practically pure fiction, others practically verbatim truth, even down to the dialogues.

The Burning of Bergthorsknoll is undoubtedly a historical fact, corroborated by earlier written sources – by, for instance, *Landnámabók* (Book of Settlements), the early-twelfth-century historical account of Iceland's first settlers and their descendants; and excavations close to the site of the present farm at Bergthorsknoll have proved that certain buildings – outhouses, probably – were burned down there hundreds of years ago,

22

although exact dating has not been possible. Probably, Njal's home stood on exactly the same spot as the present farm, on top of a low swelling mound on the sea-level plain of the Land-Isles on the south coast.

The author of *Njal's Saga* clearly made use of a number of written sources (many of them traceable) for some of the saga material – the account of the conversion of Iceland to Christianity in the year 1000, for instance (which is so like a straight 'lift' from another document that scholars have occasionally thought the account to be a later interpolation in the saga); the account of the Battle of Clontarf outside Dublin in 1014; the elaborate, confusing, and sometimes incorrect legal formulae; the genealogies, and background material for many of the subsidiary characters. He can be proved to have known and often made use of material from other sagas written in the thirteenth century.

Some of his information also came to him embedded in the occasional verses in the saga. None of them has any great literary merit, and on linguistic and stylistic grounds few of them are thought by scholars to be as old as the events of the saga; but many of them were undoubtedly composed before the saga was written – thereby suggesting the existence of flourishing oral traditions that were being occasionally replenished from the imagination. It is, however, curious that some of the verses contain information that is contradictory to the narrative; for instance, the verse ascribed to Gunnar in his burial-mound (Chapter 78), which is thought to antedate the writing of the saga, says unequivocally that Gunnar refused to leave Iceland because he was reluctant to yield to his enemies. This gives a very different account from the aesthetic, almost lyrical, version in the saga itself.

Indeed, it can be shown that he used his sources with considerable freedom and occasional mistakes, which can be accounted for by both garbled oral traditions and the natural tendency of an author to manipulate material for aesthetic purposes. His version of the institution of the Fifth Court, for instance, is obviously distorted and misdated, an attempt to make this historic event an integral part of the saga – and perhaps to give Njal a larger role in Iceland's history than he actually played. The chronology of events in the saga is at times wildly inconsistent and cannot bear too close a scrutiny (see the Note on Chronology at the end of this book); the author has sacrificed the calendar to give his narrative greater impact and significance. There are also some striking similarities to certain events of the thirteenth century – burnings, battles, disputes, even individual wounds. Some scholars have claimed that the whole pattern of dispute is unmistakably thirteenth-century – the gathering of huge bands of men on great cross-country marches, the immense mobilizations of fighting men for the crises. Some of the very minor characters are perhaps entirely fictitious and their names are obviously spurious. The late Barði Guðmundsson wrote numerous articles (recently published posthumously under the title *Njal's Saga's Author*) brilliantly elaborating the thesis that most of the events described in the saga were inspired by thirteenth-century events in which the alleged author had played a conspicuous part. However, the really important thing is that, whether or not all these people lived and behaved in the way described by the author, in *Njal's Saga* they all have a vivid and unquestionable life of their own.

From thirteenth-century sources it is clear that sagas were regarded at the time as what one might call 'serious entertainment'. Contemporary writers were fully aware of the distortions that time can create in the memories of things past, and were not particularly concerned about it.

Where strict historical accuracy could be vouchsafed, by reference to contemporary witnesses, it was valued; but artistic values were no less warmly appreciated where historicity could not be claimed – and *Njal's Saga*, unlike some others, makes no explicit claim to historical truth.

The distinction is obvious from a saga like *Sverrir's Saga*, for instance. This is a contemporary Icelandic account of the life of King Sverrir of Norway (1152–1202), compiled by a friend of the king's under the king's personal guidance; and in a later Introduction the point is specifically made that the historicity of the saga cannot be doubted, because of the reliability and immediacy of its sources – 'it could not have become garbled by oral tradition'. But the Icelandic historian Styrmir the Learned (d. 1245), writing an Epilogue to *Saint Olaf's Saga*, said, 'You can accept from this composed saga whatever you think

24

most likely, for in old sagas many things are confused. This is only to be expected where oral tradition alone supplies the material. .... I expect that holy King Olaf would not be offended by any inaccuracies in the saga, for it has been written in order to entertain others rather than to criticize the king or out of any malice.'

An Icelandic scribe who wrote out a copy of *Thidrek's Saga* probably at the same time as *Njal's Saga* was being composed had much to say about sagas as serious entertainment in an Introduction. Their value, he thought, was both moral and practical.

'Sagas about worthy men', he wrote, 'are useful to know, because they show us noble deeds and brave feats, whereas ill-deeds are manifestations of indolence; thus, such sagas point the distinction between good and evil for those who wish to understand it.'

Further: 'With sagas one man can gladden many an hour, whereas most entertainments are difficult to arrange; some are very costly, some cannot be enjoyed without large numbers of people, some only entertain a very few people for a brief time, and some entail physical danger. But saga entertainment or poetry costs nothing and holds no dangers, and one man can entertain as many or as few as wish to listen; it is equally practicable night or day, by light or in darkness.'

Such were the literary ideas in circulation at the time that *Njal's Saga* was being composed.

They can be seen in actual practice in the following incident which occurred in the year 1258 in Iceland, and which was recorded in the contemporary *Sturlunga Saga*: it tells how a certain Thorgils Skardi came to the farmhouse at Hrafnagill one evening in that year. When he arrived, his host asked him what entertainment he would prefer – saga-reading or ballad-dancing. Thorgils asked what sagas were available, and was told that the saga of Archbishop Thomas à Beckett was at hand, amongst others. This is the one that Thorgils chose, 'for he loved him more than any other holy man'. (This saga, or versions of it at least, survives to this day in several manuscripts.)

The emphasis on *reading* aloud is interesting, for it suggests that the sagas were specifically designed for public, rather than private, reading. It also suggests an explanation of the character-

25

istics of oral style which some scholars have found in the sagas; what appears to be a transcription of an existing oral tale is much more likely to have been a deliberate simulation of the earlier oral style. Formal story-telling had developed into formal saga-reading many years before *Njal's Saga* was written, and the saga bears constant marks of the concern the author showed for the listener as well as the reader.

As 'serious entertainment', *Njal's Saga* is pre-eminent. It is primarily the work of an author, not a historian. As Professor Turville-Petre of Oxford has put it, 'It was not the author's purpose to write a work of history, but rather to use an historical subject for an epic in prose.'

Perhaps, in the last resort of definition, we might call *Njal's Saga* a homily. Throughout the saga there is a bitter conflict between the forces of good and evil; physical violence is the symptom of this constant friction. In the saga, evil is consistently generated by self-aggrandisement, by the attempt to gain power or wealth. Mord Valgardsson is the most obvious example of this; it is Mord's envy of men who stand in his way, like Gunnar of Hlidarend with his fame and wealth, and Hoskuld Hvitaness-Priest with his growing authority, that motivates his destructive scheming. Hrut's journey to Norway to claim an inheritance, and his unscrupulous way of gaining his fortune (by consenting to be the elderly Queen Mother's lover) frustrate his promising marriage to Unn – who, in her second marriage, gives birth to Mord Valgardsson; and that ill-starred marriage is made possible by the money that Gunnar forcibly took from Hrut as a dowry back-claim. Hrapp's bribing of the weak-willed Thrain Sigfusson (Chapter 88) causes the clash with the Njalssons that leads to Thrain's death. Hildigunn's arrogant insistence that Hoskuld must get a chieftaincy before she will consent to marry him, and Njal's manipulation of the Constitution to achieve this, provoke Mord to malevolent enmity. Greed for money (the bait that proved fatal to Eyjolf Bolverksson) and for power invariably has disastrous consequences.

It is the unfailing source of evil in *Njal's Saga*; and it is significant that greed and power-lust were such potent causes of the civil disruption that racked Iceland in the thirteenth century and led to her loss of independence in 1262.

But money in itself could never assuage the misfortunes

26

created by money; not even the unheard-of treble compensation awarded for the death of Hoskuld Hvitaness-Priest could placate the ugly hostilities that were aroused by the killing.

In this homily, the only answer to the violence aroused by evil is active will towards good. Christianity comes to Iceland half-way through the action; and it is the Christian virtues of self-sacrifice and humility that eventually stem the tide of evil, not the pagan virtues of heroism and pride. Njal, with his weird pagan prescience and his complex intelligence, is powerless against the doom he foresees for his friend Gunnar and himself, and only broadens the scope of catastrophe by his efforts to avert it; it is only when he resigns himself to the new God, when he abandons his devious scheming and sacrifices himself and his violent sons in the fire at Bergthorsknoll, that the possibility of resolution emerges. Flosi, goaded beyond endurance by taunts at his manhood, lets his smarting pride control his actions; it is only when he sees the incredible self-sacrifice of his father-in-law, Hall of Sida, who humbly confesses his 'lack of heroism' and is prepared to waive compensation for his son's death in order to end the violence – it is only then that Flosi's good qualities reassert themselves. From then on, he lets Kari butcher his followers without retaliation, until at last Kari is ready for a reconciliation (after a pilgrimage to Rome).

Ultimately, there is an indictment of violence, and of the way of life that fostered it. Behind the rather wistful vision of past heroism lies recognition of the endless strife it provoked. It was pride that helped to spread the poison of violence, the affronted pride even of good men like Gunnar; such fierce preoccupation with honour was bound to lead to bloodshed. Throughout the saga 'good' men and 'worthy' men try hard to settle disputes peacefully, to find solutions that satisfy the 'honour' of all concerned; but too often their efforts are frustrated by someone's pride. We can see this operating at its baldest in Chapter 91 : Njal knows that his sons' quarrel with Thrain will have disastrous effects, but he realizes, too, that they have mortgaged their pride by making the quarrel public, and that therefore he must help them get public satisfaction. His contribution is merely to prearrange fresh provocation for the inevitable killing. It is a pattern of behaviour all too familiar, even today.

It would, however, be quite wrong to offer the impression

27

that this is what *Njal's Saga* is 'about' – a Christian morality. It is a facile and dangerous satisfaction to peddle some subjective interpretation of a great work. At best, one can only indicate what one believes were central attitudes. *Njal's Saga* has been vigorously quarried in the past for material to fit some theory or other, for there are any amount of 'telling' sentences with which to support a favourite cause. But it is the *completeness* of the saga that really matters; its artistry, not its argument.

Its prose has a taut epigrammatic terseness that has often proved hard to reproduce in English. It is cool, impersonal, objective, easy-paced; only in sudden explosions of harsh dialogue does the effortless lope of the narration change its unhurried stride.

And yet, under this studied urbanity, tensions gather like muscles rippling under skin; a shade of emphasis here – just a matter of word-order, so hard to transfer from an inflected language like Icelandic to an uninflected one – or a flash of irony there, breaking momentarily through the detachment. In the midst of such economy, one spendthrift sentence can speak volumes: 'two ravens flew with them all the way' (Chapter 79) as Skarp-Hedin and Hogni set out at night to avenge Gunnar; 'the fire still burned fitfully, flaring up and sinking again' (Chapter 130) as the superstitious Burners peered through the smoke and heard the voice of Skarp-Hedin chanting a verse amidst the dying flames.

One can be dramatic without exclamation marks. The author uses dialogue extensively throughout the narrative, and all the climaxes are compellingly visualized – Skarp-Hedin skimming over the ice to cut down Thrain (Chapter 92), the Njalssons marching grimly from booth to booth at the Althing seeking support (Chapter 119), Kari's eruption into the earl's hall in Orkney to kill Gunnar Lambason (Chapter 155), Bergthora storming at her sons at table to goad them into avenging an insult (Chapter 44). The scenes are innumerable; many of them could be transferred directly to the stage with scarcely an added word of dialogue – these whiplash retorts, these silences, these slow deliberate formalities that are a prelude to violence. And yet, nothing is given too much prominence; each event, each episode, each act (to use once again the theatre analogy that

28

suggests itself so often) is subdued into its proper place in the Grand Design.

The author's constructional ability is remarkable. The saga has a deep, powerful, subtly varied rhythm that keeps the action moving with unhurried fluency. It could be likened to a storm; a series of ominous gusts of wind disturbing a calm day, an atmosphere growing more and more charged with a brooding promise of thunder. However often the saga relapses into calmness and peace – as for instance with the successive episodes of Gunnar's life, 'and now there was peace for a while' – the irresistible rhythm of approaching storm takes control again. Gradually the rhythm gathers speed, the intervals of calm become fewer and farther between. There is a superbly sustained climax of storm from Chapter 108 to Chapter 145; and then, at last, it begins to blow itself out.

All this is done with great sureness of touch. So, too, are the contrast between light and shade in the narrative, the variations of mood. From the death of Gunnar we plunge into the light-hearted adventures of the younger Njalssons abroad, a brief escape that gradually becomes shadowed with trouble. From the savage avenging fury of Kari with Thorgeir Skorar-Geir we turn to the ironic comedy of Bjorn of Mork, the cowardly braggart who does not quite suffer the humiliation we expect. There is a constant interplay of battle and debate, a long thrust-and-parry court drama (surely the first court-room drama in European literature?) followed hard by an uproar of battle.

But above all, the saga is rich beyond belief in its characters. They spring to life in a few vivid sentences; some, like the old woman Sæunn in Chapter 124, are only glimpsed in a paragraph – but with what telling effect. Others, like Njal and Skarp-Hedin, Gunnar and Flosi, Hallgerd and Bergthora, grow with the saga, deepening and broadening until we seem to know them like neighbours. Consider the subtle ageing of Njal over the last forty years of his life, how he seems physically to shrink, how his intellectual vigour quietly fades into the frail resignation of the octogenarian; and yet we are hard put to it to remember exactly *how* the effect is achieved. Watch how Skarp-Hedin becomes more and more committed to his restless, contemptuous role as the frustrated Viking, the elder son who never left his father's home; the ugly mouth, the constant scornful grin,

the unnatural pallor relieved in anger by burning spots of red –
all these are gradually heightened until at the end he is almost
a nightmare figure as he stalks through the Althing, brutal,
sardonic, terrible, and doomed. And yet, in death (what a delicate touch, this) the terror of his presence vanishes, we are told;
it is as if death has released the appalling tensions that possessed
his soul during the last years of his grim life, and we see again
the person as we first met him in the saga – courageous, manly,
quick-tongued, rather likeable.

Gunnar is on a different plane. He is never allowed to
dominate in the way Njal does. His portrait, like that of Kari,
has a blurred, romantic wash; he is the hero without peer, the
knight on the tapestry. And like the true hero of old, he is never
more alive than when meeting his death.

It is, of course, essential to the balance of the saga that
Gunnar (and Kari) should engage our sympathies with less
immediacy than do Njal (and Flosi); but within these necessary
limits Gunnar is more complex than he appears at first glance.
Behind his fantastic ability in battle and his courage is his concern at taking life (Chapter 54), behind his willingness to be
guided by Njal is a deep, secret stubbornness. He is not, as one
might think, a hero who happens to be a farmer; he is a farmer
who happens to be a hero – and a reluctant one, at that.

The secondary characters – and what a host of them there is
– are never perfunctory. How subtly individual they are: Hogni,
Gunnar's son, slow and honest, who has to be carefully nursed
by Skarp-Hedin into avenging his father, but who will then be
diverted from vengeance only with the greatest reluctance; that
most engaging villain Hrapp, irrepressibly insolent even at the
moment of death; Thorhall Asgrimsson, so profoundly emo-
tional that his whole body is affected by stress – violent swoons,
a crippling boil whose brutal lancing releases his surging lust for
revenge; Hrut, gracefully maturing into wisdom after his sad-
dening youth; Bergthora, harsh but at the last gentle as she
deliberately accompanies her husband to death.

The women of *Njal's Saga*, in fact, have no less significance
than the men, although there are not many of them. No attempt
is made to romanticize them; they are forceful, intensely individual, unforgettably real. Staid old scholars have argued with
frenzied passion about Hallgerd, the enigmatic, dishonest,

ravishing Hallgerd; some have rushed to her defence with such zeal that they have even accused the author of the saga of bias against her.

And then there is Njal himself, the benevolent farmer-sage with the Celtic name of Neil. His restless brooding brain behind his bland beardless face dominates the saga, even long after his death. This is Njal's saga, and he is worthy of it.

But it is time to curb my enthusiasm and let the saga speak for itself. Its author is one of the world's great story-tellers, and the saga he wrote is one of the finest achievements of medieval literature. I can only hope that at least some of his genius has survived this translation into English.

Glasgow, 1959

MAGNUS MAGNUSSON

NOTE ON THE TRANSLATION

THIS translation is based on the standard edition of *Njal's Saga* in the Íslenzk Fornrit series – *Brennu-Njáls Saga*, Íslenzk Fornrit, Vol. 12, Reykjavik, 1954. In this splendid edition, Professor Einar Ólafur Sveinsson of the University of Iceland has provided a text as nearly definitive as we can ever expect, the fruit of a life-long study of the saga and its manuscripts. Every student of *Njal's Saga* is indebted to him for his inspired researches; to us in particular they have proved quite invaluable in dealing with the numerous problems of interpretation which abound in a work of such complexity and subtlety.

The saga has been translated into English twice previously. The first translation, *The Story of Burnt Njal*, by Sir George Webbe Dasent, 1861, has been reprinted several times in the Everyman's Library series. It was a magnificent and pioneering work, scrupulously accurate and heroically phrased; but it has a deliberately archaic flavour, a too-literal rendering of the Icelandic style and syntax, that make it unnecessarily alien to the modern reader. The other translation, *Njál's Saga*, by Carl F. Bayerschmidt and Lee M. Hollander, New York, 1955, is in a much more modern idiom. Both these works have been of great help to us, and we freely acknowledge our debt to them, even though we have frequently disagreed with their ideas.

There are two points of translation which require some comment here – the proper names, and the verses. There is no accepted standard for the treatment of Icelandic proper names, particularly place-names. Broadly speaking, our policy has been to leave uncompounded names in their Icelandic forms, but to translate or adapt wherever possible the topographical appellatives of compounded names – such as 'river', 'hill', 'dale', 'ness', 'fjord', 'tongue', 'heath', 'stead', '–by'.

We cannot lay claim to complete consistency; where consistency would have led us into absurdity or dissonance, we have preferred inconsistency. We have also dropped all accents, and transliterated the letters ð and þ into *d* and *th* respectively.

Personal nicknames have been translated wherever possible,

but personal names have not been changed (despite strong temptation to make 'Úlf' into 'Wolf'), except in accordance with generally accepted custom – dropping the nominatival ending of strong nouns. Where people or places are well known under English names, we have abandoned the Icelandic forms – 'Dover' for 'Dofrar', 'Oslo Fjord' for 'Vík', 'Baltic' for 'Eystrasalt', 'Brian' for 'Brján' (King of Ireland), 'Malcolm' for 'Melkolf' (King of Scotland) – but not where Melkolf is the name of a slave in Iceland. We have also substituted 'Kincora' for 'Kantaraborg' in Chapters 154–6 – a necessary emendation – and used just common sense for the modern equivalents of places which no longer exist individually – 'Estonia' for 'Aðalsýsla', for instance.

Translation of the verses that stud many of the Old Icelandic sagas has always been a headache. After much experimentation, we have decided not to try to imitate the intricate verse-forms and the elaborate and resourceful poetic diction (*kennings*), but to retain as much as possible of their imagery in a free prose version. A literal translation is quite meaningless to the general reader, since there is no parallel in English to the skaldic convention of 'court-metre' with its intensely esoteric metaphor.

We have provided a Glossary of the more important characters in the saga, some genealogical tables to guide the reader through the tangle of kinships, and a rough timetable of events.

We should like to record here our warm gratitude to Mr R. A. Bennett, Q.C., of Edinburgh, for his invaluable help over the proper translation of the tortuous legal passages, and for his careful scrutiny of the whole text. We also thank Miss Audrey Henshall, M.A., of the National Museum of Antiquities for Scotland, for clarifying some obscure technical points about medieval looms (Chapter 157).

Miss Bridget Gordon, B.A., B.LITT., of Glasgow University devoted much of a summer vacation to a detailed examination of the whole translation, and we are deeply indebted to her for a host of improvements. We owe thanks also to many scholars, past and present, whose work has lightened our task and from whom the Introduction has borrowed freely without individual acknowledgement; and in particular to Professor Gabriel Turville-Petre of Oxford University, whose many writings have

34

inspired the rapid development of Old Icelandic studies in this country.

We have a special debt of gratitude to Dr Sigurður Nordal, of Iceland, who first suggested and encouraged this translation. His imaginative teaching, in general and often in detail, is evident throughout this volume, and we gladly acknowledge our immense debt to him.

Maps were put at our disposal by Hið Íslenzka Fornrita-félag, to whom we make grateful acknowledgement; and we thank Mr C. E. Brown, who adapted them for this edition. Mr Charles Graham, M.A., and Mr William Hook, B.SC., helped to check the final manuscript.

We should also like to thank Dr E. V. Rieu, editor of the Penguin Classics series, for his enthusiastic support; Mr Sigur-steinn Magnússon, Icelandic Consul-General in Scotland, for many lively criticisms and suggestions, and for the liberal access he allowed us to his library; and finally our wives, for their unfailing patience and help.

M. M.
H. P.

NJAL'S SAGA

I

THERE was a man called Mord Fiddle, who was the son of Sighvat the Red. Mord was a powerful chieftain, and lived at Voll in the Rangriver Plains. He was also a very experienced lawyer – so skilful, indeed, that no judgement was held to be valid unless he had taken part in it. He had an only daughter called Unn; she was a good-looking, refined, capable girl, and was considered the best match in the Rangriver Plains.

The scene of the saga now moves west, to the Breidafjord Dales, where a man called Hoskuld Dala-Kollsson * lived at Hoskuldstead, in Laxriverdale. He had a half-brother called Hrut Herjolfsson, who lived at Hrutstead; they had the same mother. Hrut was a handsome man; he was tall, strong, and skilled in arms, even-tempered and very shrewd, ruthless with his enemies and always reliable in matters of importance.

On one occasion, Hoskuld was holding a feast for his friends; Hrut was there, sitting next to him. Hoskuld had a daughter called Hallgerd, who was playing on the floor with some other girls; she was a tall, beautiful child with long silken hair that hung down to her waist.

Hoskuld called to her, 'Come over here to me.' She went to him at once. Her father tilted her chin and kissed her, and she walked away again.

Then Hoskuld asked Hrut:

'What do you think of her? Do you not think she is beautiful?'

Hrut made no reply. Hoskuld repeated the question. Then Hrut said, 'The child is beautiful enough, and many will suffer for her beauty; but I cannot imagine how thief's eyes have come into our kin.'

---

* Hoskuld's mother was Thorgerd, the daughter of Thorstein the Red, the son of Olaf the White, the son of Ingjald, the son of Helgi and of Thora, the daughter of Sigurd Snake-in-the-Eye, the son of Ragnar Hairy-Breeks.

Thorstein the Red's mother was Aud the Deep-Minded, the daughter of Ketil Flat-Nose, the son of Bjorn Buna.

Hoskuld was furious; and for a time there was coldness between them.

Hallgerd's brothers were Thorleik (the father of Bolli), Olaf the Peacock (the father of Kjartan), and Bard.

2

On another occasion, Hoskuld and Hrut rode to the Althing together. There was a large attendance.

Hoskuld said to Hrut, 'I would like you to look to your future, brother, and find yourself a wife.'

'I have been in two minds about it for a long time,' replied Hrut. 'But now I will do as you wish. Where should we turn our attention?'

'There are many chieftains here at the Althing,' said Hoskuld, 'and we have a wide choice. But I have already decided on a match for you, a woman called Unn; she is the daughter of Mord Fiddle, a very wise man. He is here at the Althing now and his daughter is with him, so you can see her if you wish.'

Next day, as people were making their way to the Court of Legislature, the brothers saw a group of well-dressed women outside the Rangriver booth.

'There is Unn now,' said Hoskuld, 'the woman I was telling you about. What do you think of her?'

'I like the look of her,' replied Hrut. 'But I do not know that we are destined to be happy together.'

They walked on towards the court. Mord Fiddle was interpreting the law there as usual, and afterwards he went back to his booth. Hoskuld and Hrut rose and followed him. They entered the booth and greeted Mord, who was seated at the far end; he rose to meet them, took Hoskuld by the hand, and gave him the seat beside his own. Hrut sat down beside Hoskuld.

They talked about a number of things. Eventually Hoskuld said, 'I want to discuss a marriage-deal with you. Hrut wants to make an offer for your daughter's hand and become your son-in-law, and I shall not be sparing in my support.'

'I know that you are a great chieftain,' said Mord, 'but of your brother I know nothing.'

'He is a better man than I,' replied Hoskuld.

'You would have to settle a very large sum on him,' said Mord, 'for Unn will inherit everything I own.'

'I shall not keep you waiting long for my offer,' said Hoskuld. 'Hrut is to have Kambsness and Hrutstead and all the land up to Thrandargill; and in addition he owns a trading-ship which is out at sea just now.'

Hrut intervened. 'You must realize,' he said to Mord, 'that brotherly love makes Hoskuld exaggerate my virtues. But if you are prepared to consider the matter at all, I would like you to name the terms yourself.'

'I have already decided on my terms,' said Mord. 'Unn's dowry from me will be sixty hundreds,* which you are to increase by half; and if you have heirs, the whole estate is to be divided equally between the two of you.'

'I accept these terms,' said Hrut. 'Let us now call in witnesses.'

They stood up and shook hands, and Mord betrothed his daughter Unn to Hrut, the wedding to take place at Mord's home a fortnight after midsummer.

Both parties then rode home from the Althing. Hrut and Hoskuld were passing Hallbjorn Cairns on their way westward when Thjostolf, the son of Bjorn Gold-Bearer from Reykjardale, came riding towards them. He told them that Hrut's ship had arrived in Hvit River; on board was Ozur, Hrut's paternal uncle, who wanted Hrut to come to see him as soon as possible. When Hrut heard this he asked Hoskuld to accompany him, and together they rode to the ship, where Hrut welcomed his uncle warmly. Ozur invited them into his booth to drink. They had their horses unsaddled, and then went in and drank with him.

* The 'hundred' (in fact 120) refers to ells of woollen cloth, and was a common method of computing value. Six Icelandic ells (approximately three yards) were equivalent to one legal ounce, and there were eight ounces in the legal mark. Thus, Unn's dowry was 150 marks. Hrut's inheritance (later in this chapter) of 200 marks was actually 240 marks. In terms of livestock, one milch cow or six sheep were worth nearly two marks at this time. Unn's dowry was equivalent to 80 cows, Hrut's inheritance to 128 cows. *Translators' note.*

41

'And now, kinsman,' said Hrut to Ozur, 'you must ride west with me and stay with me for the winter.'

'That's out of the question,' said Ozur. 'I have to tell you that your brother Eyvind is dead. He named you as his heir, Hrut, at the Gula Assembly, but if you don't come to Norway at once your enemies there will seize the inheritance.'

'What's to be done now, Hoskuld?' asked Hrut. 'This raises difficulties, now that I have fixed my wedding date.'

'You must ride south and see Mord,' said Hoskuld. 'Ask him to alter the agreement and have Unn wait for three years as your betrothed. Meanwhile I shall ride home and bring your goods down to the ship.'

Hrut said, 'I want you to have some of this flour and timber, and anything else you would like from the cargo.'

The horses were fetched, and Hrut rode off to the south, while Hoskuld continued his journey home to the west. When Hrut reached the Rangriver Plains he was well received at Mord's house. He explained the position to Mord, and asked him for his advice.

'How much money is involved?' asked Mord.

Hrut replied that it would be two hundred marks, if he got it all.

'That is a lot compared to what I shall leave,' said Mord. 'Certainly you must go, if you wish to.'

They changed the agreement, and Unn was now to wait for three years as his betrothed. Hrut rode back to the ship and stayed there throughout the summer until it was ready to put to sea. Hoskuld brought to the ship all the goods that Hrut owned, and agreed to look after Hrut's property in the west while he was abroad. Then Hoskuld rode back home, and soon afterwards Hrut and Ozur set sail before a favourable wind. After three weeks at sea they reached the Hern Islands, and then sailed on east to Oslo Fjord.

3

THE reigning king of Norway was Harald Grey-Cloak,* the son of Eirik Blood-Axe, son of Harald Fine-Hair. Harald Grey-Cloak and his mother Queen Gunnhild † had their residence at Konungahella in the east of Norway.

News spread of the arrival in Oslo Fjord of a ship from the west, and as soon as Gunnhild heard of it she wanted to know what Icelanders were on board. She was told that one of them was Hrut, Ozur's nephew.

'I have no doubt at all that he is here to claim his inheritance,' said Gunnhild. 'A man called Soti has taken charge of it.'

She summoned her squire, Ogmund, and said to him, 'I want you to go to Oslo Fjord and meet Ozur and Hrut. Tell them that I invite them both to spend the winter with me, and that I want to befriend them. Tell them that if Hrut does what I say, I shall look after his claim and anything else he undertakes, and also get him into favour with the king.'

Ogmund set off and met Hrut and Ozur, who made him welcome as soon as they learnt that he was Queen Gunnhild's squire. He gave them the queen's message secretly, and then Ozur and Hrut considered it in private.

'It seems to me,' said Ozur, 'that our decision is already made, kinsman. I know Gunnhild's nature. The moment we refuse her invitation, she will hound us out of the country and seize all we own; but if we accept, she will treat us as handsomely as she has promised.'

Ogmund went back to report to Gunnhild the result of his mission, and told her that Hrut and Ozur would come.

'I expected no less,' said Gunnhild, 'for Hrut is said to be a shrewd and able man. And now, Ogmund, keep watch and let me know when they arrive in town.'

Hrut and Ozur set out for Konungahella. When they arrived, their kinsmen and friends came out to meet them and welcomed

* Harald Grey-Cloak ruled Norway from 961 to 970. *Translators' note.*

† Gunnhild was the daughter of Ozur Toti.

43

them warmly. They asked if the king were in residence, and were told that he was. A little later they met Ogmund, who brought them Gunnhild's greetings and a message that she would not ask them to her house until they had been to see the king, in case people started saying that she was making too much fuss of them; but she would do all she could for them, and in the meantime Hrut was to speak up boldly before the king and ask to be admitted to his court.

'And here,' he added, 'is a robe she sends you, Hrut, to wear when you go before the king.' With that he went back.

Next day Hrut said, 'Let us go before the king.'

'Very well,' said Ozur.

With ten companions, all kinsmen and friends, they went to the royal hall, where the king sat drinking after his meal. Hrut was in the lead and greeted the king. The king studied this well-dressed man carefully, and asked him his name. Hrut gave it.

'Are you an Icelander?' asked the king.

Hrut said that he was.

'What brings you here to visit us?' asked the king.

'A wish to see your splendour, my lord,' said Hrut. 'Also, I have a large inheritance to claim in this country, and I shall have need of your support if I am to secure my rights.'

'I have promised all men the protection of law in this realm,' said the king. 'Had you any other mission in coming here?'

'My lord,' said Hrut, 'I ask leave to be admitted to your court and become your liegeman.'

The king made no reply.

Gunnhild said, 'It seems to me that this man offers you a great honour. If there were many men like him in your retinue, it would be well manned indeed.'

'Is he clever?' asked the king.

'Both clever and enterprising,' she replied.

'It appears,' said the king to Hrut, 'that my mother wishes you to be given the rank you request. But in deference to my royal name and the customs of this realm, you must call on me again in a fortnight's time. You will then be made my retainer. My mother will take care of you until you come to me again.'

Gunnhild said to Ogmund, 'Show them to my house and prepare a fine feast for them there.' Ogmund went out with them and ushered them into a stone-built hall hung with most beautiful tapestries. Here stood Gunnhild's throne.

'Now you will see,' said Ogmund, 'that what I told you of Gunnhild is true. This is her throne. You are to occupy it, Hrut, and keep this seat even when she herself is present.'

A feast was set before them. They had scarcely started when Gunnhild entered. Hrut made to rise to greet her.

'Be seated,' she said. 'And keep that seat for as long as you are my guest.'

Then she sat down beside Hrut and they drank together. Later that evening she said to him, 'You shall lie with me in the upper chamber tonight, with no one else present.'

'Such matters are for you to decide,' replied Hrut.

Afterwards they went up to bed, and she locked the door. They slept there that night, and next morning they drank together, and for the whole of those two weeks they slept together in the upper chamber, alone. Gunnhild warned her attendants: 'If you breathe a word about myself and Hrut, it will be your last.'

Hrut gave her a hundred ells of fine cloth, and twelve furs. Gunnhild thanked him for the gift. Hrut embraced her and thanked her. She bade him farewell, and he went away. Next day he went before the king with thirty men, and greeted him.

The king said, 'You will now want me to carry out the promise I made you.' Hrut was then made a retainer.

'Where am I to sit?' he asked.

'My mother will decide that,' replied the king.

Gunnhild gave him a place of high honour, and Hrut spent the winter with the king, in great favour.

4

In the spring, Hrut learnt that Soti had gone south to Denmark with the inheritance. He went to see Gunnhild and told her about Soti's journey.

The queen said, 'I shall let you have two fully-manned longships, and Ulf the Unwashed, the leader of the King's Spies,* as well; there is no one braver. But go and see the king before you set out.'

Hrut went before the king and told him about Soti's going and his own plan to pursue him.

'What help is my mother giving you?' asked the king.

'Two longships, and Ulf the Unwashed to command them,' replied Hrut.

'That is generous,' said the king. 'I am going to give you another two ships; but even then you will not have too many.'

He accompanied Hrut down to the ships and bade him farewell. Hrut sailed off south with his fleet.

5

THERE was a pirate called Atli Arnvidarson † lurking in the Oresund with eight ships. He had been outlawed by the kings of Denmark and Sweden for his robberies and killings in their kingdoms.

Hrut sailed south for Oresund, and sighted a cluster of ships lying in the Sound.

'What do we do now, Icelander?' called Ulf the Unwashed.

'We carry straight on,' said Hrut. 'Nothing venture, nothing win. Ozur and I shall be in the lead with our ship, and you can take up any position you like.'

'I'm not in the habit of using others as a shield,' said Ulf, and brought his longship level with Hrut's. Together they started through the Sound.

---

* The King's Spies (*gestasveit*) were certain members of the king's retinue whose function was to look after the internal security of the kingdom. They roamed the country seeking signs of incipient rebellion and getting rid of trouble-makers – a sort of medieval F.B.I. *Translators' note.*

† Atli was the son of Earl Arnvid of East Gotaland, who had withheld tribute from King Hakon, foster-son of King Æthelstan. Arnvid and Atli had fled from Jamtland to Gotaland; then Atli led his fleet from Lake Malar out through Stocksund and south to Denmark.

Those inside the Sound saw the ships approaching, and Atli was told.

'Here's an easy chance of booty,' said Atli. 'Down with the awnings! Prepare all ships at once for action! My ship will take the middle of the line.'

The fleets converged. As soon as they were within hailing distance of each other, Atli stood up and said, 'You sail unwarily. Didn't you see there were warships in the Sound? What's the name of your leader?'

Hrut named himself.

'Whose man are you?' asked Atli.

'I am King Harald Grey-Cloak's retainer,' replied Hrut.

'Your Norwegian kings have never had much love for my father and myself,' said Atli.

'That is your ill luck, not theirs,' replied Hrut.

Atli said, 'This encounter will only have one result – and you won't be alive to tell of it.' He snatched up a spear and hurled it at Hrut's ship. The man who was in its way fell dead.

That was the start of the battle; but they found it hard to gain a foothold on Hrut's ships. Ulf the Unwashed was well to the fore, laying about him with sword and spear. Then Atli's prow-man, a man called Asolf, leapt up on to Hrut's ship and cut down four men before Hrut was aware of him and turned to face him. As they met, Asolf lunged with his spear and drove it right through Hrut's shield, before Hrut, with a single blow, struck him dead.

Ulf the Unwashed saw this and said, 'That was a heavy blow, Hrut; you have much to thank Queen Gunnhild for.'

'I have the feeling that these will be your last words,' said Hrut.

At that very moment Atli noticed a gap in Ulf's defence and hurled a spear that went right through him. The fighting now flared up even more fiercely. Atli leapt up on to Hrut's ship and scythed a path along the deck. Ozur turned to meet him and lunged at him, but was knocked off his feet by a thrust from someone else. Now Hrut faced Atli. Atli hacked at him and split his shield from top to bottom; but just then he was struck on the hand by a stone, and dropped his sword. Hrut pounced on the sword and swept off Atli's leg, and then killed him with the next blow.

Hrut and his men seized a lot of booty and kept the two best ships. They stayed on in the Sound for a short while. In the meantime, Soti and his men slipped past them and made for Norway again. They reached the East Agdir coast and went ashore. There Soti met Ogmund, Gunnhild's squire, who recognized him at once and asked him how long he intended to stay.

'Three days,' replied Soti.

'Where are you going after that?' asked Ogmund.

'West to England,' replied Soti, 'and I'm never coming back to Norway so long as Gunnhild is in power.'

Ogmund went straight to Gunnhild, who was attending a feast nearby with her son Gudrod, and told her about Soti's plans. Gunnhild asked Gudrod to go and kill Soti. Gudrod set off at once; Soti was caught unawares, taken ashore, and hanged. Gudrod seized the money and brought it to Gunnhild, who had it all sent on to Konungahella.

Hrut returned in the autumn laden with booty and went at once to see the king, who gave him a good welcome. Hrut offered the king and Gunnhild as much of the booty as they wished, and the king accepted a third of it. Gunnhild told Hrut that she had recovered his inheritance and put Soti to death; Hrut thanked her, and gave her half of it.

6

HRUT spent the winter with the king in high favour; but when spring came he grew very silent. Gunnhild noticed this, and when they were alone she asked him, 'Are you unhappy, Hrut?'

'Far from home is far from joy, as the saying goes,' replied Hrut.

'Do you want to go back to Iceland?' she asked.

'Yes,' he replied.

'Have you a woman out there?' she asked.

'No,' said Hrut.

'I believe you have, nevertheless,' said the queen, and they broke off their conversation.

Hrut went before the king and greeted him.

'What is it you wish, Hrut?' asked the king.

'I beg your leave, my lord, to go to Iceland,' said Hrut.

'Will you have greater honour there than here?' asked the king.

'No,' replied Hrut, 'but each must do as destiny decides.'

Gunnhild said, 'You cannot pull against a force like this. Give him leave to go wherever he thinks best.'

The harvest had been meagre that year, but despite that the king gave him as much flour as he wanted. Ozur and Hrut made ready for the journey to Iceland, and when all their preparations were made, Hrut went to see the king and Gunnhild. Gunnhild took him to one side.

'I want to give you this gold bracelet,' she said when they were alone, and clasped it round his arm.

'You have given me many good gifts,' said Hrut.

She put her arms round his neck and kissed him, and said, 'If I have as much power over you as I think, the spell I now lay on you will prevent your ever enjoying the woman in Iceland on whom you have set your heart. With other women you may have your will, but never with her. And now you must suffer as well as I, since you did not trust me with the truth.'

Hrut laughed, and went away. He went before the king and thanked him. The king bade him a friendly farewell and called him a very brave man, who knew well how to associate with men of rank. Hrut went straight to his ship and set sail. They had favourable winds and landed in Borgarfjord. As soon as the ship was made fast, Hrut rode west to his home, leaving Ozur to unload the ship.

Hrut rode to Hoskuldstead, where he was warmly welcomed by Hoskuld, and he told him all about his travels. They sent a message east to Mord Fiddle to prepare the wedding feast. Meanwhile the brothers rode down to the ship, and Hoskuld told Hrut of his administration of Hrut's property, which had greatly increased in value during his absence.

'Your reward will have to be less than you deserve,' said Hrut, 'but I want to give you as much flour as you will need for your household this winter.'

They laid up the ship and took all the cargo west to the Dales. Hrut remained at home at Hrutstead until six weeks before winter, and then the brothers made ready, with Ozur, to ride to Hrut's wedding. They set off with sixty men and rode all the way east to the Rangriver Plains. A large number of guests had already arrived.

The men were seated down the length of the hall, and the women sat on a dais at one end. The bride was rather downcast. The feasting and drinking began, and everything went off well. Mord Fiddle paid out his daughter's dowry, and Unn rode off west with her husband and his men. When they reached Hrutstead, Hrut handed over to her the running of the whole household; everyone was pleased at this.

But throughout that winter, the marriage between Hrut and Unn remained a marriage only in name.

When spring came, Hrut had to go to the Westfjords to collect money for his goods. Before he left, his wife asked him, 'Are you planning to be back before it is time to ride to the Althing?'

'Why do you ask?' said Hrut.

'I want to ride to the Althing myself,' she replied, 'to see my father.'

'Very well,' said Hrut. 'I shall go with you.'

'Good,' said Unn.

Hrut rode off west to the fjords, collected all his money, put it out to loan again, and then rode back home. When he got back, he made ready for the journey to the Althing and told all his neighbours to accompany him. His brother Hoskuld came too. Then he said to his wife, 'If you are still as eager to go to the Althing as you made out, then make yourself ready and come with me.' She hurriedly made ready, and they all rode to the Althing.

Unn went to her father's booth. He welcomed her warmly, but she was in rather low spirits. When her father noticed this he said, 'I have seen you look more cheerful. What is troubling you?'

Unn did not reply, but burst into tears. Then her father said, 'Why did you ride to the Althing if you won't confide in me? Do you not like it out there in the west?'

'I would give everything I own never to have gone there,' she replied.

Mord said, 'I will soon find out all about this.'

He sent a messenger to fetch Hoskuld and Hrut, who came at once. When they arrived, Mord stood up to meet them, greeted them warmly, and asked them to sit down. They talked for a long time, all in a very friendly way.

Then Mord asked Hrut, 'Why does my daughter dislike it so much out there in the west?'

'Let her speak out,' replied Hrut, 'if she has any complaints to make against me.'

But no charges were brought against Hrut. Then Hrut had his neighbours and members of his household questioned about his treatment of her. They all gave favourable witness, and said that she was allowed to do just as she pleased.

Mord said to Unn, 'Go back home and be happy with your lot. All the evidence speaks better of your husband than of you.'

After that, Hrut rode home from the Althing with his wife, and they got on well together that summer. But when winter came it was the old story all over again, and matters grew worse and worse as spring approached. Hrut had again to go west to the fjords, and announced that he would not be riding to the Althing. Unn made no comment, and when Hrut was ready he rode away.

7

SHORTLY before the Althing was due, Unn had a talk with Sigmund Ozurarson and asked him if he would ride to the Althing with her. Sigmund replied that he did not want to go if his kinsman Hrut would disapprove of it.

'I only asked this of you,' said Unn, 'because I have more claim on you than on anyone else.'

'I shall do this for you on one condition only,' said Sigmund, 'that you ride back west with me afterwards and do nothing underhand against Hrut or myself.'

She gave her promise, and they rode to the Althing. Her father, Mord Fiddle, was there. He welcomed her warmly, and invited her to stay with him in his booth during the Althing. She accepted.

'What have you to tell me of your comrade Hrut?' asked Mord.

'I have nothing but good to say of him,' replied Unn, 'in so far as he is responsible for his own actions.'

Mord was silent for a while. Then he said, 'What is troubling you, daughter? For I can see that you want no one but me to know of it. You can rely on me better than anyone else to solve your problems.'

They moved away so that their conversation could not be overheard. Then Mord said to his daughter, 'Now tell me everything about your relationship, and let nothing deter you.'

'Very well,' said Unn. 'I want to divorce Hrut, and I can tell you the exact grounds I have against him. He is unable to consummate our marriage and give me satisfaction, although in every other way he is as virile as the best of men.'

'What do you mean?' asked Mord. 'Be more explicit.'

Unn replied, 'Whenever he touches me, he is so enlarged that he cannot have enjoyment of me, although we both passionately desire to reach consummation. But we have never succeeded. And yet, before we draw apart, he proves that he is by nature as normal as other men.'

'You have done well to tell me this,' said Mord. 'I can give you a plan which will meet the case so long as you carry it out in every detail.

'First, you must ride home now from the Althing. Your husband will have returned, and he will welcome you warmly. You must be affectionate towards him and compliant, and he will think the situation much improved. On no account must you show him any indifference.

'But when spring comes you must feign illness and take to your bed. Hrut will not try to guess the nature of your illness, and will not reproach you; indeed, he will tell everyone to take the greatest care of you. Then he will set off with Sigmund west to the fjords. He will be busy fetching all his goods from the west, and will be away from home far into the summer.

'Later, when it is time for people to ride to the Althing, and when all those who intend to be there have left the Dales, you must get up from your bed and summon men to accompany you on a journey. When you are quite ready to leave, you must walk to your bedside with those who are going to travel with you. There at your husband's bedstead you must name witnesses and declare yourself lawfully divorced from him; do it as correctly as possible in accordance with the procedural rules of the Althing and the common law of the land. You must then name witnesses once again at the main door.

'With that done you must ride away. Take the path over Laxriverdale Heath and across to Holtavord Heath, for no one will search for you as far as Hrutafjord, and then carry straight on until you come to me here. I shall then take care of the case for you, and you will never fall into his hands again.'

Unn now rode home from the Althing. Hrut had already returned, and he welcomed her warmly. Unn responded well, and was affectionate towards him. They got on well together that year. But when spring came, Unn fell ill and took to her bed. Hrut rode off west to the fjords, leaving orders that she was to be well looked after.

When the Althing was due, Unn made her preparations for the journey. She followed her father's instructions in every detail, and then rode off to the Althing. The men of the district searched for her, but could not find her. Mord welcomed his daughter and asked her how she had carried out his plan.

'I have not deviated from it at all,' she replied.

Mord went to the Law Rock, and there gave notice of Unn's lawful divorce from Hrut. People thought this news indeed. Unn went home with her father, and never set foot in the west again.

8

WHEN Hrut came home, he was shocked to find his wife gone. But he kept his composure. He stayed at home for the rest of the year and discussed the matter with no one.

Next summer he rode to the Althing with his brother Hoskuld and a large following. When he arrived, he asked if Mord Fiddle were present, and was told that he was. Everyone expected that he and Mord would discuss their differences, but this did not happen.

One day, when people were assembled at the Law Rock, Mord named witnesses and gave notice of a claim against Hrut for the return of his daughter's dowry, which he assessed at ninety hundreds.* He demanded immediate payment of this sum, on penalty of a fine of three marks. He referred this action to the proper Quarter Court,† and gave lawful notice of it, in public, at the Law Rock.

When Mord had made this announcement, Hrut replied: 'You are pressing this claim concerning your daughter with greed and aggression rather than decency and fairness, and for that reason I intend to resist it. You have not got your hands on the money yet; it is still in my possesion. I declare, and let all those present at the Law Rock be witnesses, that I challenge you, Mord Fiddle, to single combat‡ for your daughter's dowry. I myself shall stake an equal sum, the winner to take all. But if you refuse to fight with me, you shall forfeit all claim to the dowry.'

Mord was silent, and conferred with his friends about the challenge. Jorund the Priest § told him, 'There is no need for you to ask our opinions; you know well enough that if you fight Hrut you will lose your life as well as the money. Hrut is a successful man; he is great by achievement, and a very good fighter.'

---

* Mord Fiddle lays claim to the whole marriage-settlement – Unn's own dowry plus Hrut's contribution. According to Icelandic law, the wife had a right to all the money involved if the husband was the 'guilty party' in the divorce. *Translators' note.*

† There was one court for each of the four Quarters of Iceland, and it was an offence to attempt to have actions heard in the wrong court (cf. Chapter 141). *Translators' note.*

‡ *Hólmganga.* Duelling seems to have been accepted as a lawful substitute for court actions in tenth-century Iceland. Formal duels (literally : 'island-going') at the Althing were fought on a sandy islet in Oxar River, which flows through the site of the Althing. *Translators' note.*

§ One of the thirty-nine priest-chieftains (cf. Introduction). Priesthood in Iceland was more a matter of secular authority than religious office in pre-Christian days. Their authority was largely inherited; they were the custodians of the laws that they themselves had created, the aristocracy of the republic, and they had in addition various functions to perform at the Althings and local Assemblies, acting as law-makers and nominating the judges for the courts. After the conversion of Iceland to Christianity in the year 1000 (cf. note on page 216) they retained their titles and secular authority. *Translators' note.*

So Mord announced that he would not fight with Hrut. There was a great shout of derision at the Law Rock, and Mord earned nothing but ignominy from this.

After that, people rode home from the Althing. Hrut and Hoskuld rode west to Reykjardale and stayed overnight at Lund, the home of Thjostolf, the son of Bjorn Gold-Bearer. It had rained heavily that day; the travellers were soaked, and long-fires* were lit for them.

Thjostolf sat between Hoskuld and Hrut. Two boys who were under his care were playing on the floor with a little girl; they were chattering loudly with the folly of youth.

One of the boys said, 'I'll be Mord and divorce you from your wife on the grounds that you couldn't have intercourse with her.'

The other boy replied, 'Then I'll be Hrut and invalidate your dowry-claim if you don't dare to fight me.'

They repeated this several times, and the household burst out laughing. Hoskuld was furious, and hit the boy who was calling himself Mord with a stick. It struck him on the face and drew blood.

'Get outside,' said Hoskuld, 'and don't try to ridicule us.'

'Come over here to me,' said Hrut. The boy did so. Hrut drew a gold ring from his finger and gave it to him.

'Go away now,' he said, 'and never provoke anyone again.'

The boy went away, saying, 'I shall always remember your noble-mindedness.'

Hrut was highly praised for this. Later they rode off home to the west, and so ends the episode of Hrut and Mord Fiddle.

9

WE return now to Hallgerd, Hoskuld's daughter, who had grown up to be a woman of great beauty. She was very tall, which earned her the nickname Long-Legs, and her lovely hair was now so long that it could veil her whole body. She was impetuous and wilful.

* *Langeldar*, a long hearth running down the centre of the main room. *Translators' note.*

She had a foster-father called Thjostolf, a Hebridean by descent. He was strong and skilled in arms; he had killed many men and paid compensation for none of them. It was said that he did little to temper Hallgerd's character.

A man called Thorvald Osvifsson lived at Fell, out in Medalfellstrand. He was a wealthy man; he owned some islands in Breidafjord known as the Bjarn Isles, from which he got dried fish and flour. He was well-built and well-bred, but apt to be quick-tempered.

One day, Thorvald and his father Osvif had a talk about where to find a wife for Thorvald. It soon became clear that Thorvald felt there was hardly anyone good enough for him.

Then Osvif asked, 'Do you want to ask for Hallgerd Long-Legs, Hoskuld's daughter?'

'Yes, I do,' replied Thorvald.

'It would not be very suitable for either of you,' said Osvif. 'Hallgerd has a will of her own, and you are stubborn and unrelenting.'

'That's where I want to try, nevertheless,' said Thorvald, 'and there's no use attempting to dissuade me.'

'The risk is all yours,' his father replied.

They went to make their marriage-proposal, and were welcomed at Hoskuldstead. They immediately told Hoskuld the purpose of their visit, and made the offer of marriage.

Hoskuld replied, 'I am well aware of your circumstances. For my part, I shall not try to conceal from you the fact that my daughter is a hard-willed woman; her looks and her manners you can judge for yourselves.'

'Name your own terms,' said Thorvald. 'I don't intend to let her temper stand in the way of this marriage-deal.'

They discussed the terms there and then. Hoskuld did not consult Hallgerd about it, because he was anxious to marry her off. They reached complete agreement on the terms, Hoskuld offered his hand, Thorvald shook it, was betrothed to Hallgerd, and then rode back home.

HOSKULD told Hallgerd about the marriage-deal.

She said, 'Now I have proof of what I have suspected for a long time: you do not love me as much as you have always said you do, since you did not think it worth while to ask me about this beforehand. Besides, this is not as good a marriage as you have promised me.'

It was obvious that she thought she was marrying beneath her.

'Your pride,' said Hoskuld, 'is not of such concern to me that I would let it interfere with any arrangements I make. I, and not you, will make the decisions whenever we differ.'

'Pride,' said Hallgerd, 'is a thing you and your kinsmen have in plenty, so it's not surprising if I have some, too.'

She left him and went to find her foster-father Thjostolf. Resentfully she told him what was to happen.

'Cheer up,' said Thjostolf. 'This will not be your only marriage, and you can be sure that you will be consulted about it next time; for I will carry out your every wish, except where your father or Hrut are concerned.'

They did not discuss the matter further.

Hoskuld made preparations for the wedding feast, and rode out to invite guests. When he came to Hrutstead he asked Hrut to come outside to talk to him. Hrut came out, and they went aside to talk. Hoskuld told him all about the contract, and invited him to the wedding.

'I hope you are not offended, kinsman,' he added, 'that I did not send you word while the deal was being arranged.'

'I would much rather have nothing to do with it at all,' said Hrut, 'for there will be no luck in this marriage, either for him or for her. But I shall attend the wedding if you think my presence would honour it.'

'I do indeed,' replied Hoskuld, and rode back home.

Osvif and Thorvald also invited guests, so that at least a hundred in all were expected.

There was a man called Svan, who lived on a farm called

Svanhill in Bjarnarfjord, to the north of Steingrimsfjord. Svan was extremely skilled in witchcraft; he was Hallgerd's maternal uncle, and a very unpleasant person to have any dealings with. Hallgerd invited him to her wedding and sent Thjostolf up north for him; the two men took to each other at once.

Now the guests arrived for the wedding. Hallgerd sat on the dais, and was a hilariously cheerful bride. Thjostolf kept going over to talk to her, and at other times he talked to Svan; and people were disturbed at this. But the wedding feast went off well. Hoskuld paid over Hallgerd's dowry with the utmost readiness, and then asked Hrut, 'Should I produce some gifts as well?'

Hrut replied, 'Hallgerd will give you plenty of opportunity in the future to waste your money; let this suffice in the meantime.'

I I

THORVALD rode home from the wedding with his bride and Thjostolf. Thjostolf rode close to Hallgerd, and they talked together all the way.

Osvif turned to his son and said, 'Are you pleased with the marriage? How did you get on together in conversation?'

'Very well,' replied Thorvald. 'She was extremely affectionate towards me. You can see that yourself from the way she laughs at every word.'

'I do not find her laughter as reassuring as you do,' said Osvif. 'But time will tell.'

They rode on until they reached home. In the evening Hallgerd sat beside her husband and placed Thjostolf on her other side.

Thjostolf and Thorvald paid each other little attention, and wasted few words on each other that winter.

Hallgerd turned out to be demanding and prodigal. She claimed everything for her own, whether it belonged to her or not, and wasted it all extravagantly. By spring, the household provisions were running out, and there was a shortage of flour and dried fish. Hallgerd went to Thorvald and said, 'You won't get anything done by sitting about; we need more flour and dried fish for the larder.'

'I laid in no less food this year than usual,' replied Thorvald, 'and it has always lasted well into the summer.'

'I don't care in the least if you and your father starved yourselves for money,' said Hallgerd.

Thorvald was furious and struck her so hard in the face that it bled. Then he walked out and called his servants to come with him. They launched a skiff, eight of his men jumped in, and they rowed out to the Bjarn Isles* to fetch the dried fish and flour.

Meanwhile Hallgerd was sitting outside the house, feeling very resentful. Thjostolf came up and saw that her face was injured.

'Why have you been so harshly treated?' he asked.

'My husband Thorvald did it,' she replied. 'And if you had cared for me at all you would have been here to help me.'

'I didn't know,' said Thjostolf. 'But now I will avenge it.'

He walked away down to the shore, taking with him an axe he owned, a massive weapon with an iron-bound shaft. He launched a six-oared boat, jumped in, and rowed out to the Bjarn Isles. When he got there, everyone was away fishing except Thorvald and his men; Thorvald was busy loading the skiff, while his men were fetching the provisions for him.

Just then Thjostolf arrived. He jumped on to the skiff and gave a hand with the loading. Then he said, 'You are slow in your work, Thorvald, and clumsy too.'

'Do you think you can do any better?' asked Thorvald.

'Anything we do, I can do better than you,' replied Thjostolf, 'and the woman who has you for a husband has made a bad marriage. You shouldn't live together much longer.'

Thorvald snatched up a short-sword which lay beside him and thrust at Thjostolf. But Thjostolf's axe was already at his shoulder, and he struck back, hitting Thorvald's arm and shattering the bone. The short-sword fell. Thjostolf raised his axe a second time and drove it into Thorvald's head, killing him instantly.

* The distance is approximately twenty-five miles. *Translators' note.*

12

AT that moment Thorvald's men came down towards the skiff with their loads. Thjostolf acted without hesitation. He hacked two-handed at the side of the skiff, smashing the planks the length of two thwarts, and then leapt into his own boat. The dark-blue sea poured into the skiff, which sank with all its cargo, and with it sank Thorvald's body before his men could see what had been done to him. They knew for certain only that he was dead.

Thjostolf rowed away up the fjord, while Thorvald's men shouted curses after him. He made no reply, but carried on rowing until he reached home. There he beached the boat and walked up to the house with his blood-smeared axe on his shoulder.

Hallgerd was outside. 'There is blood on your axe,' she said. 'What have you done?'

'I have now arranged that you can be married a second time,' replied Thjostolf.

'Then you must mean that Thorvald is dead,' she said.

'Yes,' said Thjostolf. 'And now you must think up some plan for me.'

'Certainly,' said Hallgerd. 'I am going to send you north to Svanhill in Bjarnarfjord. Svan will welcome you with open arms, and he is so formidable that no one will be able to harm you there.'

Thjostolf saddled his horse, mounted, and rode north to Svanhill in Bjarnarfjord. Svan welcomed him with open arms and asked him his news. Thjostolf told him about the killing of Thorvald and everything that had happened.

'Now that's what I call a man,' said Svan, 'someone who lets nothing stand in his way. I can promise you that if they try to reach you here, they will get nothing for their pains but ignominy.'

Meanwhile, Hallgerd told Ljot the Black, a kinsman of hers, to saddle their horses and get ready to accompany her. 'I want to ride home to my father,' she said.

He made the preparations, and Hallgerd went to her chests

and unlocked them. She called in all the members of her household and gave them each some gift. They were all sad to see her leave. Then she rode off to Hoskuldstead, where her father gave her a good welcome, for he had not yet heard the news.

'Why did Thorvald not come with you?' he asked.

'He's dead,' she replied.

'Thjostolf must be responsible for that,' said Hoskuld.

Hallgerd said that he was.

Hoskuld said, 'I can always rely on Hrut's predictions. He told me that this marriage-deal would bring terrible ill luck. But there is no point in blaming oneself after the event.'

Meanwhile, Thorvald's companions waited on the Bjarn Isles until boats arrived. They reported the killing of Thorvald and asked for a boat to take them to the mainland. They were lent one at once, and they rowed over to Reykjaness, where they went to see Osvif and told him the news.

'Evil plans have evil consequences,' said Osvif. 'And I can see what must have happened after the killing. Hallgerd will have sent Thjostolf to Bjarnarfjord, and she herself will have gone home to her father. We shall now gather a force and go north after Thjostolf.'

They agreed, and went out to ask others for support, and got a good response. Then they all rode off to Steingrimsfjord, through Ljotriverdale and Selriverdale and on past Bassastead; from there they came over the ridge into Bjarnarfjord.

At that moment Svan had a fit of yawning, and announced: 'Osvif's fetches* are attacking us.'

Thjostolf sprang to his feet and seized his axe.

'Come outside with me,' said Svan. 'We won't need much for this.'

They both went out. Svan took a goat-skin and swung it round his head, chanting:

> 'Let there be fog
> And let there be phantoms,
> Weird marvels
> To baffle your hunters.'

* *Fylgja*, the personification of a person's spirit, perceptible to those with second sight or magic power. Fetches often manifested themselves at times of crisis. *Translators' note.*

Meanwhile, Osvif and his men were riding over the hill when a thick bank of fog advanced to meet them.

'This is Svan's work,' said Osvif. 'We shall be lucky if there is nothing worse to come.'

A little later a great darkness descended on them, blinding their eyes. They toppled off their horses and lost them; some of the men strayed into swamps, others stumbled against trees; all were in danger of injury and had lost their weapons.

Then Osvif said, 'If I could find my horses and weapons, I would turn back home.'

As soon as he had said this, their sight returned a little and they found their horses and weapons. Then many of them urged that they should try to resume the attack. They set off again, but at once the same uncanny events overtook them.

This happened three times. Finally Osvif said, 'We have had no success on this expedition, but even so we must now turn back. We must resort to other plans. What I have chiefly in mind is to go to see Hoskuld and ask him for compensation for my son. One may look for honour where honour abounds.'

They rode away to the Breidafjord Dales, and there is nothing to tell of their journey until they reached Hoskuldstead. Hrut had arrived earlier from Hrutstead. Osvif asked Hoskuld and Hrut to come outside; they both went out and greeted Osvif. They went aside to talk, and Hoskuld asked Osvif where he had come from. Osvif replied that he had been to look for Thjostolf, but had been unable to find him. Hoskuld said that he would be north in Svanhill by now – 'and it is not everyone who can reach him there.'

'I have come here,' said Osvif, 'to ask you for compensation for my son.'

'I did not kill your son,' said Hoskuld, 'nor did I plot his death. But you cannot be blamed for seeking compensation somewhere.'

Hrut said, 'The nose is next to the eyes, brother; we must disarm criticism by paying this man compensation for his son. In that way we can improve your daughter's prospects. Our only course is to settle this claim now, and the less said about it the better.'

'Will you act as arbitrator, then?' asked Hoskuld.

'Certainly,' said Hrut. 'But I shall not be lenient with you, because, if the truth be told, it was your daughter who was responsible for his death.'

Hoskuld flushed dark red and was silent for a while. Finally he stood up and said to Osvif, 'Take my hand now to show that you agree to settle this by arbitration.'

Osvif stood up. 'It cannot be an impartial settlement,' he said, 'if your brother arbitrates. But your attitude has been so fair, Hrut, that I readily entrust you with the matter.'

He took Hoskuld's hand and agreed to settle, on the understanding that Hrut should arbitrate and announce the assessment before Osvif left.

Then Hrut made his assessment and announced, 'For the killing of Thorvald I award two hundred ounces of silver'* (which was considered generous compensation for a man in those days) 'You must pay it promptly and readily and in full, brother.'

Hoskuld did so. Then Hrut said to Osvif, 'I myself would like to give you a fine cloak which I brought with me from abroad.'

Osvif thanked him for the gift, and went home well pleased with the outcome. Later, Hrut and Hoskuld went to see him about the division of property, and reached a satisfactory agreement. They went back home with their share, and Osvif is now out of this saga.

Hallgerd asked Hoskuld to take Thjostolf into his household, and he granted her request. People talked a lot about the killing of Thorvald for a long time afterwards. Hallgerd's share of the property brought in good returns, and accumulated.

---

* Ounce here refers to actual weight, rather than a unit of exchange as in the note on *hundreds* on p. 41. An ounce of unrefined silver (as is meant here, probably) was worth four legal ounces, i.e. 24 ells of cloth. The compensation paid for Thorvald was equivalent to the value of 64 milch cows; in *Njal's Saga* this seems to be the norm for men of any standing. *Translator's note.*

13

THREE brothers now enter the saga – Thorarin, Ragi, and Glum, the sons of Olaf Hjalti. They were all men of great distinction and wealth. Thorarin was known as Thorarin Ragi's-Brother; he was an extremely intelligent man, and succeeded Hrafn Hængsson as Law-Speaker.*

Thorarin lived at Varmabrook, which he owned in common with Glum, who had spent many years trading abroad. Glum was tall and strong and very handsome.

The third brother, Ragi, was a great warrior. The three brothers jointly owned Eng Isle and Laugarness, in the south.

Once when Glum and Thorarin were talking together, Thorarin asked Glum if he intended going abroad as usual.

'No,' replied Glum. 'I had decided to give up trading now.'

'What do you have in mind, then?' asked Thorarin. 'Do you want to get married?'

'Yes indeed,' replied Glum, 'if I could find myself a good match.'

Thorarin then listed the women in Borgarfjord who were unmarried, and asked Glum if he wanted to marry any of them – 'and I shall ride with you to ask for her hand.'

'No, I want none of these,' replied Glum.

'Whom do you want then? Name her,' said Thorarin.

'If you want to know,' said Glum, 'her name is Hallgerd, the daughter of Hoskuld of the Dales, in the west.'

'You are certainly not learning from another man's lesson, as the saying goes,' said Thorarin. 'Hallgerd has been married already, and she contrived her husband's death.'

* *Lögsögumaðr*, the president of the Althing. The Law-Speaker was elected by the priest-chieftains for a three-year term of office (he could also be re-elected for further terms). His main duty was to recite from memory the entire code of law, one-third of the code each year, at the opening of the Althing. Hrafn Hængsson was the first Law-Speaker of Iceland; he held office from the institution of the Althing in 930 until 949. Thorarin Ragi's-Brother was Law-Speaker from 950 to 969. *Translators' note.*

'Perhaps she will not have such ill luck a second time,' said Glum. 'I am quite certain that she will not contrive my death. If you want to do me any honour, you will ride with me to ask for her hand.'

'There will be no preventing this,' said Thorarin. 'What fate ordains must come to pass.'

Glum kept raising this matter with his brother, but for a long time Thorarin was evasive. Finally, however, they gathered a company of twenty and rode west to the Dales. When they reached Hoskuldstead, they were given a good welcome by Hoskuld, and they stayed there overnight. Early next morning Hoskuld sent for Hrut, who came at once. Hoskuld was outside when he rode into the home-meadow. Hoskuld told him what visitors had arrived.

'What do they want?' asked Hrut.

'They have broached no business with me yet,' replied Hoskuld.

'Nevertheless,' said Hrut, 'you are the one they have come to see. They must be here to ask for your daughter Hallgerd's hand. What answer will you give them?'

'What do you advise?' asked Hoskuld.

'Give them a favourable answer,' replied Hrut. 'But tell them all the woman's assets and defects.'

During this conversation, the visitors came out of the house. Hoskuld and Hrut went to meet them. Hrut greeted Thorarin and Glum warmly; then they all went aside to talk.

Thorarin said, 'I have come here with my brother Glum, Hoskuld, in order to ask for the hand of your daughter Hallgerd on his behalf. I would point out to you that he is a man of worth.'

'I am aware,' said Hoskuld, 'that both of you are men of great distinction; but for my part I must tell you that I arranged my daughter's previous marriage, and it brought us great ill luck.'

'We will not let that stand in the way of our marriage-deal,' said Thorarin. 'One oath abused does not make all oaths worthless. This match can turn out well even though the other one turned out badly – and Thjostolf was most to blame for that.'

Then Hrut said, 'I would give you some advice if you are not deterred from this match by what has already happened in

65

regard to Hallgerd : if the marriage takes place, Thjostolf must not be allowed to go south with her, and he should never stay there longer than three days without Glum's permission; if he does, Glum should have the right to kill him as an outlaw. Glum may give him permission to stay longer if he likes, but I do not advise it.

'Furthermore, this time you must not fail to inform Hallgerd beforehand. Let her know all about this proposed marriage-deal now, meet Glum, and decide for herself whether she wants to marry him or not. Then she cannot put the blame on others if it does not turn out well. There must be nothing underhand about this.'

'As always,' said Thorarin, 'it is best to be guided by your advice.'

Hallgerd was sent for. She arrived accompanied by two other women; she had put on a woven blue cloak over a scarlet tunic and a silver belt. She wore her hair hanging loose on either side of her bosom and tucked under her belt. She sat down between her father and Hrut. She greeted them all graciously, spoke to them with confidence and ease, and asked them for their news. Then she stopped talking.

Glum said, 'My brother Thorarin and I have been discussing with your father the possibility of a marriage-deal, for me to marry you, Hallgerd, if you approve of it too. You must now say frankly, since you have a will very much your own, whether it is at all to your liking; and if you are averse to such a contract, we do not wish to discuss it further.'

'I know that you brothers are men of great distinction,' said Hallgerd. 'I know too that this would be a much better marriage for me than my previous one. But I also want to know what you have discussed and how far the discussion has gone. However, I have the feeling, from the look of you, that I could love you well if our temperaments did not clash.'

Glum himself told her everything that had been said about the marriage-deal, word for word, and then asked Hoskuld and Hrut if he had repeated it correctly. Hoskuld said he had.

Then Hallgerd said, 'Since you have shown me such consideration over this, father, and you, Hrut, I shall do as you advise. Let this contract stand as you have proposed.'

'I think it would be advisable,' said Hrut, 'that Hoskuld and

I name the witnesses but Hallgerd herself declare her own betrothal – if the Law-Speaker considers that correct procedure.'

'Perfectly correct,' said Thorarin.

Hallgerd's property was then valued. Glum was to put up an equal sum, and they were to share the whole estate equally. Then Glum was betrothed to Hallgerd, and the brothers rode back home to the south. Hoskuld was to hold the wedding-feast at Hoskuldstead. All was now quiet until it was time to ride to the wedding.

14

GLUM and his brothers gathered a large and select company. They all rode west to the Dales and came to Hoskuldstead, where a crowd of guests had already arrived.

Hoskuld and Hrut occupied one bench, and the bridegroom the other. Hallgerd sat on the dais, and was properly behaved. Thjostolf stalked about brandishing his axe in a sinister way, but no one paid any attention.

When the wedding-feast was over, Hallgerd went south with the brothers. When they reached Varmabrook, Thorarin asked her whether she wanted to take charge of the household.

'No,' she replied.

Hallgerd showed great restraint that winter, and was not disliked.

In the spring, Thorarin and Glum discussed their financial arrangements. Thorarin said, 'I want to hand over Varmabrook to you and Hallgerd; that will be the most convenient for you. I myself will go south to Laugarness to live, and we shall continue to own Eng Isle jointly.'

Glum agreed to this; and so Thorarin moved house to Laugarness, while Glum and his wife stayed on at Varmabrook. Hallgerd engaged more servants; she was lavish and yet resourceful.

In the summer she gave birth to a daughter. Glum asked her what the child was to be called.

'She is to be called Thorgerd, after my father's mother,' she replied, 'for Thorgerd was descended on her father's side direct from Sigurd the Dragon-Killer.'

The child was baptized and given the name of Thorgerd. She grew up at Varmabrook and became very like her mother in appearance.

Glum and Hallgerd were very happy together. And so time passed.

News came south from Bjarnarfjord about Svan: he had gone out fishing with his men that spring, and they had encountered a fierce easterly gale that drove their boat ashore at Veidilaus with the loss of all lives. Some fishermen at Kaldbak thought they had seen Svan being warmly welcomed into the innermost depths of Kaldbakhorn Mountain; other people denied this and said that it was all lies. But no one could deny that no trace of Svan was ever seen again, either living or dead.

Hallgerd was greatly distressed to hear of the loss of her uncle.

Glum offered to exchange farms with Thorarin again. Thorarin declined the offer, but added, 'If I were to outlive you, however, I would move back into Varmabrook.'

Glum told Hallgerd this.

'He certainly deserves it of us,' she replied.

15

THJOSTOLF had beaten one of Hoskuld's servants; so Hoskuld ordered him to leave. Thjostolf took his horse and his weapons and said to Hoskuld, 'This time I am going away for good.'

'That will make everyone happy,' said Hoskuld.

Thjostolf rode all the way to Varmabrook, where Hallgerd gave him a good welcome and Glum a not unfriendly one. Thjostolf told Hallgerd that her father had ordered him out, and asked her for help. She replied that she could not promise to let him stay until she had consulted Glum.

'Are you two getting on well together?' asked Thjostolf.

'We love each other very much,' she replied.

She went to see Glum, and put her arms round his neck.

'Will you grant me the favour I am going to ask of you?' she asked.

'Of course,' he replied, 'if there is honour for you in it. What is it you want?'

'Thjostolf has been ordered out of Hoskuldstead,' she replied, 'and I would like you to allow him to stay here. But I won't insist if you are opposed to it.'

'Since you are being so reasonable,' said Glum, 'I shall do as you wish. But I tell you, if he causes any trouble he will have to go at once.'

She went to Thjostolf and told him.

'You have done well,' said Thjostolf, 'as I knew you would.'

So Thjostolf stayed on there, and controlled himself to begin with; but after a while he began to make his unpleasantness felt. He showed no respect for anyone except Hallgerd; yet she never took his side when he quarrelled with others.

Thorarin took his brother Glum to task for letting Thjostolf stay on; he warned him that Thjostolf's presence would cause real trouble, as had happened before. Glum answered amiably enough, but did not alter his decision.

16

ONE year the autumn muster of sheep was poor, and many of Glum's wethers were missing. Glum said to Thjostolf, 'Go up to the mountains with my men and see if you can find any of the sheep.'

'I'm no good at chasing sheep,' said Thjostolf. 'And anyway I'm certainly not going to walk at the heels of your slaves. You go yourself, and then I'll come with you.'

This led to heated words.

Hallgerd was sitting outside; it was a fine day. Glum went up to her and said, 'Thjostolf and I have just had a quarrel. We are not sharing the same roof much longer.'

He told her everything that had happened between them. Hallgerd started to defend Thjostolf, and a quarrel flared up. Glum slapped her and walked away saying, 'I am not going to argue with you any more.'

She loved Glum so deeply that she could not restrain her tears, and wept bitterly. Then Thjostolf came up to her and said, 'You have been harshly treated, but it won't happen very often again.'

'This I forbid you to avenge,' she cried. 'You are not to take a hand in our affairs, however they may go.'

Thjostolf walked away with a grin on his face.

17

GLUM summoned his men to accompany him; Thjostolf got ready too and went with him. They all went up through southern Reykjardale past Baugagill towards Thverfell, where they split up; some went to search Skorradale, others were sent south to the Sulur Hills. All of them came upon large numbers of sheep.

Eventually Glum and Thjostolf found themselves alone. They walked south from Thverfell and discovered there some sheep which bolted from them. They tried to herd them towards the foot of the hill, but the sheep escaped to higher ground.

They each started blaming the other for this. Thjostolf said that Glum had not the strength for anything except romping on Hallgerd's belly.

'The worst companions are brought from home,' said Glum. 'To think that I should have to take insolence from you, a miserable slave!'

'You'll soon find out that I am no slave,' said Thjostolf, 'for I'll never yield an inch to you.'

Enraged, Glum hacked at him with his short-sword, but Thjostolf parried with his axe. The sword struck the axe-blade with such force that it bit an inch deep. Thjostolf at once struck back with his axe at Glum's shoulder, severing shoulder-bone and collar-bone. Blood gushed from the wound into his lungs. Glum seized hold of Thjostolf with his other arm so violently that he forced him to the ground; but he could not hold him down, for death overwhelmed him. Thjostolf took a gold bracelet off him and then covered the body with stones. Then he walked back to Varmabrook.

Hallgerd was outside. She saw the blood on his axe. Thjostolf tossed the gold bracelet to her.

'What has happened?' she asked. 'Why is your axe covered with blood?'

'I don't know how you'll take this,' replied Thjostolf. 'Glum has been killed.'

'Then you must have done it,' said Hallgerd.

'Yes,' he replied.

Hallgerd laughed. 'There's nothing half-hearted about your way of doing things,' she said.

'What can you do to help me this time?' asked Thjostolf.

'You must go to my uncle Hrut,' she replied. 'He will look after you.'

Thjostolf said, 'I don't know whether this is good advice. But still, I'll do as you say in this.'

He took his horse and rode away, and never paused until he reached Hrutstead. It was then the middle of the night. He tethered his horse behind the farm, then went round and hammered on the door. After that he walked round to the north side of the house.

Hrut had been lying awake. He jumped up at once, and pulled on his tunic and boots. He took his sword, and then wrapped a cloak around his left hand and arm. As he went out, the people in the house woke up.

He walked north round the house and caught sight of a tall figure. He realized that it was Thjostolf. Hrut asked him his news.

'I bring news of the killing of Glum,' said Thjostolf.

'Who was responsible for that?' asked Hrut.

'I killed him,' replied Thjostolf.

'Why did you come here?'

'Hallgerd sent me to you,' replied Thjostolf.

'Then she had nothing to do with the killing,' said Hrut, and drew his sword.

Thjostolf saw this and tried to get in the first blow. Quickly he swung his axe at Hrut, but Hrut dodged out of the way and struck the side of the blade so hard with his left arm that the axe flew out of Thjostolf's grasp; then he hacked right-handed at Thjostolf's leg above the knee, all but severing it, and immediately rushed hard at him to knock him down. As Thjostolf fell, Hrut struck at his head and killed him.

At that point Hrut's men came out and saw what had happened. He told them to take the body away and cover it up. Then he went to see Hoskuld and told him about the killing of Glum and of Thjostolf. Hoskuld thought Glum's death a great loss, and thanked Hrut for killing Thjostolf.

A little later, Thorarin Ragi's-Brother heard about the killing of his brother Glum. He rode off west to the Dales with eleven men, and was welcomed with open arms by Hoskuld when he reached Hoskuldstead. He stayed there overnight. Hoskuld at once sent for Hrut to come over. Hrut came immediately. Next day they all discussed Glum's death at length.

Thorarin asked, 'Will you pay me any compensation for my brother? His death is a great loss to me.'

'I did not kill your brother,' replied Hoskuld. 'Nor did my daughter contrive his death. And the moment Hrut learned about it, he killed Thjostolf.'

Thorarin fell silent, as he realized the difficulties in his claim.

Then Hrut said, 'Let us make his journey good. He has certainly suffered a great loss; it would be spoken of to our credit if we gave him gifts, and it would make him our friend for life.'

That is what they did. Hoskuld and Hrut gave him gifts, and he rode back south. In the spring, Thorarin and Hallgerd exchanged farms; she went south to Laugarness, and he moved to Varmabrook.

And Thorarin is now out of this saga.

18

MEANWHILE, Mord Fiddle fell ill and died, and this was considered a great loss. His daughter Unn, who had never married again, inherited everything. But she was very extravagant and improvident in her management of the estate, and her wealth frittered away in her hands; until finally she had nothing left except her land and some personal possessions.

A MAN called Gunnar Hamundarson was a kinsman of Unn's; his mother was Rannveig, the daughter of Sigfus.*

Gunnar lived at Hlidarend, in Fljotshlid. He was a tall, powerful man, outstandingly skilful with arms. He could strike or throw with either hand, and his sword-strokes were so fast that he seemed to be brandishing three swords at once. He was excellent at archery, and his arrows never missed their mark. He could jump more than his own height in full armour, and just as far backwards as forwards. He could swim like a seal. There was no sport at which anyone could even attempt to compete with him. It has been said that there has never been his equal.

He was a handsome man, with fair skin and a straight nose slightly tilted at the tip. He had keen blue eyes, red cheeks, and a fine head of thick flaxen hair. He was extremely well-bred, fearless, generous, and even-tempered, faithful to his friends but careful in his choice of them. He was prosperous.

Gunnar had a brother called Kolskegg, tall, strong, courageous, and reliable. There was another brother, called Hjort, still a child at this time; and a third, Orm Wood-Nose, who was illegitimate and who plays no part in this saga. He also had a sister called Arngunn, married to Hroar Tongue-Priest,† the grandson of Gardar Svafarsson, the discoverer of Iceland.‡

* Rannveig was the daughter of Sigfus, the son of Sighvat the Red (who was killed at Sandhills Ferry). Gunnar's father, Hamund, was the son of Gunnar Baugsson (who gave his name to Gunnars Holt) and of Hrafnhild, the daughter of Storolf Hængsson, brother of Hrafn the Law-Speaker and father of Orm the Strong.

† Hroar was the son of Uni the Illegitimate.

‡ The *Book of Settlements* (*Landnámabók*) gives two versions of the discovery of Iceland by the Norsemen, round about A.D. 860. One version says that it was first found by a Viking called Naddod who was driven off his course from Norway to the Faroes. The other version names Gardar Svafarsson, a Swede, as the first discoverer. But long before the Norsemen came to Iceland, it had been known to Irish monks, who would cross the Atlantic in their frail *currachs* to seek hermitage and refuge in the empty, fertile island far off the normal Viking routes. *Translators' note.*

Arngunn had a son, Hamund the Halt, who lived at Hamundar-stead.

20

A MAN called Njal, the son of Thorgeir Gollnir, lived at Berg-thorsknoll in the Land-Isles.* He also owned another farm at Thorolfsfell. He had a brother called Holta-Thorir, the father of Thorleif Crow (from whom the men of Skogar are descended), Thorgrim the Mighty, and Thorgeir Skorar-Geir.

Njal was wealthy and handsome, but he had one peculiarity: he could not grow a beard.

He was so skilled in law that no one was considered his equal. He was a wise and prescient man. His advice was sound and benevolent, and always turned out well for those who followed it. He was a gentle man of great integrity; he remembered the past and discerned the future, and solved the problems of any man who came to him for help.

His wife was called Bergthora, the daughter of Skarp-Hedin. She was an exceptional and courageous woman, but a little harsh-natured.

They had six children, three sons and three daughters, all of whom are concerned in this saga later.

2I

MEANWHILE Unn had run through all her money. She travelled to Hlidarend to see Gunnar. He gave his kinswoman a good welcome, and she stayed there overnight. Next day they sat outside and talked; eventually she told him how short of money she was.

'This is bad,' said Gunnar.

* Njal's father, Thorgeir Gollnir, was the son of Thorolf. Njal's mother was called Asgerd, the daughter of the chieftain Askel the Silent; she had come out to Iceland and settled the land to the east of Markar River, between Oldustein and Seljalandsmull.

74

'What help can you give me?' she asked.

'You can have as much as you need from the money I have out on loan,' he replied.

'No,' said Unn, 'I don't want to use up your money.'

'What do you want then?' he asked.

'I want you to recover my money from Hrut,' replied Unn.

'I hardly think that I can succeed where your father once tried and failed,' said Gunnar. 'He was a great lawyer, whereas I scarcely know a thing about law.'

'Hrut relied on force rather than law,' said Unn. 'My father was an old man then, and he was persuaded not to try to fight it out. There is no one else in my family to undertake this claim if you haven't the courage to do it.'

'I am certainly not afraid to try to get your money back,' said Gunnar, 'but I don't know how the claim should be revived.'

'Go and see Njal at Bergthorsknoll,' said Unn. 'He will know what to advise, and he is a great friend of yours.'

'I can certainly expect as good advice from him as he gives to others,' said Gunnar.

The outcome was that Gunnar took over the claim, and let Unn have as much money as she required for her household. Then she went back home.

Gunnar now rode to see Njal, who welcomed him warmly. They went aside at once to talk, and Gunnar said, 'I have come to you for some good advice.'

'I have many friends who deserve good advice from me,' said Njal. 'But for you I think I would try hardest of all.'

'I want you to know,' said Gunnar, 'that I have taken over Unn's dowry-claim against Hrut.'

'That is a very difficult task,' said Njal, 'and it could have dangerous consequences. Nevertheless, I shall give you the advice that seems to me most promising; it will work out well if you follow it in every detail, but if you don't, your life will be in danger.'

'I shall not deviate from it at all,' said Gunnar.

Njal was silent for a while. Then he said, 'I have thought it over, and this will work out well. . . .'

Njal said, 'You must set off from home with two companions as soon as possible. You must be wearing a coarse overcoat on top of a striped woollen tunic; underneath all that you must wear your good clothes, and carry a small axe. Each of you is to take two horses, one fat and the other lean, and some samples of home-made wares.

'Set off early tomorrow morning, and as soon as you have crossed west over Hvit River, pull your hat well down over your eyes. People will ask who this tall man might be; your companions are to say that it is Hawker-Hedin the Mighty, from Eyjafjord, with handiwork for sale; that he is bad-tempered and loud-mouthed and thinks that he alone knows everything; and that he is apt to cancel a sale and assault people if anything is not done exactly as he wants it.

'Ride west to Borgarfjord, offering your wares for sale everywhere but cancelling the deals often enough to let the story spread that Hawker-Hedin is an extremely unpleasant person to have any dealings with, and that his reputation is in no way exaggerated.

'Ride on to Northriverdale and then to Hrutafjord and Laxriverdale, until you reach Hoskuldstead. Stay one night there, but sit near the door and keep your head low. Hoskuld will warn his household to have nothing to do with Hawker-Hedin because he is so aggressive. Leave there the following morning and go to the farm closest to Hrutstead. Offer your wares for sale there, showing all the worst articles and trying to disguise their defects.

'The farmer will examine them closely and will notice the faults; then you snatch them away from him and start abusing him. He will say that it is little wonder that you are so rude to him when you are rude to everyone else; at that you must fly at him, even though you are not accustomed to assaulting people, but control your strength in case you are recognized or arouse suspicion.

'Someone will be sent to Hrutstead to tell Hrut that the fight had better be stopped; he will send for you at once, and you must go there immediately. You will be given a place on the lower bench, facing Hrut's high-seat. Greet him. He will give you a friendly greeting in return, and ask if you are a northerner. You reply that you are from Eyjafjord. He will then ask you whether there are a lot of good men up there; to which you reply, "A lot of perverts, that's about all."

' "Do you know Reykjardale at all?" he will ask.

' "I know the whole of Iceland," you reply.

' "Are there any great champions in Reykjardale?" he will ask.

' "Nothing but thieves and scoundrels," you reply.

'Hrut will laugh, and think this excellent entertainment. You will go on to discuss the men of the Eastfjords, and you must find something abusive to say about all of them, too. In this way your talk will lead on to the men of the Rangriver Plains, and at that point you must remark that there has been a lack of men of any note there since Mord Fiddle died.

'Hrut will ask you what makes you think that no one can fill his place, and you must reply that Mord was so clever, and so experienced a lawyer, that his chieftainship was quite faultless.

'Hrut will ask whether you are familiar at all with his own dealings with Mord.

' "I happen to know," you reply, "that Mord took your wife away from you and you could do nothing about it."

'Hrut will then say, "But did you not think it was a fault in Mord's chieftainship that he failed to recover the dowry, even though he himself brought the action?"

' "That's easily answered," you say. "You challenged him to a duel, but he was an old man and his friends advised him not to fight you, and so you threw the claim out of court."

' "That is what I said I did, anyway," Hrut will say, "and stupid people thought it was law; whereas in reality the claim could have been revived at another Althing if he had had the courage to do it."

' "Yes, I know," you must say. Then Hrut will ask you if you know anything about law.

' "They used to think so in the north," you reply. "But I

wouldn't know how to revive this claim unless you showed me how to."

'Hrut will ask what claim you are referring to, and you must say, "One that doesn't concern me at all – how Unn's dowry-claim could be revived."

' "A summons must be made either in my hearing or at my legal residence," he will say.

'Then you must say, "Recite the summons, and I'll repeat it after you."

'Hrut will then recite the summons, and you must pay close attention to the terms he uses. Then Hrut will invite you to repeat the summons. You must do so, but do it so badly that every second word is wrong. Hrut will laugh, and any suspicions of you he may have will disappear. He will tell you that it was full of mistakes. You must blame your companions for confusing you, and then ask Hrut to recite the words for you again and allow you to repeat them after him. He will have no objections, and will recite the summons himself again; you must repeat it directly after him, correctly this time, and then ask him whether you have summonsed him correctly.

'Hrut will say that no flaw can be found in it; you must then say in a low voice, so that only your companions can hear you, "I make this summons in the action assigned to me by Unn Mord's-daughter."

'Later, when the household is asleep, you and your companions must get up and leave the house silently, and carry your saddles down to the pasture. Take the fat horses and leave the lean ones behind. Ride away up beyond the grazing land and stay in the hills for three days; they will not search for you longer than that. Then you can ride back south, always travelling by night and resting by day. And we will ride to the Althing and support you in the case.'

Gunnar thanked Njal and rode back home.

23

Two days later Gunnar set out from home with two companions, and rode all the way to Blaskoga Heath. There they met some men, who asked who the tall man with the hidden face might be. His companions replied that it was Hawker-Hedin, and that there was little chance of meeting anyone worse after meeting him. Hedin made as if to set on them there and then, but both parties went on their way without incident.

Gunnar did exactly as he had been instructed. He stayed overnight at Hoskuldstead, and from there went down the valley to the farm next to Hrutstead. There he offered his wares for sale, and sold three items. The farmer found that they were defective, and called it a fraud. Hedin immediately flew at him. This was reported to Hrut. Hrut sent for Hedin, who went to see him at once and was well received.

He was given a seat facing Hrut, and their conversation followed closely the lines that Njal had predicted. Hrut explained to him how the lawsuit should be revived, and recited the summons. Hedin repeated it, but got it wrong; Hrut smiled and suspected nothing. Then Hedin suggested that Hrut should do it again, which he did; Hedin repeated the summons again after him and did it correctly this time, letting his companions witness that he was summonsing in the action assigned to him by Unn Mord's-daughter.

That night he went to bed like the rest of the household. But when Hrut was asleep, the three of them took their weapons and clothes, left the house, and went to their horses. They rode across the river and followed it on the Hjardarholt side right up the valley. They hid there between the mountains and Haukadale, in a spot where no pursuer could see them unless he stumbled on them.

Early that same night, Hoskuld woke up at Hoskuldstead and roused all his men.

'I want to tell you my dream,' he said. 'I dreamed that I saw a huge bear walk out of this house, and I felt that I knew that this creature's equal could nowhere be found. Two cubs accompanied it in a friendly way, and they all made for Hrutstead and went into the house there. With that I woke up. And now I want to ask you all if you noticed anything about that big man who was here.'

One man replied, 'I saw that there was a little gold lace and scarlet cloth showing under his sleeve, and he was wearing a gold bracelet on his right arm.'

Hoskuld said, 'That creature must have been the fetch of none other than Gunnar of Hlidarend. I can see it all now. We must ride at once to Hrutstead.'

They all walked out and went over to Hrutstead, where the door was opened to their knocking. They went inside at once. Hrut was lying in his bed-closet, and asked who had arrived. Hoskuld told him who he was, and asked what guests were present.

'Hawker-Hedin is here,' replied Hrut.

'It is someone with broader shoulders than that,' said Hoskuld. 'I suspect it will have been Gunnar of Hlidarend.'

'In that case, someone has been outwitted here,' said Hrut.

'What has happened?' asked Hoskuld.

'I showed him how to revive Unn's lawsuit,' replied Hrut. 'I summonsed myself, while he repeated the summons after me. Now he will use it to start proceedings, and it is perfectly valid in law.'

'He has certainly outwitted us,' said Hoskuld. 'But Gunnar would not have thought this up by himself. Njal must have been behind this plan, for no one can match Njal for cleverness.'

They looked for Hedin, but he had completely disappeared. Then they gathered a force and searched for three days, but without success.

Gunnar then rode south from the hills to Haukadale, east of the Pass, and north to Holtavord Heath until he finally reached home. He went to see Njal and told him that his advice had worked out well.

24

GUNNAR rode to the Althing. Hrut and Hoskuld also rode to the Althing with a large number of supporters. Gunnar raised his action, and cited the neighbours to appear in court. Hrut and Hoskuld had intended to use force against him, but they mistrusted their strength.

Gunnar now went before the Breidafjord Court and called Hrut to hear his oath and his statement of claim and all the evidence. Then he took the oath, stated his claim, and led evidence of the serving of the summons and the assignment of the action.

Njal was not present in court.

Gunnar conducted his case to the point where he invited the defence to reply. Hrut named witnesses, and declared the whole action null and void on the ground that Gunnar had omitted three witnessed statements which should have been presented in court – those originally made at the bedstead, at the main door, and at the Law Rock.

By this time Njal had arrived in court. He said that he could still save the case if they wanted to try further court tactics.

'No,' said Gunnar, 'I am going to give Hrut the same choice as he gave my kinsman Mord Fiddle. Are the brothers Hrut and Hoskuld near enough to hear me speak?'

'We hear you,' said Hrut. 'What is it you want?'

Gunnar said, 'Let all those present be witnesses that I challenge you, Hrut, to single combat, to be fought today on the islet here in Oxar River; but if you refuse to fight with me, you must pay up all the money at once.'

With that, Gunnar left the court with all his supporters. Hoskuld and Hrut also left, and that was the end of the court proceedings.

When Hrut reached his booth, he said, 'Never in all my life have I refused any man's challenge to single combat.'

'That means you are intending to fight,' said Hoskuld. 'But if I have my way there will be no duel, for you have no more chance against Gunnar than Mord Fiddle would have had against you. Instead, we will pay Gunnar the money between us.'

So the brothers went to ask their following of farmers what contribution they would make; they all replied that they would contribute whatever Hrut needed.

'Let us go, then, to Gunnar's booth,' said Hoskuld, 'and hand over the money.'

They went to the booth and asked for Gunnar, who came out to the doorway with some of his men.

'You can take the money now,' said Hoskuld.

'Pay it then,' said Gunnar. 'I am ready to receive it.'

They handed over the full amount.

'May it serve you in the manner you have earned it,' said Hoskuld.

'It will serve us well,' said Gunnar, 'for the claim was a just one.'

'Trouble will be your only reward,' said Hrut.

'That is as must be,' replied Gunnar.

The brothers walked back to their own booth. Hoskuld, smouldering with anger, said to Hrut, 'Will Gunnar never be paid out for this injustice?'

'Yes,' said Hrut, 'he will certainly be paid out; but we ourselves shall gain from it neither vengeance nor profit. Indeed, it is more than likely that he will turn to our kin for friends some day.'

They discussed it no further.

Gunnar showed the money to Njal, who said, 'This has turned out very well.'

'We have you to thank for that,' said Gunnar.

Everyone now rode home from the Althing, and Gunnar earned great credit from the outcome of the case. He handed over all the money to Unn, and refused to accept any of it for himself; but he said that he felt that he would have more claim on her and her kin in the future than on any other people. Unn agreed that this was only right.

25

A MAN called Valgard the Grey lived at Hof, beside Rang River.* He had a brother called Ulf Aur-Priest.†

Valgard the Grey, accompanied by his brother, went to ask for the hand of Unn, and she married him without consulting any of her kinsmen. Gunnar and Njal and many others strongly disapproved of the marriage, for Valgard was a malicious and unpopular man.

Valgard and Unn had a son called Mord, who plays a large part in this saga. When he grew up he treated all his kinsfolk badly, but Gunnar worst of all. He had a malicious cunning, and his advice was always calculated to cause trouble.

Now it is time to mention Njal's sons.

The eldest was called Skarp-Hedin. He was a tall, powerful man, skilful with arms, excellent at swimming and running. He was quick to make up his mind and confident in his decisions, quick to speak and scathing in his words; but for the most part he kept himself well under control.

He had curly chestnut hair and handsome eyes. His face was very pale and his features sharp. He had a crooked nose and prominent teeth, which made him ugly round the mouth. He looked every inch a warrior.

Njal's second son was called Grim. He was tall and strong and dark-haired, more handsome than Skarp-Hedin.

His third son was called Helgi. He too was a handsome man, with a fine head of hair. He was strong and skilful with arms, intelligent and even-tempered.

* Valgard the Grey was the son of Jorund the Priest, the son of Hrafn the Fool, the son of Valgard, the son of Ævar, the son of Vemund the Word-Master, the son of Thorolf Creek-Nose, the son of Thrand the Old, the son of Harald War-Tooth, the son of Hrærek the Ring-Scatterer and of Aud, the daughter of Ivar-of-the-Long-Reach, the son of Halfdan the Brave.

† Ulf Aur-Priest was the ancestor of the Oddi family. He was the father of Svart, the father of Lodmund, the father of Sigfus, the father of Sæmund the Learned. One of Valgard the Grey's descendants was Kolbein the Young.

Njal's three sons were all unmarried at this time.

Njal had a fourth son, called Hoskuld, who was illegitimate; his mother was Hrodny, the sister of Ingjald Hoskuldsson of Keldur.

Njal asked Skarp-Hedin if he wanted to marry; Skarp-Hedin asked his father to choose a wife for him. So Njal proposed on his behalf to Thorhild, the daughter of Hrafn of Thorolfsfell, and that was how he came to own another farm there. Skarp-Hedin married Thorhild, but continued to live with his father at Bergthorsknoll.

Njal asked for the hand of a wealthy widow called Astrid of Djupriverbank for his second son, Grim. Grim married her, but he too stayed on with his father at Bergthorsknoll.

26

A MAN called Asgrim Ellida-Grimsson lived at Tongue.* He had two sons, both called Thorhall and both of them promising men, and another son called Grim.

He also had a daughter called Thorhalla; she was an extremely beautiful girl, refined and capable in every way.

One day, Njal had a talk with his son Helgi.

'I have thought of a match for you, kinsman,' he said, 'if you want to follow my advice.'

'Certainly I do,' replied Helgi, 'for I know that you are both wise and well-meaning. Whom do you have in mind?'

* Asgrim was the son of Ellida-Grim, the son of Asgrim, the son of Ondott Crow. Asgrim's mother was Jorunn, the daughter of Teit, the son of Ketilbjorn the Old from Mosfell and of Helga, the daughter of Thord the Bearded, the son of Hrapp, the son of Bjorn Buna. Jorunn's mother was Alof, the daughter of the chieftain Bodvar, the son of Viking-Kari.

Asgrim had a brother called Sigfus, the father of Thorgerd, the mother of Sigfus, the father of Sæmund the Learned.

He also had a sworn-brother called Gauk Trandilsson, who is said to have been the bravest and most accomplished of men. But trouble arose between them, and later Asgrim killed Gauk.

Njal said, 'We shall ask for the hand of Thorhalla, the daughter of Asgrim Ellida-Grimsson, for she would make an excellent match.'

27

Soon afterwards they set out to ask for her hand, and rode west over Thjors River to Tongue. Asgrim was at home, and he welcomed them warmly.

They stayed there overnight. Next day they went aside to talk; Njal introduced the marriage-offer, and asked for the hand of Thorhalla for his son Helgi. Asgrim welcomed the proposal, and said that there were no other men with whom he would rather make such a marriage-deal. After some further discussion Asgrim betrothed his daughter to Helgi, and the date of the wedding was arranged.

Gunnar of Hlidarend and many other prominent people came to the wedding-feast. After the wedding, Njal offered to become foster-father to Thorhall Asgrimsson, and Thorhall went with him to live at Bergthorsknoll. He lived there for a long time, and came to love Njal more than his own father. Njal taught him law so well that he later became the greatest lawyer in Iceland.

28

A ship commanded by Hallvard the White from Oslo put in to land at the estuary near Arnarbæli. Hallvard went to Hlidarend and stayed the winter there with Gunnar. He was constantly urging Gunnar to travel abroad, and Gunnar, although he said little about it, did not seem at all reluctant. In the spring, Gunnar went to Bergthorsknoll and asked Njal whether he thought it would be advisable for him to go abroad.

'Certainly I do,' said Njal. 'You will get on well wherever you go.'

'Would you perhaps manage my property for me while I am

away?' asked Gunnar. 'I want to take my brother Kolskegg with me, and I would like you to help my mother run the farm.'

'That will not be any obstacle,' said Njal. 'I shall take care of anything you wish.'

Gunnar thanked him warmly and rode back home. The Easterner once more urged him to go abroad. Gunnar asked him whether he had sailed to many other lands. Hallvard replied that he had sailed to every land between Norway and Russia – 'and even as far as Permia'.

'Will you sail with me to the Baltic?' asked Gunnar.

'Certainly,' he replied.

So Gunnar made arrangements to travel abroad with him, and Njal took over the management of his property.

29

GUNNAR sailed abroad, with his brother Kolskegg. They landed at Tonsberg and stayed there over the winter. There had been a change of rulers in Norway; both Harald Grey-Cloak and his mother Gunnhild were dead, and Earl Hakon Sigurdarson * was now in power.†

Hallvard asked Gunnar whether he wanted to join Earl Hakon's court.

'No, I don't,' said Gunnar. 'Have you any longships?'

'I have two,' replied Hallvard.

'Then I suggest we go raiding,' said Gunnar, 'and recruit men to come with us.'

'Certainly,' said Hallvard.

They sailed into Oslo Fjord, where they took the two ships and fitted them out. They had no difficulty in manning them, for Gunnar had a fine reputation.

'Where do you want to go now?' asked Gunnar.

'East to Hising, to meet my kinsman Olvir,' said Hallvard.

* Earl Hakon Sigurdarson was ruler of Norway from 970 to 995. *Translators' note.*

† Hakon's father, Sigurd, was the son of Hakon, the son of Grjotgard and of Bergljot, the daughter of Earl Thorir and of Alof the Fecund, the daughter of Harald Fine-Hair.

'What do you want of him?' asked Gunnar.

'He is a good man,' Hallvard replied, 'and he can give us reinforcements for the expedition.'

'We will go to Hising then,' said Gunnar.

As soon as they were ready, they sailed east for Hising and were well received there. Gunnar had not been there very long before Olvir came to appreciate him greatly. Olvir questioned Hallvard about Gunnar's plans, and Hallvard replied that Gunnar wanted to go raiding for booty.

'That's not a sound plan,' said Olvir. 'You haven't the resources for it.'

'You could always make a contribution yourself,' said Hallvard.

'I have every intention of giving Gunnar some support,' said Olvir. 'You may be my kinsman, Hallvard, but I am much more impressed by Gunnar.'

'Then what are you going to contribute?' asked Hallvard.

'Two longships,' replied Olvir, 'one forty-oared and the other sixty oared.'

'How will they be manned?' asked Hallvard.

'I shall man one of them with my own men,' replied Olvir, 'and the other with neighbouring farmers. But I have heard that there is trouble on the river now, and I don't know whether you will get through or not.'

'Who is responsible for that?' asked Hallvard.

'Two brothers,' said Olvir, 'Vandil and Karl, sons of Snæ-Ulf the Old from out east in Gotaland.'

Hallvard told Gunnar about the ships Olvir had contributed, which pleased Gunnar greatly, and they prepared for the journey. When they were ready to sail, they went to see Olvir and thanked him. Olvir warned them to be on their guard against the pirate brothers.

30

GUNNAR set course down the river. He and Kolskegg were on board one of the ships, Hallvard on board another. They saw the warships ahead of them, and Gunnar said, 'Let us get ready for anything in case they come at us, but leave them alone otherwise.'

They made ready on board their ships. The Viking ships drew apart to each side, making a lane between them. Gunnar headed straight through it. Vandil seized a grappling-hook and hurled it across into Gunnar's ship, then closed at once. Gunnar drew his sword – it was a fine weapon that Olvir had given him – and without pausing to put on his helmet he jumped on to the prow of Vandil's ship and cut down the first man he met. Meanwhile, Karl had laid his ship against Gunnar's on the other side, and now he hurled a spear directly across it, aiming at Gunnar's waist. Gunnar saw the spear coming, whirled round faster than the eye could follow, caught the spear in flight with his left hand, and hurled it back at Karl's ship. The man who was in its way fell dead.

Kolskegg took hold of an anchor and heaved it into Karl's ship; one of the flukes smashed through the hull, and the dark-blue sea came pouring in. The crew had to scramble off their vessel into the other ships. Gunnar now leapt back to his own ship, and Hallvard drew alongside him. A tremendous battle developed. The men had seen their leader's courage, and each one fought as hard as he could. Gunnar laid about him, hacking and hurling, killing men on all sides, and Kolskegg gave him brave support. Karl had joined his brother Vandil on his ship, and there they fought side by side all day.

At one stage, Kolskegg was taking a rest aboard Gunnar's ship. Gunnar noticed this and said to him, 'You have been kinder to others than to yourself today, for you have quenched their thirst forever.' Kolskegg took a bowl full of mead, drained it, and returned to the fight.

Eventually Gunnar and Kolskegg boarded the ship defended by Vandil and Karl. Kolskegg worked his way down one side of it, Gunnar down the other. Vandil came to meet Gunnar and struck at him, but the sword hit his shield and stuck there fast; with a wrench of the shield, Gunnar snapped the sword at the hilt. Then Gunnar struck back; to Vandil it seemed as if there were three swords coming at him at once, and he did not know where to defend himself. The sword sliced through both his legs. Then Kolskegg ran Karl through with a spear. After that they seized much booty, and sailed on south to Denmark. From there they went east to Smaland in Sweden, and were victorious wherever they fought. They did not return that autumn, and the following summer they sailed to Reval, where they met Vikings whom they fought and defeated. After that they steered east to the island of Osel and lay there for a while behind a headland.

Then they saw a man come walking down alone from the headland. Gunnar went ashore to meet him, and they talked. Gunnar asked him his name, and the man said that he was called Tofi. Gunnar asked him what he wanted.

'It is you I want to see,' he replied. 'There are warships lying on the other side of the headland there. I'll tell you who are in command of them – two brothers called Hallgrim and Kolskegg; and I know for a fact that they are very formidable warriors. What's more, they are armed with weapons so potent that their like cannot be found anywhere else.

'Hallgrim carries a halberd which he has had charmed with spells so that no other weapon can kill him; and such is the power of its magic that one can foretell when a man is about to be killed by it, by the loud ringing noise it gives. Kolskegg carries a short-sword which is also a wonderful weapon. Their forces outnumber yours by a third. They have a hoard of treasure hidden ashore, and I know exactly where it is. But they have sent out a ship to spy round the headland, and they know all about you. They are busy preparing their ships, and they plan to attack you as soon as they are ready. So now there are two courses open to you – either to pull away from here at once, or to get ready to defend yourselves as quickly as possible. And if you defeat them, I shall lead you to all the treasure.'

Gunnar gave the man a gold ring, and then returned to his own men. He told them that there were warships on the other side of the headland – 'and they know all about us; so let us take our weapons and get ready quickly, for there is booty to be won here.'

They started to prepare, and they were no sooner ready than they saw the warships coming at them. Battle was joined; it was a long hard fight, with heavy casualties. Gunnar killed many men. Hallgrim and his brother boarded Gunnar's ship. Gunnar turned to face Hallgrim, who thrust at him with his halberd. Gunnar leapt backwards over the boom which was lying just behind him across the ship, but left his shield in front of it; Hallgrim's halberd pierced the shield and penetrated the boom. Then Gunnar hacked at Hallgrim's arm; the sword did not bite, but the blow shattered the bone and the halberd fell down. Gunnar snatched it up and ran Hallgrim through with it; and from then on, Gunnar always carried that halberd.

Meanwhile the two Kolskeggs were fighting it out, and it was touch and go who would get the better of it, until Gunnar came up and killed the Viking with one blow. After that the other Vikings begged for quarter, which Gunnar granted them; he told his men to search the dead and strip them of their possessions, but those who had surrendered were allowed to keep their own weapons and clothing and return to their homelands. They went away, leaving Gunnar in possession of all that was left.

With the end of the battle, Tofi returned to see Gunnar, and offered to guide him to the treasure the Vikings had hidden; he said that it was larger and better than the booty they had already captured. Gunnar agreed, and went ashore with Tofi, who led the way to a wood; they came to a place where a number of trees had been piled up. Tofi said that the treasure was underneath. They pulled the trees away and found a hoard of gold and silver, clothing, and good weapons, all of which they carried back to their ships.

Gunnar asked Tofi what he wanted as a reward. Tofi replied, 'I am a Dane, and I would like best of all to be taken back to my kinsmen.'

Gunnar asked how he came to be in the Baltic.

'I was captured by Vikings,' said Tofi, 'and put ashore on this island. I have been here ever since.'

31

GUNNAR took Tofi aboard, and said to Kolskegg and Hallvard, 'Now we shall head for Scandinavia.'

The prospect pleased them, and they agreed. Gunnar sailed from the Baltic with a large amount of booty. He now had ten ships, and he sailed with them to Hedeby, in Denmark, where King Harald Gormsson was in residence.

The king learned about Gunnar's arrival. He was told that Gunnar had no equal in Iceland, and so he sent messengers to Gunnar to invite him to his court. Gunnar went to him at once; the king welcomed him and gave him a seat beside his own. Gunnar stayed at the court for a fortnight, during which the king entertained himself by making Gunnar compete at various sports against his own men. But there was no one who could match him in any of them.

The king said to Gunnar, 'It seems to me that your equal would be hard to find anywhere.' He offered Gunnar wife and wealth if he would consent to settle there. Gunnar thanked the king, but said that first he had to return to Iceland to see his kinsmen and friends.

'Then you will never come back to us,' said the king.

'Fate will decide that, my lord,' said Gunnar.

Gunnar gave the king a longship and much treasure as well. In return, the king gave him his own robes, a pair of gold-embroidered gloves, a head-band studded with gold, and a Russian fur-cap.

From Hedeby, Gunnar sailed north to Hising, where Olvir welcomed him with open arms. Gunnar returned the two ships to Olvir laden with booty, and said that this was his share from the expedition. Olvir accepted the booty and said that he was a fine man, and invited him to stay there for a while.

Hallvard asked Gunnar whether he wanted to go to meet Earl Hakon. Gunnar replied that the idea appealed to him, 'for now I have been tested a little, whereas I was quite untried when you first suggested this.'

They made their preparations and sailed north to Trondheim to meet Earl Hakon, who welcomed Gunnar and invited him to stay at his court over the winter. Gunnar accepted the invitation, and soon impressed everyone highly.

At the Yule festival the earl gave him a gold bracelet. Gunnar fell in love with Bergljot, one of the earl's kinswomen, and it was obvious that the earl would have married her to Gunnar, if Gunnar had sought it at all.

32

IN the spring, the earl asked Gunnar what his plans were; Gunnar replied that he wanted to go to Iceland. The earl said that the harvest had been poor – 'and there will be very little trading. But you are to fill your ship with as much flour and timber as you wish.'

Gunnar thanked him, and prepared his ship for the voyage early. Both Hallvard and Kolskegg went with him. They reached Iceland in early summer, and made land at the estuary near Arnarbæli shortly before the Althing was due. Gunnar rode home at once with Kolskegg, leaving men to unload the ship. Everyone at home was glad at their return; they were considerate to all the household, and their travels had not made them arrogant.

Gunnar asked whether Njal were at home. When he heard that he was, he had his horse saddled and rode over to Bergthorsknoll with Kolskegg. Njal was glad at their return, and asked them to stay overnight; they did so, and Gunnar recounted their travels.

Njal said that Gunnar had proved himself to be an outstanding man – 'and now you have been well tested. But you have yet to be tested even more, for there are many who will envy you.'

'I want to be on good terms with everyone,' said Gunnar.

'Much will happen,' said Njal, 'and you will often be forced to defend yourself.'

'Then it will be important that I should have justice on my side,' said Gunnar.

'And so you will,' said Njal, 'as long as you do not have to suffer for the actions of others.'

Njal then asked Gunnar if he were going to the Althing. Gunnar said that he was, and asked if Njal were going too.

'No,' said Njal, 'and I wish that you would not, either.'

Gunnar rode back home, after giving Njal fine gifts and thanking him for taking care of his property.

Kolskegg kept urging him to ride to the Althing. 'Your honour will be enhanced, for many will come to see you there,' he said.

'It has never been my nature to show off,' said Gunnar. 'But I always like the company of worthy men.'

Hallvard, too, had come to Hlidarend, and he offered to ride to the Althing with them.

33

GUNNAR and his company rode to the Althing. When they arrived, they were so well dressed that no one there could compare with them, and people came out of every booth to marvel at them. Gunnar rode to the Rangriver booth and stayed there with his kinsmen. Many people came to see him and ask him his news; he talked gaily and cheerfully to all of them, and told them everything they wanted to know.

One day, as he was walking from the Law Rock, Gunnar went down past the Mosfell booth. There he saw some well-dressed women coming towards him; the one in the lead was the best dressed of all. As they met, this woman at once greeted Gunnar. He made a friendly reply, and asked her who she was. She said that her name was Hallgerd, and that she was the daughter of Hoskuld Dala-Kollsson. She spoke to him boldly, and asked him to tell her about his travels. Gunnar replied that he would not deny her that. So they sat down and talked.

Hallgerd was wearing a red, richly-decorated tunic under a scarlet cloak trimmed all the way down with lace. Her beautiful thick hair flowed down over her bosom. Gunnar was dressed in the robes that King Harald Gormsson had given him, with the gold bracelet from Earl Hakon on his arm.

They talked aloud for a long time, until finally he asked if she were unmarried.

'Yes,' she replied, 'and there is little risk of anyone changing that.'

'Do you think no one good enough for you?' he asked.

'Not at all,' said Hallgerd. 'But I may be a little particular about husbands.'

'How would you answer if I asked for your hand?'

'You can't be thinking of that,' she replied.

'But I am,' said Gunnar.

'If you have any wish to do that,' said Hallgerd, 'then speak to my father.'

With that they ended their conversation.

Gunnar went at once to the Dales booth and asked the men standing outside if Hoskuld were inside. They said that he was, and Gunnar went in. Hoskuld and Hrut welcomed him. Gunnar sat down between them, and there was no hint from their conversation that they had ever had any differences. Gunnar eventually asked how the brothers would answer if he were to ask for the hand of Hallgerd.

'Favourably,' said Hoskuld, 'if you are fully in earnest about it.'

Gunnar said that he certainly was – 'but from the way we parted last time, most people would think it unlikely that such a bond of kinship would ever be formed.'

'What do you think about it, kinsman?' Hoskuld asked his brother.

Hrut replied, 'I do not think this an equal match.'

'What makes you think that?' asked Gunnar.

'I shall give you a truthful answer,' replied Hrut. 'You are a brave and accomplished man, but Hallgerd is rather a mixture. I do not wish to deceive you in any way.'

'Thank you,' said Gunnar. 'But I prefer to believe that you are letting our former enmity influence you if you refuse me this match.'

'That is not so,' said Hrut. 'It is much more because I realize that you cannot help yourself at present. And even though we refused this marriage-deal, we would still wish to be your friends.'

'I have already spoken to Hallgerd,' said Gunnar, 'and she is not averse to it.'

'I can see,' said Hrut, 'that you are infatuated with one another. And you are the ones who have to face the consequences.'

Without being asked, he told Gunnar all about Hallgerd's character. At first Gunnar thought that the faults were more than enough, but eventually they came to terms about the marriage-deal. Hallgerd was then sent for, and the arrangements were discussed in her presence. As before, Hallgerd was allowed to declare her own betrothal. This wedding-feast was to be held at Hlidarend, and for the time being it was to be kept a secret. But it soon became common knowledge.

Gunnar rode home from the Althing and went to Bergthorsknoll to tell Njal about the marriage. Njal showed heavy disapproval. Gunnar asked what made him think the match so ill-advised.

'She will be the source of nothing but trouble when she comes out here to the east,' said Njal.

'She will never spoil our friendship,' said Gunnar.

'She will very nearly do so,' said Njal. 'But you will always make amends for her.'

Gunnar invited Njal to the wedding, together with as many of his household as he cared to bring with him. Njal promised to come. Gunnar rode home, and then went round the district to invite more guests.

34

A MAN called Thrain Sigfusson lived at Grjotriver in Fljotshlid. He was a grandson of Sighvat the Red, and an uncle of Gunnar.

Thrain was a man who commanded great respect. He was married to Thorhild the Poetess, a sharp-tongued woman given to lampooning in verse, and he had little love for her. They were both invited to the wedding at Hlidarend; Thorhild was to serve at the wedding-tables with Bergthora, Njal's wife.

The second son of Sigfus was called Ketil. He was married to Thorgerd, Njal's daughter, and lived at Mork, east of Markar River.

The third Sigfusson was called Thorkel, the fourth Mord, the fifth Lambi, the sixth Sigmund, and the seventh Sigurd. They were all kinsmen of Gunnar's, and every one a warrior. Gunnar had invited them all to the wedding. He had also invited Valgard the Grey and his son Mord, and Ulf Aur-Priest with his son Runolf.

The brothers Hoskuld and Hrut rode to the wedding with a large company, including Hoskuld's sons Thorleik and Olaf. The bride travelled with them, accompanied by her daughter Thorgerd, who was now fourteen years old and very beautiful, and several other women. Also at the wedding were Thorhalla, the daughter of Asgrim Ellida-Grimsson, and two of Njal's daughters, Thorgerd and Helga.

Gunnar had invited a large number of guests, and this is how he arranged the seating:

He himself sat in the middle of one bench. Beside him on one side sat Thrain Sigfusson, then Ulf Aur-Priest, then Valgard the Grey, then Mord and Runolf, and then the other Sigfussons, with Lambi farthest from the door. On the other side of Gunnar sat Njal, then the four Njalssons, Skarp-Hedin, Helgi, Grim, and Hoskuld, then Haf the Wise, then Ingjald of Keldur, and then the three sons of Holta-Thorir, Njal's brother. Thorir himself insisted on sitting farthest out of all the honoured guests, for that made the others feel satisfied with their places. Hoskuld Dala-Kollsson sat in the middle of the other bench, with his sons on one side and Hrut on the other. The rest of the order of seating is not recorded. The bride sat in the middle of the dais, with her daughter Thorgerd on one side of her and Thorhalla Asgrim's-daughter on the other. Thorhild the Poetess and Berg-thora, who were serving the guests, brought food to the tables.

Thrain Sigfusson could not take his eyes off Thorgerd, Hall-gerd's daughter. His wife Thorhild noticed this; she became very angry, and flung a couplet at him:

> 'Ogling is evil, Thrain,
> There is lust in your eyes.'

Thrain jumped to his feet and vaulted the table, named witnesses at once, and declared himself divorced from her.

'I am not tolerating any more of her obscene sarcasm,' he said. He was so vehement that he refused to remain at the feast unless she were turned out, and eventually she had to leave. After that the guests stayed in their seats, each in his place, drinking and being merry.

Then Thrain spoke up again. 'I shall make no secret of what is in my mind,' he said. 'I want to ask you, Hoskuld Dala-Kollsson, this: will you give me your grand-daughter Thorgerd in marriage?'

'I'm not so sure about that,' said Hoskuld. 'It seems to me that you have taken scant leave of the wife you had already. But what kind of a man is he, Gunnar?'

'I would rather not say anything,' replied Gunnar, 'for the man is my kinsman. You do it, Njal, everyone can believe what you say.'

Njal said, 'It can be said of this man that he is wealthy and highly accomplished and a man of great account; and therefore there is no reason to refuse this match.'

Hoskuld turned to his brother. 'What do you advise, kinsman?' he asked.

'You can accept it,' replied Hrut, 'for it is an equal match for her.'

After that they discussed the terms and reached complete agreement. Then Gunnar and Thrain rose and walked over to the dais. Gunnar asked the mother and daughter whether they consented to the match; neither of them raised any objections, and so Hallgerd betrothed her daughter to Thrain.

The seating arrangement on the dais was altered, and Thorhalla was placed between the two brides. The feast now went off excellently. When it was over, Hoskuld and his companions rode off to the west, and the Rang River people to their own homes. Gunnar enhanced his prestige by giving many of the guests gifts.

Hallgerd took charge of the household at Hlidarend, and was extravagant and overbearing. Thorgerd took over at Grjotriver and proved to be an excellent housewife.

35

BECAUSE of their close friendship, Gunnar and Njal used to take turns at inviting one another to an autumn feast. This time it was Gunnar's turn to attend Njal's feast, and so he and Hallgerd went to Bergthorsknoll.

Njal gave them a warm welcome. Helgi and his wife Thorhalla were out when they arrived, but returned soon afterwards. Bergthora went over to the dais with Thorhalla and said to Hallgerd, 'Move down for this woman.'

Hallgerd said, 'I'm not moving down for anyone, like some outcast hag.'

'I am in charge here,' said Bergthora; and Thorhalla took her seat.

Bergthora came to the table with washing-water. Hallgerd seized hold of her hand and said, 'There's not much to choose between you and Njal; you have turtle-back nails on every finger, and Njal is beardless.'

'That is true,' said Bergthora, 'and neither of us finds fault with the other for it. But your husband Thorvald wasn't beardless, yet that didn't stop you from having him killed.'

Hallgerd said, 'It does me little good to be married to the bravest man in Iceland if you don't avenge this, Gunnar.'

Gunnar jumped to his feet and vaulted the table.

'I am going home,' he said. 'You would be better off squabbling with your own household, Hallgerd, and not in other people's homes. I am too deeply in debt for all the honour Njal has done me to be provoked into folly by your taunts.'

They set off home. 'But remember this, Bergthora,' said Hallgerd in parting, 'we haven't met for the last time.'

'That will hardly be to your advantage,' said Bergthora. Gunnar did not say another word, but went back to Hlidarend and stayed at home for the rest of the winter.

Summer came, and with it the time for the Althing to assemble.

36

GUNNAR rode to the Althing. Before he left home, he said to Hallgerd, 'Behave yourself while I am away, and don't try any mischief on my friends.'

'The trolls take your friends,' she replied.

Gunnar rode away; he realized that it was no use trying to talk to her. Njal and all his sons also went to the Althing.

Meanwhile, this is what happened at home. Gunnar and Njal owned jointly some woodland on Raudaskrid, which they had never portioned out; instead, each would fell as much timber as he happened to require, and neither found anything to object to in that.

Hallgerd had an overseer named Kol, who had been in her service for a long time. He was an utter scoundrel.

Njal and Bergthora had a servant called Svart, whom they liked very much. Bergthora told him to go to Raudaskrid to fell some wood – 'and I'll send some others to bring it home.'

Svart said that he would do what she asked. He went up to Raudaskrid and started felling; he was to be there for a week.

Some beggars came west to Hlidarend from Markar River, and reported that Svart had been up on Raudaskrid, felling a lot of wood.

Hallgerd said, 'Bergthora must be trying to rob me in every-thing; but I'll see to it that Svart never chops wood again.'

Rannveig, Gunnar's mother, overheard her and said, 'House-wives around here have managed well enough without resorting to manslaughter.'

The night passed. Next morning Hallgerd talked to Kol. 'I have thought of some work for you,' she said, and gave him an axe. 'Go up to Raudaskrid. You will find Svart there.'

'What shall I do with him?' asked Kol.

'Need you ask? A scoundrel like you? You are to kill him,' she replied.

'I can do that easily enough,' said Kol, 'but I suspect it will cost me my own life.'

'You're too easily frightened,' said Hallgerd. 'You should be ashamed of yourself, after all the things I have done for you. I'll get someone else to do it, if you don't dare to.'

Enraged, Kol snatched the axe from her, jumped on to one of Gunnar's horses, and rode off east to Markar River. There he dismounted and waited in the wood until all the timber had been brought down and Svart was left there on his own. Then Kol sprang at him, saying, 'You're not the only one who can chop hard,' and buried his axe in Svart's head, killing him in-stantly. Then he rode home and told Hallgerd of the killing. She said, 'I'll look after you and keep you out of harm's way.'

'That may be,' replied Kol, 'but that's not what I dreamt before I killed him.'

Svart's companions soon returned to the wood and found him dead. They carried the body home.

Hallgerd sent a messenger to the Althing to tell Gunnar of the killing. Gunnar did not criticize Hallgerd in front of the messenger, and no one knew at first whether he approved or dis-approved. A little later he stood up and asked his men to come with him; they all went to Njal's booth, and a man was sent in to ask Njal to come out.

Njal came out at once and they went aside to talk. Gunnar said, 'I have a killing to report to you. My wife and my overseer Kol were responsible; the victim was your servant Svart.'

Njal listened in silence as Gunnar told him everything that had happened. Then he said, 'You must make sure that she does not have her own way in everything.'

Gunnar said, 'Name your own terms of compensation.'

'You will find it hard to compensate for all the damage Hallgerd will cause,' said Njal. 'Elsewhere it will bring more serious consequences than here, where we two alone are involved; but even here matters are far from being well. We must never allow ourselves to forget our frequent words of friendship; I feel sure that you will not fail, but you will be severely tested.'

Njal accepted the offer to assess the compensation himself, and said, 'I am not going to make an issue of this. You are to pay twelve ounces of silver. But I want to add this condition: that you should be no less lenient with us if you ever have to assess compensation for something that we are responsible for.'

Gunnar paid the money without demur, and rode off home. Njal and his sons also returned home from the Althing. Bergthora saw the money and said, 'That was a very modest price; the same will be paid for Kol when the time comes.'

When Gunnar arrived home he reproached Hallgerd. She replied that many better men than Svart had fallen without any compensation. Gunnar said that she might decide her own actions, 'but I shall decide how to deal with their consequences.'

Hallgerd kept on boasting about Svart's killing, and this displeased Bergthora.

One day, when Njal and his sons had gone up to Thorolfsfell to see to the farm there, Bergthora was outside and saw a man approaching on a black horse. She waited for him instead of going inside. She did not recognize him. He was carrying a spear, with a short-sword at his belt.

She asked him his name.

'My name is Atli,' he replied.

She asked where he came from.

'I am from the Eastfjords,' he replied.

'Where are you going?' she asked.

'I am unemployed,' he replied, 'and I was intending to see Njal and Skarp-Hedin to find out if they would engage me.'

'What work are you best at?' she asked.

'I am a ploughman,' he replied, 'and I can do many other things. But I won't try to conceal the fact that I am a quick-tempered man, and there are many who have felt the weight of my blows.'

'I don't blame you for not being a coward,' she said.

'Have you any say here?' asked Atli.

'I am Njal's wife,' replied Bergthora, 'and I have as much say in hiring servants as he.'

'Will you engage me, then?' he asked.

'Yes,' she replied, 'but only if you are prepared to do whatever I ask you to, even if I send you out to kill someone.'

'You have menfolk enough for that kind of work without needing me,' said Atli.

'I make my own conditions,' said Bergthora.

'We'll settle on these terms, then,' said Atli, and so she engaged him.

When Njal returned home with his sons, he asked her who this man was.

'He is one of your servants,' she replied. 'I engaged him because he claimed to be ready with his hands.'

'His work will have vigour enough,' said Njal. 'But I'm not so certain of its value.'

Skarp-Hedin liked Atli.

Njal and his sons rode to the Althing that summer. Gunnar was also at the Althing.

One day Njal produced a purse of money.

'What money is that, father?' asked Skarp-Hedin.

'This is the money that Gunnar paid me last summer for our servant,' said Njal.

'That will come in handy,' said Skarp-Hedin, and grinned.

37

MEANWHILE, at home, Atli asked Bergthora what work he was to do that day.

'I have decided on your task,' she replied. 'Go and look for Kol until you find him, for today you are to kill him if you want to please me.'

'That's very fitting,' said Atli, 'for we are both of us scoundrels. And I'll tackle him in such a way that one or other of us is killed.'

'Good luck to you,' she said. 'You won't work for nothing.'

He went to get his weapons and horse, and rode away. When he reached Fljotshlid he met some men on their way east from Hlidarend to their homes in Mork. They asked him where he was going; he replied that he was looking for an old cart-horse. They called that a petty task for a man like him – 'but you had better ask those who have spent the night out of doors.'

'Who are they?' asked Atli.

'Killer-Kol, Hallgerd's servant, has just left the shieling; he hasn't been to bed all night,' they replied.

'I'm not sure whether I dare go near him,' said Atli. 'He has a nasty temper, and I might as well learn from another man's lesson.'

'You look anything but a coward,' they said, and directed him to Kol.

Atli spurred his horse and galloped hard. When he met Kol he asked, 'Is the carting going well?'

'That's none of your business, you scum, nor anyone else's from your place,' replied Kol.

'Your hardest task is still to come,' said Atli. 'You have yet to die.'

He thrust at Kol with his spear and hit him in the waist. Kol swung his axe at him, but missed, and fell dead from his horse.

Atli rode on until he met some of Hallgerd's workmen.

'Go and see to that horse up there,' said Atli. 'Kol has fallen off its back, and he's dead.'

'Did you kill him?' they asked.

'Hallgerd will suspect that he hasn't died from natural causes,' said Atli, and rode back home. He told Bergthora, who thanked him for what he had done and what he had said.

'I don't know how Njal will take this,' said Atli.

'Njal will not mind,' said Bergthora. 'As an indication, I can tell you that he took with him to the Althing the slave-payment we accepted last summer, and which will now be used to pay for Kol. But even though a settlement is made, you must be on your guard; for Hallgerd honours no settlements.'

'Do you want to send a messenger to Njal to tell him of the killing?' asked Atli.

'No,' she replied, 'I would much rather that no compensation at all were paid for Kol.'

They did not discuss it further.

Hallgerd was told of Kol's killing and Atli's remarks; she said that she would pay him back. She sent a messenger to the Althing to tell Gunnar about the killing. He made little comment, but sent someone to tell Njal, who made no comment at all.

Skarp-Hedin said, 'Slaves are getting much more enterprising than they used to be. Once they merely brawled, and no one bothered about that, but now they insist on killing each other.' And he grinned.

Njal pulled down the purse which hung in the booth, and went out; his sons went with him. At Gunnar's booth, Skarp-Hedin said to a man standing in the doorway, 'Tell Gunnar that my father wishes to see him.'

Gunnar was told and came out at once. He greeted Njal warmly, and they went aside to talk.

Njal said, 'This is bad, that my wife should have broken our settlement and had your servant killed.'

'She shall not be blamed for that,' said Gunnar.

'Assess the compensation yourself now,' said Njal.

'Very well,' said Gunnar. 'I put an equal price on the two men, Svart and Kol; you are to pay me 12 ounces of silver.'

Njal took the purse and handed it to Gunnar, who recognized it as being the money that he himself had given Njal.

Njal returned to his booth, and their friendship remained as warm as it had been before.

When Njal returned home he reproached Bergthora, but she

said that she would never give in to Hallgerd. Hallgerd scolded Gunnar fiercely for having made a settlement over the killing, but Gunnar said that he would never break with Njal and his sons. Hallgerd stormed at him, but Gunnar paid no attention.

Gunnar and Njal took care that nothing else happened that year.

38

IN the spring, Njal said to Atli, 'I want you to go back to the Eastfjords to find work, before Hallgerd puts an end to your days.'

'I'm not afraid of that,' said Atli, 'and I would prefer to stay here, if I may.'

'That would be less advisable,' said Njal.

'I would rather die as your servant than change my master,' said Atli. 'But I want to ask you as a favour, if I am killed, not to accept slave-payment for me.'

'You shall have a freeman's compensation,' said Njal, 'and Bergthora will promise – and no doubt provide – blood-revenge for you as well.'

So Atli was made a member of the household.

Hallgerd, for her part, sent west to Bjarnarfjord for her kinsman Brynjolf the Unruly, a scoundrel of a man. This was done without Gunnar's knowledge. Hallgerd said that he would suit her well as an overseer. Brynjolf came east, and Gunnar asked him what he wanted. Brynjolf said that he had come to stay.

'You will not be any asset to our household from what I have heard of you,' said Gunnar. 'But I won't turn away any of my wife's kinsmen whom she wants to have with her.'

Gunnar was short with him, but not hostile, and in this way time passed until the Althing.

Gunnar and his brother Kolskegg rode to the Althing, where they met Njal, who was there with his sons. They passed the time together very pleasantly.

Back at Bergthorsknoll, Bergthora said to Atli, 'Go up to Thorolfsfell and work there for a week.'

Atli went off and stayed there in secret, making charcoal in the wood.

Hallgerd said to Brynjolf, 'I hear that Atli is away from home, so he must be doing some work at Thorolfsfell.'

'What do you think he is most likely to be doing?' asked Brynjolf.

'Some job or other in the wood,' she replied.

'What shall I do with him?' asked Brynjolf.

'You are to kill him,' said Hallgerd.

Brynjolf fell silent.

'Thjostolf would have been less daunted,' said Hallgerd, 'if he had still been alive.'

'I don't need any more prompting than that,' said Brynjolf. He armed himself, mounted his horse, and rode to Thorolfsfell, where he saw thick smoke to the east of the farm. He rode in that direction, dismounted, tethered his horse, and then continued on foot, using the thickest of the smoke as cover. Soon he saw the charcoal-pit, with a man standing near it; he noticed that this man had stuck his spear into the ground beside him.

Screened by the smoke, Brynjolf walked right up to him; the man was so absorbed in his work that he did not notice his approach. Brynjolf struck him on the head with an axe; Atli whirled round so sharply that Brynjolf let go of the weapon. Then Atli snatched up his spear and hurled it at Brynjolf, who threw himself flat on the ground, and the spear flew over his head.

'You were lucky that you caught me unawares,' said Atli. 'Hallgerd will be pleased when you report my death. But it is a consolation to me to know that you yourself will have the same fate soon. Now come over here and fetch the axe you dropped.'

Brynjolf did not reply, and made no attempt to retrieve the axe until Atli was dead. He rode over to Thorolfsfell and reported the killing,* then went back home and told Hallgerd, who sent a messenger to Bergthorsknoll to tell Bergthora that Kol's death was now repaid. Then she sent a messenger to the Althing to tell Gunnar about Atli's killing.

Gunnar and Kolskegg stood up.

* According to the law, it was necessary to announce the killing promptly; otherwise, the killer was guilty of the much more serious crime of 'secret murder' (morð). He was also required by law to cover the body. Translators' note.

'You could easily afford to do without Hallgerd's kinsmen,' said Kolskegg.

They went to see Njal. Gunnar said, 'I have to tell you that Atli has been killed' – and told him who did it. 'Now I want to offer you compensation for him, and I want you to assess it yourself.'

'We have already agreed to let nothing come between our friendship,' said Njal. 'But I cannot put a slave's price on Atli.'

Gunnar said that he had no objections, and offered his hand. Njal took it and named witnesses to their settlement.

Skarp-Hedin said, 'Hallgerd does not let our servants die of old age.'

'Your mother,' said Gunnar, 'will no doubt see to it that this game is played by two.'

'There will be more than enough of that,' said Njal.

Then Njal announced the figure at a hundred ounces of silver, which Gunnar paid at once. Many of those present called the figure high, but Gunnar replied angrily that worse men than Atli had been paid for with full compensation.

After that they rode home from the Althing. When Bergthora saw the money, she said to Njal, 'You will be thinking that you have kept your promise to Atli; but my promise has still to be fulfilled.'

'There is no necessity for you to keep it,' said Njal.

'But you have already guessed otherwise,' said Bergthora, 'and so it shall be.'

Hallgerd said to Gunnar, 'Did you really pay a hundred ounces of silver for Atli's killing, enough to make him out a freeman?'

'He was already free,' said Gunnar, 'and I have no intention of making Njal's servants out to be criminals.'

'There's nothing to choose between you and Njal,' said Hallgerd. 'Both of you are cowards.'

'Time will tell,' said Gunnar.

For a long time after that he treated her coldly, until she made it up with him.

Nothing further happened that year. In the spring, Njal made no further additions to his household.

Summer came, and people rode off to the Althing.

39

A MAN called Thord Freedmansson lived at Bergthorsknoll. His father, Sigtrygg, had been a slave freed by Asgerd, Njal's mother; he was drowned in Markar River, and Thord had stayed on with Njal ever since.

Thord was a tall, strong man, and had acted as foster-father to all of Njal's sons. He was in love with a kinswoman of Njal's who was housekeeper there, Gudfinna, the daughter of Thorolf. She was now pregnant.

One day Bergthora said to Thord Freedmansson, 'You are to go and kill Brynjolf.'

'I am no killer,' said Thord, 'but I will do it if you wish.'

'I do,' said Bergthora.

Thord took a horse and rode up to Hlidarend. He called Hallgerd out, and asked her where Brynjolf was.

'What do you want with him?' asked Hallgerd.

'I want him to tell me where he covered up Atli's body,' replied Thord. 'I am told he did it badly.'

She told him that Brynjolf was down in Akratongue.

'Take care he does not have the same fate as Atli,' said Thord.

'You are no killer,' said Hallgerd, 'so it does not matter where you two meet.'

'I have never seen blood shed,' replied Thord, 'and I do not yet know how it will affect me.'

He galloped out of the field and down to Akratongue.

Rannveig, Gunnar's mother, had overheard their conversation, and now said, 'You have challenged his courage sharply, Hallgerd, and I think he is a man without fear, as your kinsman will soon discover.'

Brynjolf and Thord met on the track. Thord said, 'Defend yourself, Brynjolf, for I want no unfair advantage over you.'

Brynjolf rode at Thord and aimed an axe-blow at him. Thord swung his own axe and sliced through the shaft just above Brynjolf's grip. He struck at once a second time; the axe sank deep into Brynjolf's chest, and Brynjolf fell dead from his horse.

Thord met one of Hallgerd's shepherds and declared himself

responsible for the killing; he told him where the body lay, and asked him to report the killing to Hallgerd. Then he rode home to Bergthorsknoll and reported the killing to Bergthora and others.

'May your hands prosper,' said Bergthora.

The shepherd reported the killing to Hallgerd, who said bitterly that this would lead to grave trouble if she had her way.

40

THE news soon reached the Althing. Njal asked to be told it three times; finally he said, 'More people become killers than I ever expected.'

Skarp-Hedin said, 'But the man must have been doubledoomed, to die at the hands of our foster-father who had never before seen blood shed. Most people would have expected us brothers to be first to have done this, knowing our temperament.'

'Your turn will come soon,' said Njal, 'and even then it will only be because you are driven to it.'

They went to see Gunnar and told him about the killing. Gunnar said that it was no great loss – 'but still, he was a free man.'

Njal at once offered to settle, and Gunnar accepted. He was to name the figure himself, and he set it at a hundred ounces of silver. Njal paid it at once, and that was their full settlement.

41

GUNNAR had a kinsman called Sigmund Lambason, a grandson of Sighvat the Red.

Sigmund spent much of his time trading abroad; he was a handsome, well-bred man, tall and strong. He carried himself arrogantly, was a good poet, and was proficient at most sports. But he was rowdy and sarcastic, a difficult man to get on with.

He returned to Iceland, landing in Hornafjord in the east; he had with him a Swedish companion, a very unpleasant man called Skjold. They got themselves horses and rode west from Hornafjord without pause until they reached Hlidarend in Fljotshlid. Gunnar gave them a good welcome, for his kinship with Sigmund was close, and invited Sigmund to stay the winter; Sigmund said that he would accept the invitation if his comrade Skjold could stay too.

Gunnar replied, 'From what I have heard of him, he does little to temper your character – and some tempering is precisely what you need. This is a difficult house to stay in, and I would advise you, like all my kinsmen, not to respond to my wife's promptings, for she indulges in many things that go directly against my wishes.'

'Warning wards off blame,' said Sigmund.

'Take the advice to heart then,' said Gunnar, 'for you will be severely tested. Stay by my side, and stick to my advice.'

So Sigmund and Skjold kept company with Gunnar. Hallgerd took to Sigmund at once, and it went so far that she loaded him with money and showed him no less attention than she did her own husband. People began to talk, and wondered what really lay behind it.

Hallgerd said to Gunnar, 'It is impossible to be satisfied with the hundred ounces of silver you accepted for my kinsman Brynjolf. I'm going to avenge him if I can.'

Gunnar said that he refused to argue with her about it, and walked away. He went to see Kolskegg and said to him, 'Go over to see Njal and tell him that Thord had better be on his guard despite the settlement we made, for I suspect that it might be violated.'

Kolskegg rode over and told Njal, who then told Thord. When Kolskegg set off back home Njal thanked him and Gunnar for their loyalty.

One day Njal and Thord were sitting out of doors. There was a goat which used to roam about the home-meadow, and no one was allowed to drive it away.

Thord said, 'That's very strange.'

'What do you see that seems to you so strange?' asked Njal.

'The goat seems to be lying in the hollow there, drenched in blood,' replied Thord.

Njal said that there was no goat there, nor anything else.

'Then what is it?' asked Thord.

'It means that you must be a doomed man,' said Njal. 'That was your fetch you must have seen. Be on your guard.'

'That will not help me much if that is to be my fate,' said Thord.

Hallgerd went to Thrain Sigfusson and said to him, 'I would think you a real son-in-law if you were to kill Thord Freedmansson.'

'That I will not do,' said Thrain, 'for it would earn me the anger of my kinsman Gunnar; and besides, it would be too dangerous, for this killing will soon be avenged.'

'Who will avenge it?' she asked. 'Old Beardless?'

'No, not he; but his sons will,' replied Thrain.

After that they talked for a long time with lowered voices, and no one knew what they were planning.

One day Gunnar was away from home; Sigmund and his friend Skjold stayed behind, and Thrain came over from Grjotriver. They sat outside the house with Hallgerd and talked.

Hallgerd said, 'Sigmund and Skjold have promised to kill Thord Freedmansson, the foster-father of the Njalssons, and you, Thrain, have given me your promise to be present when they do it.'

They all acknowledged that they had made her these promises.

'This is my plan, then,' said Hallgerd. 'You are to ride east to Hornafjord to see to your goods, and be away until the beginning of the Althing; for if you stay at home, Gunnar will want you to ride to the Althing with him. Njal will be away at the Althing with his sons, and Gunnar will be there too; that is when you must kill Thord.'

They agreed to carry out this plan. Then they set out for the Eastfjords; Gunnar suspected nothing, and rode away to the Althing.

Njal sent Thord Freedmansson east to the Eyjafells district, and asked him to be back the next day. Thord went east but could not get back, for the river had risen so high that it was quite impossible to ford it even on horseback. Njal waited another day, for he had intended to take Thord to the Althing with him. Then he told Bergthora to send him on to the Althing as soon as he got back.

Two days later Thord returned from the east. Bergthora told him that he was to go to the Althing – 'but first ride up to Thorolfsfell and see to the farm; don't stay more than a day or two there.'

42

WHEN Sigmund and Skjold got back from the east, Hallgerd told them that Thord was still at home, but that he was to ride to the Althing in a few days' time.

'This is your chance to get him,' she said. 'If you don't get him now, you never will.'

Some people came to Hlidarend from Thorolfsfell and told Hallgerd that Thord was there. Hallgerd went to Thrain Sigfusson and the others and said, 'Thord is now at Thorolfsfell. Your best plan is to kill him on his way home.'

'That's what we'll do,' said Sigmund.

They went out and got their weapons and horses, and rode away to lie in wait for him.

Sigmund said to Thrain, 'Don't you take any part in this; it will not need all three of us.'

'Very well,' said Thrain.

A little later, Thord came riding towards them.

Sigmund said to him, 'Give yourself up, for now it is time for you to die.'

'Certainly not,' said Thord. 'Come and fight me in single combat.'

'Certainly not,' said Sigmund. 'We shall make full use of our advantage in numbers. It's not surprising that Skarp-Hedin is so formidable, since the saying goes that one-fourth comes from the foster-father.'

'You shall feel the full force of that,' said Thord, 'for Skarp-Hedin will avenge me.'

Then they advanced on him, but Thord defended himself so well that he shattered both their spears. Then Skjold hacked off his arm, but he fought them off with his other arm for a short time until Sigmund ran him through and he fell dead to the ground. They covered him up with turf and stones.

Thrain said, 'We have done an evil deed, and the sons of Njal are not going to be pleased when they hear of it.'

They rode home and told Hallgerd, who was delighted over the killing. But Rannveig, Gunnar's mother, said to Sigmund, 'It is said that the hand is soon sorry that it struck, and so it will be here. Gunnar will manage to get you out of trouble this time; but if you ever take another of Hallgerd's baits, it will cost you your life.'

Hallgerd sent a messenger to Bergthorsknoll to report the killing, and another to the Althing to tell Gunnar. Bergthora said she would not belabour Hallgerd with abuse; that, she said, would not be vengeance enough for such a grave crime.

43

WHEN the messenger came to the Althing to tell Gunnar about the killing, Gunnar said, 'This is terrible news; I do not think I could ever hear worse. Now we must go at once to see Njal; I am sure that he will not fail us, even though he is tried so severely.'

They went to see Njal and called him out to talk. Njal came out at once, and he and Gunnar talked. There was no one else present at first except Kolskegg.

'I have harsh news to tell you,' said Gunnar. 'Thord Freedmansson has been killed. I want to offer you the right to assess your own compensation.'

Njal was silent for a while, and then said, 'It is a generous offer, and I shall accept it, even though I am sure to be reproached by my wife and my sons for doing so, as they will disapprove strongly. But I shall take that risk, for I know that I am dealing with a man of honour, and I do not want to be the cause of any breach in our friendship.'

'Do you want to have your sons present at all?' asked Gunnar.

'No,' said Njal, 'for they will not break any settlement that I make. But if they were present, they would refuse to be party to it.'

'Very well,' said Gunnar. 'Do this on your own.'

They shook hands, and agreed to make a prompt and full settlement. Then Njal said, 'I assess the compensation at 200 ounces of silver; and you will think it high.'

'I do not think it too high,' said Gunnar, and went back to his booth.

Njal's sons returned to the booth, and Skarp-Hedin asked where all that good silver his father was holding had come from.

Njal said, 'I have to tell you that your foster-father Thord has been killed. Gunnar and I have come to a settlement over it, and he has paid double compensation for the killing.'

'Who killed him?' asked Skarp-Hedin.

'Sigmund and Skjold did it,' replied Njal. 'But Thrain Sigfusson was also present.'

'They were not taking any risks,' said Skarp-Hedin. 'But how far must matters go before we can take things into our own hands?'

'It will not be very long now,' replied Njal, 'and nothing will be able to hold you back then. But it is of the greatest importance to me that you do not break this settlement.'

'Then we shall not do so,' said Skarp-Hedin. 'But if there is any further trouble, we shall remember what they have already done to us.'

'In that case I would not try to hold you back,' said Njal.

44

Now people rode home from the Althing. When Gunnar arrived back he said to Sigmund, 'You are a man of more ill luck than I had ever imagined, and you have put your gifts to evil use. I have managed to make your peace with Njal and his sons this time, but you must never allow yourself to be caught in this way again. You and I are not alike; you have a malicious and mocking tongue, but that is not my way. That is why you and Hallgerd get on so well, for you are more alike by nature.'

He rebuked him for a long time; Sigmund answered meekly, and promised to follow his advice better than he had done in the past. Gunnar said that it would do him good. After that they were on good terms for a time.

Gunnar's friendship with Njal and his sons remained firm, but the other members of their families had little warmth towards each other.

It happened one day that some beggarwomen came to Hlidarend from Bergsthorsknoll; they were talkative and sharp-tongued creatures. Hallgerd had a private room which she often used, and on this occasion her daughter Thorgerd and Thrain were sitting with her, along with Sigmund and a number of women. Neither Gunnar nor Kolskegg was there.

The beggarwomen came to this room. Hallgerd greeted them and found seats for them, and asked them their news. They said they had nothing much to tell. Hallgerd asked where they had spent the night. They replied that they had been at Berg-thorsknoll.

'What was Njal doing?' asked Hallgerd.

'He was busy sitting still,' they replied.

'What were Njal's sons doing?' asked Hallgerd. 'They at least think themselves men.'

'They look big enough, but they've never been put to any test,' they replied. 'Skarp-Hedin was sharpening his axe, Grim was putting a shaft on his spear, Helgi was riveting the hilt of his sword, and Hoskuld was strengthening the handle of his shield.'

'They must be planning some great feat,' said Hallgerd.

'We don't know,' they said.

'What were Njal's servants doing?' asked Hallgerd.

'We didn't see what all of them were doing,' they replied, 'but one of them was carting dung to the hummocks in the field.'

'What was the point of that?' asked Hallgerd.

'He said that it would make better hay.'

'Njal can sometimes be very stupid, for a man who can always give advice to others,' said Hallgerd.

'Why is that?' they asked.

'I'll tell you why, and it's quite true,' said Hallgerd: 'because he didn't cart dung on to his own chin, so that his beard would grow like other men's. So let's now call him "Old Beardless", and his sons "Little Dung-Beards". And let's have a poem from you about it, Sigmund; give us the benefit of your talent for poetry.'

Sigmund said he was quite prepared to do that, and at once composed three or four verses, all of them extremely malicious.

'You are a treasure,' said Hallgerd, 'the way you do everything I ask.'

At that point Gunnar entered the room; he had been standing outside, and had heard every word that had been said. They were all shocked when they saw him walk in, and their loud laughter died into abrupt silence.

Gunnar was furiously angry. 'You are a stupid fool,' he said to Sigmund, 'to ignore all the advice you have been given. You revile Njal's sons, and, what is even worse, Njal himself, especially after all the harm you have already done them. This is going to cost you your life. If anyone repeats these verses he will be driven from this house at once, and have my anger to reckon with as well.'

They were so afraid of him that no one dared repeat the words. And with that he left them.

The beggarwomen told themselves that they would get a reward from Bergthora if they told her about this. So they slipped away down to Bergthorsknoll and told her the whole story secretly, without being asked.

When the menfolk were at table, Bergthora said, 'Gifts have been given to you, father and sons alike; and you would scarcely be men if you did not repay them.'

'What kind of gifts?' asked Skarp-Hedin.

'You, my sons, share the one gift between you; you have all been nicknamed "Little Dung-Beards", and my husband has been nicknamed "Old Beardless".'

'We are not women,' said Skarp-Hedin, 'flying into a rage at everything.'

'But Gunnar flew into a rage on your behalf,' said Bergthora, 'and Gunnar is considered even-tempered. If you don't take vengeance for this, you will never avenge any insult.'

'Our old mother is enjoying herself,' said Skarp-Hedin, and grinned; but the sweat broke out on his forehead, and two red spots flared in his cheeks, which had seldom happened before. Grim was silent, and gnawed at his lip. Helgi did not change expression.

Hoskuld left the room with Bergthora; but she came storming in again.

Njal said, 'All in good time, woman, slow but sure. In so many cases when tempers are provoked, there are two sides to the issue, even though vengeance is taken.'

That night, when Njal was in bed, he heard an axe bump against a panel and ring loudly. Then he noticed that the shields which usually hung against another bed-closet were now gone.

'Who has taken down our shields?' he asked.

Bergthora replied, 'Your sons went out with them.'

Njal pulled on his shoes and went out at once, round to the other side of the house. He saw his sons heading up the knoll.

'Where are you off to, Skarp-Hedin?' he asked.

'To look for your sheep,' replied Skarp-Hedin.

'You would not be armed if that were your intention,' said Njal. 'You must have some other purpose.'

'We are going to fish salmon, father, if we cannot find the sheep,' said Skarp-Hedin.

'If that were true, it would be best not to let your catch escape,' said Njal.

They went on their way, and Njal went back to his bed. He said to Bergthora, 'Your sons were outside, all fully armed. You have goaded them into action.'

'I will thank them with all my heart, if they bring me back news of Sigmund's death,' said Bergthora.

45

NJAL's sons went up to Fljotshlid and stayed there that night. When it began to grow light they moved closer to Hlidarend.

That same morning, Sigmund and Skjold rose, planning to see to the stud-horses. They took bridles with them, mounted two horses that were in the home-meadow, and rode off to search the slopes for the stallion. They found him between two brooks, and brought the horses far down towards the road.

Skarp-Hedin caught sight of them, for Sigmund was wearing brightly-coloured clothing.

'Do you see that red fairy there?' he asked.

The others looked, and said that they could see him.

Skarp-Hedin said, 'Take no part in this, Hoskuld; for you

often have to travel by yourself without protection. I am going to tackle Sigmund myself – he is man's work. Grim and Helgi, you deal with Skjold.'

Hoskuld sat down, and the other three walked all the way over to Sigmund and Skjold.

Skarp-Hedin said to Sigmund, 'Take your weapons and defend yourself; you will find that more necessary now than making lampoons about us brothers.'

Skarp-Hedin waited while Sigmund armed himself. Skjold turned to face Grim and Helgi, and they fought furiously. Sigmund was equipped with helmet and shield, with a sword at his belt and a spear in his hand. He turned to meet Skarp-Hedin and thrust at him at once with the spear; Skarp-Hedin took it on his shield, then severed the spear-shaft with his axe before swinging the axe at Sigmund.

The blow struck Sigmund's shield and split it down past the handle. Sigmund drew his sword with his right hand and hacked at Skarp-Hedin; the sword pierced the shield and stuck there fast. Skarp-Hedin twisted the shield so sharply that Sigmund let go of the sword. Then Skarp-Hedin swung his axe again; it caught Sigmund on the shoulder, sheared through the tunic he was wearing, and severed the shoulder-blade. Then Skarp-Hedin jerked the axe towards himself; Sigmund was pulled forward on to both knees, but jumped to his feet again at once.

'Now you have knelt before me,' said Skarp-Hedin. 'But you will be flat on your back before we part company.'

'That's too bad,' said Sigmund.

Skarp-Hedin hacked once at his helmet, and then killed him with the next blow.

Grim sliced off Skjold's foot at the ankle, and then Helgi killed him with a sword-thrust. Skarp-Hedin had by this time cut off Sigmund's head; he noticed one of Hallgerd's shepherds, handed him the head, and told him to take it to Hallgerd, who, he said, would know whether it was the head that had made the lampoons.

But as soon as the brothers were away, the shepherd threw the head down. He had not dared to do so while they were still there. The brothers carried on until they met some men down by Markar River, and told them what had happened. Skarp-Hedin announced that he himself had killed Sigmund, and that

Grim and Helgi had killed Skjold. Then they went home and told Njal the news.

Njal said, 'May your hands prosper. And as things now stand, there is no question of giving away the right to assess compensation this time.'

Meanwhile, the shepherd went back to Hlidarend and told Hallgerd what had happened. 'Skarp-Hedin thrust Sigmund's head into my hands,' he said, 'and told me to bring it to you; but I didn't dare to, because I didn't know how you would take it.'

'It's a pity you didn't,' said Hallgerd. 'I could then have taken it to Gunnar, and he would have had to avenge his kinsman or else be despised by all men.'

She went to Gunnar and said to him, 'Sigmund, your kinsman, has been killed. It was Skarp-Hedin who killed him, and he tried to send me his head.'

'It is only what Sigmund could have expected,' said Gunnar, 'for evil plans have evil consequences. It is not the first time that you and Skarp-Hedin have shown each other spite.'

With that he walked away. He took no steps to prepare an action for manslaughter, and he refused to do anything about it at all. Hallgerd kept bringing it up and reminding him that Sigmund had fallen without compensation, but Gunnar paid no attention to her promptings.

Three Althings passed, and each time people expected Gunnar to bring an action. Then one day he found himself faced with some problem that he did not know how to handle; he rode over to see Njal, who gave him a warm welcome.

Gunnar said, 'I have come to you for some good advice about a problem I have.'

'You certainly deserve it,' said Njal, and gave him advice for his difficulty. Gunnar stood up and thanked him. Then Njal took him by the arm and said, 'Your kinsman Sigmund has lain without compensation for too long.'

'The debt was paid long ago,' said Gunnar. 'But I would not refuse any offer that did me honour.'

Gunnar had never once spoken badly of the sons of Njal. Now Njal insisted that Gunnar assess the compensation himself. Gunnar set the figure at 200 ounces of silver, but asked no compensation for Skjold. The money was paid over at once.

Gunnar announced this settlement at the Thingskalar Assembly when the attendance was largest, and stressed the restraint that Njal and his sons had shown. He told about the malicious words which had dragged Sigmund to his death, and forbad anyone ever to repeat them, on pain of outlawry.

Gunnar and Njal pledged each other always to settle by themselves any matters which might crop up between them. They never broke this pledge, and always remained firm friends.

46

A MAN called Gizur Teitsson,* known as Gizur the White, lived at Mosfell. He was a powerful chieftain.

He had a cousin called Geir the Priest,† who lived at Hlid. He and Gizur acted together in everything.

At this time, Mord Valgardsson was living at Hof, in the Rangriver Plains. He had a vicious, cunning nature. His father, Valgard the Grey, was abroad, and his mother, Unn, was dead by now. Mord bitterly envied Gunnar of Hlidarend. He was a wealthy man.

* He was the son of Teit, the son of Ketilbjorn the Old from Mosfell and of Helga, the daughter of Thord the Bearded, the son of Hrapp, the son of Bjorn Buna.

Gizur's mother was Alof, the daughter of the chieftain Bodvar, the son of Viking-Kari.

Gizur's son was Bishop Isleif Gizurarson [the first bishop of Iceland, 1056–80].

† Geir the Priest was the son of Thorkatla, the daughter of Ketilbjorn the Old from Mosfell.

47

A MAN called Otkel Skarfsson * lived at Kirkby. He was a kinsman of Gizur the White. He was prosperous, and had a son called Thorgeir, who was a promising young man.

Otkel had a friend called Skamkel, who lived at Lesser-Hof. He, too, was prosperous, but he was a malicious man, a liar, and a very unpleasant person to have any dealings with.

Otkel had a brother called Hallkel living with him, a tall, strong man. There was another brother called Hallbjorn the White, who had once brought to Iceland an Irish slave called Melkolf, who was not much liked. Hallbjorn came to stay with Otkel, bringing Melkolf with him.

Melkolf kept saying how happy he would be if Otkel were his master. Otkel liked him, and gave him a knife and belt and a set of clothing; and the slave did anything that Otkel wished. So Otkel asked Hallbjorn to sell him the slave; Hallbjorn said that he could have him for nothing, but added that he was not quite the treasure that Otkel imagined. As soon as Melkolf came into Otkel's service, his work grew worse and worse. Otkel frequently complained to Hallbjorn the White that he thought the slave lazy; Hallbjorn replied that Melkolf had worse faults than that.

This was a time of great famine in Iceland, and all over the country people were going short of hay and food. Gunnar shared out his own stocks with many people, and turned no one away empty-handed while they lasted, until he himself ran short of both hay and food. Then he asked Kolskegg to accompany him on a journey; together with Thrain Sigfusson and Lambi Sigurdarson they went to Kirkby and asked Otkel to come out. Otkel greeted them; Gunnar responded well to the

* Otkel was the son of Skarf, the son of that Hallkel who once killed Grim of Grimsness in a duel; Hallkel was a brother of Ketilbjorn the Old from Mosfell.

Otkel was married to Thorgerd, the daughter of Mar, the son of Brondolf, the son of Naddad the Faroese.

greeting and said, 'The fact is that I have come to buy hay and food, if you have any.'

'I have both,' said Otkel, 'but I will sell you neither.'

'Will you then give me some?' asked Gunnar. 'And trust me to be generous in repayment?'

'No,' said Otkel. He was being encouraged by Skamkel's malicious promptings.

Thrain Sigfusson said, 'It would serve him right if we took it by force and paid him what it was worth.'

'The men of Mosfell would have to be dead and buried,' said Skamkel, 'before you Sigfussons managed to rob them.'

'I won't have anything to do with robbery,' said Gunnar.

'Would you like to buy a slave from me?' asked Otkel.

'I have no objection to that,' said Gunnar. He bought Melkolf from Otkel, and went back home.

Njal heard about all this, and said, 'It was a bad deed to refuse to sell to Gunnar. There is little hope for others there, when men like Gunnar cannot buy.'

'Why do you have to talk so much about it?' said Bergthora. 'It would be more generous just to give Gunnar the hay and food he needs, since you are short of neither.'

'That is perfectly true,' said Njal. 'I shall certainly let him have something.'

He went up to Thorolfsfell with his sons, and they loaded fifteen horses with hay and five others with food. Then they went to Hlidarend and asked Gunnar to come out. Gunnar welcomed them warmly.

Njal said, 'Here is some hay and food I want to give you. And I want you to turn to me and never to anyone else if ever you find yourself in need.'

'Your gifts are good,' said Gunnar, 'but I value even more highly your true friendship and that of your sons.'

With that Njal returned home. The spring wore on.

48

IN the summer, Gunnar rode to the Althing. A large number of men from Sida, in the east, had stayed with him overnight, and he invited them to be his guests again on the way back from the Althing; they accepted the invitation, and they all rode off to the Althing. Njal and his sons were also there. It was an uneventful gathering that year.

Meanwhile, at Hlidarend, Hallgerd had a word with the slave Melkolf.

'I have an errand for you,' she said. 'You are to ride to Kirkby.'

'What am I to go there for?' he asked.

'You are to steal from there enough food to load two horses, particularly butter and cheese, and then set fire to the storehouse. Everyone will think it happened through carelessness, and no one will suspect that there has been a theft.'

'I may have done bad things,' said Melkolf, 'but I have never been a thief.'

'Listen to it!' said Hallgerd. 'You pretend to be innocent when you're not only a thief but a murderer as well. Don't you dare refuse, or I'll have you killed.'

He felt sure that she would do so if he did not go. That night he took two horses, put on their pack-harness, and went off to Kirkby. The dog there, recognizing him, did not bark, but ran out to welcome him. Melkolf went to the storehouse, opened it up, and loaded the two horses with food from it; then he burned the shed and killed the dog.

On his return journey along Rang River, his shoe-thong broke. He took his knife to repair it, but left the knife and belt lying there. When he reached Hlidarend he noticed that his knife was missing, but did not dare to go back to fetch it. He brought the food to Hallgerd; she was pleased.

Next morning the people of Kirkby came out of doors and saw the great damage that had been done. A messenger was sent to the Althing to tell Otkel, who took the loss calmly and said that it must have been due to the fact that the storehouse adjoined the kitchen. And that was what everyone else thought must have caused it.

When the Althing ended, a large number of people rode to Hlidarend. Hallgerd set food on the table, and brought in cheese and butter. Gunnar knew that no such provisions had been in stock, and asked Hallgerd where they had come from.

'From a source that should not spoil your appetite,' said Hallgerd. 'And besides, it's not a man's business to bother about kitchen matters.'

Gunnar grew angry. 'It will be an evil day when I become a thief's accomplice,' he said, and slapped her on the face.

Hallgerd said that she would remember that slap and pay him back if she could. They both left the room. The tables were cleared and meat was brought in instead. Everyone thought that this was because the meat was considered to have been more honestly obtained. After that, the people who had been at the Althing went on their way.

49

SKAMKEL happened to be looking for sheep up by Rang River. He noticed something glinting on the path, and dismounted to pick it up. It was a knife and belt, both of which he thought he recognized. He took them to Kirkby. Otkel was outside and welcomed him warmly.

'Do you recognize these things at all?' asked Skamkel.

'Certainly I know them,' said Otkel.

'Whose are they?' asked Skamkel.

'They belong to Melkolf the slave,' replied Otkel.

'We must get others to identify them too,' said Skamkel, 'for I am now going to give you some really good advice.'

They showed the articles to many people, all of whom recognized them.

'What do you plan to do now?' asked Skamkel.

Otkel replied, 'We shall go over to see Mord Valgardsson and ask his opinion.'

They went to Hof and showed Mord the articles, and asked if he recognized them.

'Yes,' said Mord, 'but what about them? Do you think that there is anything of yours to be found at Hlidarend?'

'This is a delicate matter to handle,' said Skamkel, 'when we are up against such powerful opponents.'

'That's true,' said Mord. 'But I know a thing or two about Gunnar's household that neither of you know.'

'We will pay you for it,' they said, 'if you will look into the matter.'

'The money would be dearly earned,' said Mord. 'But perhaps I shall look into it after all.'

They gave him three marks of silver for his promise of help. Mord then advised them to send women round the district offering small wares to housewives, and see with what they were paid – 'because,' he explained, 'people are inclined to rid themselves first of any stolen goods that may be in their possession; and that's what will happen now if a crime is involved. The women are to show me what they were given in each place, and then, if the evidence is established, I want nothing more to do with the matter.'

They agreed on this, and then Skamkel and Otkel went back home. Mord sent some women out round the district. They were away for a fortnight, and came back with bulging packs. Mord asked them where they had been given the most; they replied that it had been at Hlidarend, and that Hallgerd had been particularly generous. Mord asked what they had been given there. 'Cheese,' they replied. Mord asked to see it, and they showed it to him; there were a number of slices.

Mord took charge of the cheese, and a little later he went to see Otkel. He asked Otkel to fetch his wife's cheese-mould, and when it was brought he laid the slices into it. They fitted perfectly. They discovered that the women had been given a whole cheese.

Mord said, 'You can now see that Hallgerd must have stolen it.' They assembled all the evidence, and with that Mord said that he had fulfilled his part of the bargain, and took his leave.

Kolskegg had a talk with Gunnar, and said, 'I have bad news. Everyone is saying that Hallgerd has committed theft and was responsible for all the damage that was done at Kirkby.'

Gunnar said that he thought it all too likely, 'What should we do now?' he asked.

Kolskegg said, 'Obviously you are the one who has to make amends for your wife, and I think the best plan is to go and see Otkel and make him a good offer.'

'That is a good suggestion,' replied Gunnar. 'So be it.'

Soon afterwards, Gunnar sent for Thrain Sigfusson and Lambi Sigurdarson, and they came at once. Gunnar told them where he was planning to go; they approved. They rode off in a group of twelve, and when they reached Kirkby they asked for Otkel.

Skamkel was there too, and he said to Otkel, 'I shall go out with you; we shall need to have all our wits about us. I want to be closest to you when your need is greatest, as it is at this very moment. I would advise you to stand on your dignity.'

Then they went outside – Otkel, Skamkel, Hallkel, and Hallbjorn the White. They greeted Gunnar, who returned the greeting. Otkel asked him where he was going.

'No farther than here,' said Gunnar. 'The purpose of my visit is to tell you that the disastrous loss you suffered here was caused by my wife and that slave I bought from you.'

'I'm not surprised,' said Hallbjorn.

Gunnar said, 'Now I want to make you a fair offer. I suggest that the best men in the district should assess the compensation.'

'That sounds well,' said Skamkel, 'but it certainly is not a fair offer. You are popular with the farmers round here, but Otkel is not.'

Gunnar said, 'Then I offer to assess your compensation myself, here and now. With it I will pledge my friendship, and I will pay the entire sum at once. I offer to pay you double the amount of your losses.'

Skamkel said to Otkel, 'Don't accept. It would be beneath you to allow him self-judgement when you are entitled to it yourself.'

Otkel announced, 'I am not going to give you self-judgement, Gunnar.'

Gunnar said, 'I recognize the influence of others here, who will some day get the reward they deserve. But come, assess the compensation yourself, then.'

Otkel leaned over towards Skamkel and said, 'What do I answer now?'

'Say that it is a handsome offer,' said Skamkel, 'but refer your decision to Gizur the White and Geir the Priest; then many people will say that you are just like your grandfather Hallkel, who was a great champion.'

Otkel announced, 'This is a handsome offer, Gunnar, but nevertheless I want you to give me time to consult Gizur the White and Geir the Priest.'

'Do what you like,' said Gunnar. 'But some would say that you cannot recognize honour when you are being shown it, if you refuse the terms I have offered you.'

With that, Gunnar rode back home. As soon as he was gone, Hallbjorn said, 'What a sorry contrast in men. Gunnar made you good offers, and you refused to accept any of them. What do you expect to gain by fighting against Gunnar, a man without equal? Still, he is the sort of man who would let these offers stand if you decided to accept them after all; my advice to you is to go to see Gizur the White and Geir the Priest without delay.'

Otkel had his horse fetched, and prepared himself for the journey. His eye-sight was poor. Skamkel walked with him a short way and then said, 'I was amazed that your brother did not offer to do this task for you. I want to offer to go in your place, for I know that you find travelling difficult.'

'I accept your offer,' said Otkel. 'But be sure to keep strictly to the truth.'

'I will indeed,' said Skamkel.

He took Otkel's horse and travelling-cloak, and Otkel walked back home.

Hallbjorn was outside, and said to Otkel, 'It is bad to have a slave for your bosom-friend. We are always going to regret that you turned back. It is stupidity itself to send such a liar on a mission which you might well call a matter of life and death.'

'You would be terrified if Gunnar raised his halberd,' said Otkel, 'if you are like this already.'

'I don't know who would be the more frightened then,' said Hallbjorn, 'but one day you will learn that Gunnar wastes no time over taking aim with his halberd, once his anger is aroused.'

'You are all cowering, except Skamkel,' said Otkel.

By this time they were both furious.

50

SKAMKEL arrived at Mosfell and repeated to Gizur the White all the offers that had been made.

'It seems to me,' said Gizur, 'that these were generous offers. Why did Otkel not accept them?'

'It was chiefly because everyone wished to pay you a compliment,' replied Skamkel. 'That's why Otkel delayed his own decision, for yours will undoubtedly be the best for all concerned.'

Skamkel stayed at Mosfell overnight. Gizur sent a messenger for Geir the Priest, who came over early in the morning. Gizur told him what had happened. 'What do you think should be done now?' he asked.

'What you yourself must already have decided – to settle as best we can,' replied Geir. 'And now we shall make Skamkel repeat the whole story once more and see how he tells it this time.'

After this was done, Gizur said, 'Your version must be correct after all, although to me you look thoroughly dishonest. Appearances must be deceptive indeed if you prove to be a man of integrity.'

Skamkel rode off home. He went first to Kirkby and called Otkel out. Otkel welcomed him warmly. Skamkel said that he brought greetings from Gizur and Geir; and he added, 'There is no need to be secretive about our case. It is their wish that no settlement be accepted. Gizur's advice was that we go and serve a summons * on Gunnar for receiving stolen goods, and on Hallgerd for theft.'

'We shall do exactly what they advise,' said Otkel.

Skamkel added, 'What impressed them most of all was the

* The last day for serving an Althing summons was four weeks before the first day of the Althing. The Althing met on the eleventh Thursday of summer, i.e. late in June; the Icelandic summer was reckoned from the middle of April to the middle of October. *Translators' note.*

decisive way you behaved. I made you out to be a very great man.'

Otkel told his brothers all about this. Hallbjorn said, 'This is all an enormous lie.'

Time passed, until the last day for serving an Althing summons arrived. Otkel called on his brothers and Skamkel to ride with him to Hlidarend to deliver the summonses. Hallbjorn agreed to go, but said that they would have cause to regret the journey in the course of time. In a group of twelve they rode to Hlidarend; Gunnar was out of doors when they reached the home-meadow, but did not notice them until they had come right up to the house. He did not go inside, and Otkel at once shouted out the summons.

When it was finished, Skamkel asked, 'Was that correct, farmer?'

'You should know best,' said Gunnar. 'But one day I shall remind you of this visit, Skamkel, and of the part you have played.'

'That won't hurt us much,' said Skamkel, 'if your halberd isn't up.'

Gunnar was furious. He walked inside and told Kolskegg what had happened. Kolskegg said, 'It's a pity we were not outside with you. Their journey would have turned very sour on them if we had been at hand.'

'All in good time,' said Gunnar. 'But this journey will never be to their credit.'

A little later he went and told Njal. Njal said, 'Do not let this worry you, for it will turn out greatly to your credit before the Althing is over. We shall all support you to the full with advice and help.'

Gunnar thanked him and rode back home.

Otkel rode to the Althing with his brothers and Skamkel.

51

GUNNAR rode to the Althing accompanied by all the Sigfussons and by Njal and his sons; they all went about together, and it was said that no other group there looked as formidable.

One day Gunnar went to the Dales booth. Hrut and Hoskuld were standing beside the booth, and they welcomed Gunnar warmly. Gunnar told them all about the case.

'What does Njal advise?' asked Hrut.

'He told me to see you two brothers,' replied Gunnar, 'and tell you that he would agree to whatever you suggest.'

'I gather, then,' said Hrut, 'that he wants me, as your kinsman by marriage, to give my advice. Very well. You must challenge Gizur the White to single combat, if they don't offer you self-judgement, and Kolskegg must challenge Geir the Priest. We can get others to deal with Otkel and his men; our combined force is now so strong that you can accomplish whatever you want to do.'

Gunnar walked back to his own booth and told Njal.

Ulf Aur-Priest got wind of these plans and told Gizur. Gizur then asked Otkel, 'Who advised you to take Gunnar to court?'

'Skamkel told me that it was the advice given by you and Geir the Priest,' said Otkel.

'Where is that lying wretch now?' asked Gizur.

'He is ill in bed, in his booth,' replied Otkel.

'And may he never rise from it,' said Gizur. 'We must all go, at once, to see Gunnar and offer him self-judgement; but I'm not so sure that he will accept it now.'

There were many harsh things said to Skamkel, who remained in his sick-bed throughout the Althing. Gizur and his companions set off for Gunnar's booth. They were seen approaching and someone went in to tell Gunnar; Gunnar and all his men came outside and formed up. Gizur, who was in the lead, said, 'We have come to offer you self-judgement in this case, Gunnar.'

'Then it cannot have been your idea to serve summons on me,' said Gunnar.

'No, it was not my idea,' said Gizur, 'nor Geir's either.'

'Then you will want to give me proof to clear yourself,' said Gunnar.

'What proof do you want?' asked Gizur.

'I want you to swear an oath.'

'Certainly,' said Gizur, 'if you agree to accept self-judgement.'

'That was my original offer,' said Gunnar, 'but I feel that the issue has become much graver now.'

Njal said, 'You should not refuse the offer of self-judgement. The graver the issue, the greater is the honour involved.'

Gunnar said, 'I shall accept self-judgement, then, to please my friends. But I advise Otkel not to give me any more trouble.'

Hoskuld and Hrut were sent for, and they came. Then Gizur and Geir the Priest swore their oaths, and Gunnar made his assessment of the compensation without consulting anyone.

Announcing his decision, he said, 'This is my finding: there is liability for the cost of the storehouse and the food it contained; but for the slave's crime I will pay you nothing, because you concealed his faults. Instead, I am going to hand him back to you, on the principle that the ears fit best where they grew. In addition, I find that you served summons on me with intent to disgrace me, and for that I award myself damages to the exact value of the house and its contents destroyed in the fire.

'But if you would prefer not to accept a settlement at all, I shall offer no objections; for I have another plan to meet just such a contingency, and I shall not hesitate to carry it out.'

'We agree that you should make no payment,' said Gizur, 'but we ask that you become Otkel's friend.'

'Never, as long as I live,' said Gunnar. 'He can have Skamkel's friendship; that is what he has always relied on.'

'Anyway,' said Gizur, 'we agree to conclude a settlement, even though you alone dictate the conditions.'

They shook hands on all the terms of the settlement. Gunnar said to Otkel, 'It would be more advisable for you to go and live with your kinsmen. But if you insist on staying on at Kirkby, take care not to interfere with me again.'

Gizur said, 'That is sensible advice; let him follow it.'

Gunnar won great credit from the outcome of this case, and afterwards people went home from the Althing. Gunnar went back to his farming at Hlidarend; and everything was quiet for a while.

52

A MAN called Runolf, the son of Ulf Aur-Priest, lived at Dale, east of Markar River. He stayed overnight with Otkel at Kirkby on his way back from the Althing. Otkel gave him a jet-black ox, nine years old. Runolf thanked him for the gift, and invited him to visit Dale whenever he liked. Otkel did not act on the invitation for some time; Runolf often sent messengers to him to remind him of it, and Otkel kept promising to make a visit.

Otkel had two dun-coloured horses with a black stripe down the back; they were the best riding-horses in the district, and were so fond of each other that they were inseparable.

There was an Easterner called Audolf staying with Otkel; he was in love with Signy, Otkel's daughter. He was a tall, strong man.

53

IN the spring, Otkel said that they would ride east to visit Runolf at Dale; everyone was pleased at the prospect. Otkel's two brothers and Skamkel also went, as well as Audolf and three other men.

Otkel rode one of the dun-coloured horses, with the other running loose beside him. They made their way east towards Markar River, and Otkel galloped ahead of the others. His horses became excited and bolted off the track up towards Fljotshlid, carrying Otkel much faster than he wished.

That same day Gunnar had left home by himself, carrying a seed-basket and armed only with a hand-axe. He walked to his cornfield and started sowing the grain, after laying aside his fine-woven cloak and the hand-axe. He was busy sowing when Otkel came galloping out of control across the field; neither he nor Gunnar noticed the other. Just as Gunnar was straightening from his work, Otkel, who was wearing spurs, rode into him.

His spur struck Gunnar's ear, making a deep gash that bled freely at once.

Otkel's companions now came riding up.

'You can all see,' said Gunnar, 'that you, Otkel, have drawn blood. This is a disgrace: first you summons me, and now you trample on me and ride me down.'

Skamkel said, 'You are taking it well, Gunnar – but you looked far more fearsome at the Althing, with your halberd in your hand.'

'When next we meet,' said Gunnar, 'you shall see the halberd.'

With that they parted. Skamkel shouted, 'That's good riding, lads.'

Gunnar walked home, and told no one about the incident; and no one suspected that it had been an inflicted wound. One day he happened to tell his brother Kolskegg about it. Kolskegg said, 'You must tell this to others at once, so that you are never accused of making charges against dead men; the charges would be dismissed unless you had witnesses to testify to what had previously happened between you.'

Gunnar told his neighbours. There was little comment about it at first.

Otkel and his men were given a warm welcome at Dale, and stayed there for a week. He told Runolf everything that had happened between himself and Gunnar. Someone asked how Gunnar had reacted.

Skamkel said, 'Anyone of lesser birth would be said to have wept.'

'That is a shameful thing to say,' said Runolf, 'and you will have to acknowledge, when next you two meet, that it is not in Gunnar's nature to weep. I only hope that better men than you do not have to suffer for your malice. I think it best now that I go with you when you want to ride home, for Gunnar would not do me any harm.'

'No, thank you,' said Otkel. 'We will cross the river farther down this time.'

Runolf gave him good gifts, and said that they would never see each other again. Otkel asked him to look after his son, if anything happened.

54

OVER at Hlidarend, Gunnar was out of doors when he saw his shepherd galloping towards the house, right into the home-meadow.

'Why are you riding so hard?' asked Gunnar.

'I wanted to be loyal to you,' he replied. 'I saw a group of eight men go riding down along Markar River. Four of them were wearing brightly-coloured clothing.'

'That must be Otkel,' said Gunnar.

The shepherd said, 'I have often heard their insults. Skamkel was saying, over at Dale, that you wept when they rode you down. I tell you this because I hate such spiteful talk.'

'We must not be over-sensitive,' said Gunnar. 'But from now on you need only do whatever work you wish.'

'Shall I tell Kolskegg anything?'

'No,' said Gunnar. 'Go and have a sleep. I shall tell Kolskegg myself.'

The boy went to bed and fell asleep at once. Gunnar took the boy's horse and put his own saddle on it. He fetched his shield, buckled on the sword that Olvir had given him, and put on a helmet. Then he took his halberd, and it rang loudly. His mother heard it, and came in to him.

'You look angry, my son,' she said. 'I have never seen you look like this before.'

Gunnar went outside. With a thrust of his halberd he vaulted into the saddle and rode away. Rannveig went into the living-room. The people there were talking loudly.

'Your talk is loud,' she said. 'But the halberd spoke even louder when Gunnar was setting off.'

Kolskegg heard her. 'That promises big events,' he said.

'Good,' said Hallgerd. 'Now they will find out whether Gunnar will run away weeping.'

Kolskegg snatched up his weapons, found himself a horse, and rode off as hard as he could.

Gunnar rode straight across Akratongue and on to Geila-stofnar, then over to Rang River and down to the ford at Hof.

There were some women at the milking-pens nearby. Gunnar jumped off his horse and tethered it, just as the other men came riding up. The paths leading down to the ford were of hardened clay.

'Get ready to defend yourselves,' said Gunnar. 'The halberd is here now. Now you shall see if you can make me weep.'

They all jumped off their horses and made for him. Hallbjorn was in the lead.

'Don't you attack,' Gunnar said to him. 'You are the last person I want to harm, but I shall not spare anyone if my own life depends on it.'

'That cannot be helped,' said Hallbjorn. 'You are out to kill my brother, and it would be shameful for me to stand by idle.'

With that he thrust two-handed at Gunnar with a great spear. Gunnar jerked his shield into its path, and the spear went right through it. Then Gunnar jammed the shield down with such force that it stuck fast in the ground, drew his sword faster than the eye could follow, and slashed down on Hallbjorn's forearm, cutting off hand and wrist.

Skamkel attacked Gunnar from behind and swung at him with a huge axe. Gunnar spun round and parried with the halberd, catching the axe at the base of its blade. The axe was wrenched from Skamkel's grasp and flew into the river. Then Gunnar lunged again with the halberd; he speared Skamkel on the point, heaved him up into the air, and dashed him head-first down on the path.

Audolf the Easterner snatched up a spear and threw it at Gunnar, who caught it in flight and hurled it back. It passed right through the shield and Audolf behind it, and buried its point in the ground.

Otkel swung his sword at Gunnar, aiming just below the knee. Gunnar leapt high and the blow passed underneath him. Gunnar thrust with his halberd and drove it through him.

At that moment Kolskegg arrived. He rushed at once at Hall-kel and killed him with his short-sword. Between them, the brothers killed all eight.

One of the women who saw the fighting ran home to tell Mord Valgardsson, and begged him to separate them.

'They will only be people who are welcome to kill each other for all I care,' he said.

'You can't mean that,' she said. 'Your kinsman Gunnar and your friend Otkel are there.'

'Can you never hold your tongue, you old hag?' said Mord; and he stayed indoors on his bed throughout the fight.

When it was over, Gunnar and Kolskegg rode home. As they rode fast along the river bank, Gunnar leapt from his horse and landed upright on his feet.

'That's good riding, brother,' said Kolskegg.

Gunnar replied, 'That's what Skamkel said, to sneer at me when I said, "You have ridden me down." '

'You have avenged that now,' said Kolskegg.

'But I wish I knew,' said Gunnar, 'whether I am any the less manly than other men, for being so much more reluctant to kill than other men are.'

55

NEWS of these events spread far and wide, and many said that they had happened no sooner than expected. Gunnar rode to Bergthorsknoll and told Njal about the killings.

'You have taken drastic action,' said Njal. 'But you had great provocation.'

'What will be the consequences?' asked Gunnar.

'Do you want me to tell you what the future holds?' asked Njal. 'You will ride to the Althing. You will have the benefit of my advice there. You will gain great credit from the outcome of the case. But this will be the start of your career of killing.'

'Give me some good advice,' said Gunnar.

'I shall,' said Njal. 'Never kill more than once in the same family; and never break any settlement which good men make between you and others – particularly if you have disregarded the first of these warnings.'

Gunnar said, 'I would have thought that others were more likely to do that than I.'

'That is so,' said Njal. 'But bear in mind that if you disregard both these warnings, you will not have long to live; otherwise you will live to be an old man.'

'Do you know what will cause your own death?' asked Gunnar.

'Yes,' said Njal. 'I do.'

'What will it be?' asked Gunnar.

'Something that everyone would least expect,' said Njal.

After that, Gunnar rode home.

A messenger was sent to Gizur the White and Geir the Priest, for it was their duty to take action over Otkel's death. They met to decide what should be done, and agreed that they should take it to court. They then discussed which of them should bring the action, but both were reluctant to do so.

'It seems to me,' said Gizur, 'that there are only two courses open to us: either, that one or other of us must bring the action – and we must decide by lot which of us it is to be – or else that there will be no compensation for Otkel. We can fully expect that it will be a difficult case to prosecute, for Gunnar has many kinsmen and many friends; so the one who is not chosen must give his support to the other and not withdraw it until the case is concluded.'

They drew lots, and it fell to Geir the Priest to bring the action. A little later they rode east over the rivers to the place where the battle had been fought, beside Rang River. They dug up the bodies and named witnesses for each man's fatal wound. Then they gave notice of their charges in the presence of nine neighbours, whom they cited to be their jurymen.

They were told that Gunnar was at home with thirty men. Geir asked Gizur whether he wanted to ride there with a hundred men.

'No,' said Gizur, 'not even with that advantage in numbers.'

So they rode back home. The news that proceedings had been started spread throughout the country, and everyone felt sure that the Althing would be a stormy one.

56

A MAN called Skapti Thoroddsson * and his father, Thorodd
the Priest,† were powerful chieftains and very skilled in law.
Thorodd was considered rather a sly and spiteful man. They
both supported Gizur the White in everything.

A great number of men from Fljotshlid and the Rangriver
Plains gathered for the Althing. Gunnar was so well-liked that
they all agreed to support him. They all arrived at the Althing
and tented their booths.

In league with Gizur the White were the following chieftains :
Skapti and Thorodd, Asgrim Ellida-Grimsson, Odd from Kidja-
berg, and Halldor Ornolfsson.

One day, people assembled at the Law Rock. Geir the Priest
stood up and gave notice of a manslaughter action against
Gunnar for the killing of Orkel, a further action for the killing
of Hallbjorn the White, another for the killing of Audolf, and
yet another for the killing of Skamkel. He also announced a
manslaughter action against Kolskegg for the killing of Hallkel.
When he had given notice of all these actions, people said that
he had spoken very well. Then he made formal inquiry about
the domicile and district of the defendants. After that, people
left the Law Rock.

The Althing continued, until the day came for the courts to
sit and hear the actions. Both parties attended in full strength.
Geir and Gizur stood to the south of the Rangriver Court,
Gunnar and Njal to the north of it.

Geir the Priest called upon Gunnar to hear his oath. Then he
took the oath and stated his charges. He led evidence that notice
of the charges had been given in the presence of nine neigh-

* Law-Speaker from 1004 to 1030. During his long tenure of the
office, he wielded huge power. The author of *Njal's Saga* gives a
rather biased picture of him. *Translators' note.*

† Thorodd's mother was Thorvor, the daughter of Thormod
Skapti, the son of Olaf the Broad, the son of Olvir the Child-
Sparer.

bours, whom he now called upon to take their places as a jury.* He invited the defence to challenge the jurymen, and then he called upon them to state their findings.

The nine neighbours who had been cited came before the court. They named witnesses, and said that they were not in a position to make any finding in the action concerning Audolf, because the lawful plaintiff was in Norway and they had therefore no jurisdiction in that action. After that they announced their findings in the action concerning Otkel, and found the charge against Gunnar lawfully made. Then Geir the Priest called upon Gunnar to make his defence, and named witnesses to each stage of the prosecution case.

Gunnar in reply called upon Geir the Priest to hear his oath and the defence he was going to present. Then he took the oath and said, 'My defence against this charge is that I had previously, in the presence of witnesses, declared Otkel an outlaw for the blood-wound he inflicted on me with his spur. Furthermore, I interdict † you, Geir the Priest, from prosecuting this charge, and the judges from bringing in a verdict; and with this interdict I declare all your actions null and void. This is a lawful, binding, and absolute interdict, which it is my right to make in accordance with the procedural rules of the Althing and the common law of the land. And now I shall tell you what else I am going to do.'

'Are you going to challenge me to single combat, as usual, and refuse to submit to the law?' asked Geir.

'No,' said Gunnar, 'I am going to charge you at the Law Rock with calling upon a jury to find in an action outside their jurisdiction – the killing of Audolf; and on that charge I shall demand a sentence of three-year outlawry.'

* *Kviðdómr*. The term 'jury' is a little misleading. In Icelandic law, the jury did not give a verdict of guilty or not guilty on the whole case. Their function was to find whether there was a case to answer, and whether that case had been properly made according to the requirements of the law. *Translators' note.*

† *Lýritr*. This is an odd passage. There is no known legal precedent for Gunnar's use of an interdict in this way. He need only have submitted as his defence that Otkel was an outlaw at the time of the killing; this would have destroyed the prosecution case just as effectively (cf. also Chapter 143). *Translators' note.*

Njal said, 'It must not come to that. It would only exacerbate the dispute. It seems to me that there is much to be said for the cases on both sides. You, Gunnar, cannot escape a verdict of guilty for some, at least, of your killings; on the other hand, you have made out a case against Geir the Priest in which he, too, would be found guilty. Furthermore, you, Geir, should bear in mind that there is an outlawry action against you still pending, and that it will certainly not be dropped if you do not pay heed to my advice.'

Thorodd the Priest said, 'It seems to me that it would be in the best interests of peace if both parties came to terms. Why have you so little to say, Gizur the White?'

'It seems to me,' said Gizur, 'that our case will meet heavy opposition; it is obvious that Gunnar's friends are supporting him strongly. Our best hope of a favourable outcome is to let good men arbitrate the dispute, if Gunnar will accept that.'

'I have always been ready to make settlements,' said Gunnar. 'Certainly, the grievances for which you seek redress are heavy; but I claim that I had great provocation.'

Wise counsel prevailed, and the outcome was that all the actions were put to the arbitration of six men, who made their assessment immediately. It was decided that no compensation should be paid for Skamkel, and that the compensation for Otkel's killing and Gunnar's wound should cancel each other out. The other killings were assessed on the basis of worth.

Gunnar's kinsmen contributed enough money to pay all the compensation immediately, at the Althing. Then Geir the Priest and Gizur the White went to Gunnar and gave him pledges of peace.

Gunnar rode home from the Althing. He thanked people for their support, and gave many of them gifts.

He gained great credit from all this; and now he stayed at home, in high esteem.

57

A MAN called Starkad, the son of Bork Bluetooth-Beard,* lived at Thrihyrning. His wife was called Hallbera.† They had three sons, Thorgeir, Bork, and Thorkel, and a daughter, Hildigunn the Healer.

The sons were all arrogant, brutal men, who had no respect for the rights of others.

58

A MAN called Egil Kolsson ‡ lived at Sandgill. He had a brother called Onund of Trollwood.§ Egil was married to Steinvor, the sister of Starkad of Thrihyrning.

They had three sons, Kol, Ottar, and Hauk; they were tall men, aggressive and overbearing, and they always sided with the sons of Starkad. They had a sister called Gudrun Night-Sun, a woman of great refinement.

There were two Easterners staying with Egil at Sandgill, called Thorir and Thorgrim, on their first visit to Iceland. They were well-liked and wealthy, skilled in arms and extremely brave.

Starkad owned a good red stallion, which they all thought could beat any other horse at fighting. On one occasion, when the brothers from Sandgill were over at Thrihyrning, they dis-

* The father of Bork Bluetooth-Beard was Thorkel Bound-Foot, who was the first settler on the land around Thrihyrning Mountain.

† Hallbera was the daughter of Hroald the Red and of Hildigunn, the daughter of Thorstein Sparrow and of Unn, the daughter of Eyvind Karfi and the sister of Modolf the Wise, from whom the Modylfings are descended.

‡ Egil was the son of Kol, the son of Ottar Ball, who was the first settler on the land between Stota Brook and Reydarwater.

§ Onund of Trollwood was the father of Hall the Strong, who was with the sons of Ketil the Smooth-Tongued at the killing of Holta-Thorir.

cussed at length all the farmers in Fljotshlid; eventually the question was raised whether there was anyone who would pit his horse against theirs in a fight. Some of the men present, wanting to flatter them, said that not only would no one dare to challenge them, but that there was no one who owned such a good horse.

Then Hildigunn the Healer said, 'I know someone who would dare to match his horse against yours.'

'Name him,' they said.

'Gunnar of Hlidarend has a black stallion,' she said, 'and he would dare to challenge you or anyone else.'

'You women all seem to think that there's no one like Gunnar,' they replied. 'Just because Geir the Priest and Gizur the White were humiliated by Gunnar, it doesn't follow that we would be, too.'

'You would come off even worse,' said Hildigunn.

This led to heated words. Starkad said, 'Gunnar is the last man I would want you to pick a quarrel with, for you would find it hard to beat his good luck.'

'But you will allow us to challenge him to a horse-fight?' they asked.

'I give my permission,' said Starkad, 'but only if you promise to play fair with him.'

They gave their promise, and rode off to Hlidarend. Gunnar was at home, and came outside with Kolskegg and Hjort, his brothers. He gave them a good welcome, and asked them where they were going.

'No farther than here,' they replied. 'We have heard that you have a good stallion, and we want to challenge you to a horse-fight.'

'You can hardly have heard anything very great about my stallion,' said Gunnar. 'He is only a young horse, and completely untried.'

'But you won't refuse a fight?' they asked. 'Hildigunn told us that you were very proud of him.'

'What made you discuss that?' asked Gunnar.

'There were some men who claimed that no one would dare to match his horse against ours,' they replied.

'I would dare to, certainly,' said Gunnar, 'but that was a very spiteful remark to make.'

'Can we consider it settled, then?' they asked.

'You won't think your journey worth while unless you have your own way,' said Gunnar. 'But I make this request, that we fight our horses only to entertain others and not to make trouble for ourselves, and that you don't try to discredit me; for if you treat me in the way you treat others, I am likely to retaliate in a way you will find hard to bear. Whatever you do to me, I shall pay you back in kind.'

With that they rode back home. Starkad asked how they had got on. They replied that Gunnar had made their journey worth while. 'He promised to match his horse against ours, and we arranged when the fight was to be held. But it was obvious that he felt his own inferiority, and he was very evasive.'

Hildigunn said, 'Gunnar may often be difficult to provoke; but he hits very hard when he has to.'

Gunnar rode to see Njal; he told him about the horse-fight, and the words that had passed.

'How do you think the fight will turn out?' he asked.

'You will win it,' said Njal. 'But it will be the cause of many deaths.'

'Will it cause my death?' asked Gunnar.

'Not directly,' said Njal. 'But they will remember their old enmity and assault you with new hatred – and you will have no choice but to retaliate.'

With that, Gunnar rode home.

59

WHEN Gunnar came home, he learned that his father-in-law, Hoskuld Dala-Kollsson, had died. A few days later, Thorgerd, the wife of Thrain Sigfusson of Grjotriver, gave birth to a son. She sent a messenger to her mother Hallgerd, and asked her to choose whether the boy should be called Glum or Hoskuld. Her mother asked her to call him Hoskuld, and that was the name he was given.

Gunnar and Hallgerd had two sons, Hogni and Grani. Hogni was a quiet, capable man, cautious and reliable.

A great number of people rode to the horse-fight. Gunnar was there with his brothers and the Sigfussons, Njal and all his sons, too. Starkad and his sons arrived with Egil and his sons. They said to Gunnar that it was now time to bring the horses together, and Gunnar agreed.

Skarp-Hedin asked, 'Do you want me to be in charge of your stallion, kinsman Gunnar?'

Gunnar said he did not.

'It would be better if I handled him,' said Skarp-Hedin, 'for I can be just as violent as they.'

'You would not have to say or do much before trouble arose,' said Gunnar. 'With me, the process will be slower, even if the outcome is the same.'

The horses were brought together. Gunnar equipped himself for goading as Skarp-Hedin led the horse forward. Gunnar wore a red tunic with a broad silver belt, and carried a horse-goad in his hand. The horses started fighting, and bit at each other for a long time without needing to be goaded. It was excellent sport. Then Thorgeir and Kol arranged to give their own horse a push when the horses next rushed at each other, to see if Gunnar would be knocked down.

The horses clashed again, and Thorgeir and Kol threw their weight against their horse's rump; but Gunnar pushed his horse against theirs, and in a flash Thorgeir and Kol were flat on their backs with their horse on top of them. They jumped to their feet and rushed at Gunnar, who side-stepped them and then seized hold of Kol and threw him down so hard that he was knocked senseless. Thorgeir struck Gunnar's horse and one of its eyes came out; Gunnar hit Thorgeir with the goad, and Thorgeir fell senseless.

Gunnar went over to his stallion. 'Kill the horse,' he said to Kolskegg. 'He shall not live mutilated.'

Kolskegg killed the horse. At that point Thorgeir got to his feet and seized his weapons and made for Gunnar; but he was stopped, and people came crowding up.

Skarp-Hedin said, 'I am bored with this scuffling. Men should use proper weapons to fight each other.'

Gunnar did not move, and only one man held him, and he did not shout abuse. Njal tried to arrange a settlement, or an exchange of pledges; but Thorgeir refused to give or accept pledges, and said he would rather see Gunnar dead for that blow.

Kolskegg said, 'Mere words have never knocked Gunnar down, and they will not now, either.'

Now people rode away from the horse-match, each to his own home. No attack was made on Gunnar. And so a year passed.

Next summer, Gunnar met his brother-in-law, Olaf the Peacock, at the Althing. Olaf invited him home for a visit, but warned him always to be on his guard – 'for they will do us what harm they can, so never travel without company.'

He gave Gunnar much good advice, and they exchanged pledges of the warmest friendship.

60

ASGRIM ELLIDA-GRIMSSON was suing a man called Ulf Uggason at the Althing over an inheritance claim. It so happened that there was a technical flaw in Asgrim's case, which was unusual for him; he had cited only five neighbours to be his jurymen instead of the stipulated nine. His opponents were using this error to invalidate his case.

Gunnar said, 'I shall challenge you to single combat, Ulf Uggason, if people are not to get their just rights from you. Njal and my friend Helgi would, I know, expect me to support you, Asgrim, if they cannot be present themselves.'

'But you and I have no quarrel over this claim,' said Ulf.

'That does not matter,' replied Gunnar.

The outcome was that Ulf had to pay the whole claim.

Asgrim said to Gunnar, 'I want to invite you to my home this summer. And I shall always be on your side in lawsuits, and never against you.'

Gunnar rode home from the Althing. A little later, he met Njal, who warned him to be on his guard; he said that he had heard that the men of Thrihyrning were planning to attack him, and he urged Gunnar never to travel without company and always to carry his weapons. Gunnar promised, and added that Asgrim had invited him home – 'and I plan to go there in the autumn.'

Njal said, 'Let no one know when you are setting off, or how long you will be away; and I want you to let my sons ride with you – that would forestall any attack on you.'

They agreed on this.

The summer passed. Two months before winter, Gunnar said to Kolskegg, 'Get yourself ready; we are going to Tongue for a visit.'

'Shall we send any word to the Njalssons?' asked Kolskegg.

'No,' said Gunnar. 'They are not to get involved in any trouble on my account.'

61

GUNNAR, Kolskegg, and Hjort rode off together. Gunnar carried his halberd, and the sword that Olvir had given him. Kolskegg wore his short-sword. Hjort was fully armed. They rode to Tongue, where they were given a good welcome by Asgrim. They stayed there a short while, and then announced that it was time to go back home. Asgrim gave them good gifts, and offered to accompany them east. Gunnar said there was no need for that, and so Asgrim stayed behind.

A man called Sigurd Hog-Head, who lived near Thjors River, arrived at Thrihyrning; he had promised to spy on Gunnar's movements. He reported that Gunnar was on his way, and said that they would never have a better chance than this, for Gunnar had only two companions.

'How many men do we need for an ambush?' asked Starkad.

'Lesser men are as nothing to Gunnar,' replied Sigurd. 'It would not be safe to have fewer than thirty.'

'Where shall we ambush him?' asked Starkad.

'At Knafahills,' said Sigurd. 'They can't see us there until the very last minute.'

'Go to Sandgill,' said Starkad. 'Tell Egil to get fifteen men from there ready, and we shall meet them at Knafahills with fifteen more from here.'

Thorgeir said to Hildigunn, 'This hand will bring you proof of Gunnar's death tonight.'

'My guess is,' said Hildigunn, 'that your hand will hang as low as your head when you come back from meeting Gunnar.'

Starkad and his three sons went from Thrihyrning with eleven others to Knafahills and waited there.

Sigurd reached Sandgill and said to Egil, 'Starkad and his sons sent me here to tell you to go with your sons to Knafahills for an ambush on Gunnar.'

'How many men are needed?' asked Egil.

'Fifteen, including me,' replied Sigurd.

Kol said, 'Today I intend to take on Kolskegg.'

'You're taking on a lot, if you ask me,' said Sigurd.

Egil asked his two Easterners to come. They said that they had no quarrel with Gunnar; and Thorir added, 'You're surely needing a great deal of help, when such a host of men is to fight against three.'

Egil walked away in a rage. His wife said to Thorir, 'My daughter Gudrun was a fool to humble herself by sleeping with you, when you haven't the courage to go with your father-in-law. You're nothing but a coward.'

'I'll go with your husband, then,' said Thorir. 'But neither of us will return.'

He went to see his comrade Thorgrim, and said, 'Take the keys of my chests, for I shall never need them again. I want you to have anything from our goods you wish; but leave the country and do not think of vengeance for me, for if you remain in Iceland it will cost you your life.'

Then Thorir took his weapons and joined the others.

62

MEANWHILE, Gunnar was riding east over Thjors River. Not long after crossing it, he became very sleepy, and asked his brothers to make a halt. When they stopped, Gunnar fell fast asleep at once; but he was restless in his sleep, and Kolskegg said, 'Gunnar is dreaming now.'

'I would like to wake him,' said Hjort.

'No,' said Kolskegg, 'let him dream his dream out.'

Gunnar lay sleeping a very long time. Then he became uncomfortably hot, and threw off his cloak.

'What have you been dreaming, brother?' asked Kolskegg.

Gunnar said, 'If I had previously dreamt the dream I have just had, I would never have left Tongue with so few companions.'

'Tell us your dream,' said Kolskegg.

'I dreamt,' said Gunnar, 'that I was riding past Knafahills, and in my dream I saw a pack of wolves come out at me. I retreated down to Rang River, where they leapt at me from all sides, but we fought them off. I shot those that were in the lead, until they pressed so close that I could not use my bow. Then I drew my sword, and fought with sword in one hand and halberd in the other; I never used my shield, and did not know what was protecting me. I killed many of the wolves, and you were helping me, Kolskegg; but they overpowered Hjort and ripped open his chest, and one of them seized his heart in its jaws. Then in my dream my rage was so violent that I sliced the creature in two behind the shoulder; and with that the rest of the wolves fled.

'And now, Hjort, I think you should ride back west to Tongue.'

'No,' said Hjort. 'Though I see certain death before me, I want to stay by your side.'

They rode on together, east to Knafahills, where Kolskegg said, 'Gunnar, do you see all those spears jutting up from behind the hillocks, and men with weapons?'

'It does not surprise me that my dream is coming true,' said Gunnar.

'What shall we do?' asked Kolskegg. 'I take it you don't intend to run from them?'

'They will never be able to taunt us with that,' said Gunnar. 'We shall ride to that tongue of land down by Rang River; it's a good place for defence.'

They rode down to the river and made themselves ready. As they rode past, Kol shouted, 'Are you running away, Gunnar?'

Kolskegg replied, 'Ask that when the day is over.'

147

63

STARKAD now urged his men on, and they advanced upon the three on the headland. Sigurd Hog-Head was in the lead, with a thin round shield in one hand and a hunting-spear in the other. Gunnar sighted him and shot an arrow at him; Sigurd raised his shield when he saw the arrow curving high, but the arrow went right through the shield, pierced his eye, and came out at the back of his neck.

That was the first killing.

Gunnar shot his second arrow at Ulf-Hedin, Starkad's overseer, and hit him in the waist. Ulf-Hedin fell at the feet of a farmer, who stumbled over him; Kolskegg then hurled a stone which struck the farmer on the head and killed him.

Starkad said, 'It's not doing us any good to let Gunnar use his bow. Advance on them more briskly.'

They urged each other on. Gunnar defended himself with bow and arrows as long as he could; then he threw the bow down, took sword and halberd, and fought with both hands. It was a fierce and long battle, and Gunnar and Kolskegg killed several men.

Then Thorgeir Starkadarson said, 'I promised to bring Hildigunn your head, Gunnar.'

'She can't attach that much importance to it,' said Gunnar. 'But you will have to come a lot closer to get it.'

Thorgeir said to his brothers, 'Let's all rush him at once. He is without a shield, and we shall have him at our mercy.'

Bork and Thorkel ran forward, ahead of Thorgeir. Bork swung at Gunnar, who parried so strongly with his halberd that the sword flew from Bork's grasp. Then Gunnar noticed Thorkel on the other side within sword-reach; he pivoted on one foot and swung his sword at him. The blow fell on Thorkel's neck, and his head flew off.

Kol Egilsson said, 'Let me get at Kolskegg. I have always said that we would be equally matched in a fight.'

'We can soon find that out,' said Kolskegg.

Kol lunged at him with a spear. Kolskegg had just killed

someone, and had no time to raise his shield; the spear struck the outside of his thigh and went right through it. Kolskegg whirled round and leapt at him, swung at his thigh with the short-sword, and cut off Kol's leg.

'Did that one land or not?' asked Kolskegg.

'That's my reward for not having my shield,' said Kol. He stood for a moment on one leg, looking down at the stump.

'You don't need to look,' said Kolskegg. 'It's just as you think – the leg is off.'

Then Kol fell dead to the ground. When Egil, his father, saw this, he flung himself at Gunnar and struck at him. Gunnar countered with his halberd, drove it through his stomach, and then hoisted him up on the point and hurled him into the river.

Starkad turned to Thorir. 'You're an utter coward, Easterner,' he said, 'to sit by idle. Egil, your host and father-in-law, has just been killed.'

Thorir jumped angrily to his feet. Hjort had already killed two men. The Easterner rushed at him and struck him full in the chest, killing him instantly.

Gunnar saw this and hurled himself at the Easterner; with one sweep he sliced him in two at the waist. Next he threw the halberd at Bork, sending it right through him and pinning him to the ground. Kolskegg cut off Hauk Egilsson's head, and Gunnar sliced off Ottar Egilsson's forearm.

'Let us run,' said Starkad. 'These are not men we are fighting.'

Gunnar said, 'You will find it embarrassing to tell of this battle if you have nothing to show you have been in one.' He ran at Starkad and Thorgeir and dealt them each a wound.

With that they broke off. Gunnar and his brothers had wounded many of those who managed to escape. In all, fourteen of the attackers lost their lives in the battle, and Hjort was the fifteenth.

Gunnar rode home carrying Hjort on his shield, and raised a burial mound over him.* Many mourned his death, for he had been well liked by all.

* About a century and a half ago a number of burial mounds came to light, through erosion, near Rang River. Several skeletons were exposed, and from time to time various articles were found near the remains of these mounds. The most remarkable find was a bracelet made of bone, on which is crudely engraved a picture of

When Starkad and Thorgeir reached home, Hildigunn treated their wounds and said, 'You would give a lot now, never to have molested Gunnar.'

'Yes, indeed,' said Starkad.

64

OVER at Sandgill, Egil's widow, Steinvor, asked Thorgrim the Easterner to manage the property for her; she begged him not to go abroad, but to stay in Iceland and keep alive the memory of his comrade and kinsman.

Thorgrim replied, 'My partner Thorir prophesied that I would be killed by Gunnar if I remained in this country; and he must be right about that, since he was right about his own death.'

'I'll give you my daughter Gudrun in marriage and all the property, if you stay,' said Steinvor.

'I didn't realize you wanted to pay such a high price,' said Thorgrim. They agreed on these terms, that he should marry Gudrun, and the wedding took place that summer.

Gunnar rode over to Bergthorsknoll with Kolskegg. Njal and his sons were outside, and came to meet them with a warm welcome. Then they went aside to talk, and Gunnar said, 'I have come here to you for help and guidance.'

Njal said that he had every right to it.

'I have fallen into grave difficulties and killed many men,' said Gunnar, 'and I would like to know what you want me to do.'

'There are many who will say your hand was forced,' said Njal. 'But give me a moment while I work out a plan.'

Njal walked away by himself and pondered the problem.

two harts. The name of Gunnar's brother, Hjort, who died in this ambush at Rang River, means in Icelandic 'hart'; and the temptation to link the two is almost irresistible. Archaeologists are inclined to doubt that the design on the bracelet is from the tenth century, but have found it impossible to date with any certainty. (The bracelet is now in the National Museum of Iceland.) *Translators' note.*

When he came back, he said, 'I have given this some thought, and in my opinion it calls for bold and aggressive measures.'

He went on, 'Thorgeir has made my kinswoman Thorfinna pregnant; I am going to assign to you my action against him for seduction. I am also going to assign to you an outlawry action against Starkad, for cutting wood on my property on Thrihyrning Ridges. You can use both these actions as counter-charges. You must go over to the place where you fought; dig up the bodies there, name witnesses to the fatal wounds, and outlaw all the dead men for attacking you and your brothers with intent to wound and kill. During trial at the Althing it may be objected that you had previously struck Thorgeir a blow and thus forfeited your right to conduct your own or anyone else's action; I shall meet this objection by pointing out that during the Thingskalar Assembly I gave notice of your offer of compensation, thus restoring your legal rights. That will take care of that point.

'You must also go to see Tyrfing of Berjaness; he will assign to you an action he has pending against Onund of Trollwood, whose duty it is to take action over the killing of his brother Egil.'

Gunnar went home. A few days later he rode out with the Njalssons to the place where the bodies were buried, and dug them all up. Then he declared that the dead men had all put themselves outside the law by their assault and conspiracy to kill.

After that he rode home.

65

THAT same autumn, Valgard the Grey returned to Iceland and went home to Hof. Thorgeir went over to see him and Mord, and complained that it was an outrage for Gunnar to claim that all those he had killed had been outlaws. Valgard said that it sounded like Njal's idea, and that it would not be the last of the schemes that Njal had planned for Gunnar. Thorgeir asked Mord and Valgard for their help and support, but they were evasive for a long time and demanded a large payment.

Eventually they agreed to help, on condition that Thorgeir rode west over the rivers with them at once, to support Mord in asking for the hand of Thorkatla, Gizur the White's daughter.

They set off next day, twelve of them in all, and went to Mosfell, where they were well received and stayed the night. Then they put the marriage-offer to Gizur, and in the end it was accepted, the wedding to take place at Mosfell in a fortnight's time. They rode back home, and later they returned for the wedding; a large number of guests had already arrived, and everything went off well. Thorkatla went home with Mord and took charge of the household. Valgard went abroad in the summer.

Mord kept urging Thorgeir to start proceedings against Gunnar. Thorgeir went to see Onund of Trollwood, and asked him to start the action for the killing of Egil and his sons – 'I myself shall start the action for the killing of my brothers and the wounding of my father and me.'

Onund said he was quite ready. So they went off and gave notice of the killings, and cited the nine nearest neighbours to be their jurymen.

The news that proceedings had been started reached Hlidarend. Gunnar rode over to see Njal and told him, and asked what he wanted done now.

Njal said, 'Now you yourself must cite these nine neighbours, and name witnesses that you select Kol Egilsson as the killer of your brother Hjort. That is in accordance with the law. Then you must give notice of a manslaughter action against Kol, even though he is dead. You must then name witnesses and cite neighbours to go to the Althing to testify whether Kol and his companions were present and participating when Hjort was killed. You must also summons Thorgeir on the charge of seduction, and Onund of Trollwood on the charge provided by Tyrfing of Berjaness.'

Gunnar did everything according to Njal's instructions. Many people thought this an odd way of preparing a case.

All these lawsuits were now referred to the Althing. Gunnar rode there with Njal and his sons, and the Sigfussons. Gunnar had also sent a messenger to his brothers-in-law, asking them to come to the Althing with as much support as possible, saying that this would be a hard-fought case. Thus a large number of supporters flocked in from the west.

Mord Valgardsson rode to the Althing with Runolf of Dale and the people from Thrihyrning and Onund of Trollwood.

66

WHEN they arrived at the Althing they joined forces with Gizur the White and Geir the Priest.

Gunnar and the Sigfussons and the Njalssons all went about together in a close group, and walked so briskly that people in their path had to be careful not to be knocked over. Nothing was discussed so much all over the Althing as this great lawsuit.

Gunnar went to meet his brothers-in-law, and Olaf the Peacock and his brothers welcomed him warmly. They asked him about the battle, and he gave them a fair and detailed account; he also told them what he had done since then.

Olaf said, 'It's a great advantage to have Njal supporting you so closely and so skilfully.'

Gunnar said that he could never repay it. He then asked them for their support; they said that it was only his due.

Now the actions brought by both sides came before the court. Each side pleaded its case.

Mord asked by what right did a man like Gunnar, who had already made himself liable to outlawry for his assault on Thorgeir, bring an action.

Njal said, 'Were you at the Thingskalar Assembly last autumn?'

'Yes, I was,' said Mord.

'Did you hear how Gunnar offered compensation and a full settlement?' asked Njal.

'Yes, I did,' replied Mord.

'At that time I gave notice of Gunnar's immunity,' said Njal, 'which gives him the right to conduct legal actions.'

'That is in accordance with the law,' admitted Mord. 'But what justification was there for Gunnar to declare Kol Egilsson guilty of killing Hjort, when it was the Easterner who did the killing?[2]

'That was also in accordance with the law,' replied Njal, 'for Gunnar chose Kol in the presence of witnesses as the killer.'

'That is probably right,' said Mord. 'But on what grounds did Gunnar declare them all outlaws?'

'You should not need to ask that,' said Njal, 'since they went with intent to wound and kill.'

'But,' said Mord, 'Gunnar was never harmed.'

'Kolskegg and Hjort were Gunnar's brothers,' said Njal, 'and one was killed and the other wounded.'

'You have the law on your side,' said Mord, 'even though we find it hard to put up with.'

At that point Hjalti Skeggjason from Thjorsriverdale came forward and said, 'I have taken no sides in your lawsuits. But now I want to know how much you, Gunnar, will do at my request and for the sake of my friendship.'

'What do you ask of me?' said Gunnar.

'I ask you to submit the whole dispute to the arbitration of good men,' said Hjalti.

Gunnar replied, 'Only on condition that you never take sides against me, whomsoever I am dealing with.'

'I give you that promise,' said Hjalti.

After that, Hjalti negotiated with Gunnar's opponents, and managed to arrange a settlement. Each side gave the other pledges.

The wound on Thorgeir was set against the seduction charge, and the wound on Starkad was set against his illegal cutting of wood. Half-compensation was to be paid for Thorgeir's brothers, the other half being forfeited for their assault on Gunnar. The killing of Egil of Sandgill, and Tyrfing's action against Onund of Trollwood, cancelled each other out. The killing of Hjort was set against the killing of Kol and the Norwegian, and half-compensation was to be paid for the rest of them.

Taking part in the arbitration were Njal, Asgrim Ellida-Grimsson, and Hjalti Skeggjason.

Njal had a large sum of money loaned out to Starkad and the people of Sandgill; he gave all this money to Gunnar to help pay the compensation. Gunnar had so many friends at the Althing that he was able to pay all the compensation there and then. He gave gifts to the chieftains who had lent him their support.

Gunnar gained great credit from the outcome of this case, and everyone agreed that he had no equal in the South Quarter.

He rode home from the Althing and settled down in peace. But his adversaries bitterly grudged him the esteem he had won.

67

Now the saga returns to Thorgeir, the son of Otkel of Kirkby. Thorgeir grew to manhood tall and strong, honest and straight-forward but rather easily led. He was well liked by people of most worth, and loved by all his kinsmen.

One day Thorgeir Starkadarson of Thrihyrning went to visit his kinsman Mord Valgardsson.

'I'm not at all satisfied with the way our case against Gunnar was settled,' said Thorgeir. 'I have paid you for your support for the rest of our lives; so now I want you to think up some plan, and lay it very deep. I say this openly because I know that you are Gunnar's bitterest enemy, and he yours. I shall make it well worth your while if you do it properly.'

'Everyone knows,' replied Mord, 'that I never refuse money, and I'm not going to now. Of course, it will be very difficult to find you a way of gaining your ends without violating your pledges and settlements. However, I have heard that Kolskegg is planning to go to law in order to regain the portion of Moeidarknoll which your father was given as compensation for one of your brothers. Kolskegg is bringing the action on behalf of his mother, but it was Gunnar's idea to hold on to the land and pay cash instead. We shall wait until they carry out this plan, and then accuse him of breaking the settlement he made with you. Gunnar has also taken a cornfield from Thorgeir Otkelsson, and thus broken the settlement he made with him, too. You must go to see Thorgeir Otkelsson and get him involved in this, and make him join you in an attack on Gunnar.

'If something goes wrong with the plan, and Gunnar manages

to give you the slip this time, you must keep on trying again and again. For I can tell you this, that Njal has seen into Gunnar's future and made this prophecy : if Gunnar kills more than once in the same family and then breaks the settlement made for that killing, it will hasten him to his death. That is why you must get Thorgeir Otkelsson involved in this matter, for Gunnar has already killed Thorgeir's father; then, if the two of you ever fight against Gunnar, you must take care to protect yourself while Thorgeir advances boldly and Gunnar kills him. Gunnar will then have killed twice in the same family, and you can save yourself by flight. If this is fated to drag him to his death, he will then go on to break the ensuing settlement. We have only to sit back and wait.'

After that Thorgeir went home to Thrihyrning and told his father all this in private. They decided to carry out the plan without letting anyone else into the secret.

68

A LITTLE later, Thorgeir Starkadarson went to Kirkby to see his namesake, Thorgeir Otkelsson. They went aside and talked all day in private; finally, Thorgeir Starkadarson gave Thorgeir Otkelsson a gold-inlaid spear, and then rode back home, after exchanging pledges of warmest friendship.

At the Thingskalar Assembly in the autumn, Kolskegg made his claim to the land at Moeidarknoll; Gunnar named witnesses and offered to compensate the people of Thrihyrning with money or another piece of land lawfully assessed at the same value. Thorgeir then named witnesses and charged Gunnar with breaking their settlement. With that the Assembly ended.

A year passed. The two Thorgeirs often met, and became intimate friends.

Kolskegg said to Gunnar, 'I hear that there is great friendship between Thorgeir Otkelsson and Thorgeir Starkadarson; many people are saying that they are planning some treachery. I want you to be on your guard.'

'Death will catch up with me wherever I am,' said Gunnar, 'when it is so fated.'

They discussed it no further.

In the autumn, Gunnar gave instructions to his men to work one week at home, and the following week down in the Land-Isles to finish the hay-making there; everyone was to leave the farm, he said, except himself and the womenfolk.

Thorgeir from Thrihyrning went to see his namesake at Kirkby, and as soon as they met, they had a talk as usual.

Thorgeir Starkadarson said, 'I think we should steel ourselves for an attack on Gunnar.'

'Encounters with Gunnar all end the same way,' said Thorgeir Otkelsson. 'There are few who have come off better. Besides, I would hate to be called a pledge-breaker.'

'It is they who have broken the settlement, not we,' said Thorgeir Starkadarson. 'Gunnar stole your cornfield from you, and Moeidarknoll from my father and myself.'

They agreed to make an attack on Gunnar. Thorgeir Starkadarson then said that Gunnar would be alone at home in a few days' time. 'Meet me with eleven men,' he said, 'and I shall bring the same number.'

After that, Thorgeir rode home.

69

WHEN Kolskegg and the farmhands had been away at the Land-Isles for three days, Thorgeir Starkadarson had word of their absence and sent a message to Thorgeir Otkelsson to come to meet him at Thrihyrning Ridges; then he set off with eleven men from Thrihyrning and rode up to the Ridges to await his namesake.

Gunnar was now the only man left at Hlidarend. The two Thorgeirs rode into a wood; there a tremendous drowsiness overcame them, and they had no choice but to go to sleep. They hung their shields on branches, tethered their horses, and laid their weapons by their sides.

Njal was over at Thorolfsfell that night. He could not sleep, and wandered restlessly in and out of the house. Thorhild, Skarp-Hedin's wife, asked Njal why he could not sleep.

'My eyes are full of strange sights,' he replied. 'I see the menacing fetches of many of Gunnar's enemies. But there is something odd about them; there is ferocity in their look, but no purpose to their actions.'

A little later a man rode up to the door, dismounted, and walked in. It was the shepherd at Thorolfsfell.

Thorhild asked, 'Did you find the sheep?'

'I found something much more important,' he replied.

'What was that?' asked Njal.

'I found twenty-four men up there in the wood,' he replied. 'They had tethered their horses and were fast asleep, and had hung their shields in the branches.'

He had observed them so closely that he could describe the weapons and clothing of all of them, and Njal could tell exactly who each one was.

Njal said to the shepherd, 'What a household it would be if there were many like you! You shall never have cause to regret this service. But now I need you for an errand.'

The shepherd said he would do it.

'Go to Hlidarend,' said Njal, 'and tell Gunnar to go to Grjot-river and gather forces. Meanwhile, I shall go and meet the men in the wood and frighten them away. This has turned out very well, for their expedition will gain them nothing and lose them much.'

The shepherd went and told Gunnar in detail everything that had happened. Gunnar rode off to Grjotriver and sent out a call for men.

Meanwhile, Njal rode to meet the two Thorgeirs.

'You are careless, lying about like this,' he said. 'What was the point of this expedition, anyway? Gunnar is not a man to be trifled with, and this is a flagrant case of conspiracy to kill. You had better know that Gunnar is gathering forces; he will be here soon and will kill you, unless you flee back home.'

They jumped to their feet in panic, grabbed their weapons, mounted their horses, and fled back to Thrihyrning.

Njal went to meet Gunnar and asked him not to disband his forces. 'I shall act as go-between and try to arrange a settlement,' he added. 'They are sufficiently frightened now. The compensation for this conspiracy against your life shall be no less, since so many of them are involved, than it would be for the killing of either of the Thorgeirs, if that ever happens. I shall look after the money for you and make sure that it is available to you when needed.'

70

GUNNAR thanked him for all his help. Njal rode to Thrihyrning and told the two Thorgeirs that Gunnar was not going to disband his forces until their dispute was resolved. They were greatly alarmed; they made various offers, and begged Njal to put them to Gunnar. Njal said that he would carry only such offers as contained no treachery. They begged him to be one of the arbitrators, and promised to abide by the decision. Njal refused to arbitrate except at the Althing and with other good men present. They agreed to that.

So, with Njal acting as go-between, both sides exchanged pledges of peace and reconciliation. The terms were that Njal was to arbitrate with the help of any others he cared to name.

A little later, the two Thorgeirs met Mord Valgardsson. Mord criticized them severely for submitting to Njal's arbitration, when he was such a close friend of Gunnar's. It would do them little good, he said.

People now rode to the Althing as usual, and both parties attended. Njal asked for a hearing, and then asked all good men present what claim, in their opinion, Gunnar had against the Thorgeirs for the conspiracy against his life; they answered that in their opinion a man of Gunnar's standing had claims for heavy compensation. Njal asked whether he had a case against all of them, or whether only the two ring-leaders were liable; they answered that the leaders must carry most of the blame, but all the others some of it.

Mord said, 'Many would say that Gunnar cannot be absolved of all guilt, since he had broken settlement with the Thorgeirs.'

'It is no breach of settlement,' said Njal, 'for a man to have lawful dealings with another. With laws shall our land be built up but with lawlessness laid waste.'

Njal went on to explain how Gunnar had offered alternative land or cash payment for Moeidarknoll.

The two Thorgeirs felt that they had been deceived by Mord and reproached him bitterly. They claimed that it was his fault that they were losing their money.

Njal named twelve men to act as arbitrators in the dispute. The outcome was that each member of the expedition had to pay a hundred ounces of silver, and the two Thorgeirs twice that amount. Njal took the money into his keeping. Both sides now exchanged pledges of peace, repeating the words after Njal.

Gunnar then rode from the Althing west to the Dales, to Hjardarholt, where he was warmly welcomed by Olaf the Peacock. He stayed there for a fortnight; he rode all over the Dales, and was welcomed gladly wherever he went.

When they parted, Olaf said, 'I want to give you three gifts: a gold bracelet, a cloak that once belonged to King Myrkjartan * of Ireland, and a dog I was given in Ireland. He is a big animal, and will make as good a comrade-in-arms as a powerful man. He has human intelligence, and he will bark at every man he recognizes as your enemy, but never at your friends; he can tell from a man's face whether he means you well or not. He would lay down his life rather than fail you. His name is Sam.'

Then he said to the dog, 'Go with Gunnar and serve him as well as you can.'

The dog went to Gunnar at once and lay down at his feet.

Olaf warned Gunnar to be on his guard, and said that there were many who were envious of him – 'since you are now considered the most outstanding person in the land'.

Gunnar thanked him for his gifts and good advice, and rode back home. He stayed there for a while, and everything was quiet.

71

A LITTLE later, the two Thorgeirs met Mord, and quarrelled with him; they felt that they had lost a lot of money through him, without any returns. They demanded that Mord should

* Myrkjartan was Olaf the Peacock's grandfather, according to *Laxdæla Saga*. The Irish form of his name was Muircheartach. *Translators' note*.

devise some other scheme to do Gunnar harm. Mord agreed to do this. 'It is my advice now,' he said, 'that you, Thorgeir Otkelsson, seduce Ormhild, Gunnar's kinswoman; this will make Gunnar dislike you even more. I shall then spread the rumour that Gunnar is not going to put up with that from you; and after that, you two can make an attack on him. But not at his home; that is quite impossible as long as the dog is alive.'

They agreed to put this scheme into effect.

As the summer wore on, Thorgeir Otkelsson began to pay calls on Ormhild. Gunnar was annoyed at this, and a strong animosity sprang up between the two men, which continued throughout the winter. Next spring, Thorgeir's private meetings with Ormhild became more frequent than ever. Meanwhile, the other Thorgeir and Mord were meeting constantly; they made a plan to attack Gunnar when he rode down to the Land-Isles to see to the work his men were doing there.

One day Mord got word that Gunnar had gone to the Land-Isles. He sent to Thrihyrning to tell Thorgeir Starkadarson that this would be the best time to try an attack on him. Thorgeir set off at once with twelve men, and when they reached Kirkby they found his namesake waiting with another twelve. They discussed where to ambush Gunnar and decided to ride to Rang River and lie in wait for him there.

But when Gunnar left the Land-Isles, Kolskegg accompanied him. Gunnar carried his bow and arrows, and his halberd; Kolskegg was fully armed, and had his short-sword with him.

72

SUDDENLY, as Gunnar and Kolskegg rode up to Rang River, a stream of blood appeared on the halberd. Kolskegg asked what that could mean. Gunnar replied that when that sort of thing happened in other lands, it was called 'death rain' — 'and according to Olvir, it was a sign of imminent battle.'

They rode on until they saw the band of men by the river. They noticed that the men had tethered their horses and were sitting, waiting.

'An ambush,' said Gunnar.

'They have always been treacherous,' said Kolskegg. 'What should we do?'

'We shall race past them up to the ford,' said Gunnar, 'and face them there.'

The others saw their move and turned to follow them. Gunnar strung his bow, tossed his arrows down on the ground in front of him, and began to shoot whenever they came within range. That way he killed some and wounded several others.

Then Thorgeir Otkelsson said, 'This isn't doing us any good. We must charge them.'

They did so, with Onund the Handsome, a kinsman of Thorgeir's, in the lead. Gunnar threw the halberd at him; it split his shield in two and went right through him. Then Ogmund Tangle-Hair sprang at Gunnar from behind, but Kolskegg saw it and swept both his legs off, and then pushed him into the river, where he drowned at once. The battle grew fierce. Gunnar cut with one hand and thrust with the other; Kolskegg killed a number of men and wounded several others.

Thorgeir Starkadarson said to the other Thorgeir, 'You give little sign of having a dead father to avenge.'

'Perhaps I haven't made much progress,' said Thorgeir Otkelsson, 'but you haven't even kept up with me. I'm not going to put up with your taunts.'

With that he hurled himself furiously at Gunnar and drove his spear through Gunnar's shield and right through his arm. Gunnar twisted the shield so violently that the spear-head broke off at the socket. At that moment Gunnar noticed another man within sword-reach, and killed him with one blow. Then he seized the halberd with both hands. Thorgeir Otkelsson was now almost on him with his sword raised; Gunnar whirled on him in fury and drove the halberd right through him, hoisted him high in the air, and hurled him out into the river. The body drifted down to the ford, where it caught against a boulder; this place has been known as Thorgeirs Ford ever since.

Thorgeir Starkadarson said, 'Let us run; victory is obviously not to be ours.' They all turned and fled.

'Let us pursue them,' said Kolskegg. 'Bring your bow and arrows, you can get within range of Thorgeir Starkadarson.'

Gunnar said, 'Our purses will be empty enough by the time we have paid compensation for those who lie dead here already.'

'You will never run short of money,' said Kolskegg, 'but Thorgeir will never give up until he has contrived your death.'

'There would need to be several of his sort in my path before I took fright,' said Gunnar.

They rode home and told what had happened. Hallgerd was delighted at the news and was full of praise. But Rannveig said, 'It may be a good feat; but it gave me the unpleasant feeling that no good will come of it.'

73

NEWS of these events spread far and wide, and Thorgeir's death was mourned by many. Gizur the White and Geir the Priest rode to the place, gave notice of the killings, and cited the neighbours to attend the Althing. Then they rode back west.

Njal and Gunnar met and talked about the battle. Njal said to Gunnar, 'You must be very careful now. You have now killed twice in the same family. For your own good, remember that it will cost you your life if you do not keep the settlement that will be made.'

'I have no intention of breaking it,' said Gunnar. 'But I shall need your support at the Althing.'

'I shall keep my vow of friendship until death,' said Njal.

With that, Gunnar rode home.

The Althing drew near, and each side gathered a large number of supporters. There was much speculation at the Althing about the outcome of the case.

Gizur and Geir the Priest discussed which of them was to give notice of the action over the killing of Thorgeir. Finally Gizur took over the case and gave notice of it at the Law Rock in these words: 'I give notice of an action against Gunnar Hamundarson for unlawful assault, inasmuch as he made an unlawful assault on Thorgeir Otkelsson and inflicted on him an internal wound which did cause Thorgeir's death. I demand that Gunnar be sentenced to full outlawry on this charge, not to be fed nor forwarded nor helped nor harboured. I claim that his possessions be forfeit, half to me and half to those men in the Quarter who have a lawful right to receive confiscated goods.

'I refer this action to the proper Quarter Court. I give lawful notice of it, in public, at the Law Rock. I give notice of an action, to be heard at this session, for full outlawry against Gunnar Hamundarson.'

Again Gizur named witnesses and gave notice of an action against Gunnar Hamundarson inasmuch as he inflicted on Thorgeir Otkelsson an internal wound which did cause Thorgeir's death, at the place where Gunnar had previously made an unlawful assault on Thorgeir. Then he gave notice of this action as before. After that he made formal inquiry about the domicile and district of the defendant.

When this was over, people left the Law Rock, and everyone said that he had spoken well. Gunnar was composed, and said little.

The Althing continued, until the day came for the courts to sit. Gunnar and his men stood to the north of the Rangriver Court, Gizur and his men to the south of it.

Gizur named witnesses and called upon Gunnar to hear his oath and his charges and all the evidence he would lead. Then he took the oath, and stated his charges in the same terms as those in which he had previously given notice of the action. He led evidence that notice of them had been given, and called upon the nine neighbours to take their places as a jury. Then he invited the defence to challenge the jurymen.

74

NJAL said, 'Now we must seize the initiative. Let us go over to the jurymen.'

They went over and successfully challenged four of them; then they called upon the remaining five to find on the defence submission that Thorgeir Starkadarson and Thorgeir Otkelsson had waylaid Gunnar with intent to kill him. Without hesitation they all found in Gunnar's favour. Njal claimed that this was an unanswerable defence, and said that he would put it forward unless the other side agreed to arbitration.

Many other chieftains supported this call for a settlement, and eventually it was agreed that twelve men should arbitrate. Both parties came forward and shook hands on this agreement.

The arbitration was made and the amount of compensation determined. The entire sum was to be paid up at once at the Althing. Furthermore, Gunnar and Kolskegg were to leave the country for three years; but if Gunnar failed to leave, without good reason, his life would be forfeit to the kinsmen of the dead.

Gunnar gave no sign that he was dissatisfied with this settlement. He asked Njal for the money he had entrusted to him; Njal had accumulated interest on it, and now paid over the entire sum.

It turned out to be the exact amount that Gunnar was to pay as compensation.

Now people rode home from the Althing. Gunnar and Njal rode back together.

Njal said to Gunnar, 'Take good care, friend, not to break this settlement. Bear in mind what we have already discussed. If your first journey abroad was a success, this one will be a triumph. You will come back a man of great renown; you will live to be an old man, and no one here will be your equal. But if you break this settlement, if you don't leave the country, you will be killed here in Iceland. And that will be a sad day for those who are your friends.'

Gunnar said that he had no intention of breaking his pledges. He rode home and told the news of the settlement. Rannveig said that it was best to go abroad and leave his enemies to find someone else to quarrel with.

75

THRAIN SIGFUSSON told his wife that he intended to go abroad that summer. She agreed to this, and he arranged a passage with Hogni the White. Gunnar and Kolskegg arranged a passage with Arnfinn of Oslo.

Two of Njal's sons, Grim and Helgi, asked their father for leave to go abroad.

'There will be trouble for you on this journey,' said Njal, 'times when your lives will be in doubt. But it will bring you a certain amount of honour and renown – and probably trouble as well once you get back home.'

They kept on asking for permission, and finally Njal told them to go if they wanted to. They arranged a passage with Bard the Black and Olaf, the son of Ketil of Elda.

And now people were saying that the district was being emptied of all its best men.

Gunnar's sons, Hogni and Grani, were fully grown by this time. They were men of very different natures; Grani took after his mother, but Hogni was a fine person.

Gunnar sent his own and Kolskegg's goods down to the ship. When everything was on board, and the ship almost ready to sail, Gunnar rode to Bergthorsknoll and other places to thank all those people who had given him support.

Early next morning he made ready to ride to the ship, and told all his people that he was going abroad for ever. Everyone was dismayed at the news, but hoped that some day he would return. When he was ready to leave, he embraced them all one by one. The whole household came out to see him off. With a thrust of his halberd he vaulted into the saddle, and rode away with Kolskegg.

They rode down towards Markar River. Just then Gunnar's horse stumbled, and he had to leap from the saddle. He happened to glance up towards his home and the slopes of Hlidarend.

'How lovely the slopes are,' he said, 'more lovely than they have ever seemed to me before, golden cornfields and new-mown hay. I am going back home, and I will not go away.'

Kolskegg said, 'Do not make your enemies happy by breaking the settlement, something that no one would ever expect of you. For you can be quite sure that all of Njal's predictions will come true.'

'I am not going away,' said Gunnar. 'And I wish you would stay too.'

'Never,' said Kolskegg. 'I am not going to dishonour my pledge over this nor any other matter I am trusted in. This is the one and only thing that can separate us. Tell my kinsmen and my mother that I never mean to see Iceland again; for I shall hear of your death, brother, and there will then be nothing to draw me home.'

With that they separated. Gunnar rode home to Hlidarend, but Kolskegg carried on to the ship and sailed abroad.

Hallgerd was delighted at Gunnar's return, but his mother had little to say. Gunnar stayed at home that autumn and winter, and did not have many men with him.

Now winter withdrew. Olaf the Peacock sent a messenger to invite Gunnar and Hallgerd to come and live with him in the west, and leave Rannveig and Hogni to look after Hlidarend. Gunnar found it tempting at first, and accepted the invitation. But when the time came, he did not care to go.

At the Althing that summer, Gizur the White proclaimed Gunnar a full outlaw at the Law Rock. Before the end of the Althing, Gizur summoned all Gunnar's enemies to a meeting in Almanna Gorge : Starkad of Thrihyrning and his son Thorgeir, Mord and his father Valgard the Grey, Geir the Priest and Hjalti Skeggjason, Thorbrand and Asbrand Thorleiksson, Eilif and his son Onund, Onund of Trollwood, and Thorgrim the Easterner from Sandgill.

Gizur said, 'I propose that we attack Gunnar this summer and kill him.'

Hjalti Skeggjason said, 'I promised Gunnar here at the Althing, when he complied with an appeal I made, that I would never take part in any attack on him. I mean to keep that promise.'

Hjalti walked away. Those who were left made their plans to attack Gunnar. They shook hands, and agreed on penalties for anyone who backed out. Mord was to spy out the best opportunity for an attack. There were forty men in this confederacy. They all felt that it would be easy to catch Gunnar, now that Kolskegg and Thrain and many other friends of his were away.

People now rode home from the Althing. Njal went to see Gunnar, and told him that he had been proclaimed an outlaw and that an attack on him had been planned.

'It is good of you to give me warning,' said Gunnar.

'And now,' said Njal, 'I want Skarp-Hedin and my son Hoskuld to come and stay with you. They will pledge their lives with yours.'

'No,' said Gunnar, 'I do not want your sons killed on my account. You deserve better of me than that.'

'It makes no difference,' said Njal. 'Once you are dead, my sons will become involved in these troubles.'

'That is not unlikely,' said Gunnar. 'But I would not want to be the cause of it. I have only one request – that you look after my son Hogni. I do not say anything about Grani, for he does many things that are not to my liking.'

Njal gave his promise and rode home.

It is said that Gunnar rode to all gatherings and assemblies, and his enemies never dared to attack him. And so, for a time, Gunnar went about as if he had never been outlawed.

76

In the autumn, Mord Valgardsson sent word that Gunnar was alone at home, for all his men had gone down to the Land-Isles to finish the hay-making. Gizur the White and Geir the Priest rode east over the rivers when they heard this, and across the sands to Hof. Word was sent to Starkad at Thrihyrning. All those who had pledged themselves to make an attack on Gunnar met there and discussed how best to do it. Mord said that they would never take Gunnar unawares unless they forced the neighbouring farmer, whose name was Thorkel, to go with them, and then made him go up to Hlidarend alone to catch the dog, Sam.

They set off east for Hlidarend, and sent some men to fetch Thorkel. They seized him and gave him the choice of being killed or coming to catch the dog. Thorkel preferred to save his own life, and went with them.

There was an enclosure above the farm at Hlidarend. Here the attackers halted. Thorkel walked down to the house; the dog was lying on the roof. Thorkel lured him away into a sunken lane. Suddenly the dog saw that there were other men there; he sprang at Thorkel and bit him in the groin. Onund of Trollwood drove his axe deep into the dog's head, right down to the brain. The animal uttered a loud howl, the like of which none had ever heard before, and fell down dead.

77

INSIDE the house, Gunnar woke up.

'You have been harshly treated, Sam, my fosterling,' he said. 'It may well be fated that my turn is coming soon.'

Gunnar's house was built entirely of timber, clinker-built on the outside. There were windows near the roof-beams, protected by shutters. Gunnar slept in a loft above the main room with Hallgerd and his mother.

When the attackers approached the house they were not sure whether Gunnar was at home, and wanted someone to go right up to the house to find out. They sat down on the ground, while Thorgrim the Easterner climbed on to the roof. Gunnar caught sight of a red tunic at the window. He lunged out with his halberd and struck Thorgrim in the belly. Thorgrim dropped his shield, lost his footing, and toppled down from the roof. He strode over to where Gizur and the others were sitting.

Gizur looked up at him and asked, 'Is Gunnar at home?'

'That's for you to find out,' replied Thorgrim. 'But I know that his halberd certainly is.'

And with that he fell dead.

The others made for the house, but Gunnar warded them off with a shower of arrows, and they could not make any progress. Some climbed on to the roofs of the other buildings to attack from there, but Gunnar found them with his arrows and fought them off. After a while, they withdrew for a rest, and then attacked again; but again they could do nothing in the face of Gunnar's arrows, and they fell back once more.

Gizur the White said, 'Attack with more spirit, we are making no headway.'

They made a third assault and kept it up for a long time; but once again they drew back.

Gunnar said, 'There is an arrow lying on the roof there, one of theirs. I am going to shoot it back at them. It will be humiliating for them to be injured by their own weapons.'

His mother said, 'Don't stir them up again when they have just withdrawn.'

But Gunnar reached out for the arrow and shot it at them. It struck Eilif Onundarson and wounded him severely. He was standing by himself to one side, and the others did not realize that he had been hit.

Gizur said, 'An arm appeared over there, wearing a gold bracelet, and picked up an arrow lying on the roof. No one would look for supplies outside if there were enough inside. Let us attack again.'

Mord said, 'Let us burn him to death inside the house.'

'Never,' said Gizur, 'even though I knew that my own life depended on it. Someone as cunning as you are said to be can surely think up a satisfactory plan.'

There were some ropes lying on the ground, which were used for anchoring the house.

Mord said, 'We shall take these ropes, loop them round the ends of the roof-beams, and fasten them to boulders. Then we can winch the roof off with winding-poles.'

They fetched the ropes and put this plan into effect, and before Gunnar was aware of it they had wrenched the whole roof off the house. But still he kept them at bay with his arrows.

Then Mord again suggested that they should burn Gunnar inside his house.

Gizur replied, 'I don't know why you keep harping on something that no one else wants. That shall never be done.'

At this point, Thorbrand Thorleiksson leapt up on to the wall and slashed through Gunnar's bow-string. Gunnar seized his halberd two-handed, whirled round on Thorbrand, drove the halberd through him, and hurled him off the wall. Thorbrand's brother, Asbrand, leapt up; Gunnar lunged again with the halberd, and Asbrand thrust his shield in the way. The halberd went right through the shield and between the upper arm and forearm. Gunnar then twisted the halberd so violently that the shield split and both Asbrand's arm-bones were shattered; and he, too, toppled from the wall.

By that time, Gunnar had wounded eight men and killed two. Now he received two wounds himself, but everyone is agreed that he flinched neither at wounds nor death itself.

He said to Hallgerd, 'Let me have two locks of your hair, and help my mother plait them into a bow-string for me.' *

'Does anything depend on it?' asked Hallgerd.

'My life depends on it,' replied Gunnar, 'for they will never overcome me as long as I can use my bow.'

'In that case,' said Hallgerd, 'I shall now remind you of the slap you once gave me. I do not care in the least whether you hold out a long time or not.'

'To each his own way of earning fame,' said Gunnar. 'You shall not be asked again.'

Rannveig said, 'You are an evil woman, and your shame will long be remembered'

Gunnar defended himself with great courage, and wounded eight more so severely that many of them barely lived. He kept on fighting until exhaustion brought him down. His enemies then dealt him many terrible wounds, but even then he got away from them and held them at bay for a long time.

But in the end they killed him.

This is what Thorkel Elfara-Poet said about his defence:

> *'We have heard from the south*
> *How Gunnar, warrior of many seas,*
> *Passionate in battle,*
> *Wielded his mighty halberd.*
> *Waves of foemen broke*
> *On the cliffs of his defence;*
> *He wounded sixteen men*
> *And killed two others.'*

Gizur the White said, 'We have felled a great champion, and we have not found it easy. His last defence will be remembered for as long as this land is lived in.'

He went over to Rannveig and said, 'Will you give us room on your land to bury our two dead?'

---

* The use of women's hair as emergency bowstrings or catapult strings by besieged men is a common motif in Latin literature. On the lid of the medieval Franks Casket (a ninth-century (?) Anglo-Saxon whalebone casket) in the British Museum is a picture showing a lone defender at a window warding off a band of attackers with arrows; there is a woman in the background. *Translators' note.*

'Willingly,' she replied, 'but I would have been even more willing to give enough room for all of you.'

'You cannot be blamed for saying that,' said Gizur, 'for you have suffered a great loss.'

He gave orders that there was to be no looting or pillaging. Then they went away.

Thorgeir Starkadarson said, 'We won't be safe in our homes with the Sigfussons around unless you, Gizur, or you, Geir, stay here in the south for a while.'

'That's true,' said Gizur. They drew lots, and it fell to Geir to remain in the district. He went to Oddi and settled there.

Geir had an illegitimate son called Hroald,* who boasted that he had given Gunnar his death-blow; he went to Oddi with his father. Thorgeir Starkadarson also boasted of a wound which he claimed to have given Gunnar.

Gizur went back to Mosfell and stayed there.

The killing of Gunnar was condemned throughout the land, and many people mourned him deeply.

78

NJAL was grieved at Gunnar's death. So were the Sigfussons. They asked Njal whether he thought they should start proceedings against Gunnar's killers. Njal said they could not do that for a man who had been outlawed, and suggested that it would be better to dishonour them by killing a few of them off in revenge.

They raised a burial mound for Gunnar and sat him upright in it. Rannveig refused to allow his halberd to be buried with him; she said that only the man who was prepared to avenge Gunnar could touch it. So no one took it. Rannveig treated Hallgerd so roughly that she came near to killing her; she accused her of being responsible for Gunnar's death. Hallgerd fled to Grjotriver, taking her son, Grani, with her. A division of the property was then made; Hogni was to have the farm at

* Hroald was the son of Bjartey, the sister of Thorvald the Ailing, who was killed at Hest Brook in Grimsness [cf. Chapter 102].

Hlidarend and the stock, and Grani was to own the farms leased out to tenants.

One day the shepherd and a housemaid at Hlidarend were driving cattle past Gunnar's burial mound; it seemed to them that Gunnar was in good humour and chanting verses inside the mound. They went home and told Rannveig about this happening, and she told them to report it to Njal. They went over to Bergthorsknoll and told Njal, who asked to be told it three times. After that he talked to Skarp-Hedin in private for a long time. Then Skarp-Hedin took his axe and rode to Hlidarend with the servants.

Rannveig and Hogni were very glad to see him, and gave him a warm welcome. Rannveig asked him to make his visit a long one, and he promised to do so.

Skarp-Hedin and Hogni kept going outside. Hogni was a brave and capable man who took nothing on trust; and for that reason they had not dared to tell him of the portent.

One night, Skarp-Hedin and Hogni were standing outside, to the south of Gunnar's burial mound. The moonlight was bright but fitful. Suddenly it seemed to them that the mound was open; Gunnar had turned round to face the moon. There seemed to be four lights burning inside the mound, illuminating the whole chamber. They could see that Gunnar was happy; his face was exultant. He chanted a verse so loudly that they could have heard it clearly from much farther away:

> 'Hogni's generous father
> Rich in daring exploits,
> Who so lavishly gave battle
> Distributing wounds gladly,
> Claims that in his helmet,
> Towering like an oak-tree
> In the forest of battle,
> He would rather die than yield,
> Much rather die than yield.'

Then the mound closed again.

'Would you have believed this if others had told you of it?' asked Skarp-Hedin.

'I would have believed it if Njal had told me,' replied Hogni, 'for Njal has never been known to lie.'

'There is great significance in such a portent,' said Skarp-Hedin, 'when Gunnar himself appears before our eyes and says that he would rather die than yield to his enemies; and that was his message for us.'

'I could not achieve anything without your help,' said Hogni.

'I have not forgotten how Gunnar behaved over the death of your kinsman Sigmund,' said Skarp-Hedin, 'and I shall give you all the help I can. My father promised Gunnar that you and Rannveig would get all the help you needed.'

Then they walked back to Hlidarend.

79

SKARP-HEDIN said, 'We must set out tonight, at once; for if our enemies learn that I am here, they will be doubly on their guard.'

'I shall do anything you say,' replied Hogni.

When everyone else had gone to bed they fetched their weapons. Hogni took down Gunnar's halberd, and it rang loudly. Rannveig sprang up in a towering rage.

'Who is taking the halberd?' she demanded. 'I forbade anyone to touch it.'

Hogni replied, 'I am taking it to my father, so that he can have it in Valhalla and carry it to combat there.'

'But first you are going to carry it yourself,' said Rannveig, 'to avenge your father, for it has just predicted death for someone – or for several.'

Hogni went out and told Skarp-Hedin of this exchange with his grandmother. Then they set out for the farm at Oddi. Two ravens flew with them all the way.

They reached Oddi in the dead of night, and drove all the sheep right up to the house. Hroald and Tjorvi came hurrying out of the house and drove the animals back up the lanes. Both men were armed.

Skarp-Hedin started up in their path. 'You don't need to look more closely,' he said, 'it's just as you think.'

With that he killed Tjorvi with one blow. Hroald had a spear in his hand; Hogni attacked him, and Hroald lunged. Hogni sliced the spear-shaft in two with the halberd, and then ran him through with it.

They left them lying there dead, and made their way up to Thrihyrning. Skarp-Hedin climbed on to the roof of the farmhouse, and began to pluck at the grass. The people inside thought it must be the sheep. Starkad and Thorgeir took their clothing and weapons and ran out into the yard. Then Starkad saw Skarp-Hedin, and, in terror, tried to turn back. But Skarp-Hedin cut him down beside the wall. Then Hogni came face to face with Thorgeir, and killed him with the halberd.

From there they rode to Hof, where Mord was already out of doors. He begged for mercy, and offered full compensation. Skarp-Hedin told Mord of the four men they had already killed, and threatened to send him on the same journey unless he offered Hogni self-judgement – if Hogni would accept it.

Hogni said that he had not intended to come to any terms with his father's killers, but finally he accepted the offer of self-judgement.

80

NJAL negotiated with those whose duty it was to take action over the killing of Starkad and Thorgeir, and persuaded them to accept a settlement. A district Assembly was called, and arbitrators were appointed. All the factors were taken into consideration, including the attack on Gunnar, even though he had been an outlaw at the time. The compensation that was finally awarded in this dispute was paid in full by Mord – because judgement in his case was delayed until the former case had been decided; the two awards were then made to tally. This was their final settlement.

At the Althing there was much discussion about the dispute between Hogni and Geir the Priest; in the end, a settlement was made, which proved lasting. Geir the Priest lived at Hlid for the rest of his life, and he is now out of this saga.

Njal arranged a marriage for Hogni with Alfeid, the daughter of Vetrlidi the Poet. Hogni and Alfeid had a son, Ari, who sailed to Shetland and married there; one of his descendants was Einar the Shetlander, a very brave man.

Hogni always kept his close friendship with Njal, and he is now out of this saga.

81

Now the saga returns to Kolskegg. He reached Norway and stayed the winter in Oslo Fjord. The following summer he went south to Denmark, where he committed his allegiance to King Svein Fork-Beard, and was held in high esteem.

One night he dreamt that a man came to him, radiant with light, and roused him.

'Arise and follow me,' he said.

'What do you want of me?' asked Kolskegg.

'I shall find you a bride, and you shall be my knight.'

Kolskegg agreed – and with that he awoke. He went to see a sage and told him the dream. This wise man interpreted it to mean that Kolskegg was to journey to southern lands and become God's knight.

Kolskegg was baptized in Denmark. But he never found happiness there, and moved on east to Russia, where he stayed for one winter. From there he travelled to Constantinople, where he joined the Emperor's army. The last that was heard of him was that he had married there and become a leader in the Varangian Guard. He stayed there for the rest of his life; and he is now out of this saga.

82

Now the saga returns to the time when Thrain Sigfusson went to Norway. He reached Halogaland in the north, and then continued south towards Trondheim and on to Lade. When Earl Hakon heard of the arrival, he sent messengers over to find out who the newcomers were; they came back and told the earl who they were. The earl then sent for Thrain.

Thrain came to the court, and the earl asked him about his kin. Thrain replied that he was a close kinsman of Gunnar of Hlidarend.

'That will stand you in good stead,' said the earl, 'for I have met many Icelanders, and not one of them has been his equal.'

'Will you permit me to stay at your court this winter, my lord?' asked Thrain.

The earl accepted him, and Thrain stayed the winter there in high favour.

A Viking named Kol, the son of Asmund Ash-Side of Smaland, lay in the Gotaelv, in Sweden, with five ships and a strong force of men. From there he made a raid on Norway; he landed at Fold and surprised Hallvard Soti in his sleeping-loft. Hallvard defended himself well, until they set fire to the house; then he surrendered, and they put him to death. They seized a lot of booty, and then sailed back to Lodose. When Earl Hakon heard of this, he declared Kol an outlaw throughout his kingdom and put a price on his head.

Some time later the earl said, 'Gunnar of Hlidarend is too far away now; he would have killed this outlaw for me if he had been here. But now Gunnar himself will be killed by the Icelanders; it is a pity he never came back to me.'

'I may not be Gunnar,' said Thrain, 'but I am Gunnar's kinsman, and I am willing to take on this task myself.'

'Excellent,' said the earl. 'I shall equip you well for the expedition.'

His son Eirik intervened. 'You make many fine promises, father,' he said, 'but you tend to be less consistent in fulfilling them. The mission is a difficult one; this Viking is a ruthless and formidable opponent. You will have to be very particular in your choice of men and ships.'

'I am still determined to go, even though the prospects are not good,' said Thrain.

The earl gave him five ships, all well manned. Thrain was accompanied by Gunnar Lambason and Lambi Sigurdarson; Gunnar Lambason was Thrain's nephew and had lived with him from an early age, and they were very fond of each other.

Eirik Hakonarson helped them, inspecting the crews and their weapons and making any changes he thought fit. When they were ready to sail, he provided them with a pilot.

They sailed south along the coast, and wherever they landed they had the earl's permission to obtain whatever they needed. They set course east for Lodose. There they heard that Kol had gone south to Denmark, and so they followed him. When they came south to Helsingborg, they met some men in a boat, who told them that Kol was in the neighbourhood and was planning to stay there for a while.

It was a clear day and Kol saw their ships approaching. He said that he had dreamt about Earl Hakon the previous night, and that these must be the earl's men. He ordered his forces to arm themselves, and they made ready. There was long and indecisive fighting. Then Kol leapt on to Thrain's ship and scattered the crew, killing many of them. He was wearing a gilded helmet. Thrain realized that the moment was crucial; rallying his men, he himself led the attack on Kol. Kol swung at Thrain and split his shield in two; but then he was struck on the hand by a stone, and dropped his sword. Thrain struck at him, and cut off his leg. After that they killed him. Thrain cut off his head and kept it, but threw the body overboard.

They seized a lot of booty, and then headed north to Trondheim, where they went to see the earl. The earl welcomed Thrain warmly. Thrain showed him Kol's head, and the earl thanked him for what he had done. Eirik said that it was worth more than mere words; the earl agreed. He took them down to the yards, where some good ships were being built for him. One of them, though not designed like a longship, had a prow carved in the shape of a vulture's head and richly decorated.

The earl said, 'You have a taste for the ornate, Thrain, just like your kinsman Gunnar of Hlidarend. I want to give you this ship as a gift. It is called the *Vulture*. With it goes my friendship, and I want you to stay with me as long as you wish.'

Thrain thanked the earl for his kindness, and said that he had no desire to return to Iceland for the time being. The earl had a journey to make to his eastern boundaries to meet the king of Sweden. Thrain accompanied him that summer, commanding the *Vulture*, and sailed his ship with such verve that few could keep up with him; he was bitterly envied. But it was always obvious how highly the earl regarded Gunnar of Hlidarend, for he heavily rebuffed all those who tried to molest Thrain.

Thrain stayed with the earl throughout the winter. In the spring, the earl asked him whether he wanted to stay on, or go back to Iceland. Thrain replied that he had not yet made up his mind, and that he was waiting for news from Iceland first. The earl told him to do whatever he preferred, and Thrain remained with him.

Then word came from Iceland that Gunnar of Hlidarend was dead; many thought this news indeed. The earl now did not want Thrain to go back to Iceland, and so Thrain remained at court.

83

MEANWHILE, Grim and Helgi, Njal's sons, had left Iceland the same summer that Thrain had gone abroad. They took passage on a trading ship with Bard the Black and Olaf, the son of Ketil of Elda. They ran into violent northerly gales that drove them off their course, and then met fog so dense that they could not tell their position. After they had been out at sea a long time, they found themselves in shallow waters, and were sure that they must be near land.

The Njalssons asked Bard whether he had any idea what country they were approaching.

'It could be one of many,' replied Bard, 'considering the winds we have had. It might be Orkney, or Scotland, or Ireland.'

Two days later they saw land on both sides of them, with underwater reefs in the sound. They anchored outside the broken water. That night the storm abated, and by morning there was a calm. Then they saw thirteen ships coming out towards them.

'What shall we do now?' asked Bard. 'These men look as if they are going to attack us.'

They started arguing whether to defend themselves or surrender, but before they had reached any decision, the Vikings were upon them. Each side asked the other what the leaders were called. The leaders of the merchants, Bard and Olaf, gave their names, and then asked who the Viking captains were. They announced themselves as Grjotgard and Snækolf, sons of

Moldan of Duncansby in Scotland and kinsmen of King Malcolm of Scotland.

'We offer you a choice,' said Grjotgard. 'Either you go ashore and hand over your goods to us, or else we will attack you and kill everyone we lay hands on.'

Helgi replied, 'The merchants choose to defend themselves.'

'Damn your tongue,' said the merchants to Helgi. 'What kind of defence can we put up? Life is worth more than money.'

Then Grim started shouting at the Vikings, to prevent them hearing the angry protests of the merchants. And Bard and Olaf said, 'Don't you realize that the Icelanders will ridicule you for your behaviour? Take your weapons and defend yourselves instead.'

So they all took their weapons and pledged themselves not to surrender while they still had strength to fight.

84

THE Vikings hurled spears at them, and the battle started. The merchants defended themselves bravely. Snækolf sprang at Olaf and ran him through with his spear, but Grim thrust at Snækolf so fiercely with a spear that the Viking was knocked overboard. Helgi now joined Grim; together they swept the Vikings back, and were always at hand where the need was greatest. The Vikings again called on the merchants to surrender, but the reply came that they would never yield.

At that moment they looked out to sea, and saw ships come sweeping round the headland from the south, no fewer than ten in all, rowing hard and making straight for them. War-shields lined the gunwales, and at the mast of the leading ship stood a man with a magnificent head of hair, who wore a silk tunic and a gilded helmet and carried a spear inlaid with gold.

This man asked, 'Who are the players in this uneven game?'

Helgi gave his own name, and said that their opponents were Grjotgard and Snækolf.

'Who are your captains?' asked the newcomer.

Helgi replied, 'Bard the Black is one – he's still alive; but the other one, Olaf, has just been killed. And I have a brother with me, called Grim.'

'Are you Icelanders?'

'Yes, we are,' replied Helgi.

The stranger asked who their father was. When they told him, he knew at once who they were and said, 'You bear a famous name.'

'Who are you?' asked Helgi.

'I am Kari Solmundarson,' he replied.

'Where have you come from?'

'From the Hebrides,' said Kari.

'Your arrival is welcome,' said Helgi, 'if you will give us some help.'

'As much as you need,' said Kari. 'What do you want me to do?'

'Attack the Vikings,' said Helgi.

Kari agreed.

They laid alongside the Vikings and the battle started all over again. When they had fought for some time, Kari leapt on to Snækolf's ship. Snækolf turned to meet him and struck at him, but Kari jumped backwards over the boom which was lying across the ship, and Snækolf's sword embedded itself in the boom. Kari then swung at him; his sword crashed down on Snækolf's shoulder with such force that it sliced off the arm. Snækolf died instantly. Grjotgard hurled a spear at Kari, but Kari saw it coming and sprang high into the air, so that the spear missed him. Just then Helgi and Grim joined Kari; Helgi rushed at Grjotgard and ran him through with his sword, killing him. Then they went from ship to ship; the Vikings begged for mercy, which was granted them, but all their booty was taken. After that they brought all the ships into the lee of the islands.

85

THE ruler of Orkney at that time was Earl Sigurd Hlodvisson.* Kari was one of his retainers, and had been collecting tribute for him from Earl Gilli in the Hebrides.

Kari invited the Njalssons to come to Mainland, in Orkney, and said that Earl Sigurd would give them a good welcome. They accepted, and went with him to Mainland. Kari took them to the earl, and told him who they were.

'How did they meet you?' asked the earl.

'I found them in the Minch,' said Kari, 'fighting the sons of Moldan and putting up a fine defence. They seemed to be everywhere in the ship, and were always at hand where the need was greatest. I ask leave for them to be admitted to your court.'

'Just as you please,' said the earl. 'You have accepted so much responsibility for them already.'

They spent the winter with the earl in high esteem. But as time passed, Helgi became silent. The earl could not fathom the reason, and asked Helgi why he was so silent, and if he were dissatisfied with life at court.

'I like it here,' said Helgi.

'Then what is on your mind?' asked the earl.

'Have you lands in Scotland to defend?' asked Helgi.

'I am under that impression,' said the earl. 'What of it?'

'In that case,' replied Helgi, 'the Scots have killed your Steward and stopped any messages from crossing the Pentland Firth.'

'Do you have second sight?' asked the earl.

'It has never yet been tested,' replied Helgi.

'I shall enhance your honour, if you are right,' said the earl. 'But if you are not, I will make you pay for this.'

'Helgi is not that kind of man,' said Kari. 'What he says must be true, for his father is prescient.'

* Earl Sigurd was the son of Hlodvir, the son of Thorfinn the Skull-Splitter, the son of Torf-Einar, the son of Earl Rognvald of More, the son of Eystein the Noisy.

The earl then sent messengers south to Stroma, to Arnljot, his Steward there, and Arnljot sent spies south over the Pentland Firth. They discovered that Havard of Freswick, Earl Sigurd's brother-in-law, had been killed by Earl Hundi and Earl Melsnati. Arnljot sent word to Sigurd asking him to come south with a large army to drive these earls out of the realm. As soon as Sigurd heard this, he gathered a large force from all the islands.

86

EARL SIGURD set off south with his army. With him went Kari and the Njalssons. They landed in Caithness. The earl's territories in Scotland also included Ross, Moray, Sutherland, and Argyll. Scotsmen from these districts joined them and reported that the earls were nearby with a large army. Earl Sigurd led his forces towards them, and at Duncansby Head the two armies clashed. It was a fierce battle. The Scots had detached a part of their forces to attack Earl Sigurd's unguarded flank, and many of Sigurd's men fell there, until the Njalssons led a counter-attack and routed the enemy. The battle was now at its height, and Helgi and Grim returned to Earl Sigurd's standard and fought well. Then Kari came face to face with Earl Melsnati; Melsnati hurled a spear at him, but Kari caught it in flight and sent it back, right through him.

At that, Earl Hundi fled. Earl Sigurd pursued, until news came that King Malcolm was gathering an army at Duncansby. The earl conferred with his men, and they all thought it better to turn back, rather than meet such a large force. So they withdrew. When they reached Stroma, the earl distributed the spoils and then sailed north to Mainland. Kari and the Njalssons went with him. The earl held a great feast there; and at it he gave Kari a fine sword and a spear inlaid with gold, Helgi a gold bracelet and a cloak, and Grim a shield and a sword. Then he made Grim and Helgi his retainers, and thanked them for their brave support.

They stayed with the earl that winter and part of the next summer, and then joined Kari on a foray. They raided far and wide that summer, and carried all before them. They fought against Gudrod, the king of the Isle of Man, and defeated him, and then turned for home laden with booty. They stayed with Earl Sigurd over the winter, in high favour.

In the spring, the Njalssons asked leave to go to Norway. The earl said that they were free to go wherever they wished, and gave them a good ship and a sturdy crew. Kari told them that he himself would be sailing to Norway that summer with tribute for Earl Hakon, and they arranged to meet there. Then the Njalssons set sail for Norway, and made land at Trondheim.

87

A MAN called Kolbein Arnljotarson, from Trondheim, had sailed out to Iceland in the same summer that Kolskegg and the Njalssons had gone abroad. He spent the winter east in Breiddale, and the following summer he prepared to sail back from Gautavik. They were on the point of setting sail when a man rowed out and made fast to the ship; then he climbed on board to see Kolbein. Kolbein asked him his name.

'My name is Hrapp,' he replied.

'What do you want with me?' asked Kolbein.

'I want you to take me to Norway,' said Hrapp.

'Whose son are you?'

'I am the son of Orgumleidi, the son of Geirolf the Warrior,' replied Hrapp.

'What is your trouble?' asked Kolbein.

'I have killed a man,' said Hrapp.

'What man?' asked Kolbein. 'And who will be taking action over it?'

'I have killed Orlyg, the son of Olvir, the son of Hrodgeir the White,' replied Hrapp. 'And the men of Vopnafjord will be taking action over it.'

'I suspect,' said Kolbein, 'that whoever takes you abroad will have cause to regret it.'

'I am a friend to my friends,' said Hrapp, 'but I repay in kind those who injure me. Anyway, I am quite willing to pay for my passage. I have plenty of money for that.'

So Kolbein agreed to take him. A little later they set sail before a favourable wind. Out at sea, Hrapp ran short of provisions, so he helped himself from those who were nearest. They jumped up cursing, a fight started, and at once Hrapp had two of them down.

This was reported to Kolbein. Kolbein invited Hrapp to share his own food, and Hrapp accepted.

They made land in Norway and cast anchor off Agdenes. Then Kolbein asked, 'Where is the money you offered me for your passage?'

'Out in Iceland,' replied Hrapp.

'I won't be the last person you will try to cheat,' said Kolbein. 'But I shall let you have your passage free.'

Hrapp thanked him. 'And what do you think I should do now?' he asked.

'First of all,' said Kolbein, 'I advise you to get off this ship as fast as you can, for all the Easterners are going to give you a bad name. My second piece of advice is that you never betray your master.'

Hrapp went ashore with his weapons. He had a massive axe with an iron-bound shaft. He made his way over to Gudbrand of the Dales, who was one of Earl Hakon's closest friends; they owned jointly a temple which was never opened except when the earl was there – the largest temple in Norway apart from the one at Lade. Gudbrand had a son called Thrand and a daughter called Gudrun.

Hrapp went to see Gudbrand and greeted him well. Gudbrand asked him who he was. Hrapp gave his name, and said that he was from Iceland. Then he asked Gudbrand to take him into his household.

'You don't look like a man of good luck,' said Gudbrand.

'Then it looks as if I've been hearing lies about you,' said Hrapp, 'for I was told that you took in anyone who asked, and that you were the noblest man there was. I shall have to correct that story if you turn me away now.'

'Stay if you must,' said Gudbrand.

'Where am I to sit?' asked Hrapp.

'On the lower bench opposite my high-seat,' said Gudbrand.

Hrapp went to his seat. He had a fund of stories, and at first Gudbrand and many others found him entertaining to listen to.

But after a while they tired of his malicious humour. Later, Hrapp started making advances to Gudrun, and people said that he was seducing her. When Gudrun heard this he scolded her severely for responding to Hrapp's advances, and warned her to have nothing at all to do with him except in the presence of others. Gudrun promised faithfully, but it was not long before their secret intercourse was resumed. Then Gudbrand ordered his overseer, Asvard, to go with her wherever she went.

One day she asked leave to go to amuse herself in the nut-grove. Asvard accompanied her. Hrapp went to look for them and found them in the wood; he caught her by the hand and drew her away by herself. Asvard went in search of her and found them lying together in a thicket. He rushed up with his axe raised and swung at Hrapp's leg, but Hrapp quickly twisted away and dodged the blow. Then he jumped to his feet and snatched up his own axe; Asvard tried to get away, but Hrapp's axe bit clean through his backbone.

Gudrun said, 'That blow has killed your chance of staying with my father any longer. But he is going to be even more displeased when he hears that I am pregnant.'

'He's not going to hear it from others,' said Hrapp. 'I shall go and tell him all this myself.'

'Then you'll never escape with your life,' she said.

'I'll take that risk,' he replied.

He took her back to the other women, and then went to the house alone. Gudbrand was sitting on his high-seat, and there were only a few people in the room. Hrapp walked up to him with his axe raised over his shoulder.

'Why is there blood on your axe?' asked Gudbrand.

'I have been curing Asvard's backache with it,' he replied.

'Not out of any kindness,' said Gudbrand. 'I suppose you killed him?'

'Yes,' said Hrapp.

'Why?' asked Gudbrand.

'You will probably think it small cause,' said Hrapp. 'He wanted to cut off my leg.'

'What had you done before that?'

'Something that did not concern him at all,' said Hrapp.

'You can at least tell me what it was,' said Gudbrand.

'If you really want to know,' said Hrapp, 'I was lying with your daughter, and he disapproved of it.'

'To your feet, men,' said Gudbrand. 'Seize him and put him to death.'

'You're not letting me benefit much from being your son-in-law,' said Hrapp. 'But you haven't the men to have this done quickly.'

The others sprang to their feet, but Hrapp backed away and out of the door. They ran after him, but he got away into the forest and they lost him. Gudbrand collected men and had the wood combed, but they never found him, for the wood was large and dense. Hrapp made his way under cover of the forest until he reached a clearing; there was a house there, with a man outside it chopping wood.

Hrapp asked him his name. The man replied that he was called Tofi, and asked Hrapp for his name in return. Hrapp gave it, and then asked the farmer why he lived so far away from other people.

'Because,' said Tofi, 'I feel I'm not in anyone's way here.'

'Let's not beat about the bush,' said Hrapp. 'I'll tell you about myself first. I have been with Gudbrand of the Dales, and I've just run away from there because I killed his overseer. But I know that we are both scoundrels, because you would not be burying yourself away here unless you were on the run from somebody yourself. So I shall offer you a choice: either we go shares on everything here, or else I shall give you away.'

'What you say is quite true,' said the farmer. 'I abducted the woman who is here with me, and there have been many people looking for me ever since.'

After that he took Hrapp into the house; it was small but sturdily built. He told his wife that Hrapp would be staying with them.

'That man will bring ill luck wherever he goes,' she replied. 'But have it your own way.'

Hrapp moved in with them. But they saw little of him, for he was often away. He still managed to have meetings with Gudrun. Gudbrand and his son Thrand set ambushes for him, but they never got their hands on him. And so it went on for a year. Gudbrand sent word to Earl Hakon to tell him of the trouble Hrapp was giving him. The earl declared Hrapp an out-law and put a price on his head; he even said that he himself would come and track him down. But he did nothing about it, for he thought it simple enough for the others to catch Hrapp when the man took so few precautions.

88

THAT same summer, the Njalssons sailed from Orkney to Nor-way, and spent the summer trading there. At the same time, Thrain Sigfusson was preparing to sail back to Iceland and was almost ready to leave.

Meanwhile, Earl Hakon was attending a feast at Gudbrand's home. During the night, Hrapp the Killer went to their temple. Inside it, he saw the statue of Thorgerd Holgi's-Bride enthroned, massive as a fully-grown man; there was a huge gold bracelet on her arm, and a linen hood over her head. Hrapp stripped off the hood and the bracelet. Then he noticed Thor in his chariot, and took from him another gold bracelet. He took a third bracelet from Irpa. He dragged all three of the idols outside and stripped them of their vestments; then he set fire to the temple and burned it down.

Dawn was breaking when he went away. As he was crossing a cornfield, six fully-armed men jumped up and attacked him. Hrapp defended himself well, and in the end he had killed three, mortally wounded Thrand, Gudbrand's son, and chased the two survivors into the forest to prevent them from reaching the earl with the news.

He came back and said to Thrand, 'I could kill you now if I wanted to, but I'm not going to. I shall show more respect for our family ties than you and your father have.'

Hrapp made for the forest again; but he found that more men had arrived to cut him off from the woods, and he didn't dare to risk it. Instead, he went to ground in a thicket and lay there for a while.

Early that morning, Earl Hakon and Gudbrand went out to the temple and found it burned down, with the three idols lying outside stripped of all their riches.

Then Gudbrand said, 'Our gods are powerful indeed. They have walked unaided from the flames.'

'The gods had nothing to do with it,' said Earl Hakon. 'A man must have fired the temple and carried the gods out. But the gods are in no haste to take vengeance; the man who did this will be driven out of Valhalla for ever.'

At that moment four of the earl's men came running up with the bad news that they had found three of their men lying dead in the cornfield and Thrand mortally wounded.

'Who has done this?' asked the earl.

'Killer-Hrapp,' they replied.

'Then he must have been the one who burned down the temple,' said the earl.

They thought him quite capable of it.

'Where is he now?' asked the earl.

They replied that Thrand had told them that Hrapp had hidden himself in a thicket. The earl went there to look for him, but Hrapp was gone. The earl ordered a search to be made, but they could not find him. Then the earl himself joined the search. He told the others to take a rest for a moment; then he walked away by himself and forbade anyone to follow him. He was away for some time. He fell to his knees and covered his eyes with his hands. Then he returned to the others and said, 'Follow me.' They went with him. He turned sharply off the course they had been following, and led them to a dell. There they flushed Hrapp, who had hidden there earlier. The earl sent his men in pursuit, but Hrapp ran so fast that they got nowhere near him.

Hrapp made for Lade, where Thrain Sigfusson and the Njalssons had their ships ready to sail. Hrapp ran up to the Njalssons and said, 'Save me, good people, for the earl is after my life.'

Helgi looked at him and said, 'It strikes me that you are a bringer of ill luck. It would be wiser to have nothing to do with you.'

'Then I wish all my ill luck on to your heads,' said Hrapp.

Helgi said, 'I am quite capable of paying you back later.'

Hrapp then went over to Thrain Sigfusson and begged him for protection.

'What is the trouble?' asked Thrain.

'I have burned down one of the earl's temples,' said Hrapp,

'and killed a few of his men. He is leading the chase himself, and will be here at any moment now.'

'It would scarcely be proper for me to help you,' said Thrain, 'considering how well the earl has treated me.'

Hrapp then showed Thrain the treasures he had removed from the temple, and offered to give them to him. Thrain refused to accept them unless he was allowed to pay for them.

Then Hrapp said, 'I'm not going to move from this spot. They shall kill me here before your eyes, and all men will speak of you with contempt.'

At that moment they caught sight of the earl and his men, and Thrain made up his mind to take Hrapp into his care. He ordered the boat to be cast off, and took Hrapp out to the ship.

'The best way to hide you,' said Thrain, 'is to knock the bottom out of two barrels and put you inside them.'

Hrapp crawled into the barrels, which were then lashed together and lowered over the side.

Now the earl and his men arrived. He went over to the Njalssons and asked them if Hrapp had been there; they said that he had. The earl asked which way he had gone, but they said that they had paid no attention.

'The man who tells me where Hrapp is now,' said the earl, 'will stand high in my favour.'

Grim whispered to Helgi, 'Why should we not tell? I suspect that Thrain will not repay us with much kindness, anyway.'

'That is still no reason for telling,' said Helgi. 'Thrain's life is at stake.'

'But the earl is likely to turn his vengeance on us,' said Grim, 'for he is now so angry that someone will have to suffer.'

'That makes no difference,' said Helgi. 'But we shall move our ship out and be ready to sail with the first wind.'

They pulled out and anchored behind an island, and waited there for a breeze.

The earl went round all the ships and questioned the crews, but everyone denied any knowledge of Hrapp.

Finally the earl said, 'Now we shall go and see my comrade Thrain. Thrain will hand the man over if he knows of him.'

They took a longship and pulled out to the merchantman. Thrain saw the earl coming, stood up, and greeted him warmly. The earl returned the greeting, and then said, 'We are searching for a man called Hrapp, an Icelander. He has done us every conceivable injury. We want to ask you to hand him over or tell us where he is.'

'You will remember, my lord,' said Thrain, 'how I killed an outlaw for you; I risked my life to do it, and in return you honoured me greatly.'

'You shall have still greater honour this time,' said the earl.

Thrain racked his brains, for he could not be sure what the earl would appreciate most. In the end, however, he denied that Hrapp was there and invited the earl to search the ship. The earl made only a cursory search and went ashore again. He walked off by himself in such a rage that no one dared speak to him.

Then he said, 'Take me to the Njalssons. I am going to force the truth out of them.'

He was told that they had already left harbour.

'We cannot do that, then,' said the earl. 'But there were two water-casks slung alongside Thrain's ship, where a man could easily have been hidden. If Thrain was hiding Hrapp, that is where it must have been. We shall go out to see Thrain once again.'

Thrain saw that the earl was coming over again, and said, 'If the earl was angry before, he will be twice as angry now. The life of every single man on board is at stake this time.'

They promised to keep the secret, for everyone was now thoroughly frightened. They took some sacks out of the pile of cargo and put Hrapp there instead, covering him with other sacks that were of little weight. By the time the earl arrived, they had finished stowing Hrapp amongst the cargo.

Thrain greeted the earl warmly. The earl was curt in his reply, and they saw that he was very angry indeed.

The earl said to Thrain, 'Hand over Hrapp. I know for a fact that you are hiding him.'

'Where could I have hidden him, my lord?' asked Thrain.

'You are the man to answer that,' replied the earl, 'but at a guess I should say that you had him hidden in these water-casks the last time.'

'I do not want you to accuse me of lying, my lord,' said Thrain. 'I would much rather you searched the ship.'

The earl came on board and made a search, but found nothing.

'Do you acquit me of the charge now?' asked Thrain.

'Far from it,' said the earl, 'but I cannot understand why we do not find him. I seem to see through it all when I go ashore, but when I come back here I see nothing.'

He had himself ferried back to land. He was now so furious that no one could speak to him. His son, Svein, said, 'It's an odd way to behave, to make innocent men suffer for one's anger.'

Once again the earl walked off by himself. Almost at once he came back and said, 'We shall row out to them again.'

They started rowing. 'Where could he have been hidden?' asked Svein.

'It does not matter now,' said the earl, 'for they will have moved him by this time. But there were two sacks lying loose beside the cargo, and Hrapp must have taken their place in the pile.'

Thrain said to his crew, 'The earl and his men are launching their boat again. They must be going to pay us another visit. We shall take Hrapp out of the cargo and put something else in his place, but leave the two sacks lying loose where they were.'

They did this, and Thrain said, 'Now we shall put Hrapp in the sail furled to the top-yard.'

They had done this by the time the earl arrived. He was now in a terrible rage.

'Are you going to hand him over now, Thrain?' he demanded. 'Your position is getting more serious.'

'I would have handed him over a long time ago if he had been in my keeping,' said Thrain. 'Where could he have been?'

'In the cargo,' replied the earl.

'Then why did you not look for him there?' asked Thrain.

'It did not occur to me at the time,' said the earl.

They searched the whole ship, but still did not find him.

Then Thrain asked, 'Will you acquit me of the charge now, my lord?'

'Certainly not,' said the earl, 'because I know that you have hidden the man, even though I cannot find him. But I would rather that you broke faith with me than I with you.'

With that he went ashore again.

'Now I see it all,' he said. 'He had Hrapp hidden in the sail.'

Just then a breeze sprang up, and Thrain put out to sea. It was then that he uttered this couplet, which has been remembered ever since:

> 'Give the Vulture his wings,
> Nothing can make Thrain yield.'

When the earl heard what Thrain had said, he commented, 'My failure was not due to my lack of wisdom, but rather to this alliance of theirs, which will eventually drag them both to destruction.'

Thrain had a fast voyage, and when he reached Iceland he went home to his farm. Hrapp went with him and stayed there for a year. Next summer Thrain provided him with a farm at Hrappstead, and Hrapp went to live there; but he spent most of his time at Grjotriver, and caused nothing but trouble there. There were some who said that he and Hallgerd were very close, and that he slept with her; but others contradicted this.

Thrain gave the Vulture to his kinsman Mord the Careless; this was the Mord who killed Odd Halldorsson out east at Gautavik in Berufjord.

All Thrain's kinsmen now looked on him as a chieftain.

89

Now the saga returns to the point where Thrain slipped from Earl Hakon's grasp. The earl said to his son Svein, 'We shall take four longships and row after the Njalssons and put them to death. They must have been party to this with Thrain.'

'It is never a good idea to throw the blame on to innocent men and let the guilty escape,' said Svein.

'I give the orders here,' said the earl.

They set off in pursuit of the Njalssons, and after a search found them anchored behind an island.

It was Grim who first sighted the earl's ships.

'There are warships on the way,' he said. 'I see that it is the earl, and he is certainly not coming in peace.'

'It is said that the brave man always resists, whoever the opponents may be,' said Helgi, 'and so shall we.'

They all said that they would accept his decision, and took up their weapons.

The earl drew near and called out to them to surrender. Helgi replied that they would defend themselves to the last. The earl then offered amnesty to anyone who refused to fight for Helgi, but Helgi was so beloved that they all preferred to die with him. The earl and his men then attacked, but the defenders resisted bravely, and the Njalssons were always at hand where the fighting was fiercest. Again and again the earl repeated his offer of amnesty, but always the reply came back the same, that they would never surrender.

Aslak of Langey kept attacking and managed to board the ship three times. Then Grim said, 'You are attacking so bravely that you deserve to achieve your end.' He snatched up a spear and sent it flying at Aslak's throat. Aslak died instantly. A little later Helgi killed Egil, the earl's standard-bearer. At that point Svein, the earl's son, led an attack. He ordered his men to smother them with shields, and in that way they were captured alive.

The earl wanted to put them to death at once, but Svein urged against this, pointing out that it was after sunset.

'Kill them tomorrow, then,' said the earl. 'But tie them up securely for the night.'

'What must be, will be,' said Svein. 'But I have never met braver men than these, and it would be a great loss to put them to death.'

'They have killed two of our bravest men,' said the earl, 'and for that they must die.'

'They proved themselves that much the braver,' said Svein. 'But your wish will have to be obeyed.'

The Njalssons were bound and chained. After that the earl retired. When the earl had fallen asleep, Grim said to Helgi, 'I would like to escape if I could.'

'We must look for a way, then,' said Helgi.

Grim said that there was an axe lying nearby with its edge pointing upwards. He wriggled over to it and managed to sever the bowstring that tied him, but in doing so he gashed his arms deeply. Then he freed Helgi. After that they crawled overboard and reached the shore without raising the alarm. There they broke the chains off their ankles and walked over to the other side of the island.

Dawn was just breaking. They saw a ship there and found that Kari Solmundarson had arrived. They went straight to him and told him of their ordeal and showed him their wounds. They added that the earl and his men would still be asleep.

'It is disgraceful that you should have to suffer for the misdeeds of others,' said Kari. 'What do you want to do now?'

'Attack the earl and kill him,' they replied.

'That will not be granted us,' said Kari, 'but you certainly do not lack courage. Anyhow, we'll go and see whether he is still there.'

They went there, but the earl had already gone.

Then Kari sailed in to Lade to meet the earl, and delivered the tribute from the west.

The earl asked, 'Have you taken the Njalssons into your care?'

'Yes,' replied Kari.

'Will you hand them over to me?' asked the earl.

'No,' said Kari.

'Will you swear an oath that you never considered attacking me?' asked the earl.

Eirik, the earl's son, intervened. 'You have no right to ask that,' he said. 'Kari has always been our friend. This would never have arisen if I had been present at the time; the Njalssons would have been left unmolested, and the guilty ones would have got their due punishment. It seems much more proper to give the Njalssons handsome gifts for their humiliating ordeal and the wounds they have suffered.'

'You are right,' said the earl. 'But I don't know whether they would be willing to settle.'

He told Kari to find out whether the Njalssons would agree to a settlement. Kari went to Helgi and asked if he would accept damages from the earl.

'I would accept them from his son Eirik,' said Helgi. 'But I want nothing to do with the earl.'

Kari told Eirik their reply.

'Very well,' said Eirik. 'Helgi can receive redress at my hands if he so prefers. Tell them that I invite them to stay with me, and that my father will do them no harm.'

They accepted this offer, and went to stay with Eirik until Kari was ready to sail west. Then Eirik held a feast for Kari and gave him and the Njalssons gifts. After that, Kari and the Njalssons sailed to Orkney, where Earl Sigurd gave them a cordial welcome. They stayed with Earl Sigurd that winter. In the spring, Kari asked the Njalssons to come raiding with him, but Grim would only agree if Kari came to Iceland with them afterwards. Kari gave his promise, and so they went raiding with him.

They raided around Anglesey in the south and all round the Hebrides, then made for Kintyre and landed there. They fought the inhabitants and gathered rich booty before returning to their ships. From there they went south to Wales * and raided, and then to the Isle of Man, where they fought and defeated King Gudrod of Man, killing his son Dungal and taking good spoils. From there they headed north to Coll, where they met Earl Gilli; he made them welcome, and they stayed there for a while. The earl then sailed with them to Orkney to meet Earl Sigurd. In the spring, Earl Sigurd gave his sister Nereid to Earl Gilli in marriage. Earl Gilli then returned to the Hebrides.

90

THAT summer, Kari and the Njalssons prepared to sail to Iceland. When they were ready they went to the earl. He gave them handsome gifts, and they parted in warm friendship.

Then they set sail. They had favourable winds and the voyage did not take long. They landed at Eyrar, where they got horses and rode from the ship home to Bergthorsknoll. Everyone was delighted to see them. Then they fetched home their cargo and laid up the ship.

Kari stayed with Njal that winter. In the spring he asked for the hand of Helga, Njal's daughter. Grim and Helgi supported

* *Bretland.* This has always been assumed by scholars to be Wales, but there are strong indications that here and elsewhere in the Icelandic sagas it refers to the area in south-west Scotland then occupied by Britons, known as the Kingdom of Strathclyde. *Translators' note.*

the marriage-offer; so Helga was betrothed to Kari, and the wedding day was arranged. The feast was held a fortnight before midsummer. The couple lived with Njal that winter. Then Kari bought some land at Dyrholmar, out east in Myrdale, and raised a farm there. They put overseers in charge of it, and they themselves continued to live with Njal.

91

HRAPP had a farm at Hrappstead, but spent most of his time at Grjotriver, where he caused nothing but trouble. Thrain liked him.

On one occasion when Ketil of Mork was at Bergthorsknoll, the Njalssons told him about their ordeal in Norway, and said that they had heavy claims against Thrain Sigfusson if ever they cared to make them. Njal said that it would be best if Ketil himself had a word with his brother Thrain. Ketil promised to do so.

They gave him time to have his talk with Thrain. A little later they brought the matter up with Ketil again. Ketil replied that he did not care to repeat much of their conversation. 'It was obvious,' he said, 'that Thrain felt I put too much value on my relationship to you.'

They realized how difficult the situation was, and discussed it no further with Ketil; but they asked their father what they should do about it. They said they were not satisfied to leave the matter as it now stood.

'This is not easy,' replied Njal. 'If you were to kill them now, it would be considered an unprovoked killing. My advice is that you get as many people as possible to talk to them about this, so that it becomes widely known if their comments are abusive. Then Kari is to discuss it with Thrain, for Kari can control his temper. The hostility will keep growing, and they will heap abuse on you when others discuss it with them; for they are stupid men.

'People may even start saying that my sons are shy of action, and you will have to bear with that for a while; for there are always differences of opinion once the act is done. You should let it be understood that you intend to take action only if you are provoked. But if you had asked for my advice at the very beginning, you would never have raised the matter at all, and so you would never have compromised yourselves. But now you are already committed to a trying situation; humiliations will be heaped on you, until you have no alternative but to cut through your difficulties with weapons. That is why we must cast such a wide net.'

They discussed it no further. Soon everyone in the district was talking about this.

One day the brothers suggested that Kari should go over to Grjotriver. Kari said that he could think of more congenial journeys, but agreed to go since it was part of Njal's plans. He went to see Thrain and they discussed the matter, but they were unable to agree. When Kari returned the Njalssons asked him how he had got on with Thrain. Kari said that he would rather not repeat what had been said. 'It is more than likely you will hear it said again to your faces,' he added.

Thrain had fifteen able-bodied men in his household, and eight of them accompanied him wherever he rode. Thrain was extremely ostentatious; when he rode, he always wore a blue cloak and gilded helmet, and carried the spear that Earl Hakon had given him, a splendid shield, and a sword at his belt.

He was usually accompanied also by Gunnar Lambason and Lambi Sigurdarson and Grani Gunnarsson of Hlidarend; but his closest companion was Killer-Hrapp. One of his men was called Lodin; Lodin and his brother Tjorvi never left Thrain's side. It was Killer-Hrapp and Grani Gunnarsson who were the most vicious in their abuse of the Njalssons, and it was chiefly due to them that no offer of compensation was made.

The Njalssons repeatedly asked Kari to ride with them to Grjotriver. Eventually he agreed, and said that it was as well for them to hear Thrain's answer in person. The five of them – Kari and the four Njalssons – made ready for the journey, and rode to Grjotriver. The farm had a wide porch which could hold a number of men standing side by side. A woman who was outside saw them approaching and went to tell Thrain. Thrain ordered his men to group themselves on the porch and bring their weapons with them. They did so.

Thrain stood in the middle of the doorway. On either side of him stood Killer-Hrapp and Grani Gunnarsson, then Gunnar Lambason, then Lodin and Tjorvi, then Lambi Sigurdarson, and then the others ranged alongside, for all the men were at home.

The five walked up towards them. Skarp-Hedin was in the lead, followed by Kari, then Hoskuld, then Grim, and then Helgi. As they came up, there was not a single word of greeting from the group on the porch.

Skarp-Hedin said, 'We are all welcome.'

Hallgerd, who was also standing on the porch and had been whispering to Hrapp, replied, 'None of us here says you are welcome.'

'Your words don't count,' replied Skarp-Hedin, 'for you are either an outcast hag or a harlot.'

'You'll be paid back for those words before you go home,' she said.

Helgi said, 'It was you I came to see, Thrain, to find out if you are prepared to pay me any compensation for the ordeal I suffered in Norway on your account.'

'I would never have thought,' said Thrain, 'that you brothers would put a market-price on your manhood. How long are you going to keep up this begging?'

'Many people would say that you had an obligation to offer us redress,' said Helgi, 'considering that your life was at stake.'

Then Hrapp said, 'It shows the difference in our luck. The blow fell where it belonged; that's why you landed in trouble and we got out of it.'

'I would scarcely call it good luck,' said Helgi, 'to break faith with the earl and make friends with you instead.'

'Don't you think that you should address your claim to me?' asked Hrapp. 'I am quite ready to pay you in the kind I think proper.'

'The only dealings we shall have together,' replied Helgi, 'will not turn out a bargain for you.'

'Don't waste words on Hrapp,' said Skarp-Hedin. 'We'll exchange his grey hide for a red one.'

'Hold your tongue, Skarp-Hedin,' said Hrapp. 'I won't hesitate to apply my axe to your skull.'

'Time will tell,' said Skarp-Hedin, 'which of us will survive to build the other's cairn.'

'Go home, "Little Dung-beards",' said Hallgerd. 'That's what we're going to call you from now on; and we'll call your father "Old Beardless".'

But they did not leave until the others had all associated themselves with this insult – all except Thrain, who tried to restrain his companions. Then the Njalssons and Kari went away and rode home. They told their father what had happened.

'Did you name any witnesses to these insults?' asked Njal.

'No, none,' said Skarp-Hedin. 'We are going to plead this case only with weapons.'

Bergthora said, 'Everyone must be thinking that you are all scared to lift your weapons by now.'

'Spare yourself the trouble of goading your sons,' said Kari. 'They are eager enough already.'

After that Njal and his sons and Kari talked together in undertones for a long time.

92

THERE was a great deal of talk about this dispute, and everyone felt sure that the situation was now beyond repair.

Runolf of Dale, the son of Ulf Aur-Priest, was a friend of Thrain's. He had invited Thrain to his home, and it was arranged that he should go there in the third or fourth week of winter. Thrain asked Killer-Hrapp, Grani Gunnarsson, Gunnar Lambason, Lambi Sigurdarson, Lodin, and Tjorvi to travel with him; there were eight men in all, and Thorgerd and Hallgerd were also to go. Thrain let it be known that he also intended to visit his brother Ketil at Mork, and made it clear how many days he planned to be away from home.

They were all fully armed. They rode east over Markar River, where they met some beggarwomen who asked to be ferried over to the west bank. They did this for them, and then rode on to Dale, where they were warmly welcomed. Ketil of Mork was already there. They stayed there for two days. Both Runolf and Ketil asked Thrain to make a settlement with the Njalssons, but Thrain said that he would never pay them anything. He was curt in his replies, and said that he thought himself a match for the Njalssons anywhere.

'That may be,' said Runolf, 'but I am of the opinion that no one is a match for the Njalssons now that Gunnar of Hlidarend is dead. The chances are that this will bring death for you or for them.'

Thrain said he was not afraid of that. Then he went up to Mork and stayed there for two days. After that he rode back down to Dale, and in both places he was given handsome gifts when he left.

Markar River was at that time flowing between banks of ice, with occasional ice-strips bridging the channel. Thrain said that he was going to ride home that evening. Runolf tried to dissuade him, and said that it would be more prudent not to keep to the plan he had announced.

'No,' said Thrain, 'that would be a sign of fear.'

The beggarwomen who had been helped over Markar River came to Bergthorsknoll. Bergthora asked them where they had come from. From the east, from the Eyjafells district, they replied.

'Who helped you over Markar River?' asked Bergthora.

'The most conceited people alive,' they replied.

'Who would they be?' asked Bergthora.

'Thrain Sigfusson and his companions,' they replied. 'But we were annoyed at all the unpleasant things they were saying about your husband and your sons.'

'Few people are spoken of in the way they would choose,' said Bergthora.

The women went on their way, and Bergthora gave them good gifts. She also asked them how long Thrain intended to be away. They replied that he would be away for four or five days. Bergthora reported this to her sons and Kari, and they talked together secretly for a long time.

Early in the morning of the day that Thrain and his party were riding home, Njal woke up at the sound of Skarp-Hedin's axe bumping against the panel. Njal rose and went out, and saw that his sons and Kari were all fully armed. Skarp-Hedin was in the lead, dressed in a blue jacket and carrying a round shield, with his axe hoisted on his shoulder. Next to him was Kari, wearing a silk jacket and a gilded helmet; there was a lion painted on his shield. Behind him walked Helgi, wearing a red tunic and a helmet, and carrying a red shield decorated with a hart. They all wore coloured clothing.

Njal called out to Skarp-Hedin, 'Where are you going, kinsman?'

'To look for sheep,' he replied.

'You said that once before,' said Njal, 'but then you hunted men.'

Skarp-Hedin laughed and said, 'Do you hear that? He's not so innocent, the old man.'

Kari asked, 'When was the other time you said that?'

'When I killed Sigmund the White, Gunnar's kinsman,' replied Skarp-Hedin.

'What for?' asked Kari.

'He had killed Thord Freedmansson, my foster-father,' said Skarp-Hedin.

Njal went back inside, and the others made their way to the slopes of Raudaskrid and waited. From there they could keep watch on Thrain's journey west from Dale.

It was a clear, sunny day; and now Thrain came riding down from Dale towards the river.

Lambi Sigurdarson said, 'There are shields flashing in the sun up on Raudaskrid. It must be an ambush.'

'In that case,' said Thrain, 'we shall swing down and follow the river. If they have any business with us, they will then have to come out to meet us.'

They turned, and followed the river down.

Skarp-Hedin said, 'They have seen us now; they are turning off their course. There is nothing else for it but to run down and intercept them.'

'Most people prefer to ambush with more favourable odds,' said Kari. 'We are five against eight.'

They headed for the river. Downstream they could see an ice-floe spanning the river channel, and they decided to cross there. Thrain and his men took up position on the sheet-ice opposite this bridge.

'What can these men want?' said Thrain. 'There are only five of them against the eight of us.'

'I believe they would risk an attack against even greater odds,' said Lambi Sigurdarson.

Thrain took off his cloak and his helmet.

It so happened that Skarp-Hedin's shoe-thong broke as they ran down along the river, and he stopped.

'What keeps you back, Skarp-Hedin?' asked Grim.

'I am tying up my shoe,' he replied.

'We'll go on ahead,' said Kari. 'I do not think he will be any slower than we.'

They turned down towards the ice-bridge, running as fast as they could. Skarp-Hedin jumped up as soon as he had tied his shoe, and hoisted his axe. He raced down straight towards the river, which was much too deep to be forded anywhere along that stretch. A huge sheet of ice had formed a low hump on the other side of the channel. It was as smooth as glass, and Thrain and his men had stopped on the middle of this hump. Skarp-Hedin made a leap and cleared the channel between the ice-banks, steadied himself, and at once went into a slide: the ice was glassy-smooth, and he skimmed along as fast as a bird.

Thrain was then about to put on his helmet. Skarp-Hedin came swooping down on him and swung at him with his axe. The axe crashed down on his head and split it down to the jaw-bone, spilling the back-teeth on to the ice. It all happened so quickly that no one had time to land a blow on Skarp-Hedin as he skimmed past at great speed. Tjorvi threw a shield into his path, but Skarp-Hedin cleared it with a jump without losing his balance and slid to the other end of the sheet-ice.

Kari and the others came running up.

'That was man's work,' said Kari.

'Now it's your turn,' said Skarp-Hedin.

They made for Thrain's men. Grim and Helgi singled out Hrapp and attacked him at once. Hrapp swung his axe at Grim, but Helgi, seeing this, hacked off Hrapp's arm. The axe fell to the ground.

Hrapp said, 'What you have done certainly needed doing; that hand has brought harm and death to many.'

'This will put an end to all that,' said Grim, and ran him through with a spear. Hrapp fell dead.

Tjorvi turned to face Kari and let fly a spear, but Kari leapt high and the spear passed underneath. Then Kari sprang at him and plunged his sword deep into his chest, killing him instantly.

Skarp-Hedin seized hold of Gunnar Lambason and Grani Gunnarsson. 'I have caught a couple of puppies here,' he said. 'What shall I do with them?'

'You could choose to kill them both if you wanted them out of the way,' replied Helgi.

'I cannot bring myself to kill Grani and support his brother at the same time,' said Skarp-Hedin.

'Some day you will wish you had killed him,' said Helgi, 'for he will never keep faith with you, nor will any of the others here.'

'They will never frighten me,' said Skarp-Hedin.

So they spared the lives of Grani Gunnarsson, Gunnar Lambason, Lambi Sigurdarson, and Lodin.

They went back home, and Njal asked what had happened. They told him everything.

'This is very serious,' said Njal, 'and it will probably lead to the death of one of my sons – or even worse.'

Gunnar Lambason brought Thrain's body to Grjotriver, where they raised a burial mound over him.

93

KETIL of Mork was Thrain's brother; but he was married to Njal's daughter, Thorgerd, and he found himself in a difficult situation. He rode to see Njal and asked him if he intended to offer compensation for Thrain's killing.

Njal said, 'I shall make such reparation as is required that all may be well; and I want you to persuade your brothers to accept a settlement, for they are parties to the claim.'

Ketil agreed gladly. They decided that Ketil should go to see all those involved and bring about a settlement. He rode home and summoned all his brothers to a meeting at Hlidarend. He explained the position to them, and Hogni gave him full support. Finally arbitrators were selected and a meeting was arranged. Full compensation was awarded for the killing of Thrain, and all those who had legal title to a share accepted it. Then pledges of good faith were exchanged and everything done to make them binding. Njal paid out the entire amount readily; and now there was peace for a while.

One day Njal rode to Mork to see Ketil; they talked together all day. In the evening Njal rode back home. No one knew what they had been discussing, but Ketil went over to Grjotriver and talked to Thorgerd, Thrain's widow.

'I always loved my brother Thrain,' he said, 'and now I want to show it, by offering to adopt his son Hoskuld.'

'I shall let you do that,' she replied, 'but you will have to give the boy all the support in your power when he grows up; avenge him if he is slain, give him dowry-money when he marries. All this you must swear on oath.'

Ketil agreed to all this, and took Hoskuld home with him. The boy stayed with him at Mork for some time.

94

ONE day Njal rode to Mork again; he was made welcome, and stayed the night. In the evening, the boy Hoskuld came up to Njal, and Njal spoke to him. He showed the boy a gold ring he was wearing on his finger. The boy took the ring and examined it, and then put it on.

'Will you accept the ring as a gift?' asked Njal.

'Yes, I will,' said the boy.

'Do you know what caused your father's death?' asked Njal.

The boy replied, 'I know perfectly well that Skarp-Hedin killed him. But there is no need to bring that up again, for it has all been settled with full compensation.'

'Your answer is better than my question,' said Njal, 'and you will grow up to be a good man.'

'I am pleased that you prophesy well of me,' said the boy, 'for I know that you can see into the future and that you never lie.'

'And now,' said Njal, 'I want to adopt you as my foster-son, if you are willing.'

Hoskuld said that he would accept this and any other kindness that Njal bestowed on him. The arrangements were made and Hoskuld went home with Njal. Njal brought him up as his foster-son; he loved the boy dearly, and shielded him from all harm. His own sons took the boy with them wherever they went and gave him every privilege.

And so time passed, until Hoskuld was fully grown. He became tall and strong and very handsome, with a fine head of hair. He was gentle-tongued and generous, a man of great composure and extremely skilled in arms; he always had a good word for everyone, and everyone liked him. He and the Njalssons never disagreed over anything.

95

A MAN called Flosi, the son of Thord Frey's-Priest,* lived at Svinafell. He was married to Steinvor, the daughter of Hall of Sida.†

Flosi was a powerful chieftain. He was tall and strong, and a very forceful man. He had a half-brother called Starkad,‡ and four other brothers, called Thorgeir, Stein, Kolbein, and Egil.

Starkad had a daughter called Hildigunn, a woman of great beauty and spirit. She was exceptionally skilful with her hands. She was harsh-natured and ruthless; but when courage was called for, she never flinched.

* Thord Frey's-Priest was the son of Ozur, the son of Asbjorn, the son of Heyjang-Bjorn, the son of Helgi, the son of Bjorn Buna. Flosi's mother was Ingunn, the daughter of Thorir of Espihill, the son of Hamund Hell-Hide, the son of Hjor, the son of Half (leader of 'Half's Warriors'), the son of Hjorleif the Lecherous. The mother of Thorir of Espihill was Ingunn, the daughter of Helgi the Lean, the first settler in Eyjafjord.

† Steinvor was an illegitimate daughter of Hall of Sida. Her mother was Solvor, the daughter of Herjolf the White.

‡ Starkad had the same father as Flosi, but his mother was Thraslaug, the daughter of Thorstein Sparrow Geirleifsson and of Unn, the daughter of Eyvind Karfi, one of the original settlers in Iceland, and the sister of Modolf the Wise.

96

A MAN called Hall of Sida,* Flosi's father-in-law, was married to Joreid, the daughter of Thidrandi the Wise.†

Hall of Sida had a brother called Thorstein Broad-Paunch; he was the father of Kol, whom Kari was later to kill in Wales.

Hall of Sida had five sons – Thorstein, Egil, Thorvard, Ljot, and Thidrandi (who, it is said, was killed by the elf-women).

There was a man called Thorir, known as Holta-Thorir. His sons were Thorgeir Skorar-Geir, Thorleif Crow (from whom the men of Skogar are descended), and Thorgrim the Mighty.

97

ONE day Njal said to his foster-son Hoskuld, 'I want to find a good match for you and provide you with a wife.'

'I leave it in your hands,' said Hoskuld. 'Where are you thinking of seeking a match?'

Njal replied, 'There is a woman called Hildigunn, the daughter of Starkad, the son of Thord Frey's-Priest. She is the best match I know of.'

'You decide, foster-father,' said Hoskuld. 'I shall accept whatever choice you wish to make.'

'That is the match we shall try for, then,' said Njal.

A little later Njal asked the Sigfussons, his own sons, and Kari Solmundarson to accompany him. They rode east to Svinafell, where they were well received. Next day Njal and

---

* Hall of Sida was the son of Thorstein Bodvarsson and of Thordis, the daughter of Ozur, the son of Hrodlaug, the son of Earl Rognvald of More, the son of Eystein the Noisy.

† Thidrandi the Wise was the son of Ketil Rumble, the son of Thorir Thidrandi of Veradale.

Joreid's brothers were Ketil Rumble of Njardvik, and Thorvald, the father of Helgi Droplaugarson. Joreid's sister was Hallkatla, the mother of Thorkel and Thidrandi Geitisson.

Flosi went aside to talk, and eventually Njal said, 'The purpose of our visit is to make a proposal of marriage, to link our family with yours, Flosi. We are asking for the hand of your niece, Hildigunn.'

'On whose behalf?' asked Flosi.

'For Hoskuld Thrainsson, my foster-son,' replied Njal.

'This is a good offer,' said Flosi. 'On the other hand there are dangerous flaws in your family relationships. What can you tell me of Hoskuld?'

'Nothing but good,' replied Njal, 'and I am prepared to settle as large a sum on him as you think proper, if you care to consider the matter at all.'

'We shall send for Hildigunn,' said Flosi, 'and see what she thinks of the man.'

Hildigunn was sent for. When she arrived Flosi told her of the proposal.

'I have my pride,' said Hildigunn, 'and I am not sure whether this proposal suits me, considering the kind of people involved – particularly since this is a man without authority. You made me a promise that you would never marry me to a man without the rank of chieftain.'

'If you don't want to marry the man, that in itself is sufficient reason for me to refuse the offer,' said Flosi.

'I am not saying that I don't want to marry Hoskuld – if they provide him with a chieftainship,' said Hildigunn. 'But otherwise I will not consider it.'

Njal said, 'Give me then three years' grace to deal with the matter.'

Flosi agreed to this.

'I want to stipulate,' said Hildigunn, 'that we settle here in the east if the marriage takes place.'

Njal said that he would rather leave that to Hoskuld to decide. Hoskuld said that he trusted many men, but none so well as his foster-father Njal.

With that they rode back west.

Njal tried everywhere to obtain a chieftainship for Hoskuld, but no one was prepared to part with one.

Summer passed, until the Althing was due. There was heavy litigation that year, and as usual many people came to consult Njal; but Njal, against all likelihood, gave them advice which each time led to deadlock between plaintiff and defendant. Bitter quarrels arose when legal agreement could not be reached, and people rode home from the Althing with their differences unsettled.

The months passed until the next Althing was due. Njal attended it. It was uneventful at first, until Njal said it was high time that people gave notice of their lawsuits. But there were many who said there was little point in doing that, since no one could make any progress with actions that were brought before the court – 'and we prefer to settle our claims with weapons now,' they said.

'That must never happen,' said Njal. 'It would be quite wrong to have no law in the land. But your complaints are more than justified, and it imposes a responsibility on those of us who know the law and are the lawmakers. I think that all we chieftains should hold a meeting and discuss this problem.'

The Court of Legislature met. Njal spoke: 'I want to point out to you, Skapti Thoroddsson, and all you other chieftains, that in my opinion an impossible situation has arisen. When we raise actions in the Quarter Courts, they become so involved that no one can get a verdict or even make any headway. It seems to me essential to institute a Fifth Court and refer to it those actions which cannot be settled in the Quarter Courts.'

Skapti Thoroddsson said, 'How would you appoint this Fifth Court, since the Quarter Courts are founded on the original chieftainships, with three dozen judges for each Quarter?'

'My solution,' replied Njal, 'would be to establish new chieftainships, to be held by the best qualified men in each Quarter; and anyone who wished to do so would have the right to transfer his allegiance to the new chieftains.'

'We shall accept this plan,' said Skapti. 'But what is to be the court procedure, and what kind of cases would be referred to this court?'

Njal replied, 'It would be an appeal court dealing with all cases from the Quarter Courts of procedural irregularity, and of perjury and offences by jurymen. Any lawsuit in which a unanimous verdict could not be reached in the Quarter Courts would also be referred to the Fifth Court. Further, cases of offering or accepting bribes for support in court actions, and of harbouring runaway slaves or debtors, would be heard in the Fifth Court.

'In this court the most solemn of all oaths shall be taken, and the probity of the witnesses must be sworn to on the word of honour of two others. The court would also give judgement in favour of the party whose pleading is technically correct against another who has committed technical errors.

'Court procedure shall be the same as in the Quarter Courts, except that plaintiff and defendant shall each have the right to challenge six of the four dozen judges appointed to the Fifth Court; and if the defendant does not wish to exercise this right, the plaintiff must challenge six more. But if the plaintiff fails to do so, his case shall be dismissed, for the judges may not number more than three dozen.

'The Court of Legislature shall be arranged in such a way that those who are chosen to make the law or grant exemptions from it shall sit on the middle bench; only the wisest and most sensible shall be chosen for this. The Fifth Court shall sit there too. If the Court of Legislature disagrees over the making of law or the granting of exemptions, the issue shall be decided by a majority vote. But if anyone is prevented from entering the Court or thinks himself coerced, he may veto the proceedings, within hearing of the court, and with that veto invalidate any decisions the court may have made.'

All these proposals were made law, and then Skapti Thoroddsson incorporated the Fifth Court into the Constitution.* Later, people assembled at the Law Rock to institute the new chieftainships. In the North Quarter, they were allotted to the Mel family in Midfjord and the Laufas family in Eyjafjord.

Then Njal asked to be heard and said, 'Most people know of

* The institution of the Fifth Court (fimmtardómr) is usually dated c. 1005. It certainly took place after the conversion of Iceland to Christianity, not before it as in Njal's Saga. Ari the Learned (cf. Note on p. 216) says that it was Skapti Thoroddsson who was responsible for this constitutional development during his long tenure of office as Law-Speaker. Njal's Saga gives a broadly accurate but rather confusing version of the provisions governing the Fifth Court. It is not suggested in any other source that Njal took any part in this historic event; indeed, it is clear from the rest of the saga that Njal was not a chieftain. Translators' note.

the trouble there was between the Grjotriver men and my sons, who killed Thrain Sigfusson. In spite of that, we made a full settlement, and I adopted Hoskuld Thrainsson as my foster-son. Now I have arranged a good marriage for him, provided that he can obtain a chieftainship somewhere. But no one is willing to part with his chieftainship; so now I want to ask you to grant me leave to institute a new chieftainship at Hvitaness for Hoskuld.'

There was unanimous consent. So Njal instituted the Hvitaness chieftainship for Hoskuld, and from then on he was known as Hoskuld Hvitaness-Priest.

After that, people rode home from the Althing. Njal did not wait long before riding east to Svinafell with his sons. He reminded Flosi of the marriage-proposal, and Flosi said that he would make good his promise. Hildigunn was then formally betrothed to Hoskuld, and the wedding day was arranged.

They rode back home, and the next time they rode to Svinafell it was for the wedding. After the feast, Flosi readily paid out Hildigunn's full dowry. The couple went to Bergthorsknoll, where they stayed for that year. Hildigunn and Bergthora got on well together.

Next summer Njal bought some land at Ossaby and gave it to Hoskuld. Hoskuld made his home there, and Njal chose all the servants for him. The whole family were on such intimate terms that no one made any decisions without consulting all the others. For a long time after Hoskuld had moved to Ossaby, each thought only of the others' prestige. The Njalssons always accompanied Hoskuld on his journeys. So intense was their friendship that they invited each other to a feast every autumn, and loaded each other with valuable gifts.

And so it went on for a long time.

98

A MAN called Lyting, who lived at Samstead, was married to Thrain Sigfusson's sister, Steinvor. He was a big, powerful man, wealthy, but unpleasant to deal with.

One day Lyting held a feast at Samstead. He had invited

Hoskuld Hvitaness-Priest and the Sigfussons, and they all came. Grani Gunnarsson, Gunnar Lambason, and Lambi Sigurdarson were also there.

It so happened that Hoskuld Njalsson and his mother Hrodny had a farm at Holt. Hoskuld was in the habit of riding from Bergthorsknoll to Holt, and his journey took him right past the farmhouse at Samstead. Hoskuld had a son called Amundi, who had been born blind but was well-built and powerful.

Lyting had two brothers, Hallstein and Hallgrim. They were men of violence, and kept company with Lyting because no one else could bear them.

On the day of the feast, Lyting spent most of his time outside, only occasionally going inside the house. Finally he took his seat at the table; then a woman came in from outside and said, 'You men should have been outside just now to see that peacock riding past the farm.'

'What peacock are you talking about?' asked Lyting.

'Hoskuld Njalsson has just ridden past,' replied the woman.

'He often rides past the farm,' said Lyting, 'and I find it a constant provocation. I make you an offer here and now, Hoskuld Thrainsson, to ride with you if you want to avenge your father and kill Hoskuld Njalsson.'

'Certainly not,' said Hoskuld. 'It would be a vile way of repaying my debt to my foster-father. A curse on all your feasts.' He jumped up from the table, called for his horses, and rode home.

Then Lyting said to Grani Gunnarsson, 'You were present when Thrain was killed, and it must still be fresh in your memory – you too, Gunnar Lambason, and you, Lambi Sigurdarson. I propose that we ride out to meet Hoskuld Njalsson and kill him on his way home tonight.'

'No,' said Grani, 'I'm not going to attack the Njalssons and break a settlement made by good men.'

The other two and the Sigfussons made similar replies, and they decided to ride away. When they had gone Lyting said, 'Everyone knows that I received no compensation for the death of my brother-in-law Thrain. I shall never be content until he is avenged.'

He called on his two brothers and three of the servants to accompany him. They followed the track that Hoskuld would use, and lay in ambush for him in a hollow north of the farm. There they waited for him until evening. As Hoskuld came riding towards them they all sprang up fully armed and attacked him. Hoskuld defended himself so briskly that for a long time they could not bring him down. He wounded Lyting on the arm and killed two of the servants before he was cut down. They had given him sixteen wounds, but they did not cut off his head. After the fight they went into the woods east of Rang River and hid there.

That same evening Hrodny's shepherd found Hoskuld lying dead. He went home and told her that her son had been killed.

'No, he is not dead,' said Hrodny. 'Was his head off?'

'It was not,' replied the shepherd.

'I shall know if he is dead when I see him,' she said. 'Go and get my horse and the sled.'

He made everything ready, and they drove to the place where Hoskuld lay. She looked at his wounds and said, 'It is just as I thought, he is not quite dead. Njal can heal worse wounds than these.'

They picked up the corpse, laid it on the sled, and drove to Bergthorsknoll. There they dragged the body into a sheep-shed and placed it in a sitting position against the wall. Then they both went up to the house and knocked. A servant came to the door. Hrodny pushed past him at once and went over to Njal's bed.

'Are you awake?' she asked.

Njal said that he had been asleep but was awake now – 'but what are you doing here so early in the morning?'

Hrodny said, 'Get up from my rival's bed and come outside with me. Bring the woman and your sons too.'

They all got up and went outside. Skarp-Hedin said, 'Let us take our weapons with us.' Njal made no comment. They hurried back inside and came out again fully armed.

Hrodny led the way to the sheep-shed. She went in, and told them to follow. She raised her lantern and said, 'Here is your son Hoskuld, Njal. He has been given many wounds, and needs healing.'

Njal said, 'I see only the marks of death on him, no signs of life at all. Why did you not close his eyes and nostrils? They are still open.'

'I was leaving that to Skarp-Hedin,' she replied.

Skarp-Hedin stepped forward and performed the last duties. Then he asked his father, 'Who do you think killed him?'

'Lyting of Samstead and his brothers must have killed him,' replied Njal.

Hrodny said, 'I entrust to you, Skarp-Hedin, the task of avenging your brother; and even though he was not legitimate, I am sure that you will do it well, for you are not a man to give up easily.'

Bergthora said, 'You men amaze me. You kill when killing is scarcely called for, but when something like this happens you chew it over and brood about it until nothing comes of it. Hoskuld Hvitaness-Priest will be here as soon as he hears about it; he will ask you to settle the matter peacefully, and you will grant his request. So if you really want to do anything, you must do it now.'

'Our mother is trying to spur us on,' said Skarp-Hedin, 'and not without good reason.'

They hurried out of the sheep-shed. Hrodny went into the house with Njal and stayed there the rest of the night.

99

MEANWHILE, Skarp-Hedin and his brothers made their way towards Rang River.

'We will stop for a moment,' said Skarp-Hedin, 'and listen.' Then he added, 'We must move quietly; I can hear voices farther upriver. Would you rather deal with Lyting or with his two brothers?'

They said they would prefer to deal with Lyting.

'He is the bigger catch,' said Skarp-Hedin, 'and I would be annoyed if he escaped. I have more trust in myself to prevent him from getting away.'

'If we get within range,' said Helgi, 'we shall see to it that he does not give us the slip.'

They walked in the direction of the voices that Skarp-Hedin had heard, and caught sight of Lyting and his brothers near a stream. Skarp-Hedin at once leapt over the stream on to the gravelly slope on the other side. At the top of this slope stood Hallgrim and the others. Skarp-Hedin slashed at Hallgrim's thigh and severed it; and with his other hand he seized hold of Hallkel. Lyting lunged at Skarp-Hedin, but at that moment Helgi came up and parried the thrust with his shield.

Lyting picked up a stone with his other hand and clubbed Skarp-Hedin with it. Skarp-Hedin lost his hold on Hallkel, who tried to escape up the slope but had to scramble on his hands and knees. Skarp-Hedin swept his axe at him and sliced through his backbone. Now Lyting turned and fled, with Grim and Helgi in pursuit. Each managed to wound him once, but Lyting got away from them across the river to the horses, and galloped all the way to Ossaby.

Hoskuld Hvitaness-Priest was at home. Lyting went straight to him and told him what had happened.

'You might have known it,' said Hoskuld. 'You rushed into this without thinking. It is proof of the saying that the hand is soon sorry that it struck – and now you must be wondering what chance you have of saving yourself.'

'It's true that I barely escaped with my life,' said Lyting. 'And now I want you to make a settlement for me with Njal and his sons, one which would allow me to retain my farm.'

'Very well,' said Hoskuld. He had his horse saddled, and rode to Bergthorsknoll with five companions. Njal's sons had returned home by then and were in bed. Hoskuld went at once to see Njal, and they went aside to talk.

Hoskuld said to Njal, 'I am here to plead for Lyting, my aunt's husband. He has done you grave injury, broken the settlement, and killed your son.'

Njal said, 'Lyting no doubt feels by now that he has suffered a great loss in the death of his brothers. But if I offer any chance of settlement, I do it for your sake alone; and I stipulate beforehand that Lyting's brothers shall be counted as outlaws, and that Lyting shall get no redress for his wounds and shall also have to pay full compensation for Hoskuld.'

'I want you alone to make the terms,' said Hoskuld.

'I shall do it now,' said Njal, 'since you want me to.'

'Have you any wish to have your sons present?' asked Hoskuld.

'Their presence would not make a settlement easier,' said Njal, 'but they will honour any settlement I make.'

'Let us clear up the matter now,' said Hoskuld, 'and you can give Lyting pledges of peace on behalf of your sons.'

'Very well,' said Njal. 'Lyting is to pay two hundred ounces of silver for the killing of Hoskuld. He may remain at Samstead if he likes, but I think it wiser for him to sell his land and leave the district; not that he need fear that I or my sons shall break our pledges to him – but I think it possible that someone might turn up in the district whom he would have to guard against. Rather than give the impression that I am outlawing him from the district, however, I grant him leave to remain in the area. But he does so entirely at his own risk.'

After that, Hoskuld went back home. The Njalssons woke up and asked their father what had happened. He told them that Hoskuld, his foster-son, had been there.

'He will have been pleading for Lyting,' said Skarp-Hedin.

'Yes,' said Njal.

'That was unfortunate,' said Grim.

Njal said, 'Hoskuld could not have tried to protect him if you had killed Lyting as you were meant to do.'

'We will not reproach our father,' said Skarp-Hedin.

It should be said that this settlement was never broken.

100*

In Norway there had been a change of rulers. Earl Hakon was in his grave, and Olaf Tryggvason had succeeded to the throne. Hakon had met his death at the hands of the slave Kark, who slit his throat at Rimul in Gauldale.

---

* The conversion of Iceland to Christianity, Chapters 100–5: scholars have shown that this account is clearly taken from another written source – a source which was in all essentials based on the account written by Iceland's first vernacular historian, Ari the Learned, in his *Book of Icelanders* (*Islendingabók*) in 1130 or thereabouts. Ari the Learned (cf. Chapter 114) was born in 1067 – sixty-seven years after this event; he was brought up by Hall Thorarinsson at Haukadale, who lived to be ninety-four and who

It was also learnt that there had been a change of religion in Norway. The old faith had been discarded, and King Olaf had also converted to Christianity the western lands – Shetland, Orkney, and the Faroe Islands.

Njal heard many people say that it was monstrous to forsake the old beliefs. But Njal replied, 'In my opinion the new faith is much better; happy the man who receives it. And if the men who spread this faith come out to Iceland, I shall do all I can to further it.'

He said this on many occasions; and often he would leave the company of others and meditate aloud.

That same autumn a ship put in to land in the Eastfjords at Berufjord, at a place called Gautavik. The captain was called Thangbrand, the son of Count Willibald of Saxony. Thangbrand had been sent out to Iceland by King Olaf Tryggvason as a missionary. He was accompanied by an Icelander called Gudleif Arason,* an extremely brave and formidable warrior.

At Beruness lived two brothers, called Thorleif and Ketil Holmsteinsson.† They summoned a district meeting and forbade anyone to trade with the newcomers.

Hall of Sida, who lived at Thvattriver in Alptafjord, learnt about this. He rode to the ship with thirty men and went at once to meet Thangbrand.

'Is the trading going badly?' asked Hall.

Thangbrand said that it was.

could remember being baptized at the age of three by the missionary Thangbrand (cf. Chapter 102). Ari was also the pupil of Teit Isleifsson, son of Bishop Isleif Gizurarson, the first Icelandic Bishop of Iceland and the son of Gizur the White (cf. Chapter 46). There is no reason to doubt that Iceland's conversion took place very much in the way here described. The circumstances are remarkable enough; it is also worth noting that Iceland never reverted, even temporarily, to paganism as did the Scandinavian countries when the pressures exerted by King Olaf Tryggvason (killed that same year), and fears of the millennium, were withdrawn. *Translators' note.*

* Gudleif was the son of Ari, the son of Mar, the son of Atli, the son of Ulf the Squint-Eyed, the son of Hogni the White, the son of Otrygg, the son of Oblaud, the son of King Hjorleif the Lecherous of Hordaland.

† Holmstein was the son of Ozur of Breiddale.

'I shall tell you why I came here,' said Hall. 'I want to invite you all to stay at my house, and I shall take the responsibility for marketing your goods.'

Thangbrand thanked him, and went to Thvattriver.

One morning that autumn, Thangbrand went out early and ordered a tent to be pitched. Then he sang Mass with great ceremony, for it was an important feast-day.

Hall asked him, 'In whose honour are you celebrating this day?'

'The angel Michael,' replied Thangbrand.

'What power has this angel?' asked Hall.

'Great power,' said Thangbrand. 'He weighs everything you do, both good and evil, and he is so merciful that the good weighs more heavily with him than the evil.'

'I would like to have him as my friend,' said Hall.

'You can do that easily,' said Thangbrand. 'Give yourself to him in God's name this very day.'

Hall said, 'I want to stipulate that you pledge your word on his behalf that he shall become my guardian angel.'

'I give you my promise,' said Thangbrand.

After that, Hall and all his household were baptized.

101

NEXT spring Thangbrand toured the country evangelizing, and Hall of Sida accompanied him. When they came west across Lonsheath to Stafafell the farmer there, a man called Thorkel, opposed the new faith strongly and challenged Thangbrand to a duel. Thangbrand defended himself with a crucifix instead of a shield, but even so he managed to defeat Thorkel and kill him.

From there they went to Hornafjord and were guests at Borgarhofn, to the west of Heinabergsand. Hildir the Old lived there, the father of Glum, who later was to go to the Burning with Flosi. Hildir and all his household took the new faith.

From there they went to the Fell District and stayed at Kalfafell as guests of Kol Thorsteinsson, Hall of Sida's nephew. Kol and all his household took the new faith.

From there they went to Breidriver, the home of Ozur Hroaldsson, another of Hall's kinsmen. Ozur accepted preliminary baptism.*

From there they went to Svinafell, where Flosi accepted preliminary baptism and promised to support them at the Althing.

From there they went west to the Skogar District, and were guests at Kirkby, the home of Surt Asbjarnarson.† Surt was already a Christian.

From the Skogar District they carried on to Hofdabrekka. By that time news of their journey had travelled far ahead of them.

A man called Sorcerer-Hedin lived at Kerlingardale. The heathens there hired him to put Thangbrand and his followers to death. He went up on to Arnarstakk Heath and held a great sacrifice there. While Thangbrand was riding westwards, the ground suddenly burst open under his horse. Thangbrand leapt off the horse and reached safety on the brink of the chasm, but the horse and all the gear were swallowed up in the earth and never seen again.

Then Thangbrand praised God.

102

GUDLEIF went in search of Sorcerer-Hedin; he found him on the heath and chased him down to Kerlingardale River. When he came within range, Gudleif hurled a spear through him.

From there they went on to Dyrholmar; they held a meeting there and Thangbrand preached the faith. Ingjald the son of Thorkel Haeyjar-Tyrdil was converted there.

From there they went on to Fljotshlid and preached the faith. The strongest opposition came from Vetrlidi the Poet and his son Ari; so they killed Vetrlidi. This verse was composed about it:

*Prímsigning. Prima signatio – the sign of the Cross was made, but there was no baptism. These catechumens would be allowed to attend church. Translators' note.

† Surt's father was Asbjorn, the son of Thorstein, the son of Ketil the Foolish. All these men had been Christians.

> *The tester of shields came south*
> *To bring home the tools of war*
> *To the prayer-forge*
> *In the poet-warrior's breast.*
> *Then the tester of battle-faith*
> *Brought the hammer of death*
> *Crashing down on the anvil*
> *Of Vetrlidi's head.*

From there Thangbrand went on to Bergthorsknoll, and Njal and all his household took the new faith. Mord and his father Valgard opposed the new faith strongly.

From there they went west over the rivers to Haukadale, where they baptized Hall Thorarinsson, who was then three years old.

From there they went on to Grimsness. Thorvald the Ailing gathered a force against them there, and sent word to Ulf Uggason to fall on Thangbrand and kill him. Thorvald sent him this verse:

> '*This message I send*
> *To my friend Ulf Uggason,*
> *That wolf with armoured pelt*
> *Of whom I have no fear:*
> *Drive the cowardly cur*
> *That howls against our gods*
> *Over the cliff of death,*
> *While I take care of the other.'*

Ulf Uggason answered him with another verse:

> '*I refuse to rise*
> *To the tempting fly*
> *Of the message I was sent,*
> *Feathered with bright poetry.*
> *I am too wise a fish*
> *To gobble the angler's bait;*
> *These are troubled waters,*
> *But I can avoid being caught.'*

'I have no intention of being Thorvald's catspaw,' said Ulf. 'He had better be careful that his tongue does not choke him.'

The messenger went back to Thorvald the Ailing and told him what Ulf had said. Thorvald had a large body of men with him and declared that he was going to ambush Thangbrand and Gudleif on Blaskoga Heath. As Thangbrand and Gudleif came riding out of Haukadale they met a man riding down towards them; this man asked for Gudleif and said to him, 'For the sake of your brother Thorgils of Reykjahills I bring you warning that your enemies are setting ambushes everywhere for you, and that Thorvald the Ailing is waiting with his men at Hest Brook, in Grimsness.'

'We will not let that deter us from riding to meet him,' said Gudleif.

They turned down towards Hest Brook. Thorvald had already crossed the stream. Gudleif said to Thangbrand, 'There is Thorvald now. Let us rush him.' Thangbrand hurled his spear right through Thorvald, Gudleif hacked his arm off at the shoulder, and Thorvald died.

After that they rode to the Althing. Thorvald's kinsmen were on the point of attacking Thangbrand, but Njal and the men from the Eastfjords stood by him.

Hjalti Skeggjason came out with this verse:

> *'I don't mind mocking the gods,*
> *For I think that Freyja's a bitch;*
> *It must be one or the other —*
> *Odin's a dog or else Freyja.'*

Hjalti went abroad that summer, with Gizur the White. That same summer Thangbrand's ship, the *Bison*, was wrecked off Bulandsness, in the east.

Thangbrand travelled through all the western districts. Steinunn, the mother of Poet-Ref, came to see him. She lectured to him for a long time and tried to convert him to paganism. Thangbrand listened to her in silence, but when she had finished he spoke at length, turning all her own arguments against her.

'Did you ever hear,' she asked, 'how Thor challenged Christ to a duel, and Christ did not dare to accept the challenge?'

'I have heard,' said Thangbrand, 'that Thor would be nothing but dust and ashes if God did not permit him to live.'

'Do you know who wrecked your ship?' she asked.

'Who do you think?' asked Thangbrand.

'I will tell you,' she replied:

> 'It was Thor's giant-killing hammer
> That smashed the ocean-striding Bison;
> It was our gods who drove
> The bell-ringer's boat ashore.
> Your Christ could not save
> This buffalo of the sea from destruction;
> I do not think your God
> Kept guard over him at all.'

She added:

> 'Thor seized the great ship,
> Shook its frame
> And beat its timbers,
> And hurled it on the rocks;
> That ship will never
> Sail the seas again,
> For Thor's relentless thrashing
> Smashed it into fragments.'

With that, Steinunn and Thangbrand parted. Thangbrand and his men travelled west to Bardastrand.

103

AT Hagi on Bardastrand lived Gest Oddleifsson, a very wise man, who could foretell men's destinies. He held a feast for Thangbrand and his company, and they went to Hagi sixty strong. It was reported that 200 heathens were there already, and that a berserk* was also expected; his name was Otrygg,

* In Norse times, berserks were highly valued as warriors for their capacity to run amok and fight with maniacal frenzy, impervious to pain. The Icelandic word apparently means 'bear-shirted' (not 'bare-shirted') — wearing a bear's pelt or disguised as a bear. It has been suggested that originally the wearing of such a pelt was thought to transmit the qualities of the animal to the wearer; but there is no extant record of a pelt actually being worn in battle. Translators' note.

and everyone was terrified of him. It was even said of him that he feared neither fire nor sword.

The heathens were extremely afraid of him. Thangbrand asked whether the people wanted to accept the new faith, but all the heathens opposed it strongly.

Thangbrand said, 'I shall give you a chance of testing which is the better faith. We shall kindle three fires. You heathens are to hallow one of the fires, I shall hallow the second, and the third fire is to remain unhallowed. If the berserk is afraid of the fire I hallow, but walks unscathed through your fire, then you must accept the new faith.'

'That is fair,' said Gest. 'I accept on behalf of my household and myself.'

When Gest had spoken, there was loud approval from many of the others.

Then news came that the berserk was approaching the house. The fires were lit and kindled to a blaze. The men took their weapons and jumped on to the benches to await his arrival. The berserk came rushing fully armed into the hall; he strode at once through the fire which the heathens had hallowed, but when he came to the fire that Thangbrand had hallowed he did not dare walk through it and said that he was burning all over.

He brandished his sword to strike at the benches, but the sword caught in a crossbeam as he swung it upwards. Thangbrand struck him on the arm with a crucifix and, miraculously, the sword dropped from the berserk's grasp; then Thangbrand plunged a sword into his chest and Gudleif slashed off his arm. Many more joined in and helped to kill the berserk.

Then Thangbrand asked if they would now take the new faith. Gest replied that he never made promises he did not intend to keep. So Thangbrand baptized Gest and all his household and many others. Later, Thangbrand discussed with Gest whether he should travel west to the fjords. Gest advised against it and said that the people there were hard and unpleasant to deal with. 'And if it is fated that this new faith be accepted,' he added, 'it will be accepted at the Althing, and all the chieftains from every district will be present.'

'I have already pleaded at the Althing,' said Thangbrand, 'and that is where my difficulties were greatest.'

'But you have done most of the work, even though it shall

fall to others to succeed in making it law,' said Gest. 'A tree does not fall at the first stroke, as the saying goes.'

Gest gave Thangbrand fine gifts at his departure. Thangbrand went south again, first to the South Quarter and then to the Eastfjords. He was a guest at Bergthorsknoll, where Njal gave him fine gifts, and then rode east to Alptafjord to stay with Hall of Sida. He had his ship repaired – the heathens called it the Iron Basket – and on it he sailed abroad with Gudleif.

104

AT the Althing that summer, Hjalti Skeggjason was outlawed for blaspheming the gods.

Thangbrand told King Olaf Tryggvason of the ill-treatment he had suffered at the hands of the Icelanders, and said that they were so steeped in sorcery that the earth had burst open under his horse and swallowed the animal. The king was so enraged that he ordered all the Icelanders in Norway to be seized and thrown into dungeons, and was going to put them to death. Then Gizur the White and Hjalti Skeggjason came forward and offered to go surety for their countrymen and sail to Iceland to preach the faith. The king was pleased at the offer and reprieved all the other Icelanders.

Gizur and Hjalti prepared their ship for the journey to Iceland, and were quickly away. They landed at Eyrar in the eleventh week of summer. They got themselves horses at once, and rode off to the Althing thirty strong, leaving the ship to be unloaded by others; and they sent word to all the Christians to hold themselves in readiness. Hjalti stayed behind at Reydarmull, because he had learned that he had been outlawed for blasphemy; but when the others reached Vellandkatla, below Gjabakki, Hjalti came riding after them and said that he did not want to let the heathens think he was afraid of them.

Many Christians met them there, and they rode to the Althing in a large column. The heathens had also massed their forces. A battle which would have involved the whole Althing was imminent, but it did not occur.

105

A MAN called Thorgeir the Priest* lived at Ljosawater.

The Christians tented their booths at the Althing; Gizur and Hjalti stayed in the Mosfell booth. Next day both sides went to the Law Rock, and both of them, Christians and heathens, named witnesses and renounced their community of laws. The Law Rock was in such uproar as a result that no one could make himself heard. People then dispersed, and everyone thought the situation looked very ugly.

The Christians chose Hall of Sida to be their Law-Speaker; but Hall went to see Thorgeir the Priest of Ljosawater, and gave him three marks of silver to proclaim what the law should be. It was taking a risk, for Thorgeir was a heathen.

For a whole day, Thorgeir lay with a cloak over his head. No one spoke to him. Next day, people gathered at the Law Rock.

Thorgeir asked to be heard, and said, 'It seems to me that an impossible situation arises if we do not all have one and the same law. If the laws are divided the peace will be divided, and we cannot tolerate that. Now, therefore, I want to ask heathens and Christians whether they will accept the law which I am going to proclaim.'

They all agreed. Thorgeir insisted on oaths and binding pledges from them; they all agreed to that, and gave him their pledge.

'The first principle of our laws,' declared Thorgeir, 'is that all men in this land shall be Christian and believe in the one God – Father, Son, and Holy Ghost – and renounce all worship

* He was the son of Tjorvi, the son of Thorkel the Long; his mother was Thorunn, the daughter of Thorstein, the son of Sigmund, the son of Gnupa-Bard. Thorgeir's wife was Gudrid, the daughter of Thorkel the Black from Hleidrargard, the brother of Orm Trunk-Back, the father of Hlenni the Old from Saurby; Orm and Thorkel were both sons of Thorir Snippet, the son of Ketil Seal, the son of Ornolf, the son of Bjornolf, the son of Grim Hairy-Cheek, the son of Ketil Trout, the son of Hallbjorn Half-Troll from Hrafnista.

of idols. They shall not expose children at birth* nor eat horse-flesh. The penalty for carrying on these practices openly shall be outlawry, but they shall not be punishable if they are done in private.'

(Within a few years all these heathen practices were absolutely forbidden, in private as well as in public.)

Thorgeir then dealt with the observance of the Lord's Day and fast days, Christmas and Easter, and all the important feast-days.

The heathens felt they had been grossly betrayed, but despite that the new faith became law, and the whole land became Christian.

After that, people went home from the Althing.

106

THREE years later, Amundi the Blind, the son of Hoskuld Njalsson, happened to be present at the Thingskalar Assembly. He asked to be taken round all the booths; when he came to the booth where Lyting of Samstead was staying, he asked to be led into the booth and taken to Lyting.

'Is Lyting of Samstead here?' he asked.

'What do you want with me?' asked Lyting.

'I want to know what compensation you will pay me for my father,' replied Amundi. 'I am his illegitimate son, and I have received no compensation yet.'

'I have already paid in full for killing your father,' said Lyting, 'and your grandfather and uncles received the money, while nothing was paid for my own brothers. Certainly, I committed a grave crime, but I had to pay dearly for it.'

'I am not asking if you paid them any compensation,' said

*Exposure of children at birth was probably never a very common practice in Iceland, although it is mentioned in a few sagas – usually with the qualification that it was disapproved of. According to Ari the Learned, neither child-exposure nor the eating of horse-flesh was banned at all, neither in private nor in public, by Thorgeir in his first code of Christian observances. Child-exposure was probably used mainly for slave offspring. *Translators' note.*

Amundi. 'I know that you came to terms with them. I am asking what compensation you are prepared to pay me.'

'None whatever,' replied Lyting.

'I cannot understand how that can be right and just before God,' said Amundi, 'for you have struck me close to my heart. And I can tell you this, that if my eyes were blest with sight, I would get full compensation for my father or else take blood-revenge. May God judge between us.'

He walked out of the booth. At the door he turned once more, and at that moment his eyes opened.

'Praise be to the Lord my God,' he said. 'His will is revealed.'

He ran back into the booth right up to Lyting, and sank his axe up to the hammer into Lyting's head; then he wrenched the axe out, and Lyting fell forward, dead.

Amundi walked back to the door of the booth. When he reached the exact place where his eyes had opened, they closed again, and he remained blind for the rest of his life.

He asked to be taken to Njal and his sons, and told them of the killing of Lyting.

'No one can blame you for what you did,' said Njal, 'for such things are foreordained. It is a warning to others in similar circumstances never to rebuff those who are so close of kin.'

Then Njal offered terms to Lyting's kinsmen. Hoskuld Hvitaness-Priest helped to persuade them to accept compensation, and it was put to arbitration. Half of the compensation was remitted because of the just claim that Amundi was found to have had against Lyting. After that, pledges were exchanged, and Lyting's kinsmen gave pledges of peace to Amundi.

People then rode home from the Assembly, and there was peace for a long time.

107

VALGARD the Grey returned to Iceland. He was still a heathen. He went to Hof to visit his son Mord, and stayed there that winter.

He said to Mord, 'I have ridden all over the district, and I can hardly recognize it as the same. I went to Hvitaness, and there

I saw many new booths and much activity. Then I went to the Thingskalar Assembly ground, and there I saw all our booths falling into ruin. What is the meaning of this disgrace?'

'New chieftaincies and a Fifth Court have been instituted here,' replied Mord, 'and people have been withdrawing their allegiance from me and giving it to Hoskuld Hvitaness-Priest.'

Valgard said, 'It is poor repayment for the chieftaincy I entrusted to you that you have administered it so feebly. I want you now to pay back Njal's family in a way that will drag them all to destruction; to do that, you must divide them by slander, and make the Njalssons kill Hoskuld. There are many who will have to take action over Hoskuld's death, and the death of the Njalssons would inevitably follow.'

'I shall never be able to contrive that,' said Mord.

'I shall tell you how to go about it,' said Valgard. 'You must invite the Njalssons home and give them gifts when they leave. But you must withhold your slander until a close friendship has developed between you, and they trust you no less than themselves. In this way you can revenge yourself on Skarp-Hedin for the money he forced out of you after Gunnar's death. You will never regain your authority in the district until every one of them is dead.'

They pledged themselves to carry out this plan.

Mord said, 'I would like you to take the new faith, father. You are an old man now.'

'No,' said Valgard, 'I would rather have you discard it and see what happens then.'

Mord refused to do that. Valgard broke all Mord's crosses and sacred symbols for him. Then Valgard fell ill and died, and a burial mound was raised over him.

108

SOME time later, Mord rode to Bergthorsknoll and met Skarp-Hedin and his brothers. He talked to them all day with flattering words, and said that he wanted to see much more of them. Skarp-Hedin took all this well, but said that Mord had never sought their company before. Eventually, Mord managed to insinuate himself into their confidence to such an extent that they never made any decisions until he too had been consulted.

Njal always disliked Mord's visits, and always showed his disapproval.

On one occasion when Mord was visiting Bergthorsknoll, he said to the Njalssons, 'I have arranged a feast at Hof to honour my father's memory. I want to invite you brothers and Kari to attend, and I can promise you that you will not leave without gifts.'

They promised to go, and Mord rode home to prepare the feast. He invited many farmers, and there was a large crowd at the feast. The Njalssons and Kari were also there. Mord gave Skarp-Hedin a large gold brooch, Kari a silver belt, and Grim and Helgi fine gifts. When they returned home they praised these gifts highly and showed them to Njal. Njal said that they had probably bought them dearly – 'but take care you do not repay him in the way he wants.'

109

A LITTLE later Hoskuld and the Njalssons exchanged invitations; the Njalssons' feast was first.

Skarp-Hedin owned a black four-year-old stallion, a big handsome animal that had never been tested in a fight. Skarp-Hedin gave Hoskuld this horse and two mares as well. The others all gave Hoskuld gifts, and repeated their pledges of friendship.

Later, Hoskuld invited them home to Ossaby. There was a large number of guests there already, and the house was crowded. Hoskuld's hall was roofless at the time, and he had prepared sleeping-quarters in three out-houses. All those who had been invited came to the feast, and it was a great success. When the guests were leaving, Hoskuld chose fine gifts for them; then he escorted the Njalssons on their way home, accompanied by the Sigfussons and all the other guests. They told each other that no one would ever be allowed to come between them.

A little later, Mord called at Ossaby, and asked Hoskuld out to talk to him. They went aside to talk, and Mord said, 'What a difference there is between you and the Njalssons. You gave them fine gifts, but their gifts to you were contemptuous.'

'What makes you say that?' asked Hoskuld.

'They gave you a black horse which they called a promising colt,' said Mord, 'and they did that to show their contempt for you, for they think that you too are young and inexperienced. I can also tell you that they envy you your chieftainship; Skarp-Hedin assumed the office at the Althing when you failed to turn up for a meeting of the Fifth Court, and he has no intention of ever letting it go.'

'That is not true,' said Hoskuld. 'I received it back at the autumn district Assembly.'

'Then you had Njal to thank for that,' said Mord. 'Besides, they broke the settlement with Lyting.'

'I do not think that was their doing,' said Hoskuld.

'But you cannot deny,' said Mord, 'that when you went with Skarp-Hedin east to Markar River, an axe slipped out from under his belt. He had intended to kill you.'

'That was his wood-chopper,' said Hoskuld, 'and I had already seen him putting it there. And let me tell you at once,' he went on, 'that as far as I am concerned you will never say anything so evil of the Njalssons that I shall believe it. And even if you are telling the truth, and it turns out to be a choice between killing them or being killed by them, I would much rather endure death at their hands than do them any harm. And you, Mord, are all the more evil for saying what you have said.'

Mord went home. A little later he went to see the Njalssons, and had a long talk with them and Kari.

'I am told,' said Mord, 'that Hoskuld has been saying that you, Skarp-Hedin, broke settlement with Lyting; and I have also discovered that he thought you had planned a treacherous attack on his life when you were travelling together to Markar River. But in my opinion it was no less treacherous of Hoskuld to invite you to a feast and make you sleep in the out-house farthest from the hall, where faggots were being piled up all night with the intention of burning you alive inside. It was only Hogni Gunnarsson's arrival during the night that put a stop to their plans, because they were afraid of him.

'And later, when Hoskuld escorted you on your way with a large company, he was planning another attack on you, and had arranged for Grani Gunnarsson and Gunnar Lambason to do the killing; but in the event, their courage failed them and they did not dare to attack you.'

At first the Njalssons rejected everything he said; but in the end they came to believe it. From then on, they showed great coldness towards Hoskuld, and they scarcely spoke to him whenever they met. Hoskuld made no attempt to appease them.

This went on for some time. In the autumn, Hoskuld rode east to attend a feast at Svinafell, and Flosi welcomed him warmly. Hildigunn came too.

Flosi said to Hoskuld, 'Hildigunn tells me that you and the Njalssons are estranged, and this disturbs me. I want to make you an offer : you can have the farm at Skaptafell instead of riding back west, and I shall send my brother Thorgeir to take over the farm at Ossaby.'

'Then people would say that I was fleeing from Ossaby because I was afraid,' said Hoskuld, 'and I don't want that.'

'Then,' said Flosi, 'this is likely to lead to disaster.'

'That is a pity,' said Hoskuld, 'for I would rather that no compensation at all were paid for me than be the cause of suffering to others.'

A few days later, Hoskuld prepared to leave for home. Flosi gave him a scarlet cloak bordered with lacework down the front. Hoskuld rode back to Ossaby, and there was peace for a while. He was so well liked that he had few enemies, but the same bad feeling between him and the Njalssons persisted throughout the winter.

Njal had adopted Thord, Kari's son. He was also foster-father to Thorhall, the son of Asgrim Ellida-Grimsson. Thorhall was a man of great vitality and courage; he had learned so much law from Njal that he was now one of the three greatest lawyers in Iceland.

Spring came early that year, and farmers sowed their corn early.

ONE day Mord came to Bergthorsknoll, and at once took the Njalssons and Kari aside to talk. Mord started slandering Hoskuld as usual, and had many new tales to tell. He kept urging Skarp-Hedin and the others to kill Hoskuld, and warned them that Hoskuld would get his blow in first if they did not attack at once.

'You can have your way,' said Skarp-Hedin, 'if you agree to come with us and take part in it yourself.'

'I am prepared to do even that,' said Mord.

They pledged themselves to this agreement, and Mord was to come back that same evening.

Bergthora asked Njal, 'What are they discussing out there?'

'They have not taken me into their confidence,' said Njal. 'But I was seldom excluded when their plans were wholesome.'

Skarp-Hedin did not go to bed that evening, nor did his brothers and Kari. During the night Mord Valgardsson arrived; the Njalssons and Kari took their weapons, and they all rode away together. They travelled without pause to Ossaby, and waited behind a fence there.

The sun was up, and it was a fine morning.

111

HOSKULD HVITANESS-PRIEST woke up early that morning. He dressed himself and put on the cloak that Flosi had given him. With a seed-basket in one hand and a sword in the other he went out to his cornfield and started to sow.

Skarp-Hedin had agreed with the others that they all should strike him. Now he jumped up from behind the fence. Hoskuld saw him and started to move away, but Skarp-Hedin ran up to him and said, 'Don't trouble yourself to run away, Hvitaness-Priest.'

With that he struck. The blow fell on Hoskuld's head.

Hoskuld sank to his knees. 'May God help me and forgive you all,' he said.

They all rushed at him and cut him down.

Then Mord said, 'I have an idea.'

'What is it?' asked Skarp-Hedin.

'I think I should go home first, and then go up to Grjotriver and report what has happened and pretend to be horrified. I am quite certain that Thorgerd will ask me to give notice of the killing and that is what I shall do, for that is the surest way of invalidating their legal action. I shall also send someone to Ossaby to find out how soon they plan to take action there; he can learn from them what has happened, and I shall pretend that this was how I came to hear of it.'

'Do so by all means,' said Skarp-Hedin.

The Njalssons and Kari went home. When they arrived, they told Njal the news.

'Sorrowful news,' said Njal. 'This is a terrible thing to hear, for I can truthfully say that it grieves me so deeply that I would rather have lost two of my own sons to have Hoskuld still alive.'

'There is some excuse for you,' said Skarp-Hedin. 'You are an old man now, and it is no wonder you take it to heart.'

'It is not merely old age that makes me grieve,' said Njal, 'so much as the fact that I know far better than you what this will lead to.'

'What will it lead to?' asked Skarp-Hedin.

'My death,' said Njal, 'and the death of my wife and all my sons.'

Kari asked, 'What do you foretell for me?'

'They will find it hard to cope with your good luck,' said Njal. 'You will prove more than a match for all of them.'

This was the only thing that grieved Njal so much that he could never speak of it unmoved.

112

HILDIGUNN woke up and found that Hoskuld had left the bed. 'I have had cruel and ominous dreams,' she said. 'Go and look for Hoskuld.'

A search was made round the farm, but Hoskuld could not be found. By that time Hildigunn was dressed; she went over to the cornfield with two men, and there they found Hoskuld dead. Just then Mord's shepherd arrived and told her that the Njalssons had ridden away from there – 'and Skarp-Hedin called me over and declared that he had done the killing.'

'It would have been man's work,' said Hildigunn, 'if only one man had done it.'

With her husband's cloak she wiped away all the blood and gathered into it all the blood-clots; then she folded the cloak and put it away in a chest. Then she sent a messenger to Grjotriver to report what had happened. Mord had arrived there earlier and had already told the news. Ketil of Mork was also there.

Thorgerd said to Ketil, 'Hoskuld is dead, as we now know, so bear in mind what you promised when you took him away for fostering.'

'I probably promised more than enough at that time,' said Ketil, 'for I never thought that a day like this would ever come; but I am in a difficult position now, for I am married to Njal's daughter, and the nose is next to the eyes, as the saying goes.'

'Then do you want Mord to give notice of the killing?' asked Thorgerd.

'I am not so sure of that,' said Ketil. 'I have the impression that Mord causes more harm than good.'

But as soon as Mord talked to him, Ketil, like so many others, trusted him at once; and they agreed that Mord should give notice of the killing and make all the preparations for raising an action at the Althing. Mord then rode down to Ossaby with ten men. The nine neighbours who lived closest to the scene arrived. Mord showed them Hoskuld's wounds and named witnesses to them, and for each wound he named the man who had inflicted it, with one exception – the wound that he himself had inflicted, which he now pretended to know nothing about. He charged Skarp-Hedin with the actual killing, and his brothers and Kari with the other wounds. Then he cited the nine neighbours to attend the Althing, and rode home.

He scarcely ever saw the Njalssons, and when they happened to meet, they were short with each other. That was part of their plan.

The killing of Hoskuld was talked about and condemned

throughout the land. The Njalssons went to see Asgrim Ellida-
Grimsson and asked him for support.

'You can be sure of my suport in all important matters,' said
Asgrim. 'But my mind is uneasy about this, for there are many
who will have to take action over this killing, and it has been
bitterly condemned throughout the land.'

After that the Njalssons went back home.

113

A MAN called Gudmund the Powerful* lived at Modruvellir in
Eyjafjord. His wife was called Thorlaug.†

Gudmund was a great and wealthy chieftain. He kept a hundred servants at Modruvellir. He completely dominated all the
other chieftains to the north of Oxnadale Heath; some he forced

* He was the son of Eyjolf, the son of Einar, the son of Audun
Rotin, the son of Thorolf Butter, the son of Thorstein Skrofi, the
son of Grim Kamban. Gudmund's mother was Hallbera, the daughter of Thorodd Helmet and of Reginleif, the daughter of Sæmund
the Hebridean (Sæmundarhlid in Skagafjord is named after him).
The mother of Eyjolf (Gudmund's father) was Valgerd, the daughter of Runolf and of Valborg, the daughter of Jorunn the Illegitimate, the daughter of King Oswald the Saint and of Bera, the
daughter of King Edmund the Saint. The mother of Einar (Gudmund's grandfather) was Helga, the daughter of Helgi the Lean
(the first settler in Eyjafjord), the son of Eyvind the Easterner and of
Rafarta, the daughter of King Kjarval of Ireland; Helga's mother
was Thorunn Hyrna, the daughter of Ketil Flat-Nose, the son of
Bjorn Buna, the son of the chieftain Grim, the son of Hervor, the
daughter of Thorgerd, the daughter of King Haleyg of Halogaland.

† She was the daughter of Atli the Strong, the son of Eilif Eagle,
the son of Bard of Al, the son of Ketil Fox, the son of Skidi the
Old. Thorlaug's mother was Herdis, the daughter of Thord of Hofdi,
the son of Bjorn Butter-Box, the son of Hroald Backbone, the son
of Bjorn Iron-Side, the son of Ragnar Hairy-Breeks, the son of
Sigurd Ring, the son of Randver, the son of Radbard. The mother of
Herdis (Thorlaug's mother) was Thorgerd, the daughter of Skidi
and of Fridgerd, the daughter of King Kjarval of Ireland.

to leave their farms, others he forced to give up their chieftaincies, still others he put to death. All the greatest families in Iceland are descended from him – the men of Oddi, the Sturlungs, the men of Hvamm, the men of Fljot, Bishop Ketil, and many other outstanding men.

Gudmund was a friend of Asgrim Ellida-Grimsson, and Asgrim was hoping to get support from him.

114

A MAN called Snorri, known as Snorri the Priest,* lived at Helgafell (until Gudrun Osvif's-daughter † bought it from him and lived there for the rest of her life; Snorri then moved to Hvammsfjord and lived at Sælingsdale Tongue).

Snorri was a great friend of Asgrim Ellida-Grimsson, and Asgrim was relying on him for support. Snorri was reckoned the wisest man in Iceland, not counting those who were prescient; he was a reliable friend, but a ruthless enemy.

A great number of people were riding to the Althing that summer from all quarters of the land, and many court actions were being raised.

* Snorri's father was Thorgrim, the son of Thorstein Cod-Biter, the son of Thorolf Mostrar-Beard, the son of Ornolf Fish-Driver (Thorgils Reydarsida, according to Ari the Learned). Thorolf was married to Osk, the daughter of Thorstein the Red. The mother of Thorgrim (Snorri's father) was Thora, the daughter of Olaf Feilan, the son of Thorstein the Red, the son of Olaf the White, the son of Ingjald, the son of Helgi and of Thora, the daughter of Sigurd Snake-In-The-Eye, the son of Ragnar Hairy-Breeks. Snorri's mother was Thordis, the sister of Gisli Sursson.

† The heroine of Laxdæla Saga. Translators' note.

FLOSI was deeply disturbed and angered by the news that Hoskuld had been killed; but he kept his composure. He was told how proceedings had been started for Hoskuld's killing, but he had little to say about them.

He sent word to his father-in-law, Hall of Sida, and Hall's son, Ljot, to attend the Althing in strength. Ljot was considered the most promising of the future chieftains in the east; it had been prophesied of him that if he survived three visits to the Althing he would become the greatest chieftain in his family and live the longest. He had already attended the Althing once, and this would be the second year.

Flosi also sent word to Kol Thorsteinsson, Glum (the son of Hildir the Old), Geirleif (the son of Onund Trunk-Back), and Modolf Ketilsson. They all rode to meet Flosi, and Hall of Sida also promised to come with a large following.

Flosi rode to Kirkby to see Surt Asbjarnarson, and sent for his nephew Kolbein Egilsson to join him there. Then he rode to Hofdabrekka, the home of Thorgrim the Showy (the son of Thorkel the Handsome), and asked Thorgrim to accompany him to the Althing. Thorgrim agreed, and said, 'I have often seen you more cheerful, Flosi; but your gloom is not unjustified.'

Flosi replied, 'Certainly I would give all I possess for this thing never to have happened. The seeds of evil have been sown, and evil will be the harvest.'

From there Flosi rode over Arnarstakk Heath and reached Solheim that evening, where he stayed overnight with his great friend Lodmund Ulfsson. Next morning Lodmund rode with him to Dale, the home of Runolf, the son of Ulf Aur-Priest, where they stayed the night.

Flosi said to Runolf, 'Now we can hear the true story of the killing of Hoskuld Hvitaness-Priest. You are a truthful man, and you are close to the source; so I can believe anything you tell me of what caused their enmity.'

'There is no point in mincing my words,' said Runolf. 'Hoskuld was killed for less than no cause; all men mourn his death, but none more than Njal, his foster-father.'

'Then they will find it hard to get support,' said Flosi.

'Yes,' said Runolf, 'unless something happens.'

'What has been done so far?' asked Flosi.

'The neighbours have been cited and notice given of the killing.'

'Who did that?'

'Mord Valgardsson,' replied Runolf.

'How safe is that?' asked Flosi.

'Mord is my kinsman,' said Runolf, 'but, to be truthful, I must admit that he causes more harm than good. But I want to urge you, Flosi, to compose your anger and take the course that will lead to the least trouble; for Njal and other good men will make generous offers.'

Flosi said, 'Ride to the Althing, Runolf; the advice you give will carry much weight with me, if nothing happens to make things worse.'

They discussed it no further, and Runolf promised to ride to the Althing; he sent word to his kinsman Haf the Wise, who came to him at once.

Flosi set off from Dale to Ossaby.

116

HILDIGUNN was waiting outside.

'I want all the men to be out here when Flosi rides in,' she said. 'The women are to clean the house and put up the hangings, and make ready a high-seat for Flosi.'

Soon Flosi came riding into the home-meadow. Hildigunn went to meet him.

'You are welcome, kinsman,' she said. 'My heart rejoices at your coming.'

'We shall eat here and then ride on,' said Flosi.

The horses were tethered. Flosi went inside. He sat down, and threw the high-seat away from him on to the dais.

'I am neither king nor earl,' he said, 'and there is no need to make me a high-seat. There is no need to mock me, either.'

Hildigunn was beside him. 'It is a pity you are offended,' she said. 'We did this in all sincerity.'

Flosi replied, 'If you are being sincere with me and your motives are good they will speak for themselves, and condemn themselves if they are evil.'

Hildigunn laughed an icy laugh. 'This is nothing,' she said. 'We shall get closer yet before we part.'

She sat down beside Flosi, and they talked in undertones for a long time.

After that the tables were set up, and Flosi and his men washed themselves. Flosi examined the towel; it was full of holes, and one end had been ripped away. He threw it down on the bench and refused to use it; instead he tore a piece off the table-cloth, dried his hands on it, and tossed it to his men. Then he sat down at the table and told his men to eat.

At that moment Hildigunn came into the room and went up to Flosi, pushed her hair back from her eyes, and wept.

Flosi said, 'You are sad now, kinswoman, you are weeping. It is only right that you should weep over a good husband.'

'What redress will you get me?' she asked. 'How much help will you give me?'

'I shall press your claims to the full extent of the law,' said Flosi, 'or else conclude a settlement which in the eyes of all good men will satisfy every demand of honour.'

Hildigunn said, 'Hoskuld would have avenged you with blood if he were in your place now.'

'You are a ruthless woman,' said Flosi. 'It is clear now what you are after.'

Hildigunn said, 'Arnor Ornolfsson from Forsriverwoods never did your father as grave an injury as this, and yet your brothers Kolbein and Egil killed him at the Skaptafell Assembly.'

She walked from the room and unlocked her chest. She took out the cloak, the gift from Flosi, which Hoskuld had been wearing when he was killed, and in which she had preserved all his blood. She came back with the cloak and went up to Flosi without a word; Flosi had finished eating and the table had been cleared. She threw the cloak around his shoulders, and the clotted blood rained down all over him.

'This is the cloak you gave to Hoskuld, Flosi,' she said, 'and now I give it back to you. He was wearing it when he was killed. I call upon God and all good men to witness that I charge you in the name of all the powers of your Christ and in the name of your courage and your manhood, to avenge every one of the wounds that marked his body – or be an object of contempt to all men.'

Flosi threw off the cloak and flung it back into her arms. 'Monster,' he cried. 'You want us to take the course which will turn out worst for all of us. "Cold are the counsels of women."'

He was so agitated that his face changed colour rapidly; one moment it was red as blood, then pale as withered grass, then black as death. He and his men went out to their horses and rode away to Holtsford; here they waited for the Sigfussons and other friends.

Flosi sent word to Ingjald of Keldur* to join him. He came at once with fourteen men, all members of his household. Ingjald was tall and powerful, rather reserved in his own home, a very brave man and open-handed to his friends. Flosi welcomed him warmly and said, 'Grave problems beset us, kinsman, which we shall find hard to solve. I ask you not to withdraw your support before our difficulties are over.'

Ingjald said, 'I am in a difficult position myself, because of my relationship with Njal and his sons, and for other important reasons which have to be taken into account.'

'I had thought, when I gave you my niece in marriage,' said Flosi, 'that you promised to support me in everything.'

'It is more than likely that I shall,' said Ingjald. 'But I want to ride home first and go on to the Althing from there.'

* He was the brother of Hrodny, the mother of Hoskuld Njalsson. He and Hrodny were the children of Hoskuld the White, the son of Ingjald the Strong, the son of Geirfinn the Red, the son of Solvi, the son of Gunnstein the Berserk-Killer.

Ingjald was married to Thraslaug, the daughter of Egil, the son of Thord Frey's-Priest and of Thraslaug, the daughter of Thorstein Sparrow and of Unn, the daughter of Eyvind Karfi and a sister of Modolf the Wise.

117

THE Sigfussons heard that Flosi was at Holtsford, and rode to meet him there; their party consisted of the Sigfusson brothers (Ketil of Mork, Lambi, Thorkel, Mord, and Sigmund), Lambi Sigurdarson, Gunnar Lambason, Grani Gunnarson, and Vebrand Hamundarson.

Flosi rose to meet them and welcomed them gladly. They walked down to the river. Flosi questioned them, and their account of the killing tallied exactly with that given by Runolf of Dale.

Flosi said to Ketil of Mork, 'I have a question to put to you: how strongly do you and your brothers feel about this case?'

'I want to see a reconciliation arranged,' replied Ketil. 'But I have sworn never to abandon this cause until it is settled one way or another, and to this I pledge my life.'

'You are truly a man,' said Flosi. 'It is good to have men like you.'

Grani Gunnarsson and Gunnar Lambason said in the same breath, 'We demand outlawry, and blood-vengeance as well.'

Flosi said, 'We cannot expect to have it both ways.'

'When they killed Thrain at Markar River,' said Grani, 'and then his son Hoskuld, I made up my mind that I would never be reconciled with these people. I would gladly be present when they are all being killed.'

'You have been close enough to take vengeance yourself,' said Flosi, 'if you had the courage and manhood for it. I feel that you and many others are now demanding something that you would later give much never to have taken part in. I realize only too well that even though we kill Njal and his sons, they are men of such family and standing that we shall be faced with such consequences that we shall be forced to grovel at the feet of many men and beg them for help before we get clear of trouble. And you can also be sure that many who now are rich would be stripped of wealth, and some would lose their lives as well.'

Mord Valgardsson came to meet Flosi and said that he wanted to ride with him to the Althing with all his following. Flosi accepted the offer, and proposed that Mord should give his daughter Rannveig in marriage to Starkad of Stafafell, Flosi's nephew; Flosi's purpose was that he thought he could thus guarantee Mord's loyalty and resources.

Mord took this favourably, but referred it to Gizur the White, and asked Flosi to discuss it at the Althing. Mord was married to Gizur's daughter, Thorkatla.

Mord and Flosi rode side by side to the Althing, and talked together all day long.

118

NJAL said to Skarp-Hedin, 'What plans have you in mind now, you brothers and Kari?'

'We do not use dreams much to guide our plans,' replied Skarp-Hedin. 'But if you want to know, we are going to ride to Tongue to meet Asgrim Ellida-Grimsson, and carry on from there to the Althing. Are you going yourself, father?'

'Yes, I shall ride to the Althing,' said Njal, 'for honour demands that I do not abandon you while I am still alive. I rather think that there are many who will have a good word for me there, and that you will benefit rather than suffer from my presence.'

Thorhall Asgrimsson, Njal's foster-son, was nearby. The Njalssons were laughing at him for wearing a coarse striped cloak, and asked him how long he was going to keep it on.

'I shall have discarded it,' replied Thorhall, 'by the time I have to seek redress for the death of my foster-father.'

'You will always rise to the occasion when the need is greatest,' said Njal.

They all made ready for the journey; they were nearly thirty strong. They rode to Thjors River, where they were joined by two of Njal's kinsmen, Thorleif Crow and Thorgrim the Mighty, sons of Holta-Thorir. They offered the Njalssons their support and men, which they accepted. They all forded Thjors River and rode on to Laxriverbank, where they rested. They were met there by Hjalti Skeggjason, who conferred with Njal for a long time in undertones.

Hjalti then said, 'It is always my policy to be frank about my thoughts. Njal has asked me for help; I have agreed, and have promised him my support. He has paid me and many others in advance with all his good counsel.'

Hjalti told Njal about Flosi's movements. They sent Thorhall on ahead to Tongue to announce that they would arrive there that evening. Asgrim made ready at once, and was standing outside when Njal rode into the home-meadow. Njal was wearing a blue cape and a felt hood, and carried a small axe in one hand. Asgrim lifted Njal off his horse, carried him indoors, and placed him on the high-seat. The Njalssons and Kari followed them in. Asgrim went out again and found Hjalti on the point of leaving, thinking that there were too many people there already. Asgrim took hold of the reins and told him that he would not let him go away; he ordered the horses to be unsaddled and led Hjalti into the house, and seated him beside Njal. Thorleif and his brother sat with their men on the opposite bench.

Asgrim sat down on a stool in front of Njal and asked, 'What do you feel about this case?'

'I am uneasy,' said Njal, 'for I fear that there are men of ill luck involved. Send for all those who owe you allegiance, and ride with me to the Althing.'

'I had intended to,' said Asgrim, 'and I can promise you that I shall never abandon your cause as long as I have any men left to follow me.'

All those in the room thanked him, and said that he had spoken like a true man.

They stayed there overnight, and next day all Asgrim's supporters arrived. Then they all rode off to the Althing where their booths were already tented.

119

FLOSI had already arrived at the Althing and manned his booth. Runolf was in charge of the Dale booth, and Mord of the Rangriver booth. Hall of Sida had come farthest from the east, nearly the only one from there; but he had brought a large following from his own district, and joined forces with Flosi at once. He urged Flosi to seek a settlement and peace; he was an understanding and benevolent man. Flosi gave him a friendly answer, but would not commit himself. Hall asked who else had promised him help; Flosi mentioned amongst others Mord Valgardsson, and said that he had asked on behalf of his nephew Starkad for the hand of Mord's daughter. Hall said that the woman was a good match, but that any dealings with Mord would be disastrous – 'and you will find that out before this Althing is over.'

They discussed it no further.

One day Njal and his sons had a long secret talk with Asgrim. Then Asgrim jumped to his feet and said to the Njalssons, 'Let us go and find ourselves some friends, lest we are outnumbered in court; for this case will be a hard-fought one.'

Asgrim went out, followed by Helgi Njalsson, then Kari Solmundarson, then Grim Njalsson, then Skarp-Hedin, then Thorhall Asgrimsson, then Thorgrim the Mighty, and then Thorleif Crow. They went to the booth of Gizur the White and walked inside. Gizur stood up to welcome them and invited them to sit and drink.

'This is no time for that,' said Asgrim, 'and no time for mumbling, either. What help can I expect from you, kinsman?'

'My sister Jorunn would expect me not to shrink from helping you,' replied Gizur. 'You and I shall stand side by side, now and always.'

Asgrim thanked him and left the booth.

'Where shall we go now?' asked Skarp-Hedin.

'To the Olfus booth,' said Asgrim.

They went there, and Asgrim asked if Skapti Thoroddsson were in. He was told that he was, and they went into the booth. Skapti was sitting on the dais and welcomed Asgrim, who returned the greeting. Skapti invited him to sit beside him; Asgrim replied that he did not mean to stay long – 'but it is you I came to see, nevertheless.'

'Let us hear your errand,' said Skapti.

'I need your help,' said Asgrim, 'for myself and my kinsmen.'

'I have no intention,' said Skapti, 'of letting your troubles into my house.'

Asgrim said, 'These are mean words; you are of least use when the need is greatest.'

'Who is that man,' asked Skapti, 'the fifth in the line, that tall, fierce-looking, troll-like man with the pale, ill-starred look?'

'Skarp-Hedin is my name,' he replied, 'and you have often seen me here at the Althing. But I must be sharper than you, for I have no need to ask you your name. You are called Skapti Thoroddsson, but once you called yourself Bristle-Head, when you had just killed Ketil of Elda; that was the time you shaved your head and smeared it with tar, and bribed some slaves to cut you a strip of turf to cower under for the night. Later you fled to Thorolf Loptsson of Eyrar, who took you in and then smuggled you abroad in his flour sacks.'

With that they all left the booth.

'Where shall we go now?' asked Skarp-Hedin.

'To Snorri the Priest's booth,' said Asgrim.

They went to Snorri's booth. Asgrim asked a man standing in the doorway if Snorri were in, and was told that he was. Asgrim walked into the booth, followed by the others.

Snorri was sitting on the dais. Asgrim went up to him and greeted him well; Snorri welcomed him cordially and invited him to sit. Asgrim said that he did not mean to stay long – 'but it is you I came to see, nevertheless.'

Snorri asked him to state his errand.

'I would like you to come to court with me,' said Asgrim, 'and give me your support, for you are a clever and very resourceful man.'

Snorri replied, 'Our own lawsuits are going badly just now, and we are under strong pressure from many of our opponents; and for that reason we are reluctant to shoulder the troubles of men in other Quarters.'

'That is not unreasonable,' said Asgrim, 'for you don't owe us anything.'

'I know that you are a good man,' said Snorri, 'and I can promise that I shall not take sides against you nor support your enemies.'

Asgrim thanked him.

Then Snorri said, 'Who is that man, fifth in the line, the pale, sharp-featured man with a grin on his face and an axe on his shoulder?'

'My name is Hedin,' he replied, 'but some call me Skarp-Hedin in full. Have you anything else to say to me?'

'I think you look very ruthless and formidable,' said Snorri, 'but my guess is that you have exhausted your store of good luck, and that you have not long to live.'

'Well and good,' said Skarp-Hedin, 'for death is a debt we all have to pay. But you would be better employed avenging your father than making me such prophecies.'

'You are not the first man to tell me that,' said Snorri, 'and it cannot make me angry.'

With that they left the booth, and got no promise of support. They made their way to the Skagafjord booth, which was owned by Haf the Wealthy.* They walked inside. Haf was sitting in the centre of the booth and was talking to someone. Asgrim went up to him and greeted him; Haf welcomed him and invited him to sit.

'No,' said Asgrim, 'I have come to ask your help for myself and my kinsmen.'

Haf replied promptly that he wanted no part of their troubles – 'but I would like to know who that pale-faced man is, fifth in the line, who looks evil enough to have come straight out of some sea-cliff?'

Skarp-Hedin replied, 'Never mind that, milksop; I would dare to face you anywhere, and it would not frighten me in the least though there were more than one of your sort in my path; and you would be better employed fetching back your sister Svanlaug, whom Eydis Iron-Sword and Anvil-Head kidnapped from your home.'

'Let us go,' said Asgrim. 'There is no hope of help here.'

From there they walked to the Modruvellir booth, and asked if Gudmund the Powerful were in. They were told that he was, and went in. There was a high-seat in the middle of the booth, and Gudmund was sitting on it. Asgrim went up to him and greeted him. Gudmund welcomed him and invited him to sit.

---

* He was the son of Thorkel, the son of Eirik from Goddales, the son of Geirmund, the son of Hroald, the son of Eirik Bristle-Beard, who killed Grjotgard in Soknardale in Norway. Haf the Wealthy's mother was Thorunn, the daughter of Asbjorn the Bald of Myrk-river, the son of Hrossbjorn.

'I do not wish to sit,' said Asgrim. 'I want to ask for your help, for you are an enterprising and powerful chieftain.'

'I will certainly not be against you,' said Gudmund. 'But if I feel like giving you some help, we can easily discuss that later.'

He seemed well disposed towards them. Asgrim thanked him for his words.

'There is one man in your group that I have been looking at for some time,' said Gudmund. 'He seems to me unlike most other men I have ever seen.'

'Which one is that?' asked Asgrim.

'He is fifth in the line,' said Gudmund, 'chestnut-haired and pale-faced, huge and powerful, and so manly-looking that I would rather have him in my following than any ten others. But he looks a man of ill luck.'

'I am well aware that you are referring to me,' said Skarp-Hedin, 'but we are both men of ill luck, each in his own way. I stand condemned, as is only right, for the killing of Hoskuld Hvitaness-Priest; but Thorkel Braggart and Thorir Helgason have spread some very unpleasant tales about you, for which you yourself must stand condemned.'

With that they left the booth.

'Where shall we go now?' asked Skarp-Hedin.

'To the Ljosawater booth,' said Asgrim.

That booth belonged to Thorkel Braggart,* who had been abroad and won fame in foreign lands.

He had killed a robber east in Jamtland Forest, and then travelled east to Sweden, where he joined forces with Sorkvir the Old. Together they harried in the Baltic. One evening, on the coast of Finland, it was Thorkel's turn to fetch water for the crew; he encountered a fabulous monster and was only able to kill it after a long struggle. From there he travelled south to Estonia, where he killed a flying dragon. After that he

* He was the son of Thorgeir the Priest of Ljosawater, the son of Tjorvi, the son of Thorkel Long; Thorgeir's mother was Thorunn, the daughter of Thorstein, the son of Sigmund, the son of Gnupa-Bard. Thorkel Braggart's mother was Gudrid, the daughter of Thorkel the Black from Hleidrargard, the son of Thorir Snippet, the son of Ketil Seal, the son of Ornolf, the son of Bjornolf, the son of Grim Hairy-Cheek, the son of Ketil Trout, the son of Hallbjorn Half-Troll.

returned to Sweden, then to Norway, and then to Iceland, where he had these feats carved above his bed-closet and on a chair in front of his high-seat.

He and his brothers also fought against Gudmund the Powerful at the Ljosawater Assembly, and the Ljosawater men won the day; it was on that occasion that Thorkel Braggart and Thorir Helgason had slandered Gudmund.

Thorkel claimed that there was no one in Iceland whom he would not dare to meet in single combat or before whom he would yield ground. He was called Thorkel Braggart because no one with whom he had to deal escaped the weight of his tongue or his arm.

I20

ASGRIM ELLIDA-GRIMSSON and the others walked to Thorkel's booth. Asgrim told them, 'This booth belongs to Thorkel Braggart. He is a great warrior, and it would make a great difference to us if we got his help. We must handle this extremely carefully, for he is a self-willed and difficult man. I must ask you, Skarp-Hedin, not to interfere in the conversation.'

Skarp-Hedin grinned. He was wearing a blue tunic with a silver belt, blue-striped trousers, and black top-boots. He was carrying a small round shield and the axe with which he had killed Thrain Sigfusson and which he called 'Battle-Troll'. His hair was combed well back and held in place by a silk headband. He looked every inch a warrior, and everyone knew him at first sight. He kept exactly to his position in the line.

They went into the booth and up to the far end. Thorkel was sitting in the centre of the dais, with his men ranged alongside him. Asgrim greeted him, and Thorkel returned the greeting.

'The reason we have come here,' said Asgrim, 'is to ask if you will come to court to support us.'

'Why should you need my help, when you have already been to Gudmund?' asked Thorkel. 'Surely he promised you some help?'

'We got no help from him,' said Asgrim.

'Then Gudmund must have thought your cause very unpopular,' said Thorkel. 'And he was right; for it was a hideous crime. Now I see what brought you here: you thought that I would be less particular than Gudmund and quite prepared to back an unjust cause.'

Asgrim fell silent. He did not like the way things were going.

Thorkel went on, 'Who is that big baleful man, fifth in the line, the one with the pale, sharp, ill-starred, evil look?'

'I am called Skarp-Hedin,' he replied, 'and you have no cause to pick on me, an innocent man, with your insults. I at least have never threatened my own father's life, as you once did, nor ever fought with him, as you once did. You have rarely attended the Althing or taken part in lawsuits, and you must feel more at home milking the cows at Oxarriver with your scanty household. You would be better employed picking out of your teeth the bits of mare's arse you ate before you came here – your shepherd saw you at it, and was amazed at such disgusting behaviour.'

Thorkel sprang to his feet in fury and snatched up his short-sword. 'This is the sword I got in Sweden,' he said. 'I killed a great warrior to get it, and since then I have used it to kill many more. And when I get at you I shall run you through with it and pay you back for your obscene insults.'

Skarp-Hedin stood there grinning, with his axe raised and said, 'This is the axe I carried when I leapt twelve ells over Markar River * and killed Thrain Sigfusson while eight men stood by and could not lay a hand on me. And I have never raised weapon against anyone and missed my mark.'

He burst past his brothers and Kari and charged up to Thorkel. 'And now, Thorkel Braggart,' he said, 'put away your sword and sit down, or I shall drive my axe into your head and split you to the shoulders.'

Thorkel sheathed his sword and sat down promptly. It was the only time in his life that such a thing happened.

Asgrim and the others walked out of the booth.

'Where shall we go now?' asked Skarp-Hedin.

'Home to our booth,' said Asgrim.

'Back to our booth, tired of begging,' said Skarp-Hedin.

* By Icelandic reckoning, eighteen feet. Translators' note.

Asgrim turned to him and said, 'You were rather too ready with your tongue in some places, but where Thorkel was concerned I think you gave him just what he deserved.'

They returned to their booth and told Njal everything that had happened.

'Fate will take its own course,' said Njal.

Gudmund the Powerful was told of Skarp-Hedin's encounter with Thorkel, and said, 'You all know how things went between us and the Ljosawater men; but I never suffered anything like the humiliation at their hands that Thorkel did from Skarp-Hedin. This is excellent.'

He turned to his brother, Einar Thværing, and said, 'Take all my men and give your support to the Njalssons when the court sits. And if they need any help next summer, I shall give them support myself.'

Einar agreed, and sent word to Asgrim.

'There are not many chieftains like Gudmund,' said Asgrim. Then he told Njal.

121

NEXT day, Asgrim and the others held a meeting with Gizur the White, Hjalti Skeggjason, and Einar Thværing. Mord Valgardsson was also present; he had by then withdrawn from the legal action and assigned it to the Sigfussons.

Asgrim said, 'I am addressing you first, Gizur and Hjalti and Einar, to let you know how our case stands. As you know, it was Mord who began proceedings, but the fact of the matter is that Mord himself took part in the killing of Hoskuld; it was he who inflicted the wound which was never attributed to any known assailant. In my opinion, the prosecution case must clearly be invalidated on that account.'

'We must announce this at once,' said Hjalti.

Thorhall Asgrimsson said that it would be foolish to make this fact public before the court sat.

'What difference does it make?' asked Hjalti.

'If they find out right away that there was a flaw in the preliminaries,' replied Thorhall, 'they can salvage the case by sending someone home at once to repeat the procedures there and cite the neighbours for a second time to attend the Althing. That would make the proceedings correct.'

'You are a shrewd man, Thorhall,' they said. 'We shall follow your advice.' They went back to their booths.

The Sigfussons gave notice of their charges at the Law Rock, and made formal inquiry about the domicile and district of the defendants. The court was to sit on the Friday evening to hear the action.

Until then, the Althing remained quiet. Many people tried to bring about a reconciliation. Flosi was stubborn, but not so outspoken as some of the others. The situation looked unpromising.

Friday evening came, and the court sat. The whole Althing attended. Flosi and his men stood to the south of the Rangriver Court, accompanied by Hall of Sida, Runolf of Dale, and those others who had promised him support. To the north of the court stood Asgrim, Gizur the White, Hjalti, Einar Thveræing, and all their men. Meanwhile the Njalssons, Kari, Thorleif Crow, and Thorgrim the Mighty sat fully armed in their booth, a formidable group.

Njal had invited the judges to take their places. The Sigfussons now brought their action; they named witnesses, and called upon the Njalssons to hear their oath; then they took the oath and stated their charges. They led evidence that notice of the action had been given, called upon the nine neighbours to take their seats as a jury, and then invited the defence to challenge the jurymen.

Thorhall Asgrimsson named witnesses, and interdicted the jury from making a finding, on the ground that the man who had given notice of the action was himself in breach of the law and liable to outlawry.

'Whom do you mean?' asked Flosi.

Thorhall replied, 'Mord Valgardsson took part with the Njalssons in the killing of Hoskuld, and inflicted on him the wound which was never attributed to any known assailant when witnesses to the wounds were named. You cannot dispute the fact that your case is invalidated.'

122

THEN Njal stood up and spoke: 'I appeal to you, Hall of Sida and Flosi and all the Sigfussons and all our own men – do not go away until you have heard me out.'

They stayed, and Njal went on, 'It seems to me that this case has reached deadlock; and that is scarcely surprising, for it has grown from an evil seed. I want you all to know that I loved Hoskuld more dearly than my own sons; and when I learnt that he had been killed, it was as if the sweetest light of my eyes had been extinguished. I would rather have lost all my sons, to have Hoskuld still alive. And now I beg you, Hall of Sida, and you, Runolf of Dale, Gizur the White, and Einar Thveræing, and Haf the Wise – give me a chance to make settlement over this killing on behalf of my sons; and it is my desire that the arbitration be done by those who are best fitted to do it.'

Gizur and Einar and Haf, each in turn, spoke at length and urged Flosi to accept a settlement, promising him their friendship in return. Flosi did not appear unwilling, but made no promises.

Then Hall of Sida said to Flosi, 'Will you now keep your word, and grant me the favour you once promised me when I helped your kinsman Thorgrim Stout-Ketilsson to escape from the country after killing Halli the Red?'

'Indeed I shall, father-in-law,' said Flosi, 'for you would never ask anything of me that would not enhance my honour.'

'Then,' said Hall, 'I want you to accept a settlement quickly and let worthy men arbitrate, and thereby gain for yourself the friendship of all good men.'

Flosi said, 'I want you all to know that I shall comply with the wishes of my father-in-law, Hall of Sida, and other good men, and let six men from each side, lawfully nominated, arbitrate this case. It seems to me that Njal fully deserves that I should grant him this.'

Njal thanked them all, and the others who were present added their thanks and said that Flosi had done well.

Flosi said, 'I will now name my arbitrators. First of all I name my father-in-law, Hall of Sida, and then Ozur of Breid-river, Surt Asbjarnarson of Kirkby, Modolf Ketilsson of Asar, Haf the Wise, and Runolf of Dale. Everyone will agree that these men are the best fitted for this task amongst my supporters.'

Then he asked Njal to name his arbitrators. Njal stood up and said, 'First of all I name Asgrim Ellida-Grimsson, and then Hjalti Skeggjason, Gizur the White, Einar Thveræing, Snorri the Priest, and Gudmund the Powerful.'

After that, Njal and Flosi and the Sigfussons shook hands, and Njal pledged his word on behalf of his sons and Kari. It was agreed that these twelve men should arbitrate.

It would not be too much to say that the whole Althing was delighted at this.

Messengers were sent to Snorri and Gudmund, who were in their booths. It was decided that the arbitrators should sit in the Court of Legislature, and that all others should leave.

123

SNORRI THE PRIEST spoke. 'We are all here now,' he said, 'the twelve arbitrators to whom this case has been referred. I want to appeal to you all to create no difficulties that would stand in the way of a full settlement between the two sides.'

Gudmund asked, 'Is there any wish to impose either district outlawry or full exile?'

'No,' said Snorri, 'neither, for such sentences have often been disobeyed, and thus given rise only to further killings and further enmities. No, I suggest that we award such huge compensation that no man's death shall ever have been so costly in this land as Hoskuld's.'

His words were well received. They discussed it further, but could not agree which one of them should make the first proposal about the size of the compensation. Finally they drew lots, and it fell to Snorri to make a proposal.

'I do not intend to take any more time over this,' said Snorri. 'I shall tell you what my suggestion is. I think there should be treble compensation for Hoskuld's death, six hundred ounces of silver in all. It is now up to you to change this, if you think it too much or too little.'

They replied that they did not want to make any changes.

'And furthermore,' said Snorri, 'the whole sum must be paid up here at the Althing.'

Gizur said, 'I think that is hardly feasible; for they can scarcely have enough money with them here to pay it all.'

'I know what Snorri wants,' said Gudmund. 'He wants all of us arbitrators to contribute as much as we are generous enough to give, and many others will then do the same.'

Hall of Sida thanked him, and declared himself willing to give as much as the one who gave most. All the arbitrators then agreed to the proposal. After that they left; they decided that Hall of Sida should announce their assessment at the Law Rock.

The bell was rung, and everyone came to the Law Rock. Hall stood up and said, 'We have reached unanimous agreement on this case, and have decided on a sum of 600 ounces of silver. We arbitrators shall pay half of this amount, and the whole sum must be paid up here at the Althing. It is now my request to all those present, that everyone contribute something in the name of God.'

Everyone approved. Hall of Sida named witnesses to the settlement, that none should ever violate it. Njal thanked them for their arbitration. Skarp-Hedin stood nearby in silence, and grinned.

People left the Law Rock and went to their booths. The arbitrators brought to the farmers' churchyard the money they had promised to contribute. The Njalssons and Kari gave whatever they had with them, which amounted to a hundred ounces of silver. Njal added all the money he had, which came to another hundred ounces of silver. After that, all this money was carried to the Court of Legislature, and others gave so much that it was not a penny short.

Finally Njal took a silk cloak and a pair of boots and placed them on top of the pile.

Then Hall suggested that Njal should fetch his sons – 'and I shall go for Flosi, and both sides can exchange pledges of peace.'

Njal walked back to his booth and said to his sons, 'Now our case has been found a happy solution. We have been reconciled, and all the money is gathered together. Each side is now to go and pledge peace and good faith to the other. I want to ask of you now not to spoil all this in any way.'

Skarp-Hedin stroked his brow and grinned in reply. Then they all walked to the Court of Legislature.

Hall went to find Flosi and said, 'Come to the Court of Legislature now, for all the money has been paid in full and gathered into one place.'

Flosi asked the Sigfussons to come with him. They all left the booth and walked towards the court from the east, as Njal and his sons approached from the west. Skarp-Hedin moved over to the middle-bench and stood there.

Flosi entered the Court of Legislature to look at the money, and said, 'This is a great sum of good money, and handsomely paid, as was to be expected.'

Then he picked up the cloak * and asked whose contribution that might be. No one answered him. Again he waved the cloak and asked who had given it, and laughed; but still no one answered. Then he said, 'Does none of you really know who owned this garment? Or does none of you dare to tell me?'

'Who do you think gave it?' asked Skarp-Hedin.

'If you want to know,' said Flosi, 'I will tell you what I think. I think it was your father who gave it, "Old Beardless", for few can tell just by looking at him whether he is a man or woman.'

'It is wrong to mock him in his old age,' said Skarp-Hedin, 'and no real man has ever done that before. You can be quite

* In all probability a silk cloak was a highly decorative and expensive garment that could be worn by a man or a woman. It was not unusual for a gift to be added to the required sum, to set a seal of friendship on a settlement. The cloak's dual purpose must have suggested an insult to Flosi – particularly as the Njalssons had got off so lightly, financially, in the settlement (they only paid between them 100 ounces of silver, half the normal compensation for a man of standing). *Translators' note.*

sure that he is a man, for he has fathered sons on his wife; and we have let few of our kinsmen lie unavenged at our doors.'

He snatched the cloak away and tossed a pair of blue trousers at Flosi, saying that he would have greater need of them than a cloak.

'Why should I need them more?' asked Flosi.

Skarp-Hedin replied, 'You certainly will if you are, as I have heard, the mistress of the Svinafell Troll,* who uses you as a woman every ninth night.'

Then Flosi kicked the pile of money and said he would not take a penny of it; he said they would take no other compensation for Hoskuld than blood-vengeance. He refused to give or accept any pledges of peace, and said to the Sigfussons, 'Back to our booths. We shall stand or fall together.'

They went back to their booths.

Hall of Sida said, 'There are men of too much ill luck involved in this.'

Njal and his sons walked back to their booth.

'I have long had the feeling that this case would go badly for us,' he said, 'and so it has turned out.'

'Not at all,' said Skarp-Hedin. 'They will never have any legal grounds for prosecuting us.'

'Then,' said Njal, 'it will end in disaster for everyone.'

Those who had contributed the money talked about taking it back again. But Gudmund said, 'I shall never bring on myself the disgrace of taking back what I have given, either now or any other time.'

'That is well spoken,' they said. After that, no one wanted to take back his own contribution.

Snorri the Priest said, 'It is my advice that Gizur the White and Hjalti Skeggjason look after this money until the next Althing. I have a feeling that it will not be long before it will be needed.'

Hjalti took half the money into his keeping, and Gizur the rest. Then people went to their booths.

* Most of Skarp-Hedin's insults contain some imputation of perversion – an unforgivable taunt. This particular insinuation, that a man behaved like a woman every ninth night, was specifically forbidden in the laws, and must have been not uncommon. It occurs in two other sagas. *Translators' note.*

124

FLOSI summoned all his supporters to Almanna Gorge. When he arrived, his men were already there, a hundred in number.

Flosi asked the Sigfussons, 'What kind of help from me would you appreciate most?'

Gunnar Lambason replied, 'We shall never be satisfied until every one of the Njalssons is killed.'

'I give my promise to the Sigfussons,' said Flosi, 'never to abandon this cause until one side or the other is destroyed. I also want to know whether there is anyone here who is not willing to give his support.'

They all said that they would support the Sigfussons.

'Let every man come over to me,' said Flosi, 'and swear an oath never to withdraw from this cause.'

They all went up to Flosi and swore oaths.

'We shall also pledge by hand-clasp,' said Flosi, 'that anyone who backs out shall forfeit life and property.'

The following were the chieftains with Flosi: Kol, the son of Thorstein Broad-Paunch (and nephew of Hall of Sida); Hroald Ozurarson of Breidriver; Ozur, the son of Onund Trunk-Back; Thorstein Geirleifsson the Handsome; Glum Hildisson; Modolf Ketilsson; Thorir, the son of Thord Illugi of Mortongue; Kolbein and Egil, Flosi's kinsmen; Ketil Sigfusson and his brothers Mord, Thorkel, and Lambi; Grani Gunnarsson; Gunnar Lambason and his brother Sigurd; Ingjald of Keldur; and Hroar Hamundarson.

Flosi said to the Sigfussons, 'Choose yourselves a leader, the man you think best fitted for the task, for we must have one person to lead us.'

Ketil of Mork replied, 'If it were up to us brothers to decide, we would all choose you to lead us. There are many good reasons for this; you are descended from a great family, and you are a great chieftain yourself, shrewd and resolute. We also think that you would take best care of our interests in this.'

'It seems only reasonable that I agree to your request,' said

Flosi. 'I shall now tell you what course we should adopt. It is my advice that everyone ride home from the Althing and see to his farm during the summer while the hay-making is on; that is what I shall do myself, too. On the Sunday eight weeks before winter I shall have Mass sung for me at home and then ride west over Lomagnup Sand. Each of us is to take two horses. I shall not add to our number beyond those who have pledged themselves here, for our company is quite strong enough if no one lets us down. I shall ride all day Sunday and all night too, and by mid-evening of the second day of the week I shall be at Thrihyrning Ridges. By that time, all those who have pledged themselves to this cause should have arrived there; and if anyone who has joined is missing, he shall forfeit his life, if we have our way.'

Ketil asked, 'How will it be possible for you to leave your home on Sunday and reach Thrihyrning Ridges by the second day of the week?'

'I shall ride up from Skaptrivertongue and north of Eyjafells Glacier down to Godaland,' replied Flosi, 'and it can be done if I ride briskly. And now I shall tell you my whole plan; when we are all there, we shall ride to Bergthorsknoll with all our company and attack the Njalssons with fire and sword and not withdraw until they are all dead. You must keep this plan secret, for all our lives depend on it. Let us now take our horses and ride home.'

They all went back to their booths. Flosi ordered the horses to be saddled and they set off for home without waiting for anyone else. Flosi did not want to meet his father-in-law, Hall of Sida, for he was sure that Hall would discourage any drastic action.

Njal rode home from the Althing with his sons, and they all stayed at Bergthorsknoll that summer. Njal asked Kari whether he would be riding east at all to his farm at Dyrholmar.

'No, I shall not ride east,' replied Kari. 'Your sons and I shall stand or fall together.'

Njal thanked him, and said that this was what he had expected of him. There were nearly twenty-five able-bodied men at Bergthorsknoll all the time, including the servants.

One day Hrodny, the mother of Hoskuld Njalsson, came to Keldur. Her brother Ingjald welcomed her warmly; she did not return his greeting, but asked him to come outside with her. Ingjald went with her, and together they moved away from the farm. Then she clutched hold of him and they sat down.

'Is it true,' she asked, 'that you have sworn an oath to attack Njal and his sons and kill them?'

'Yes,' he replied, 'it is true.'

'How utterly despicable you are,' she said. 'Njal has saved you from outlawry three times.'

'The position now,' said Ingjald, 'is that if I do not, my own life is at stake.'

'No,' said Hrodny. 'You will live – and live to be called a man of honour, if you refuse to betray the man to whom you owe most.'

She took from her bag a tattered, blood-stained linen cap.

'This is the cap that Hoskuld Njalsson was wearing when they killed him,' she said. 'It seems to me less honourable for you to side with those who were involved in that.'

'Very well,' said Ingjald. 'I shall not join the attack on Njal, whatever the consequences; but I know that they will make trouble for me later.'

Hrodny said, 'You could do Njal a great service now if you tell him their plans.'

'I refuse to do that,' said Ingjald. 'I would be an object of contempt to all men if I revealed what they trusted me to keep secret. But it is manly to withdraw from this knowing well that vengeance will follow. However, tell Njal and his sons that they would be well advised to be on their guard all this summer and keep many men in the house.'

Hrodny went to Bergthorsknoll and told Njal this whole conversation. Njal thanked her and said that she had done well – 'for Ingjald is the last person who has any just cause to raise his hand against me.'

Hrodny went home, and Njal told his sons what had happened.

There was an old woman at Bergthorsknoll called Sæunn. She knew a lot about many things, and had second sight. She was very old by this time, and the Njalssons called her senile because she talked so much; but what she predicted often came true. One day she snatched up a cudgel and made her way round the house to a pile of chickweed that lay there, and started beating it and cursing it for the wretched thing that it was. Skarp-Hedin laughed at this, and asked her why she was so angry with the chickweed.

The old woman replied, 'This chickweed will be used as the kindling when they burn Njal and my foster-child Bergthora inside the house. Quickly, take it away and throw it into some water or burn it.'

'No,' said Skarp-Hedin, 'for if that is what is ordained, something else will be found to kindle the fire even if this chickweed is not here.'

The old woman kept nagging them all summer to take the chickweed indoors, but they never got round to doing it.

125

AT Reykir in Skeid lived a man called Runolf Thorsteinsson, who had a son called Hildiglum. On the Sunday night twelve weeks before winter, Hildiglum was outside the house; then he heard a tremendous crash, and the earth and the sky seemed to quiver. He looked to the west, and thought he saw a ring of fire with a man on a grey horse inside the circle, riding furiously. He rushed past Hildiglum with a blazing firebrand held aloft, so close that Hildiglum could see him distinctly; he was as black as pitch, and Hildiglum heard him roaring out:

> 'I ride a horse
> With icy mane,
> Forelock dripping,
> Evil-bringing.
> Fire at each end,
> And poison in the middle,
> Flosi's plans
> Are like this flying firebrand –
> Flosi's plans
> Are like this flying firebrand.'

Before Hildiglum's eyes, it seemed, the rider hurled the firebrand east towards the mountains; a vast fire erupted, blotting the mountains from sight. The rider rode east towards the flames and vanished into them.

Hildiglum returned to the house and went to his bed, where he fainted and lay unconscious for a long time. When he recovered he could remember every detail of the apparition he had seen, and told his father about it. His father asked him to tell it to Hjalti Skeggjason.

Hildiglum went to Hjalti and told him. Hjalti said, 'You have seen the witch-ride, and that is always a portent of disaster.'

126

Two months before the beginning of winter, Flosi made ready for his journey west, and summoned all those men who had promised to make it with him. They all came to Svinafell, each with two horses and good weapons, and stayed there overnight. Early on Sunday morning Flosi had matins said and then sat down to table. He told each member of the household what work was to be done during his absence, and then went to his horses.

Flosi and his company set off west towards Sand. He warned them not to ride too hard at first, saying that they would have enough of that to do before the journey's end. He said that all should wait for anyone who had to drop back. They rode west to the Skogar District and reached Kirkby, where Flosi asked all his men to attend church and pray.

They did so. Then they remounted and rode up into the mountains, passing Fiskiwaters on the west side and then heading due west for Sand, keeping Eyjafells Glacier on their left. From there they descended to Godaland and on to Markar River, and reached Thrihyrning Ridges early in the afternoon of the second day. They waited there until mid-evening, by which time everyone had arrived except Ingjald of Keldur. The Sigfussons denounced him, but Flosi told them not to abuse him in his absence – 'we shall pay him back later, nonetheless.'

127

MEANWHILE, over at Bergthorsknoll, Grim and Helgi were away on a visit to Holar, where their children were being fostered; they had told Njal that they would not be back that night. They spent the whole day at Holar.

Some beggarwomen came there, who claimed to have travelled a long way; the brothers asked them what news they had, and they replied that they had none to speak of, apart from one thing that had seemed unusual.

The Njalssons asked what that might be, and told them to keep nothing back. They agreed.

'We have just come down from Fljotshlid,' said the women, 'and there we saw all the Sigfussons riding fully-armed, making for Thrihyrning Ridges; they were in a group of fifteen. We also saw Grani Gunnarsson and Gunnar Lambason, in a group of five, all heading the same way. One might say that everyone is on the go these days.'

Helgi Njalsson said, 'In that case, Flosi must have arrived from the east, and they will all be going to join him. Grim and I ought now to be with Skarp-Hedin.'

Grim agreed, and they set off home.

At Bergthorsknoll, Bergthora was saying to the members of her household, 'You are all to choose your favourite food to-night, for this is the last evening on which I shall serve a meal for my household.'

Those who heard her denied this strenuously.

'It shall be so, nevertheless,' she replied, 'and I could tell you much more if I wished to; but let it suffice as proof, that Grim and Helgi will be home tonight before this meal is over. If that comes true, the rest of what I have said will come true.'

After that, she brought food to the table.

Suddenly Njal said, 'How strange! I seem to see all four corners of the room before my eyes, and both the gable-walls are down, and there is blood all over the table and the food.'

Everyone was greatly perturbed except Skarp-Hedin, who told them that they must not wail or do anything disgraceful that people would talk about afterwards – 'for our behaviour will be judged by stricter standards than that of others, and that is as it should be.'

Grim and Helgi arrived home before the tables were taken away, and everyone was greatly taken aback. Njal asked why they had been in such a hurry to return, and they told him what they had heard.

Njal told everyone not to go to bed that night.

128

MEANWHILE, Flosi was saying to his men, 'We shall now ride to Bergthorsknoll, to reach there by nightfall.'

When they arrived, they rode into a hollow in the knoll,* where they tethered their horses and waited late into the night.

'Now we shall walk slowly up to the house,' said Flosi, 'keeping close together, and see what they do.'

Njal was standing outside with his sons and Kari and all the servants ranged in front of the house. They were nearly thirty in all.

Flosi halted and said, 'We shall note carefully what action they take, for I suspect that we shall never get the better of them if they stay out of doors.'

'This would turn out a sorry trip if we did not dare to make an attack on them,' said Grani.

'We shall certainly attack them,' said Flosi, 'even though they remain outside. But we would have to pay a heavy price, and not many would live to tell the tale, whichever side wins.'

Njal said to his men, 'How many do you think they are?'

'They are a tightly-knit force,' said Skarp-Hedin, 'and strong in numbers, too; but they suspect that they will have a hard task to overcome us, and that is why they have halted.'

'I do not think so,' said Njal. 'I want everyone to go inside, for they found it hard to overcome Gunnar of Hlidarend, even though he was only one against many. This house is just as

* There certainly is no hollow there today capable of concealing a hundred men and two hundred horses, and there probably never was. *Translators' note.*

strongly built as his was, and they will never be able to overcome us.'

'That is the wrong way to look at it,' said Skarp-Hedin. 'The men who attacked Gunnar were chieftains of such character that they would have preferred to turn back rather than burn him in his house. But these people will not hesitate to use fire if they cannot overcome us in any other way, for they will resort to any means to destroy us. They will assume, and quite rightly, that it will cost them their lives if we escape. And I for one am reluctant to be suffocated like a fox in its den.'

Njal said, 'Now you are going to override my advice and show me disrespect, my sons – and not for the first time. But when you were younger you did not do so, and things went better for you then.'

'Let us do as our father wishes,' said Helgi. 'That will be best for all of us.'

'I am not so sure of that,' said Skarp-Hedin, 'for he is a doomed man now. But still I do not mind pleasing my father by burning in the house with him, for I am not afraid of dying.'

To Kari he said, 'Let us all keep close together, brother-in-law, so that we do not get separated.'

'That is what I had intended,' said Kari, 'but if fate wills it otherwise, then it shall be so and nothing can be done about it.'

'Then you avenge us,' said Skarp-Hedin. 'And we shall avenge you if we survive.'

Kari agreed. Then they all went inside and stood guard at the doors.

Flosi said, 'Now they are doomed, for they have gone indoors. We shall advance on the house at once and form up in strength round the doors to make sure that not one of them escapes, neither Kari nor the Njalssons; for otherwise it will cost us our lives.'

Flosi and his men came up to the house and surrounded the whole building, in case there might be a secret door somewhere. Flosi himself and his own men went up to the front of the house. Hroald Ozurarson rushed at Skarp-Hedin and lunged at him with a spear; Skarp-Hedin hacked the spear-shaft in two and sprang at him, swinging his axe. The axe fell on Hroald's shield and dashed it against him; the upper horn of the axe caught him full in the face, and he fell back dead at once.

Kari said, 'There is no escaping you, Skarp-Hedin; you are the bravest of us all.'

'I don't know about that,' said Skarp-Hedin, and he was seen to draw back his lips in a grin.

Kari and Grim and Helgi lunged often with their spears and wounded many men, and Flosi and the attackers were kept at bay.

Flosi said, 'We have suffered heavy losses amongst our men, several wounded and one dead, the one we would least have wanted to lose. It is obvious that we cannot defeat them with weapons; and there are many here who are showing less fight than they said they would. Now we must resort to another plan. There are only two courses open to us, neither of them good: we must either abandon the attack, which would cost us our own lives, or we must set fire to the house and burn them to death, which is a grave responsibility before God, since we are Christian men ourselves. But that is what we must do.'

129

THEN they kindled a fire and made a great blaze in front of the doors.

Skarp-Hedin said, 'So you're making a fire now, lads! Are you thinking of doing some cooking?'

'Yes,' said Grani, 'and you won't need it any hotter for roasting.'

'So this is your way,' said Skarp-Hedin, 'of repaying me for avenging your father, the only way you know; you value more highly the obligation that has less claim on you.'

The women threw whey on the flames and doused the fire.

Kol Thorsteinsson said to Flosi, 'I have an idea. I have noticed that there is a loft above the cross-beams of the main room. That is where we should start a fire, and we can use the heap of chickweed behind the house as kindling.'

They brought the chickweed up and set fire to it, and before those inside knew what was happening, the ceiling of the room was ablaze from end to end. Flosi's men also lit huge fires in front of all the doors. At this, the womenfolk began to panic.

Njal said to them, 'Be of good heart and speak no words of fear, for this is just a passing storm and it will be long before another like it comes. Put your faith in the mercy of God, for He will not let us burn both in this world and the next.'

Such were the words of comfort he brought them, and others more rousing than these.

Now the whole house began to blaze. Njal went to the door and said, 'Is Flosi near enough to hear my words?'

Flosi said that he could hear him.

Njal said, 'Would you consider making an agreement with my sons, or letting anyone leave the house?'

'I will make no terms with your sons,' replied Flosi. 'We shall settle matters now, once and for all, and we are not leaving until every one of them is dead. But I shall allow the women and children and servants to come out.'

Njal went back inside the house and said to his household, 'All those with permission to go out must do so now. Leave the house now, Thorhalla Asgrim's-daughter, and take with you all those who are allowed to go.'

Thorhalla said, 'This is not the parting from Helgi I had ever expected; but I shall urge my father and my brothers to avenge the killings that are committed here.'

'You will do well,' said Njal, 'for you are a good woman.'

She went out, taking many people with her.

Astrid of Djupriverbank said to Helgi, 'Come out with me. I will drape you in a woman's cloak and put a head-scarf over you.'

Helgi protested at first, but finally yielded to their entreaties. Astrid wrapped a scarf round his head, and Thorhild laid the cloak over his shoulders. Then he walked out between them, along with his sisters Thorgerd and Helga and several other people.

When Helgi came outside, Flosi said, 'That's a very tall and broad-shouldered woman – seize her.' When Helgi heard this, he threw off the cloak; he was carrying a sword under his arm, and now he struck out at one of the men, slicing off the bottom of the shield and severing his leg. Then Flosi came up and struck at Helgi's neck, cutting off his head with one blow.

Flosi went up to the door and called Njal and Bergthora over to speak to him; when they came, he said, 'I want to offer you leave to come out, for you do not deserve to burn.'

'I have no wish to go outside,' said Njal, 'for I am an old man now and ill-equipped to avenge my sons; and I do not want to live in shame.'

Flosi said to Bergthora, 'You come out, Bergthora, for under no circumstances do I want you to burn.'

Bergthora replied, 'I was given to Njal in marriage when young, and I have promised him that we would share the same fate.'

Then they both went back inside.

'What shall we do now?' asked Bergthora.

'Let us go to our bed,' said Njal, 'and lie down.'

Then Bergthora said to little Thord, Kari's son, 'You are to be taken out. You are not to burn.'

The boy replied, 'But that's not what you promised, grandmother. You said that we would never be parted; and so it shall be, for I would much prefer to die beside you both.'

She carried the boy to the bed. Njal said to his steward, 'Take note where we lay ourselves down and how we dispose ourselves, for I shall not move from here however much the smoke or flames distress me. Then you can know where to look for our remains.'

The steward said he would.

An ox had recently been slaughtered, and the hide was lying nearby. Njal told the steward to spread the hide over them, and he promised to do so.

Njal and Bergthora lay down on the bed and put the boy between them. Then they crossed themselves and the boy, and commended their souls to God. These were the last words they were heard to speak. The steward took the hide and spread it over them, and then left the house. Ketil of Mork seized his arm and dragged him clear, and questioned him closely about his father-in-law Njal; the steward told him everything that had happened.

Ketil said, 'Great sorrow has been allotted us, that we should all share such terrible ill luck.'

Skarp-Hedin had seen his father go to lie down and the preparations he had made.

'Father is going early to bed,' he said. 'And that is only natural, for he is an old man.'

Skarp-Hedin and Kari and Grim snatched up the blazing brands as soon as they fell and hurled them at those outside. After a while the attackers threw spears at them, which they caught in flight and hurled back. Flosi told his men to stop – 'for we shall always come off worse in every exchange of blows with them. You would be wiser to wait until the fire conquers them.'

They did as he said.

Now the main beams fell down from the roof.

Skarp-Hedin said, 'My father must be dead now, and not a groan or a cough has been heard from him.'

They went over to the far end of the room. One end of the cross-beam had fallen there, and it was almost burned through in the middle. Kari said to Skarp-Hedin, 'Use that beam to jump out, and I shall give you a hand and come right behind you. That way we can both escape, for the smoke is all drifting in this direction.'

'You go first,' said Skarp-Hedin, 'and I shall follow you at once.'

'That is not wise,' said Kari, 'for I can go out some other way if this does not succeed.'

'No,' said Skarp-Hedin, 'you go out first, and I shall be right on your heels.'

Kari said, 'It is every man's instinct to try to save his own life, and I shall do so now. But this parting will mean that we shall never see each other again. Once I jump out of the flames, I shall not feel inclined to run back into the fire to you; and then each of us must go his own way.'

'I shall laugh, brother-in-law, if you escape,' said Skarp-Hedin, 'for you will avenge us all.'

Kari took hold of a blazing brand and ran up the sloping cross-beam; he hurled the brand down from the wall at those who were in his way outside, and they scattered. Kari's clothes and hair were on fire by now, as he threw himself down off the wall and dodged away in the thick of the smoke.

Someone said, 'Was that a man jumping down from the roof?'

268

'Far from it,' said someone else. 'It was Skarp-Hedin throwing another brand at us.'

After that, no one suspected anything.

Kari ran until he reached a small stream; he threw himself into it and extinguished his blazing clothes. From there he ran under cover of the smoke until he reached a hollow, where he rested. It has ever since been called Kari's Hollow.

130

MEANWHILE, Skarp-Hedin had jumped on to the cross-beam directly behind Kari, but when he reached that part of the beam which was most severely burned, it broke beneath him. Skarp-Hedin managed to land on his feet and made a second attempt at once, by taking a run at the wall. But the roof-beam came down on him and he toppled back once more.

'It is clear now what is to be,' said Skarp-Hedin, and made his way along the side wall.

Gunnar Lambason jumped up on to the wall and saw Skarp-Hedin. 'Are you crying now, Skarp-Hedin?' he asked.

'No,' said Skarp-Hedin, 'but it is true that my eyes are smarting. Am I right in thinking that you are laughing?'

'I certainly am,' said Gunnar, 'and for the first time since you killed Thrain.'

'Then here is something to remind you of it,' said Skarp-Hedin.

He took from his purse the jaw-tooth he had hacked out of Thrain, and hurled it straight at Gunnar's eye; the eye was gouged from its socket on to the cheek, and Gunnar toppled off the wall.

Skarp-Hedin went over to his brother Grim. They joined hands and stamped on the fire. But when they reached the middle of the room, Grim fell dead. Skarp-Hedin went to the gable-end of the house; then, with a great crash, the whole roof fell in. Skarp-Hedin was pinned between roof and gable, and could not move an inch.

Flosi and his men stayed by the blaze until broad daylight.

Then a man came riding towards them. Flosi asked him his name, and he replied that he was Geirmund, a kinsman of the Sigfussons.

'You have taken drastic action here,' said Geirmund.

'People will call it a drastic action, and an evil one too,' said Flosi. 'But nothing can be done about it now.'

Geirmund asked, 'How many people of note have perished here?'

Flosi said, 'Among the dead here are Njal and Bergthora, their sons Helgi, Grim, and Skarp-Hedin, Kari Solmundarson and his son Thord, and Thord Freedman. We are not sure about those others who are less well known to us.'

'You have listed amongst the dead a man who to my certain knowledge has escaped,' said Geirmund, 'for I talked to him only this morning.'

'Who is that?' asked Flosi.

'Kari Solmundarson,' said Geirmund. 'My neighbour Bard and I met him with his hair burnt off and his clothes badly charred, and Bard lent him a horse.'

'Had he any weapons with him?' asked Flosi.

'He was carrying the sword "Life-Taker",' said Geirmund, 'and one of its edges was blue and discoloured. We said that the metal must have softened, but Kari replied that he would soon harden it again in the blood of the Sigfussons and the other Burners.'

'What did he tell you of Skarp-Hedin and Grim?' asked Flosi.

'He said that they were both alive when he left them,' replied Geirmund, 'but that they must be dead by now.'

'What you have told us,' said Flosi, 'gives us little hope of being left in peace; for the man who has escaped is the one who comes nearest to being the equal of Gunnar of Hlidarend in everything. You had better realize, you Sigfussons and all the rest of our men, that this Burning will have such consequences that many of us will lie lifeless and others will forfeit all their wealth.

'I suspect that none of you Sigfussons will now dare to stay on at your farms, and I certainly cannot blame you for that. So I invite you all to stay with me in the east, and let us all stand or fall together.' They thanked him.

Then Modolf Ketilsson said:

> *'One pillar of Njal's house*
> *Was not destroyed in the fire*
> *That devoured all the others,*
> *The fire the bold Sigfussons lit.*
> *Now at last, Njal,*
> *Brave Hoskuld's death is avenged;*
> *Fire swept through the building,*
> *Bright flames blossomed in the house.'*

'We must find other things to boast about than burning Njal to death,' said Flosi, 'for there is no achievement in that.'

Flosi climbed on to the gable wall with Glum Hildisson and several others.

'Is Skarp-Hedin dead yet, do you think?' asked Glum.

The others said that he must have been dead for some time.

The fire still burned fitfully, flaring up and sinking again. Then they heard this verse being uttered somewhere down amongst the flames:

> *'The woman will find it hard*
> *To stop the cloudburst of her tears*
> *At this outcome*
> *Of the warrior's last battle. . . .'* *

Grani Gunnarsson said, 'Was Skarp-Hedin alive or dead when he spoke that verse?'

'I shall not make any guesses about that,' replied Flosi.

Grani said, 'Let us look for Skarp-Hedin and the others who were burned to death in there.'

'No,' said Flosi, 'and only stupid men like you would make such a suggestion, at a time when forces must be gathering throughout the district; and he who lingers here will be so terrified that he will not know which way to run. It is my advice that we all ride away as quickly as possible.'

Flosi and all his men hurried to their horses. Flosi asked Geirmund, 'Is Ingjald at home at Keldur?'

Geirmund said that he expected so.

'That is the man who has broken all his oaths and faith with us,' said Flosi. 'What do you want to do with him?' he asked

---

* The text of the rest of the stanza is too garbled to be intelligible. *Translators' note.*

the Sigfussons. 'Do you want to let him off, or shall we go for him and kill him?'

They all replied that they wanted to attack him. Flosi and the others jumped on their horses and rode off. Flosi was in the lead. He headed for Rang River and up along the bank. Then he saw a man come riding down on the other side of the river, and recognized Ingjald of Keldur. Flosi shouted to him; Ingjald halted and turned to face them.

Flosi said to him, 'You have broken our agreement, and have thereby forfeited life and property. The Sigfussons are here, and want to kill you. But I can see that you were in a difficult position, and I am prepared to spare your life if you give me self-judgement.'

'I shall ride to join Kari sooner than give you self-judgement,' said Ingjald. 'And my answer to the Sigfussons is that I shall not be more afraid of them than they are of me.'

'Stay where you are then,' said Flosi, 'if you are not a coward, and I will send you a present.'

'I shall not move an inch,' said Ingjald.

Thorstein Kolbeinsson, Flosi's nephew, rode up carrying a spear; he was one of the bravest and most respected men in Flosi's band. Flosi took the spear from him and hurled it at Ingjald; it came at him from the left, and struck his shield just below the handle. The shield split, and the spear went right through Ingjald's thigh and sank into the saddle-tree.

Flosi said to Ingjald, 'Did that touch you?'

'It did,' said Ingjald, 'but I call that only a scratch, not a wound.'

Ingjald wrenched the spear from his thigh and said to Flosi, 'Now you stay still if you are not a coward.'

He hurled the spear back across the river. Flosi saw the spear coming straight at his waist and pulled his horse back. The spear flew past in front of him and missed, but struck Thorstein Kolbeinsson in the waist. Thorstein fell from his horse, dead. Ingjald galloped off into the woods and made his escape.

Flosi said to his men, 'We have suffered a great loss already; and this is enough to make us realize that ill luck is on our side. It is my advice now that we ride to Thrihyrning Ridges; we can watch from there any movements in the district, for they will have gathered a huge force against us by now. They will assume that we have ridden east to Fljotshlid from Thrihyrning Ridges, and will expect us to be riding north to the mountains and from there to the eastern districts. Most of their forces will go that way, but some of them will take the coast route east to Seljalandsmull, although they will think it less likely to find us there. But my plan is that we ride up into Thrihyrning Mountain and wait there until sunset on the third day.'

They did this.

131

Now the saga returns to Kari. He left the hollow and walked until he met Bard, and they talked together in the way Geirmund had described to Flosi. From there Kari rode to see Mord Valgardsson, and told him what had happened. Mord was loud in his lamentation, but Kari said that there were more manly things than weeping for the dead, and asked him to gather forces and bring them all to Holtsford.

Then he set off for Thjorsriverdale to see Hjalti Skeggjason. As he was riding along Thjors River, he noticed a man riding hard in pursuit. He waited for him, and saw that it was Ingjald of Keldur, his thigh covered with blood. Kari asked him who had wounded him. Ingjald told him.

'Where did you two meet?' asked Kari.

'At Rang River,' replied Ingjald. 'He threw a spear across the river at me.'

'Did you not retaliate?' asked Kari.

'I threw the spear back,' said Ingjald, 'and they said that a man had been struck by it and killed.'

'Did you not see who it was?'

'It looked to me like Thorstein Kolbeinsson, Flosi's nephew,' replied Ingjald.

'May your hands prosper,' said Kari.

They rode off together to see Hjalti Skeggjason, and told him what had happened at Bergthorsknoll. Hjalti was appalled at the news, and said that it was imperative to pursue them and kill every one of them. He gathered forces, summoning every

273

available man, and they rode off at once with Kari to join Mord Valgardsson. They met at Holtsford, where Mord was already waiting with a large force.

They split up to search. Some rode the coast route east to Seljalandsmull, some went up to Fljotshlid, and others went further up round Thrihyrning Ridges and from there down to Godaland and north all the way to Sand. Some rode as far as Fiskiwaters before turning back; others rode east along the coast to Holt, where they told Thorgeir Skorar-Geir what had happened and asked whether the Burners had ridden past.

Thorgeir said, 'I may not be much of a chieftain, but Flosi would have more sense than to ride past in front of my eyes just after killing my uncle Njal and my cousins. The only thing you can do is to turn back, for you have been searching much too far afield. But tell Kari to ride here and stay with me, if he wishes; and if he does not want to come east, I shall look after his farm at Dyrholmar if he likes. Tell him that I shall give him all support and ride to the Althing. As he knows, the duty of taking action over these deaths belongs to us brothers; we intend to enforce outlawry if we can, and follow that up with blood vengeance. But I will not accompany you now, for I know that nothing can be done at present; they will be very much on their guard now.'

They rode back and met the others at Hof. They all felt that they had brought disgrace on themselves by failing to find the Burners. Mord disagreed. Many of them urged that they should go to Fljotshlid and seize the property of all those who had taken part in the Burning. The decision was left to Mord, and he called the plan extremely ill-advised. They asked him why he said that.

'If their farms are left intact,' replied Mord, 'they will visit them and their womenfolk, and we shall be able to hunt them down there after a while. You must not for a moment doubt my complete loyalty to Kari, for my own safety is involved too.'

Hjalti told Mord to keep to his promises. He invited Kari to stay with him, and Kari agreed to go there for the time being. Kari was also told what Thorgeir had offered; he replied that he would take advantage of the offer later, and that he would feel confident indeed if there were many like Thorgeir.

Then they dispersed their forces.

Flosi and his men saw everything that was happening from their vantage point up on the mountain. Flosi said, 'We shall take our horses and ride away, for it is safe to do so now.'

The Sigfussons asked if they would be safe to go to their farms and give some orders about the work there.

'Mord will be expecting you to visit your womenfolk,' replied Flosi. 'I imagine that it is on his advice that your farms are not being plundered. My advice is that no one should go off on his own, and that you all ride east with me.'

They all followed his advice and rode off, north of the glacier and then east to Svinafell. Flosi at once sent off men to gather supplies, so that there should be no lack of anything.

Flosi never boasted of what they had done; nor did he ever show a trace of fear. He stayed at home that winter until Christmas.

132

KARI asked Hjalti to go with him to search for Njal's bones – 'for everyone will accept your account and your impressions.'

Hjalti readily agreed to go, and to bring Njal's remains to church.

They set off, fifteen in all, and rode east over Thjors River, where they summoned others to accompany them until they numbered a hundred, including Njal's neighbours.

They reached Bergthorsknoll at noon. Hjalti asked Kari whereabouts under the ruins Njal's body would be lying, and Kari showed them. They dug through a deep layer of ashes, and underneath they found the ox-hide; the flames had shrivelled it. They lifted it up, and found Njal and Bergthora lying there, quite unmarked by the flames. They all gave praise to God for this, and thought it a great miracle. Then they lifted up the boy who had been lying between them; one finger, which he had stretched out from under the hide, had been burned off.

Njal and Bergthora were carried out, and everyone came up to see the bodies.

'How do these bodies impress you?' asked Hjalti.

'We would rather hear your verdict first,' they replied.

'I shall put it into plain words,' said Hjalti. 'I think that Berg-thora's body is rather better preserved than could have been expected; but Njal's countenance and body appear to have a radiance which I have never seen on a dead man before.'

They all agreed.

Then they looked for Skarp-Hedin. The servants showed them the place where Flosi and his men had heard the verse uttered. The roof had collapsed there beside the gable wall, and that was where Hjalti told them to dig. They did so, and found the body of Skarp-Hedin. He had held himself upright against the wall; his legs were almost burnt off below the knees, but the rest of him was unburnt. He had bitten hard on his lip. His eyes were open but not swollen. He had driven his axe into the gable with such violence that half the full depth of the blade was buried in the wall, and the metal had not softened. His body was carried out, with the axe. Hjalti picked up the axe and said, 'This is a rare weapon. Few could wield it.'

'I know the man to wield it,' said Kari.

'Who is that?' asked Hjalti.

'Thorgeir Skorar-Geir,' replied Kari. 'He is the outstanding member of that family now.'

They stripped Skarp-Hedin's body, for the clothes had not been burnt off. He had crossed his arms, with the right one over the left. They found two marks on his body, one between the shoulders, the other on his chest, both of them burn-marks in the shape of a cross; they came to the conclusion that he had branded them on himself. They all agreed that they found it less uncomfortable to see Skarp-Hedin dead than they had expected; for no one felt any fear of him.

They searched for Grim, and found his remains in the middle of the main room. Opposite him, under the side wall, they found Thord Freedman, and in the weaving-room they found the old woman Sæunn and three other people. They found the remains of eleven people in all.

They took all the bodies to church. Hjalti then rode home, and Kari went with him.

Ingjald's wounded leg swelled up, and he came to Hjalti, who healed it for him. But for the rest of his life Ingjald walked with a limp.

Kari rode to Tongue to see Asgrim. Thorhalla had already

gone back there and told the news. Asgrim received Kari with
open arms and invited him to stay there for that year. Kari
said he would. Asgrim also invited all the people who had been
living at Bergthorsknoll. Kari said that it was a generous offer –
'and I accept it on their behalf.' The whole household moved
over to Tongue.

Thorhall Asgrimsson was so shocked when he heard that his
foster-father, Njal, had been burned to death, that his whole
body swelled up; a stream of blood spouted from his ears and
could not be staunched, until he fell down unconscious and the
flow ceased of its own accord. Then he got up and said that he
had not behaved like a man. 'My only wish now is to take
vengeance for what has just happened to me upon those who
burned Njal to death.'

The others said that no one would call his behaviour disgraceful; but Thorhall replied that no one could stop people
talking.

Asgrim asked Kari what support he could rely on from east
of the rivers. Kari said that Mord Valgardsson and Hjalti Skeggjason would give him whatever help they could, and also Thorgeir Skorar-Geir and his brothers. Asgrim said that it was a
formidable force.

'What support can we expect from you?' asked Kari.

'All that I can possibly give,' said Asgrim, 'and to that I
pledge my life.'

'Do so,' said Kari.

'I have also enlisted Gizur the White's help,' said Asgrim,
'and asked him how we should go about this.'

'Good,' said Kari. 'What did he advise?'

'He suggested that we let things rest until spring,' replied
Asgrim, 'and then ride east and start proceedings against Flosi
for the killing of Helgi; cite the neighbours to attend the
Althing, give notice of the actions for the Burning, and cite the
same neighbours to be your jurymen. I also asked Gizur who
should bring the manslaughter action, and Gizur said that Mord
should do it, even though he is unwilling. He said, "Mord must
bear the brunt, for he has behaved worst in all this; Kari is
always to be angry with him whenever they meet, and that,
combined with other pressures that I intend to apply, will
drive him into it." '

Kari said, 'We shall follow your advice for as long as you care to give us the benefit of your leadership.'

It is said of Kari that he could not sleep at nights. Asgrim woke up once and heard that Kari was still awake. Asgrim asked, 'Does sleep come hard to you at nights?'

Kari replied:

> *'Sleep is denied my eyes*
> *Throughout the night,*
> *For I cannot forget*
> *That great shield of a man;*
> *Ever since the warriors*
> *With the blazing swords*
> *Burned Njal in his house,*
> *I cannot forget my grief.'*

Kari spoke of no one so often as of Njal and Skarp-Hedin. He never spoke ill of his enemies, and never uttered threats against them.

133

ONE night at Svinafell, Flosi was restless in his sleep. Glum Hildisson roused him, but it was a long time before Flosi awoke. He asked Glum to fetch Ketil of Mork.

When Ketil came, Flosi said, 'I want to tell you my dream.'

'By all means,' said Ketil.

'I dreamed,' said Flosi, 'that I was at Lomagnup. I went outside, and as I looked up towards the cliffs they opened, and a man came out of them. He was wearing a goat-skin and carried an iron staff in his hand. He was shouting, calling to my men several at a time, summoning them by name. First he called Grim the Red and Arni Kolsson; then, strangely enough, he called Eyjolf Bolverksson and Ljot, Hall of Sida's son, and some half dozen others. He paused for a while; then he called five more of my followers, and among them were the Sigfussons, your brothers. Then he called another five men, including Lambi and Modolf and Glum. Then he called three more. Finally he called Gunnar Lambason and Kol Thorsteinsson.

'Then he came up to me. I asked him his news. He said that he would tell me. I also asked him his name; he replied that he was called Iron-Grim. I asked where he was intending to go, and he replied that he was on his way to the Althing.

' "What are you going to do there?" I asked.

'He replied, "First I shall clear the jury, and then the court, and then the field for battle."

'Then he said :

> *"Soon a great warrior*
> *Will tower over the land,*
> *And you will see the ground*
> *Strewn with severed heads.*
> *The clamour of blue swords*
> *Will echo in the hills;*
> *The dew of blood*
> *Will lace the limbs of men."*

'He struck the ground with his staff, and there was a great crash. He walked back into the cliffs, and I was overcome with dread. And now I want you to tell me what you think is the meaning of my dream.'

'I have a premonition,' said Ketil, 'that all those who were called are doomed men. I think it advisable that we tell no one of this dream for the time being.'

Flosi agreed.

And so the winter months passed. After Christmas, Flosi said to his men, 'I think we should now leave Svinafell, for I feel that we can have little respite now. Let us go in search of support; and you will now learn the truth of what I once said, that we should be forced to grovel for help at the feet of many men before all this is ended.'

134

THEY all made ready to leave. Flosi was wearing breeches with stockings attached because he intended going on foot; he knew that this would make it less irksome for those who had to walk. They went first to Knappavoll, reached Breidriver the next evening, and from there went on to Kalfafell, then to Bjarnaness in Hornafjord, then Stafafell, in Lon, and from there to Thvattriver to see Hall of Sida; Flosi was married to Hall's daughter, Steinvor.

Hall welcomed them warmly. Flosi said, 'I want to ask you, father-in-law, to accompany me to the Althing with all the men you can call on.'

'Now the old saying is proved, that the hand is soon sorry that it struck,' said Hall, 'for those men in your following who now hang their heads are the very ones who urged you on to evil. As for my support, I am under obligation to provide you with as much help as I can.'

'What do you think I should do,' asked Flosi, 'as things now stand?'

'Go north all the way to Vopnafjord,' replied Hall, 'asking every chieftain for support; you will have need of them all yet before this Althing is over.'

Flosi rested there for three days. Then he travelled east to Geitahellur and on to Berufjord, where he and his men stayed the night. From there they went east to Heydale, in Breiddale, to the home of Hallbjorn the Strong, who was married to Oddny, the sister of Sorli Brodd-Helgason.

Here Flosi was well received. Hallbjorn had many questions to ask about the Burning; Flosi gave him an exact account of it all. Hallbjorn asked him how far north into the fjords he was planning to go; he replied that he was making for Vopnafjord. Then Flosi took a purse from his belt and said that he wished to give it to him. Hallbjorn took the money, but said that he had no cause to expect gifts from Flosi – 'I would, however, like to know how you want me to repay this.'

'I have no need of money,' said Flosi, 'but I would like you to ride to the Althing with me and give me your support – even though I have no claims on you through blood or marriage ties.'

'I give you my promise,' said Hallbjorn. 'I shall ride to the Althing and give you my support, as if you were my own brother.'

Flosi thanked him. From there he and his men travelled to Breiddale Heath and on to Hrafnkelstead, the home of Hrafnkel

Thorisson.* Flosi was well received there, and he asked for Hrafnkel's presence and support at the Althing. Hrafnkel was evasive for a long time, but eventually he promised that his son Thorir would go with all the men they had a call on, and would provide the same support as the other chieftains in the district.

Flosi thanked him, and then journeyed on to Bersastead, the home of Holmstein Spak-Bersason, who welcomed him warmly. Flosi asked for Holmstein's help. Holmstein replied that Flosi had long ago earned the right to that help.

From there he and his men went to Valthjofstead, the home of Sorli Brodd-Helgason, Bjarni's brother; Sorli was married to Thordis, the daughter of Gudmund the Powerful of Modruvellir.

Flosi and his men were well received there. The following morning, Flosi sounded Sorli about accompanying him to the Althing, and offered to pay him for it.

'I cannot say,' replied Sorli, 'until I know whose side my father-in-law, Gudmund the Powerful, is taking, for I shall be supporting him whatever side he is on.'

'I can see from your replies that you are under woman's rule here,' said Flosi. He rose to his feet and told his men to gather up their clothes and their weapons. Then they left, without any promise of help.

They passed the lower end of Lagarwater and travelled over the heath to Njardvik. Two brothers lived there, Thorkel the Sage and Thorvald, the sons of Ketil Thrym;† their mother was called Yngvild.‡ Flosi was well received there. He told them his mission, and asked for their support; at first they refused, and only finally agreed to help him when he had given them three marks of silver each.

Yngvild, their mother, was present, and when she heard them promise to ride to the Althing she started weeping.

'Why do you weep, mother?' asked Thorkel.

'I dreamed,' she replied, 'that your brother Thorvald was wearing a red tunic; and this tunic was so tight that it looked

* Hrafnkel was the son of Thorir, the son of Hrafnkel Hrafnsson.
† Ketil Thrym was the son of Thidrandi the Wise, the son of Ketil Thrym, the son of Thorir Thidrandi.
‡ Yngvild's father was also called Thorkel the Sage.

as if he had been sewn into it. He was also wearing red hose bound with shabby tapes. I was distressed to see him looking so uncomfortable, but I could not do anything to help him.'

They laughed and called it nonsense, and said that her babblings would not stop them riding to the Althing.

Flosi thanked them warmly. From there he travelled to Vopnafjord, and came to Hof, the home of Bjarni Brodd-Helgason.* Bjarni welcomed Flosi with open arms. Flosi offered him money for his support.

'I have never bartered my manhood or my support for bribes,' replied Bjarni. 'Now that you are in need of help, I shall treat you as a friend and ride to the Althing with you, and stand by you as I would by my own brother.'

'You are putting me completely in your debt,' said Flosi, 'but I had expected something like this of you.'

From there, Flosi went to Krossavik to see Thorkel Geitisson, who had always been a great friend of his. Flosi told him his mission; Thorkel replied that it was his duty to help Flosi with every means at his command and not to forsake his cause. And when they parted, Thorkel gave Flosi fine gifts.

Flosi now went south from Vopnafjord and up into the Fljotsdale district, where he stayed overnight with Holmstein Spak-Bersason, and told him that everyone had responded to his appeal for help except Sorli Brodd-Helgason. Holmstein said that the reason for that was that Sorli did not relish violence. Holmstein gave Flosi fine gifts.

Flosi travelled up Fljotsdale and over to the southern fells across Oxar Lava, then down Svidinhornadale and out along the west side of Alptafjord. He did not break his journey until he came to his father-in-law, Hall, at Thvattriver.

There Flosi and his men rested for a fortnight. Flosi asked

*Bjarni was the son of Brodd-Helgi, the son of Thorgils, the son of Thorstein the White, the son of Olvir, the son of Eyvald, the son of Oxen-Thorir. Bjarni's mother was Halla, the daughter of Lyting. Brodd-Helgi's mother was Asvor, the daughter of Thorir, the son of Gruel-Atli, the son of Thorir Thidrandi. Bjarni was married to Rannveig, the daughter of Thorgeir, the son of Eirik of Goddales, the son of Geirmund, the son of Hroald, the son of Eirik Bristle-Beard.

Hall what steps he would advise him to take now, and how he should conduct himself.

'My advice is that you should stay at your home with the Sigfussons,' replied Hall, 'and that they should send men to see to their farms. But the first thing to do is to get back home; and when you ride to the Althing, you must all ride together and not disperse your band, and on the way the Sigfussons can visit their wives. I myself shall ride to the Althing with my son Ljot and all our followers, and give you all the help in my power.'

Flosi thanked him, and Hall gave him fine gifts when they parted. Flosi then left Thvattriver, and there is nothing to tell of his journey back to Svinafell. He stayed at home for the rest of that winter, and the following summer until the Althing was due.

135

ONE day, Kari Solmundarson and Thorhall Asgrimsson rode to Mosfell to see Gizur the White. He welcomed them with open arms, and they stayed for a long time.

On one occasion, when they were discussing the Burning of Njal, Gizur said that it was great good fortune that Kari had escaped. Then this verse came to Kari's lips:

> 'My heart was raging
> When I left Njal's house
> Against my will,
> While the timbers sweated smoke
> And while the warriors
> Burned to their deaths.
> Listen to my words:
> I am telling my grief.'

Then Gizur said, 'No one can blame you for being obsessed by these memories. We shall not talk about it any more at present.'

Kari then said that he was going home. Gizur said, 'I am going to take the liberty of giving you some advice now. Leave by all means if you wish to, but do not go home; go right out east to the Eyjafells district to see Thorgeir Skorar-Geir and Thorleif Crow at Holt. They are to ride west with you, for they are the plaintiffs in the action, and Thorgrim the Mighty, their brother, should come with them. You are all to go and visit Mord Valgardsson, and give him this message from me : that he is to take over the manslaughter action against Flosi for the killing of Helgi. If he raises any objections, you must fly into a rage and pretend that you are about to put your axe in his head; and you can add that he may be assured of my anger as well if he makes any difficulties. You must also tell him that I will fetch my daughter Thorkatla and bring her home with me; he will not be able to bear that, for he loves her like the eyes in his own head.'

Kari thanked him for his advice; but with Gizur, Kari never discussed the question of support, for he assumed that Gizur would show him the same friendship in that as in other matters.

Kari and his men rode east over the rivers to Fljotshlid and from there over Markar River and on to Seljalandsmull and east to Holt. Thorgeir Skorar-Geir welcomed them with great warmth; he told them about Flosi's journey and how much backing he had received in the Eastfjords. Kari said that it was no wonder Flosi was looking for help, considering how much he would have to answer for.

'The worse they do, the better,' said Thorgeir.

Kari told him about Gizur's plan. After that they all rode west to the Rangriver Plains to see Mord Valgardsson. Mord gave them a good welcome. Kari gave him the message from Gizur the White, his father-in-law. Mord made difficulties : it was harder, he said, to prosecute Flosi than any ten other men.

'You are behaving exactly as Gizur expected,' said Kari. 'There is badness in you everywhere, for you are frightened and cowardly at heart. You shall now get your proper reward, for Thorkatla is going straight back to her father.'

Thorkatla made ready at once, and said that she had been prepared to leave Mord for a long time. Mord's attitude changed quickly; he begged them not to be angry with him, and agreed at once to take over the action.

284

'Now that you have taken over the action,' said Kari, 'prose-cute it fearlessly, for your life is at stake.'

Mord promised to put his whole heart and soul into doing it well and honourably.

After that, Mord summoned the nine nearest neighbours. He took Thorgeir's hand and named two witnesses – 'to witness that Thorgeir Thorisson assigns to me a manslaughter action against Flosi Thordarson for the killing of Helgi Njalsson, with all the evidence pertinent to that action. You assign this action to me to prosecute it or settle it, making full use of all the evidence, as if I were the rightful plaintiff; you assign it law-fully and I take it over lawfully.'

Then Mord named witnesses – 'to witness that I give notice of an action against Flosi Thordarson for unlawful assault, in-asmuch as he inflicted on Helgi Njalsson a brain wound, in-ternal wound, or marrow wound, which did cause Helgi's death. I give notice of this in the presence of five neighbours' – and he named them all by name – 'I give lawful notice of this action as assigned to me by Thorgeir Thorisson.'

Once more Mord named witnesses – 'to witness that I give notice of an action against Flosi Thordarson for a brain wound, internal wound, or marrow wound, which did cause Helgi Njalsson's death, at the place where Flosi had previously made an unlawful assault on Helgi. I give notice of this in the presence of five neighbours' – and he named them all by name – 'I give lawful notice of this action as assigned to me by Thorgeir Thorisson.'

Then Mord named witnesses for a third time –'to witness that I cite these nine nearest neighbours' – and he named them all by name – 'to ride to the Althing and to find as a jury whether or not Flosi Thordarson made an unlawful assault on Helgi Njalsson at the place where Flosi inflicted on Helgi a brain wound, internal wound, or marrow wound, which did cause Helgi's death.

'I cite you to make all the findings which you are required by law to make and which I shall require you to make before the court, and which properly pertain to this action. I cite you law-fully, in your presence and hearing, in this action as assigned to me by Thorgeir Thorisson.'

Then Mord named witnesses again – 'to witness that I cite

these nine nearest neighbours to ride to the Althing and to find as a jury whether or not Flosi Thordarson inflicted on Helgi Njalsson a brain wound, internal wound, or marrow wound, which did cause Helgi's death, at the place where Flosi had previously made an unlawful assault on Helgi. I cite you to make all the findings which you are required by law to make and which I shall require you to make before the court, and which properly pertain to this action. I cite you lawfully, in your presence and hearing, in this action as assigned to me by Thorgeir Thorisson.'

Then Mord said, 'Proceedings have now been started, as you requested. I now want to ask you, Thorgeir Skorar-Geir, to come to me on your way to the Althing; we can then combine our forces and travel together as closely as possible. My following will be ready promptly for the opening of the Althing, and you can rely on me in everything.'

They were satisfied at this. They all swore not to forsake each other until released by Kari, and each pledged his life to the others. Then they all parted in friendship and made arrangements for meeting at the Althing.

Thorgeir rode back east, but Kari rode west over the rivers to Asgrim at Tongue, who welcomed him most warmly. Kari told him everything that Gizur had advised, and described the start of proceedings.

'I fully expected that Gizur would not fail,' said Asgrim 'and he has once more proved me right. What news have you from the east about Flosi?'

'He travelled all the way up to Vopnafjord,' replied Kari, 'and almost all the chieftains have promised to ride to the Althing and support him. They also expect to get help from the men of Reykjardale, Ljosawater, and Oxarfjord.'

They discussed a great many things. And now the Althing drew near.

Thorhall Asgrimsson developed an inflammation of the leg, so acute that above the ankle his leg was as thick and swollen as a woman's thigh, and he could only walk with the help of a stick. Thorhall was a tall, powerful man, dark-haired and sallow-complexioned, as quiet-spoken as he was hot-tempered. He was one of the three greatest lawyers in Iceland.

When the time came near for people to start riding to the

Althing, Asgrim said to Kari, 'You should ride to the Althing early and tent our booths; take my son Thorhall with you, for I know that you will treat him with every consideration, lame as he is, and we shall have very great need of his help at the Althing. Twenty others will accompany you.'

They made their preparations for the journey and then rode off to the Althing, where they tented their booths and made everything ready.

136

FLOSI set off from the east, accompanied by the hundred men who had been with him at the Burning. They rode all the way to Fljotshlid, where the Sigfussons spent a day seeing to their farms. In the evening they rode west over Thjors River and slept there that night. Early next morning they took their horses and rode on their way.

Flosi said to his men, 'We will now ride to Tongue and pay an unwelcome visit to Asgrim.'

This suggestion pleased them, and they rode on until they came within reach of Tongue.

Asgrim was standing outside with some of his men, and they noticed the group of riders as soon as they came within sight. Asgrim's men said, 'That must be Thorgeir Skorar-Geir.'

'I certainly do not think so,' said Asgrim. 'These men are laughing and joking, but Njal's kinsmen, men like Thorgeir, will never laugh until Njal has been avenged. My guess is quite different, however unlikely it may sound to you; I think that these men are Flosi and his Burners on their way to force their attentions on us. Let us all go inside.'

They went in. Asgrim ordered the house to be swept, the tapestries to be hung, the tables to be set up, and food to be brought in; and he put extra seats facing the benches in the main room.

Flosi came riding into the home-field and told his men to dismount and go in. They did so. Flosi and his men entered the room. Asgrim was sitting on the dais. Flosi looked at the benches and saw that everything was ready for their needs.

Asgrim offered them no greeting, but said to Flosi, 'The tables are set because there should always be food for anyone who needs it.'

Flosi and all his men sat down at the tables, and laid their weapons against the walls. Those who could not find room on the benches sat on the extra seats; and four armed men stood guard in front of Flosi during the meal.

Asgrim never spoke throughout the meal, but his face was as red as blood. When they had finished, women cleared the tables and brought in water for washing. Flosi did everything as unhurriedly as if he were in his own home.

There was a wood-chopper lying in a corner of the dais; Asgrim snatched it up with both hands, jumped to the edge of the dais, and swung a blow at Flosi's head. Glum Hildisson saw the assault coming; he sprang to his feet, caught hold of the axe above Asgrim's hands, and in a flash had turned the edge on Asgrim himself, for Glum was a powerful man. Many others then jumped to their feet and made for Asgrim, but Flosi forbade anyone to harm him – 'for we have tried him beyond endurance and he acted only as he should have, and has proved that he is certainly no coward.'

To Asgrim he said, 'We shall go our ways now unharmed; but we shall meet again at the Althing, and there we shall fight this out in earnest.'

'Very well,' said Asgrim. 'And I only hope that by the end of the Althing you will have been humbled.'

Flosi made no reply to this. He and his men left the house, mounted their horses, and rode away. They travelled to Laugarwater, where they spent the night. Next morning they rode down to Beitivellir and halted; here they were joined by several other groups, including Hall of Sida and all the men from the Eastfjords.

Flosi welcomed them warmly, and told them about his journey and his dealings with Asgrim. Many of them praised Flosi for his boldness. But Hall said, 'I disagree. I think it was a stupid thing to do. They will remember their grievances vividly enough without being reminded of them anew, and those who provoke them like this are only inviting further trouble.'

Hall left them in no doubt that he thought Flosi had gone much too far.

From there they all travelled together to the Upper Plains, where they formed up and rode into the Althing. Flosi had previously made arrangements for the Stronghold booth * to be made ready. The men from the Eastfjords rode to their own booths.

137

MEANWHILE, Thorgeir Skorar-Geir came riding from the east with a large following; his brothers Thorleif Crow and Thorgrim the Mighty were also with him. They rode to Hof to meet Mord Valgardsson, and waited there until he was ready. Mord had gathered every able-bodied man in the district, and the brothers found him confident and determined.

They travelled together west over the rivers and waited for Hjalti Skeggjason, who arrived soon afterwards. They welcomed him warmly, and rode off in a body to Reykir in Byskupstongue, where they waited for Asgrim to join them.

Then they all rode west over Bruar River, and Asgrim told them all about his encounter with Flosi. Thorgeir said, 'I only hope we have a chance to put their manhood to the test before this Althing is over.'

They rode on to Beitivellir, where they were joined by Gizur the White with a huge following. They talked together for a long time. Then they rode to the Upper Plains, where they all formed up and rode into the Althing.

Flosi and his men ran to arms, and a pitched battle seemed inevitable; but Asgrim and his men refused to be drawn, and rode straight to their booths. The rest of the day passed quietly, without any fighting. By then, chieftains from every Quarter of the land had arrived, and this was the most crowded Althing within living memory.

* *Byrgisbúð*. It stood on a tongue of lava sheltered by natural outcrops of rock. Traces can still be seen to this day of a manmade rampart that protected the fourth side. *Translators' note.*

138

A MAN called Eyjolf Bolverksson * was one of the three greatest
lawyers in Iceland. He was a man who commanded great respect, and his knowledge of law was outstanding. He was extremely handsome, tall, and strong, with all the makings of a
fine chieftain. He was also very fond of money, like the rest of
his kinsmen.

One day Flosi went to Bjarni Brodd-Helgason's booth. Bjarni
welcomed him with open arms, and Flosi sat down beside him.
They talked of several things, and then Flosi said, 'What are we
to do now?'

'It is a difficult problem,' replied Bjarni. 'But the most sensible
thing would be, I think, to try to enlist more support, for they
are gathering forces against you. I also want to ask you, Flosi,
if you have any outstanding lawyer amongst your following,
for there are only two courses open to you now : either to seek
a settlement – and that would be an excellent idea – or else to
fight the case in court if any defence can be established, even
though this might be considered sheer obstinacy. In my opinion
this is the course you must choose, for you have already shown
so much defiance that it would not be proper for you to back
down now.'

'You asked about lawyers,' said Flosi. 'I can tell you right
away that we have none in our group, and I know of none to
count on in the Eastfjords except your kinsman Thorkel
Geitisson.'

'We shall not consider him at all,' said Bjarni. 'He knows his
law well enough, but he is much too cautious. Besides, no one
need think that Thorkel is going to be made the target for
attack; but he will support you as bravely as the best, for he is
no coward. I can tell you this : it will mean death for the man

---

* He was the son of Bolverk, the son of Eyjolf the Grey of
Otradale, the son of Thord Gellir, the son of Olaf Feilan. Eyjolf's
mother was Hrodny, the daughter of Midfjord-Skeggi, the son of
Hide-Bjorn, the son of Skutad-Skeggi.

who undertakes the defence of the Burners, and I would not wish that on my kinsman Thorkel. We shall have to look elsewhere.'

Flosi said that he had no idea who the best lawyers were.

'There is a man called Eyjolf Bolverksson,' said Bjarni. 'He is the greatest lawyer in the Westfjords Quarter. We would need to pay him a large amount to persuade him to take the case, but we should not let that deter us. Also, we must always go fully-armed to court and be continually on our guard, but never fight unless we are forced to do so in self-defence. I shall now come with you to seek help, for it seems to me that we have no more time to lose.'

They left the booth and went to see the men of Oxarfjord. Bjarni talked to Lyting and Blæing and Hroi Arnsteinsson, and they promptly promised what he asked for.

Then they went to see Kol, the son of Killer-Skuti, and Eyvind Thorkelsson, the grandson of Askel the Priest, and asked them for support. They demurred for a long time, but in the end they accepted three marks of silver and committed themselves to their cause.

Then they went to the Ljosawater booth and stayed there for a while. Flosi asked the Ljosawater men for support, but they proved stubborn and hard to persuade.

Flosi spoke now in growing anger. 'Shame on you,' he said. 'You are aggressive and lawless enough at home in your own district, but at Althings you refuse to give anyone support, even when you are asked. If you now overlook the insults that Skarp-Hedin heaped on you men of Ljosawater, you will always be talked of with contempt at Althings, behind your backs and even to your faces.'

He also talked to them in private and offered them money for their help, and coaxed them with flattering words. In the end they promised their support, and then worked up such enthusiasm that they declared they would even fight for Flosi if that became necessary.

Bjarni said to Flosi, 'Well done! You are a great chieftain indeed, bold and determined, a man who lets nothing stand in his way.'

After that they went west over Oxar River to the Hlad booth. They could see a number of men standing outside it. There was one who was wearing a scarlet cloak and a gold headband, and carried a silver-wrought axe.

'This is fortunate,' said Bjarni. 'There is Eyjolf Bolverksson now.'

They went over to him and greeted him. Eyjolf recognized Bjarni at once and welcomed him. Bjarni took Eyjolf by the arm and led him up to Almanna Gorge, telling Flosi to follow with his men; Eyjolf's men came too. They were told to stay up on the edge of the Gorge and keep a look-out. The leaders went on until they reached a path which led down from the higher side of the Gorge. Flosi said that this was a good place to sit, for it had a commanding view. They sat down by themselves – just the four of them.

Then Bjarni said to Eyjolf, 'We have come to you, friend, because we are in great need of your help in everything.'

'There is a wide choice of good men at the Althing now,' said Eyjolf, 'and you will have no difficulty in finding men who would strengthen you much more than I can.'

'That is not so,' said Bjarni, 'for you have many qualities that make you as great a man as any other here at the Althing. In the first place, you are as well-born as all those who are descended from Ragnar Hairy-Breeks. Your forefathers have always played a part in major issues both at the Althing and at home in their districts, and were never on the losing side. There-fore we think it likely that you will have the winning touch of your kinsmen.'

'These are handsome words,' said Eyjolf, 'but I feel that I deserve little part of them.'

Flosi said, 'It is hardly necessary to explain what we have in mind. We want to ask you to support us in our case – to come to court with us, seize on any points of defence that may occur, plead them on our behalf, and stand by us at the Althing in everything that may turn up.'

Eyjolf jumped to his feet in fury and said that no one need think that he could be used as a catspaw to do something he was not obliged to do. 'And now I see,' he said, 'what prompted all these flattering words you used towards me.'

Hallbjorn the Strong took hold of him and set him down again between himself and Bjarni, and said, 'No tree falls at the first stroke, my friend. Just sit here beside us for a while.'

Flosi drew from his arm a gold bracelet and said, 'I want to give you this bracelet, Eyjolf, for your friendship and help, and to show you that I have no wish to deceive you. You would do well to accept it, for there is no man at this Althing whom I have ever given so fine a gift.'

The bracelet was so thick and well-made that it was worth twelve hundred yards of best homespun cloth.* Hallbjorn placed it on Eyjolf's arm.

Eyjolf said, 'It is only proper for me to accept this bracelet in the face of such courtesy. And you can fairly expect that I shall take over the defence and do everything that may be required.'

'Now you are both being sensible,' said Bjarni. 'And there are two others here, Hallbjorn and myself, who are well suited to be witnesses to the fact that you are taking over the defence.'

Eyjolf and Flosi then stood up and shook hands. Flosi assigned to Eyjolf the defence and also any actions that might arise from it (for often a defence in one action becomes a prosecution in another). Eyjolf took over all the evidence pertinent to such actions, whether for the Quarter Courts or the Fifth Court. Flosi lawfully assigned the case, and Eyjolf lawfully took it over.

Then Eyjolf said to Flosi and Bjarni, 'Now that I have taken over the action as you requested, I would like you to keep the fact secret for a while. And if the case goes to the Fifth Court, you must take particular care not to let it be known that you have paid me for my help.'

They all stood up. Flosi and Bjarni went to their own booths, but Eyjolf went to Snorri the Priest's booth and sat down beside him. They talked of many things.

Snorri suddenly took hold of Eyjolf's arm and turned up the sleeve, and saw that he was wearing a large gold bracelet.

'Was this bracelet bought, or was it given to you?' he asked.

Eyjolf was embarrassed, and said nothing.

'It is obvious,' said Snorri, 'that you must have got it as a gift. I only hope that it does not cost you your life.'

Eyjolf jumped up and moved away, not wishing to discuss it.

* This was striped and of better quality than the staple woollen cloth, and it was valued at five ells to the legal ounce instead of six. This bracelet was thus worth 19 cows. *Translators' note.*

Snorri, when he saw Eyjolf rise, said, 'By the time the courts are over, you will be in little doubt what sort of a gift you have accepted.'

Eyjolf walked away to his own booth.

139

MEANWHILE, Asgrim Ellida-Grimsson and Kari Solmundarson held a meeting with Gizur the White, Hjalti Skeggjason, Thorgeir Skorar-Geir, and Mord Valgardsson.

Asgrim spoke first. 'We can talk quite openly,' he said, 'for only those who are in each other's full confidence are present. I want to ask you if you know anything of Flosi's plans, for in my opinion it is time we decided on our own plan of action.'

Gizur the White replied, 'Snorri the Priest sent me a message to say that Flosi had received strong support from the North, and that Eyjolf Bolverksson, Snorri's kinsman, had been given a gold bracelet by someone and was trying to keep it a secret. Snorri thought it likely that Eyjolf Bolverksson is intended to act for the defence, and that the bracelet was given as payment for his services.'

They all agreed that this must be right.

Gizur said to them, 'My son-in-law, Mord, has undertaken what everyone agrees will be the hardest part of the case – the prosecution of Flosi himself. I want you all now to distribute the other actions amongst yourselves, for it will soon be time to give notice of them at the Law Rock. We shall also have to seek more support for ourselves.'

'Very well,' said Asgrim. 'But we would like to ask you to take part when we go asking for support.'

Gizur promised to do so. Then he selected all the wisest men amongst their supporters to accompany him; they included Hjalti and Asgrim and Kari and Thorgeir Skorar-Geir.

'We shall go first to the booth of Skapti Thoroddsson,' said Gizur.

They went to the Olfus booth. Gizur was in the lead, followed by Hjalti, then Kari, then Asgrim, and then Thorgeir and his brothers. They walked into the booth. Skapti was sitting on the dais. When he saw Gizur, he rose to his feet and welcomed him and the others warmly, and asked Gizur to sit beside him. Gizur sat down, and said to Asgrim, 'You present to Skapti our request for support, and I shall contribute any remarks I think fit.'

Asgrim said, 'The reason we have come here is to ask you for support and help, Skapti.'

'You thought me difficult enough the last time,' said Skapti, 'when I refused to get involved in your troubles.'

'This is a different matter now,' said Gizur. 'We are now seeking redress for the death of Njal and Bergthora, both burned alive without cause, and for the death of their three sons and many other good men. You surely cannot want to refuse people help; surely you will want to support your kinsmen by blood and marriage.'

'I made up my mind,' said Skapti, 'when Skarp-Hedin taunted me with smearing tar on my head and hiding under a strip of turf, and when he said that I had been so frightened that Thorolf Loptsson had had to carry me on board his ship in flour-sacks and transport me thus to Iceland – I made up my mind then that I would never seek redress for his death.'

'There is no point in bringing that up now,' said Gizur, 'for the man who said it is now dead. You will surely want to give support to me at least, even though you don't want to do anything for others.'

'This case does not really concern you at all, Gizur,' replied Skapti, 'unless you insist on getting yourself mixed up with these men.'

This infuriated Gizur. 'You are not the man your father was,' he said, 'even though your father was not considered perfect. But at least he never failed people when they most needed his help.'

'You and I have little in common,' said Skapti. 'You like to think of yourselves as men who have taken part in great events – you, Gizur the White, for overcoming Gunnar of Hlidarend, and you, Asgrim, for killing your own sworn-brother, Gauk.'

'Where fault can be found the good is ignored,' said Asgrim. 'But many people would say that I did not kill Gauk until my hand was forced. To refuse us your help is understandable; but there can be no excuse for refusing it with insults. I only hope

that you will be utterly discredited before this Althing ends –
and get no compensation for your humiliation, either.'

Gizur and the others all stood up and left. They went to
Snorri the Priest's booth and walked in. Snorri was sitting on the
dais. He recognized them at once, stood up to meet them, bade
them all welcome, and offered them seats beside him. They discussed current news, and then Asgrim said to Snorri, 'The
reason my kinsman Gizur and I have come here is to ask you
for support.'

'You have every good cause to ask,' replied Snorri, 'since you
are seeking redress for such a family as you have lost. We have
often benefited from Njal's good counsel, though few seem to
remember that now. But I don't know what sort of help you
feel most in need of.'

'Our need would be greatest,' replied Asgrim, 'if there should
be a pitched battle at the Althing.'

'Certainly, that would be the crucial point for you,' said
Snorri. 'You will no doubt be prosecuting the case very force-
fully, and the defence will reply in kind; neither side will be
prepared to give way. You will find this intolerable and will
assault them; you will not have any alternative, for they want
to compensate killings with insults and hand out humiliation
for your loss of kinsmen.'

They had the impression that Snorri was not urging restraint.

Then Gizur said, 'Well spoken, Snorri. You are always at your
best, and make your authority most felt, when the issue is
greatest.'

'I would like to know,' said Asgrim, 'what help you would
give us if events turn out as you predict?'

Snorri said, 'I shall do you this act of friendship since your
honour will be wholly at stake. I shall not come to the court
with you; and if a fight breaks out at the Althing, you must not
attack before you are absolutely confident of the result, for
there are some great fighters on the other side. But if you are
forced to give ground, you had better retreat in this direction,
for I shall have my men drawn up here in battle array ready
to come to your help. If on the other hand your opponents
retreat, I expect they will try to reach the natural stronghold
of Almanna Gorge; for if they manage to get there, you would
never be able to defeat them. I shall take it upon myself to bar

their way to this vantage ground with my men, but we shall not pursue them if they retreat north or south along the river. And as soon as I estimate that you have killed off as many of them as you can afford to pay compensation for without exile or loss of your chieftaincies, I shall intervene with all my men to stop the fighting; and you must then obey my orders, if I do all this for you.'

Gizur thanked him warmly, and said that Snorri's advice was in their best interests. Then they all left the booth.

'Where shall we go now?' asked Gizur.

'To the Modruvellir booth,' replied Asgrim.

They went there.

140

WHEN they entered the booth, they saw Gudmund the Powerful sitting talking to his foster-father Einar Konalsson, a very shrewd man. They walked up the booth to Gudmund, who made them welcome and cleared the booth to give them all seats.

They exchanged news. Then Asgrim said, 'There is no point in prevaricating; the reason we have come here is to ask for your full support.'

'Have you approached any other chieftains?' asked Gudmund.

They replied that they had been to see Skapti and Snorri the Priest, and told him in confidence everything that had been said.

'The last time you approached me,' said Gudmund, 'I was small-minded and made difficulties; this time I shall make up for my previous obstinacy with all the greater willingness. I shall accompany you to the courts with all my followers and give you whatever help I can, fight for you if need be and even pledge my life with yours. And I shall pay out Skapti by making his son, Thorstein Hollow-Mouth, fight on our side, for he will not dare to go against my wishes, since he is married to my daughter Jodis. That will make Skapti want to stop the fighting.'

They thanked him and then talked for a long time in private.

Gudmund urged them not to beg for help from any other chieftains – he said it was belittling. 'We shall take our chance on the men we have already,' he said. 'Always be armed when you go to court, but do not fight as things stand at present.'

Then they left and went home to their booths. For the time being, this was known to only a few people.

The Althing continued.

141

ONE day when everyone was at the Law Rock, the chieftains were ranged as follows: Asgrim Ellida-Grimsson, Gizur the White, Gudmund the Powerful, and Snorri the Priest were standing close up to the Law Rock, while the men from the Eastfjords stood further below.

Mord Valgardsson stood beside his father-in-law Gizur the White. Mord was an extremely fine speaker. Gizur told him that he should now give notice of the manslaughter actions, and asked him to speak loudly and clearly so that all might hear him.

Mord named witnesses – 'to testify that I give notice of an action against Flosi Thordarson for unlawful assault, inasmuch as he assaulted Helgi Njalsson at the place where he assaulted Helgi and inflicted on him an internal wound, brain wound, or marrow wound, which did cause Helgi's death. I demand that Flosi be sentenced to full outlawry on this charge, not to be fed nor forwarded nor helped nor harboured. I claim that all his possessions be forfeit, half to me and half to those men in the Quarter who have a lawful right to receive his confiscated goods. I refer this manslaughter action to the proper Quarter Court. I give lawful notice of it, in public, at the Law Rock. I give notice of an action, to be heard at this session, for full outlawry against Flosi Thordarson, as assigned to me by Thorgeir Thorisson.'

There was loud approval at the Law Rock for the eloquent and forceful way Mord had spoken.

Mord continued: 'I call upon you to testify that I give notice of an action against Flosi Thordarson, inasmuch as he inflicted on Helgi Njalsson an internal wound, brain wound, or marrow wound, which did cause Helgi's death, at the place where Flosi had previously made an unlawful assault on Helgi. I demand that you be sentenced to full outlawry on this charge, Flosi, not to be fed nor forwarded nor helped nor harboured. I claim that all your possessions be forfeit, half to me and half to those men in the Quarter who have a lawful right to receive your confiscated goods. I refer this action to the proper Quarter Court. I give lawful notice of it, in public, at the Law Rock. I give notice of an action, to be heard at this session, for full outlawry against Flosi Thordarson, as assigned to me by Thorgeir Thorisson.'

With that, Mord sat down. Flosi had given him a good hearing, and never uttered a word throughout.

Thorgeir Skorar-Geir then stood up and named witnesses – 'to testify that I give notice of an action against Glum Hildisson, inasmuch as he took fire and kindled it and applied it to the buildings at Bergthorsknoll on the occasion when they burned to death Njal Thorgeirsson and Bergthora Skarp-Hedin's-daughter and all those people who died therein. I demand that he be sentenced to full outlawry on this charge, not to be fed nor forwarded nor helped nor harboured. I claim that all his possessions be forfeit, half to me and half to those men in the Quarter who have a lawful right to receive his confiscated goods. I refer this action to the proper Quarter Court. I give lawful notice of it, in public, at the Law Rock. I give notice of an action, to be heard at this session, for full outlawry against Glum Hildisson.'

Kari Solmundarson raised actions against Kol Thorsteinsson, Gunnar Lambason, and Grani Gunnarsson, and everyone commented that he spoke remarkably well. Thorleif Crow raised actions against all the Sigfussons, while his brother Thorgrim the Mighty raised actions against Modolf Ketilsson, Lambi Sigurdarson, and Hroar Hamundarson (the brother of Leidolf the Strong). Asgrim Ellida-Grimsson raised actions against Leidolf, Thorstein Geirleifsson, Arni Kolsson, and Grim the Red.

They all spoke well. After that, other men gave notice of their actions, and this occupied most of the day. Then people went back to their booths.

Eyjolf Bolverksson walked with Flosi to his booth. They went over to the east side of the booth, and Flosi asked him if he could see any flaws in the proceedings so far.

'No, none,' replied Eyjolf.

'What should we do now?' asked Flosi.

'This is a difficult problem,' said Eyjolf, 'but I still have a plan to suggest. You are to transfer your chieftaincy to your brother Thorgeir, and attach yourself to the following of the chieftain Askel Thorketilsson of Reykjardale, in the North Quarter. If your opponents do not get to hear of this, they will probably make a fatal error, by pleading the case in the East Quarter Court instead of the North Quarter Court. This is a possibility they will overlook, and a Fifth Court charge can be lodged against them for pleading in the wrong court. We could use this as a counter-charge, but only as a last resort.'

'It could be that we are already repaid for that bracelet,' said Flosi.

'I do not know about that,' said Eyjolf. 'But I shall give you every possible legal assistance, so that everyone will say that no man could have done more. You must now send for Askel, and Thorgeir and one other man must also come here immediately.'

A little later Thorgeir arrived, and took over Flosi's chieftaincy. Then Askel came, and Flosi attached himself to his following. No one else knew about these arrangements.

142

THE time now passed uneventfully until the courts were due to sit. Then both sides made ready and armed themselves, and put battle-emblems on their helmets.

Thorhall Asgrimsson said, 'Don't be too hasty in anything, and be careful to make no mistakes. But if things go wrong for you, let me know at once and I shall send you fresh counsel.'

Asgrim and the others looked at him; his face was as red as blood, and tears like hailstones burst from his eyes. He asked them to bring him his spear, the one that Skarp-Hedin had given him; it was a most valuable weapon.

As they left, Asgrim said, 'My kinsman Thorhall was not easy in his mind when we left him behind in the booth, and I do not know what he will do. Let us now go and support Mord Valgardsson and act as if nothing else mattered, for Flosi is a bigger catch than all the others put together.'

Asgrim sent a messenger to Gizur the White and Hjalti and Gudmund the Powerful. They all met and went at once to the East Quarter Court, where they took their places at the south side. Flosi and all the men of the Eastfjords went to the north side of the court; with Flosi were the men from Reykjardale, Oxarfjord, and Ljosawater, and also Eyjolf Bolverksson.

Flosi leaned over to him and said, 'This is promising. It looks as if things are going exactly the way you surmised.'

'Keep quiet about it,' said Eyjolf. 'We may still be forced to fall back on that plan.'

Mord Valgardsson named witnesses and proposed that lots be drawn to determine the order in which those with outlawry actions to bring should plead them. He made this proposal lawfully, in the hearing of the judges. Thereupon lots were cast, and it fell to Mord to be the first to plead.

Mord then named witnesses again – 'to testify that I reserve to myself the right to correct any mistakes I may make in my pleading, whether overstatements or errors. I reserve to myself the right to amend any of my pleading until I have given my case its proper legal wording. I name these witnesses on behalf of myself or whomsoever else may require the benefit of this reservation.'

Mord continued: 'I name witnesses to testify that I call upon Flosi Thordarson, or whomsoever else has taken over the defence on his behalf, to hear my oath and my charges and all the evidence I shall lead against him. I call upon him lawfully in the hearing of all the judges in this court.'

Mord continued: 'I name witnesses to testify that I swear this oath on the Book, a lawful oath: I declare before God that I shall plead this case as truthfully and fairly and lawfully as I can, and that I shall fulfil all the demands of the law as long as I am at this Althing.'

Then he spoke as follows: 'I cited Thorodd as my first witness and Thorbjorn as my second witness, to testify that I gave notice of an action against Flosi Thordarson for unlawful assault at the place where Flosi made an unlawful assault on

Helgi Njalsson and inflicted on him an internal wound, brain wound, or marrow wound, which did cause Helgi's death. I demanded that Flosi be sentenced to full outlawry on this charge, not to be fed nor forwarded nor helped nor harboured.

'I claimed that all his possessions be forfeit, half to me and half to those men in the Quarter who have a lawful right to receive his confiscated goods. I referred this action to the proper Quarter Court. I gave lawful notice of it, in public, at the Law Rock. I gave notice of an action, to be heard at this session, for full outlawry against Flosi Thordarson, as assigned to me by Thorgeir Thorisson. I gave notice of it in the same terms as I have now used in stating my charges. I duly present this outlawry action before the East Quarter Court in the presence of Jon, in the form in which I gave notice of it.'

Mord continued, 'I cited Thorodd as my first witness and Thorbjorn as my second witness, to testify that I gave notice of an action against Flosi Thordarson for inflicting on Helgi Njalsson an internal wound, brain wound, or marrow wound, which did cause Helgi's death, at the place where Flosi had previously made an unlawful assault on Helgi. I demanded that Flosi be sentenced to full outlawry on this charge, not to be fed nor forwarded nor helped nor harboured. I claimed that all his possessions be forfeit, half to me and half to those men in the Quarter who have a lawful right to receive his confiscated goods. I referred this action to the proper Quarter Court. I gave lawful notice of it, in public, at the Law Rock. I gave notice of an action, to be heard at this session, for full outlawry against Flosi Thordarson, as assigned to me by Thorgeir Thorisson. I gave notice of it in the same terms as I have now used in stating my charges. I duly present this outlawry action before the East Quarter Court in the presence of Jon, in the form in which I gave notice of it.'

Then the witnesses named by Mord went before the court and gave evidence, one reciting the testimony and both confirming it – 'Mord named Thorodd as the first witness and me as the second, and I am called Thorbjorn' (and he gave his father's name). 'Mord cited us to testify that he gave notice of an action against Flosi Thordarson for unlawful assault, inasmuch as Flosi made an unlawful assault on Helgi Njalsson at the place where he inflicted on Helgi an internal wound, brain wound, or marrow wound, which did cause Helgi's death. He demanded that Flosi be sentenced to full outlawry on that charge, not to be fed nor forwarded nor helped nor harboured. He claimed that all his possessions be forfeit, half to himself and half to those men in the Quarter who have a lawful right to receive his confiscated goods. He referred this action to the proper Quarter Court. He gave lawful notice of it, in public, at the Law Rock. He gave notice of an action, to be heard at this session, for full outlawry against Flosi Thordarson, as assigned to him by Thorgeir Thorisson. He gave notice of it in the same terms as he used in stating his charges, and as we have now used in our testimony. We have now given our evidence accurately, and we are both agreed on it. This evidence that notice was given we duly give before the East Quarter Court in the presence of Jon, in the form in which Mord gave notice.'

For a second time they gave their evidence in court that notice had been given of the action, but this time they referred to the wounds first and the assault second; but otherwise all the terms were the same as they had used in their previous testimony. They duly gave it before the East Quarter Court, in the form in which Mord had given notice.

Then the witnesses of the assignment of the action to Mord went before the court. One recited the evidence and then both confirmed it, and they declared that Mord Valgardsson and Thorgeir Thorisson had cited them to testify that Thorgeir had assigned to Mord a manslaughter action against Flosi Thordarson for the killing of Helgi Njalsson. 'He assigned to Mord this action with all the evidence pertinent to it. He assigned the action to Mord to prosecute it or settle it, making full use of all the evidence, as if he were the rightful plaintiff. Thorgeir assigned the action lawfully and Mord took it over lawfully.'

They duly gave this evidence of assignment before the East Quarter Court in the presence of Jon, as Thorgeir and Mord had cited them to testify.

They made all their witnesses take the oath before giving evidence, and the judges as well.

Once again Mord named witnesses – 'to testify that I call upon the nine neighbours I cited in this action I have brought against Flosi Thordarson, to take their seats as a jury on the west bank of the river, and I invite the defence to challenge these jurymen. I make this invitation lawfully in court, in the hearing of the judges.'

Mord named witnesses again – 'to testify that I invite Flosi Thordarson, or whomsoever else has taken over the defence on his behalf, to challenge the jurymen I have assembled on the west bank of the river. I make this invitation lawfully in court, in the hearing of the judges.'

Then Mord named witnesses again – 'to testify that all the preliminaries pertaining to the action have now been completed : the defence has been called upon to hear my oath, the oath taken, the charges stated, the evidence of notice led, the evidence of assignment led, the jury assembled, and the defence invited to challenge the jurymen.

'I name these witnesses to testify to all the stages of the prosecution case, and also to witness that I should not be considered to have abandoned the case if I should leave the court to seek further evidence or for any other reason.'

Then Flosi and his men walked over to the place where the jury was seated. Flosi said, 'The Sigfussons should know whether these neighbours have been assembled here rightly or not.'

Ketil of Mork said, 'There is one juryman here who sponsored Mord Valgardsson at his baptism, and another who is second cousin to him.'

They worked out his kinship and confirmed it on oath. Eyjolf Bolverksson then named his witnesses and proposed that the jury should stay in their places at present until they had all been challenged. Then he named witnesses again – 'to testify that I disqualify these two men from the jury ' (and he named them both, and their fathers' names as well) 'on the grounds that one of them is second cousin to Mord and that the other stands in spiritual relationship to him, which disqualifies him from sitting on this jury. According to the law, you two have no right to sit on the jury, because a valid challenge has now been made against you. I disqualify you in accordance with the procedural rules of the Althing and the common law of the land. I disqualify you in the case assigned to me by Flosi Thordarson.'

This caused a great stir; everyone said that Mord's case had been ruined, and all agreed that the defence had the upper hand over the prosecution.

Asgrim said to Mord, 'They have not won yet, even though

they think they have now forced an advantage. We must first see my son Thorhall and find out what he advises.'

A reliable man was sent as messenger to Thorhall. He gave Thorhall a detailed account of what was happening in court, how Flosi and his men thought they had disqualified the jury.

'I will see to it that you don't lose the case on that account,' said Thorhall. 'Tell them that they should not let themselves be tricked by lawyers' quibbles, for this time Eyjolf's cleverness has failed him. Go back as fast as you can. Tell Mord Valgardsson to go before the court and name witnesses to testify that the disqualification of the jury was invalid' – and he told the messenger precisely how they should proceed. The messenger went and reported Thorhall's proposals.

Then Mord Valgardsson went before the court and named witnesses – 'to testify that I declare invalid Eyjolf Bolverksson's disqualification of the jury, on the ground that he challenged them for their kinship not to the plaintiff himself but to the pleader. I call these witnesses on behalf of myself or whomsoever else may require the benefit of this objection.'

After that he led this evidence in court. Then he walked over to where the jury was sitting, and told those who were standing to take their seats again because they were rightful jurymen according to the law.

Then everyone said that Thorhall had scored a great success; and everyone felt that the prosecution now had the upper hand over the defence.

Flosi said to Eyjolf, 'Do you think this a valid point of law?'

'Certainly,' replied Eyjolf. 'It was something we overlooked, I admit. But the game isn't over between us yet.'

Eyjolf then named witnesses – 'to testify that I disqualify these two men from the jury' (and he named them) 'on the ground that you are dependants and not householders. I deny you the right to sit on the jury, because a valid challenge has now been made against you. I disqualify you in accordance with the procedural rules of the Althing and the common law of the land.'

Eyjolf said that he would be greatly surprised if they could refute this point. Everyone now said that the defence had the upper hand over the prosecution. Everyone praised Eyjolf highly, and said that no one could compete with him in legal skill.

Mord Valgardsson and Asgrim sent a messenger to Thorhall to tell him this latest move. When Thorhall heard this, he asked what property the two jurymen owned, or whether they were destitute. The messenger replied that one of them made his livelihood from some milch cows and ewes, and that the other owned one third of the land which they farmed together; he provided his own board, and the two of them shared a hearth and a shepherd with the lessee of the farm.

Thorhall said, 'They have overlooked a point, just as they did the last time, and I can quash this challenge right away, even though Eyjolf boasted so loudly that it was irrefutable.'

He told the messenger in detail how they should proceed. The messenger went back and told Mord and Asgrim what Thorhall had advised them to do.

Mord went before the court and named witnesses – 'to testify that Eyjolf Bolverksson's disqualification of the jury is invalid, because he challenged men who have every right to be on it. The law says that any man has the right to be on a jury if he owns three hundreds of land or more, even though he owns no milch animals. The law also says that any man has the right to be on a jury if he owns milch animals, even though he owns no land.'

Then he led this evidence in court. Thereupon he walked over to the place where the jury was sitting, and told the two to take their seats again because they were rightful jurymen according to the law.

Uproar broke out at this, and everyone said that Flosi had been practically routed. They all agreed that the prosecution now had the upper hand over the defence.

Flosi asked Eyjolf, 'Is this the law?'

Eyjolf admitted that he had not the knowledge to be sure. So they sent a messenger to Skapti the Law-Speaker to ask him if this were the law. He sent back word that it certainly was, although there were few people who knew it. This was reported to Flosi and Eyjolf.

Eyjolf then asked the Sigfussons about the other neighbours who had been cited. The Sigfussons replied that four jurymen had been wrongly cited – 'since there are others still at home who live closer to the scene.'

Eyjolf then named witnesses to testify that he disqualified all these four men from the jury, and used the correct legal formula for the challenge. Then he said to the remaining jurymen : 'You are under an obligation to render justice to both sides. Now you must go before the court when you are called, and name witnesses to testify that you are not in a position to make any finding, because only five of you have been lawfully cited whereas there should have been nine.

'And if Thorhall can save the case now,' he added, 'he can win any case there is.'

It was obvious that Flosi and Eyjolf were jubilant. There was a clamour of agreement that the proceedings over the Burning had collapsed, and that the defence now had the upper hand over the prosecution.

Asgrim said to Mord, 'They cannot know what they have to boast about until Thorhall has been consulted. Njal once said that he had taught Thorhall law so well that he would prove to be the best lawyer in Iceland if it ever came to the test.'

A messenger was sent to Thorhall to tell him what had happened and about their boasting and the general opinion that the proceedings over the Burning had collapsed.

'Excellent,' said Thorhall, 'but they will still not gain any credit from this. You go back now and tell Mord to name witnesses and swear on oath that the majority of the jury was lawfully cited. He is then to lead this evidence in court, and he will thus save the case. He himself will be fined three marks for every juryman he cited wrongly, but he cannot be prosecuted for that at this session of the Althing. Now go back to them.'

The messenger returned and reported Thorhall's words in every detail. Mord went before the court and named witnesses, and swore on oath that the majority of the jury had been lawfully cited. He claimed that he had thus saved the prosecution case – 'and our opponents will have to pride themselves on something other than that we have committed some grave blunder here.'

There was loud agreement that Mord was giving a good account of himself in the case, and that Flosi and his men were resorting to mere lawyers' quibbles and cheating.

Flosi asked if this were the law, but Eyjolf replied that he did not know for certain and said that the Law-Speaker would have to settle that point. Thorkel Geitisson went on their behalf and told the Law-Speaker the situation, and asked if there were any legal basis for Mord's submission.

'There are more great lawyers alive today than I thought,' replied Skapti. 'I can tell you that this is so precisely correct that not a single objection can be raised against it. But I had thought that I was the only person who knew this specialty of the law now that Njal is dead, for to the best of my knowledge he was the only other man who knew it.'

Thorkel went back to Flosi and Eyjolf and told them that it was indeed the law.

Then Mord Valgardsson went before the court and named witnesses – 'to testify that I call upon the neighbours I cited in the action I have brought again Flosi Thordarson, to state their findings, either for or against. I call upon them lawfully in court, in the full hearing of all the judges.'

Mord's jurymen went before the court. One of them announced their findings and the others confirmed them, as follows: 'Mord Valgardsson cited nine of us freemen to form this jury; but four have been disqualified, and we are only five now. Evidence has been led regarding those four who were to have made a finding with us. We are now bound by law to state our findings. We were cited to find whether or not Flosi Thordarson made an unlawful assault on Helgi Njalsson at the place where Flosi inflicted on Helgi an internal wound, brain wound, or marrow wound, which did cause Helgi's death.

'He cited us to make such findings as we are required by law to make and which he required us to make before the court, and which properly pertain to this action. He cited us lawfully, in our hearing, in the action assigned to him by Thorgeir Thorisson. We have all now taken the oath and made our findings, and we are all agreed. We find against Flosi, and find the charge against him lawfully made. We jurymen present our nine-man findings to this effect before the East Quarter Court in the presence of Jon, as Mord cited us to do. This is the finding of us all,' they said.

They announced their findings once more, this time referring to the wounds first and the assault second, but otherwise in exactly the same terms. They found against Flosi, and found the charge against him lawfully made.

Then Mord Valgardsson went before the court and named witnesses to testify that the jurymen he had cited in the action he had brought against Flosi Thordarson had stated their findings and found the charges against Flosi lawfully made. He named these witnesses on behalf of himself – 'or whomsoever else may require the benefit of these findings.'

Once more Mord named witnesses – 'to testify that I invite Flosi Thordarson, or whomsoever else has taken over the defence on his behalf, to submit his defence to the action I have brought against him; for now all the stages which by law pertain to the prosecution case have been completed – all the evidence has been led, the jury assembled, and witnesses named to testify to the findings and to each stage of the prosecution case. But I reserve the right to re-open the prosecution case if any point occurs in the defence which I may require to answer. I make this request lawfully in court, in the hearing of the judges.'

'It amuses me, Eyjolf,' said Flosi, 'to think how they will grimace and tear their hair when you present our defence.'

143

EYJOLF BOLVERKSSON went before the court and named witnesses – 'to testify that it is an unanswerable defence in law, that you have pleaded this case in the East Quarter Court when it should have been pleaded in the North Quarter Court, since Flosi has attached himself to the following of the chieftain Askel. Here now are the witnesses who were present and who can testify that Flosi first transferred his chieftaincy to his brother Thorgeir and then attached himself to Askel's following. I name these witnesses on behalf of myself or whomsoever else may require the benefit of this submission.'

Eyjolf named witnesses again – 'to testify that I call upon Mord, who is pleading this action, or whomsoever else may be the plaintiff, to hear my oath and the defence I shall submit and all the evidence I shall lead. I call upon him lawfully in court, in the hearing of the judges.'

Eyjolf named witnesses again – 'to testify that I swear this oath on the Book, a lawful oath : I declare before God that I shall defend this case as fairly and truthfully and lawfully as I can, and that I shall fulfil all the demands of the law as long as I am at this Althing.'

Eyjolf continued : 'I cite these two men as witnesses, to testify that I submit as an unanswerable defence in law the fact that this case was pleaded in the wrong Quarter Court. On this ground I claim that the action is invalidated. I duly submit this defence in this form before the East Quarter Court.'

Then he led all the evidence that pertained to this defence, and named witnesses to testify that all the stages of the defence case had now been completed.

Eyjolf named witnesses again – 'to testify that I interdict the judges from bringing a verdict in the action brought by Mord and his associates, on the ground that an unanswerable defence in law has been established. This is a lawful, binding, and absolute interdict, which it is my right to make in accordance with the procedural rules of the Althing and the common law of the land.'

Then he called upon the court to consider his defence.

Asgrim and his men then brought the other actions against the Burners, and they took their regular course.

144

MEANWHILE, Asgrim and his men sent a messenger to Thorhall to tell him of this latest development.

'I was too far away this time,' said Thorhall. 'The case would never have taken this turn if I had been present. I see their strategy now : they intend to charge you in the Fifth Court with committing a procedural irregularity. They will also be planning to divide the judges over the actions for the Burning so that no verdict can be brought, for their tactics make it clear that they will stop at nothing, however dishonest. Go back at once and tell Mord to charge both Flosi and Eyjolf with using bribes in court, and demand a sentence of three years' outlawry. Tell him to charge them further with leading evidence that was irrelevant to the case, thereby committing a procedural irregularity. Tell him also that I pointed out that a man found guilty on two charges carrying a sentence of three years' outlawry shall be sentenced to full outlawry. But you must be first with your charges, so that they can be heard and judged before theirs are.'

The messenger went back and repeated this to Mord and Asgrim. They went at once to the Law Rock, where Mord named witnesses – 'to testify that I charge Flosi Thordarson with bribing Eyjolf Bolverksson here at the Althing for his help in court. I demand that he be sentenced to three years' outlawry on this charge, not to be forwarded nor granted asylum unless the full amount of the fine be paid at the court of confiscation; failing which, he shall be sentenced to full outlawry. I claim that all his possessions be forfeit, half to me and half to those men in the Quarter who have a lawful right to receive his confiscated goods.

'I refer this action to the Fifth Court, where it properly belongs. I refer this action for immediate trial and full sentence. I refer it lawfully, in public, at the Law Rock.'

He similarly charged Eyjolf Bolverksson with accepting the bribe; and this action, too, he referred to the Fifth Court.

He further charged Flosi and Eyjolf with leading evidence at the Althing which was irrelevant to the case, thereby committing a procedural irregularity. On this charge, too, he demanded a sentence of three years' outlawry.

Then they went to the Court of Legislature, where the Fifth Court was in session.

Meanwhile, in the Quarter Court, after Asgrim and Mord had left, the judges were unable to agree on their verdict. Some of them wanted to find in favour of Flosi, others in favour of Mord and Asgrim. In the end they had to declare the court divided. Flosi and Eyjolf delayed there during the time when the charges against them were being announced at the Law Rock.

A little later, they were informed that they had each been charged at the Law Rock with two Fifth Court charges.

Eyjolf said, 'It was ill luck that we delayed here for so long while they were getting ahead of us with their charges. Thorhall's cunning shows itself in this; for no one can equal him in shrewdness. Now they have gained the advantage of being first to plead their cases, and that was all-important to them. Nevertheless, we shall go to the Law Rock and start proceedings against them, even though it may not do us much good now.'

They went to the Law Rock, and Eyjolf charged them with committing a procedural irregularity. Then they went to the Fifth Court.

Meanwhile, when Mord and Asgrim reached the Fifth Court, Mord named witnesses and called for a hearing for his taking of the oath and the statement of his charges and all the evidence he intended leading against Flosi and Eyjolf. He made his request lawfully in court, in the full hearing of all the judges.

In the Fifth Court, corroborators had to confirm all oaths, under oath themselves.

Mord then named witnesses – 'to testify that I swear this Fifth Court oath : may God be my help, in this world and the next, that I shall plead this case as fairly and truthfully and lawfully as I can. I believe that Flosi is guilty of this charge, if my facts are correct. I have not offered money in this court to help me in this case, nor shall I do so; neither have I received money, nor shall I do so, whether for lawful or unlawful purposes.'

Mord's two corroborators went before the court and named witnesses – 'to testify that we swear this oath on the Book, a lawful oath : may God be our help, in this world and the next, that we on our word of honour believe that Mord will plead this case as fairly and truthfully and lawfully as he can, and that he has not offered money in this court to help him in this case and will not do so; and that he has neither received money, nor will he do so, whether for lawful or unlawful purposes.'

Mord had cited as a jury nine neighbours who lived near Thingvellir. Now Mord named witnesses and stated the four charges he had made against Flosi and Eyjolf, using the same terms in his statement as he had used in his announcement of them. He duly presented these three-year outlawry charges before the Fifth Court in the same form as he had used when announcing them at the Law Rock.

Mord then named witnesses and called upon the nine neighbours to take their places as a jury on the west bank of the river. Then he named witnesses again and invited Flosi and Eyjolf to challenge the jurymen. They came over to challenge the jurymen and examined them carefully, but they were unable to raise any objections and retired in exasperation.

Mord named witnesses and called upon the nine neighbours he had cited to state their findings as a jury, either in favour or against.

Mord's jurymen then went before the court. One of them announced their findings and the others confirmed them. They had all taken the Fifth Court oath, and now they found the charge against Flosi lawfully made and found against him. They duly presented their findings before the Fifth Court in the presence of the person before whom Mord had stated his charges. Then they announced their findings in all the actions, as they were required by law to do, and everything was done in accordance with the law. Eyjolf Bolverksson and Flosi were alert for any flaw in the proceedings, but could find none.

Mord named witnesses – 'to testify that the nine neighbours I cited as a jury for the charges I made against Flosi Thordarson and Eyjolf Bolverksson have now announced their findings, and have found the charges against them lawfully made.'

He named witnesses again – 'to testify that I invite Flosi Thordarson, or whomsoever else has taken over the defence on his behalf, to submit his defence, for now the prosecution case has been completed : the defence has been called upon to hear my oath, the oath taken, the charges stated, the evidence of announcing them led, the jury assembled, the defence invited to challenge, and the jury's findings announced and witnessed.'

And he named witnesses to testify to all the stages of the prosecution case.

Then the person in whose presence the charges had been stated rose to his feet and recapitulated the case. First he repeated how Mord had called for a hearing for his taking of the oath and his statement of charges and all the evidence. He recounted how Mord and his corroborators had taken the oath. He next recounted how Mord had stated his charges, and said that he was using the same terms as Mord had used in his statement of the charges and in his previous announcement of them at the Law Rock – 'and in this form Mord stated his charges before the Fifth Court, using the same terms as in his announce-ment.' Then he recalled that evidence had been led of the announcement, and repeated the terms of the announcement which had also been used in the evidence about it – 'and which I have now used in my recapitulation. They duly gave their evidence before the Fifth Court in the same form as Mord had used for his announcement.' Then he recalled how Mord had called upon the jury to take their places, and then invited Flosi or whomsoever else had taken over the defence on his behalf to challenge the jurymen. Then he recounted how the neighbour-jurymen had gone before the court and stated their findings and found the charges against Flosi lawfully made – 'and they duly presented the findings of this nine-neighbour jury before the Fifth Court in this form.' Then he recounted how Mord had named witnesses to the announcement of the jury's findings, and how he had then named witnesses to all the stages of the case and invited the defence to reply.

Mord then named witnesses – 'to testify that I forbid Flosi Thordarson, or whomsoever else has taken over the defence on his behalf, to raise any further objections in law, for now all the relevant stages of the case have been completed, with this recapitulation as the final stage.'

Then the recapitulation of this final submission was duly made.

Mord named witnesses and called upon the judges to pass judgement on the case.

Gizur the White said, 'You will have to do more than that, Mord, because four dozen judges cannot give a verdict, as the law stands.'

Flosi said to Eyjolf, 'What do we do now?'

'The position is very delicate just now,' replied Eyjolf, 'and I think we should wait for the time being; for I have a sus-picion that they are about to make a blunder in the prosecution. Mord has just called for an immediate verdict, whereas he should first exclude six of the judges and then invite us before witnesses to exclude another six. We are going to refuse to do that, and it will then be his duty to exclude a further six. That is the point that he will probably overlook, and if he does, their whole action will be invalidated; for a verdict can be given only by three dozen judges.'

'You are a clever man, Eyjolf,' said Flosi. 'There are few men who are your equals.'

Mord Valgardsson named witnesses – 'to testify that I exclude the following six judges from the court' (and he named them all by name). 'I deny you a seat in the court. I exclude you in accordance with the procedural rules of the Althing and the common law of the land.'

Then he invited Flosi and Eyjolf, before witnesses, to exclude a further six judges from the court, but Flosi and Eyjolf abstained from doing so.

Then Mord called for the verdict. And when the verdict had been given, Eyjolf Bolverksson named witnesses and claimed that the verdict was null and void and the whole action invalidated, on the ground that forty-two judges had given the verdict instead of only thirty-six, as the law demanded – 'and we shall now bring our own Fifth Court actions against them and have them all sentenced to outlawry.'

Gizur the White said to Mord, 'You have blundered terribly by making this error. This is disastrous ill luck. What are we to do now, kinsman Asgrim?'

'We shall send a messenger to my son Thorhall at once,' replied Asgrim, 'and find out what he wants us to do.'

145

SNORRI THE PRIEST now learnt how the court actions were going. He began to draw up his forces in battle array between Almanna Gorge and the Hlad booth; he had already told his men what they were to do.

Meanwhile, the messenger came to Thorhall and told him what had happened – that they were all going to be outlawed and that the manslaughter action had been dismissed. When Thorhall heard this he was so shocked that he could not speak a word. He sprang out of bed, snatched with both hands the spear that Skarp-Hedin had given him, and drove it deep into his own leg. The flesh and the core of the boil clung to the blade as he gouged it out of his leg, and a torrent of blood and matter gushed across the floor like a stream. Then he strode from the booth without a limp, walking so fast that the messenger could not keep pace with him, and hurried to the Fifth Court.

There he encountered Grim the Red, one of Flosi's kinsmen. As soon as they met, Thorhall lunged at him with the spear. It struck Grim's shield, split it in two, and went right through Grim himself, so that the blade protruded from between his shoulders. Thorhall flung him off the spear, dead.

Kari Solmundarson caught sight of this and said to Asgrim, 'Your son Thorhall has just arrived, and has killed a man already. It would be a disgrace if he alone had the courage to avenge the Burning.'

'Never!' said Asgrim. 'We shall attack them at once.'

Orders were shouted throughout the army, and the battle-cry roared out. Flosi and his men turned to face them, urging each other on fiercely.

Kari Solmundarson came face to face with Arni Kolsson and Hallbjorn the Strong. The moment Hallbjorn saw Kari he struck at him, aiming at the leg; Kari leapt high, and Hallbjorn missed. Kari turned on Arni Kolsson and hacked at his shoulder, cleaving shoulder-bone and collar-bone and splitting open the chest. Arni fell down dead at once. Then Kari struck at Hallbjorn; the blow sliced through his shield and cut off Hallbjorn's big toe. Then Holmstein Spak-Bersason hurled a spear at Kari, but Kari caught it in mid-air and returned it, killing a man in Flosi's following.

Thorgeir Skorar-Geir now encountered Hallbjorn the Strong, and lunged at him one-handed with such force that Hallbjorn was knocked down and only just managed to get to his feet; he fled at once. Then Thorgeir met Thorvald Thrum-Ketilsson and struck at him at once with 'Battle-Troll', the axe that Skarp-Hedin had owned. Thorvald put his shield in the way; the axe split the shield in two, but the upper horn caught him in the chest and pierced it. Thorvald fell, dead.

Asgrim and his son Thorhall, with Hjalti and Gizur the White, were attacking Flosi and the Sigfussons and others of the Burners. The fighting there was bitter, and it ended with Flosi and his men retreating before the ferocity of the onslaught. Gudmund the Powerful, Mord Valgardsson, and Thorgeir Skorar-Geir were attacking the men from Oxarfjord and the

Eastfjords and Reykjardale, and there, too, the fighting was bitter.

Kari Solmundarson met Bjarni Brodd-Helgason. Kari seized a spear and lunged at him, striking his shield; and had Bjarni not wrenched the shield to one side, the spear would have gone right through him. He struck back at Kari, aiming at the leg; Kari jerked his leg away and spun on his heel, making Bjarni miss.

Kari at once struck back at him. Someone ran forward and put up a shield in front of Bjarni. Kari's blow split the shield in two, and the point of the sword caught the man's thigh, ripping the whole leg open; he fell at once and was a cripple for the rest of his life. Kari then grasped a spear with both hands and lunged at Bjarni, who had no choice but to fling himself sideways under the thrust; and when he regained his feet, he fled.

Thorgeir Skorar-Geir attacked Holmstein Spak-Bersason and Thorkel Geitisson, and eventually put them both to flight. Gudmund the Powerful's men jeered at them loudly.

Thorvard Tjorvason from Ljosawater was severely wounded in the arm by a spear said to have been thrown by Halldor, the son of Gudmund the Powerful. But Thorvard never received any compensation for that wound; the crowd was very thick.

Some of the things that happened are related here, but there were far many more that have not been reported.

Flosi had told his men to make for the natural stronghold of Almanna Gorge if they were forced back, for there they could be attacked from one side only. But the group led by Hall of Sida and his son Ljot, in retreat before the onslaught of Asgrim's men, had turned down along the east bank of Oxar River.

Hall said, 'It would be a tragedy to see the whole Althing fighting. I think, kinsman Ljot, that we should appeal for help to separate the two sides, even though we might be abused for it by some people. Wait for me here at the head of this bridge while I go over to the booths to get some help.'

'If I see that Flosi and his men are in need of our support, I shall run to their help at once,' replied Ljot.

'You must do what you think best,' said Hall. 'But I beg you to wait for my return.'

Now the ranks of Flosi's men broke in flight and they all fled west over Oxar River, with Asgrim and Gizur the White and their whole army in pursuit. Flosi and his men retreated towards the gap between Snorri's booth and the Hlad booth. But Snorri the Priest had drawn up his forces there so densely that they could not pass through.

Snorri called out to Flosi, 'Why are you in such a rush? Who is chasing you?'

'As if you did not know that already,' replied Flosi. 'Is it you who is responsible for preventing us from reaching the safety of Almanna Gorge?'

'It is not my doing,' replied Snorri, 'but I know whose doing it is. I can tell you without being asked that it is the work of Thorvald Cropped-Beard and Kol.'

Both these men had been dead for many years; they had both been utter scoundrels.*

Then, turning to his own men, Snorri shouted, 'Hack at them and thrust at them and drive them away from here. They will not resist for long, with the others attacking from below. But don't pursue them. Let them fight it out themselves.'

Thorstein Hollow-Mouth, Skapti Thoroddsson's son, was fighting on the side of Gudmund the Powerful, his father-in-law. When Skapti heard this, he made for Snorri the Priest's booth, intending to ask Snorri to come with him and stop the fighting. The battle was at its height as he was approaching the door of Snorri's booth, and Asgrim and his men were advancing fast from below.

Thorhall Asgrimsson said, 'There is Skapti Thoroddsson now, father.'

'So I see, kinsman,' replied Asgrim, and at once hurled a spear at Skapti. It struck him just below the thickest part of the calf and went right through both legs. Skapti was thrown to the ground and could not get up again. The bystanders could do nothing but drag him headlong into the booth of some sword-grinder.

* A slightly garbled reference. Thorvald Cropped-Beard had burned his brother Gunnar alive in his house in the Eastfjords; their grandfather, Thorir Cropped-Beard, had murdered a slave called Kol, for which he was outlawed and his property confiscated for the benefit of the Althing. Snorri mockingly suggests that it is their evil spirits, still assumed to be haunting the Althing, that are thwarting Flosi's escape. *Translators' note.*

Then Asgrim and his men attacked so violently that Flosi and his men fled south along the river to the Modruvellir booth. There was a man called Solvi standing beside a booth, cooking meat in a large cauldron; he had just taken the meat out, but the water was still boiling furiously. Solvi caught sight of the fleeing Eastfjords men who were almost on him by then.

Solvi said, 'Are all these Eastfjords men cowards, fleeing along here? Even Thorkel Geitisson is running. What a lie to say of him, as so many have done, that he is bravery itself, for now he is fleeing faster than anyone else.'

Hallbjorn the Strong was nearby at that moment, and said, 'You shall never be able to say that all of us are cowards.' With that he seized hold of Solvi, lifted him high in the air, and pitched him head-first into the cauldron. Solvi died at once. Just then Hallbjorn was attacked, and had to start fleeing once more.

Flosi hurled a spear at Bruni Haflidason, one of the men in Gudmund the Powerful's forces; it struck him in the waist and killed him. Thorstein Hlennason pulled the spear out of the body and hurled it back at Flosi, hitting him in the leg and wounding him severely. Flosi fell, but got up again at once. Then they all retreated towards the Vatnsfjord booth.

At this, Ljot and Hall of Sida crossed to the west bank of the river with all their men. As they reached the lava bed, a spear came hurtling from Gudmund the Powerful's forces; it struck Ljot in the waist and he fell down dead at once. It was never discovered who had done this killing.

Flosi and his men retreated past the Vatnsfjord booth. Thorgeir Skorar-Geir said, 'There is Eyjolf Bolverksson now, Kari. Reward him for that bracelet.'

Kari snatched a spear from someone and hurled it at Eyjolf. It struck him in the waist and went right through him; Eyjolf fell down dead at once.

Now there was a slight lull in the fighting. At that, Snorri the Priest arrived with his forces, together with Skapti, and they rushed up between the two sides so that they could not get at each other. Hall of Sida also came up and helped to separate them, and a provisional truce was arranged for the duration of the Althing. The dead were laid out and carried to church, and the wounds of those who were injured were dressed.

Next day everyone went to the Law Rock. Hall of Sida stood up and asked for a hearing, which was granted at once. He said, 'There have been harsh happenings here, in loss of life and law-suits. Now I shall let it be seen that I am no hero; I want to ask Asgrim and those others who are behind these lawsuits, to grant us a settlement on even terms.' He pleaded with them eloquently and persuasively.

Kari replied, 'Even though all the others accept settlements, I shall never do so. You are trying to equate the Burning with these killings, and that we could never tolerate.'

Thorgeir Skorar-Geir said the same.

Then Skapti Thoroddsson stood up and said, 'You would be better not to have deserted your kinsmen, Kari, and not to except yourself from a settlement now.'

Kari replied :

> 'Why should you, of all men,
> Heap abuse on me for fleeing –
> Weapons have been drawn
> For far less cause than this;
> You, the cowardly red-beard,
> Who crept into a booth
> When the long tongues of steel
> Sang in battle chorus.

> 'Skapti was easily put off,
> And cowered behind his shield,
> When others were reluctant
> To go out and stop the fighting;
> And cooks had to drag
> This prone prince of battle
> Into some juggler's booth –
> It was the plainest cowardice.

> 'Men have joked
> About the Burning of Njal
> And Grim and Helgi;
> But they do wrong,
> And when this Althing
> Comes to an end,
> There will be grunting
> To a different tune in Svinafell.'

There was loud laughter at this. Snorri the Priest smiled, and murmured in an undertone that carried to many:

> 'Skapti's good at stopping fights,
> But Asgrim stopped him – with a spear.
> Holmstein didn't really want to flee,
> And Thorkel didn't really want to fight.'

There was even louder laughter.

Hall of Sida said, 'Everyone knows the great grief that I myself have suffered. My son Ljot is dead. Many would think that he ought to be the most costly of all those who have lost their lives here. But to bring about a settlement I am prepared to claim no compensation for my son, and yet give pledges of peace to those men who are my adversaries. I appeal to you, Snorri the Priest, and other good men, to bring about a settlement between us.'

With that he sat down. There was loud approval at his words, and everyone praised his good-will highly.

Then Snorri the Priest stood up and made a long and eloquent speech, urging Asgrim and Gizur and those others who were acting on their behalf, to agree to a settlement.

Asgrim said, 'I made up my mind, when Flosi invaded my home, that I would never make any settlement with him. But now, because of what you and others of my friends have said, Snorri the Priest, I do not want to dissociate myself from a settlement.'

Thorleif Crow and Thorgrim the Mighty also said that they would join in a settlement, and strongly urged their brother Thorgeir Skorar-Geir to do the same. But Thorgeir refused, and said that he would never forsake Kari.

Then Gizur the White said, 'Now Flosi can see what choice he has, whether or not he is prepared to make a settlement in which all are not included.'

Flosi replied that he was willing to do so. 'The fewer good men I have against me, the better,' he said.

Gudmund the Powerful said, 'For my part I am prepared to guarantee compensation for those killings that have taken place here at the Althing, on condition that the dismissals of the actions for the Burning be revoked.'

Gizur the White, Asgrim, and Hjalti all gave their support to this, and a settlement was arranged on those terms. It was agreed to refer the disputes to the arbitration of twelve men, consisting of Snorri the Priest and other worthy men. The killings on each side were offset against each other, and money paid for any which were left over.

They also arbitrated in the actions for the Burning. Njal was to be paid for with treble compensation, and Bergthora with double compensation. The killing of Skarp-Hedin was equated with the killing of Hoskuld Hvitaness-Priest. Grim and Helgi were each to be paid for with double compensation, and there was to be single compensation for every other person killed. No settlement was made concerning the death of Kari's son, Thord.

Furthermore, Flosi and all the Burners were ordered to leave the country, but they did not have to go that summer unless he so wished; however, if they had not left after three years, Flosi and all the Burners would incur full outlawry, and their sentence could be announced at the spring Assembly or autumn Assembly, whichever was preferred. Flosi was to stay abroad for three years; but Gunnar Lambason, Grani Gunnarsson, Glum Hildisson, and Kol Thorsteinsson were never to be allowed to return.

Then Flosi was asked if he wished to claim compensation for his own wound, but he replied that he did not want to make money out of his own person.

It was laid down that no compensation should be paid for Eyjolf Bolverksson, because of his unfairness and dishonesty.

The settlement was now confirmed by hand-shakes, and it was never broken.

Asgrim and the others gave Snorri the Priest fine gifts. He gained great honour from these proceedings.

Skapti Thoroddsson received no compensation for his wound.

Gizur the White, Hjalti, and Asgrim invited Gudmund the Powerful to their homes. He accepted the invitations, and each of them gave him a gold bracelet. Then Gudmund rode off north to his home, and was praised by everyone for his conduct throughout the proceedings.

Thorgeir Skorar-Geir invited Kari home; but first they accompanied Gudmund all the way north to the mountains. Kari gave Gudmund a gold brooch, and Thorgeir gave him a silver belt, both very valuable, and they parted in warmest friendship. Gudmund then rode on home to the north, and he is now out of this saga. Kari and Thorgeir turned south from the mountains down to Hreppar, and from there to Thjors River.

Meanwhile, Flosi and all the Burners rode east to Fljotshlid, where Flosi told the Sigfussons to see to their farms. Then he learnt that Thorgeir and Kari had ridden north with Gudmund, and everyone assumed that they would be staying in the north. The Sigfussons therefore asked leave to go east to the Eyjafells district to collect money which was outstanding to them at Hofdabrekka. Flosi gave them permission, but warned them not to linger there. Flosi then rode up through Godaland, across the mountains and north of Eyjafells Glacier, and did not pause until he reached his home at Svinafell.

It remains to be said that after Hall of Sida had forgone any compensation for his son in order to bring about a settlement, everyone at the Althing contributed something to compensate him. It amounted to no less than eight hundred ounces of silver – a quadruple compensation. But all the others who had been on Flosi's side received no compensation for injury, and were extremely dissatisfied about it.

The Sigfussons stayed at home for two days, and on the third day they rode east to Raufarfell and stayed there overnight. They were in a group of fifteen and had no fears for their safety. They rode off late in the day, intending to reach Hofdabrekka that night. But in Kerlingardale they paused to rest, and fell into a deep sleep.

146

THAT same day, Kari and Thorgeir rode east over Markar River and on to Seljalandsmull. There they met some women, who recognized them at once and said, 'You aren't in such high spirits as the Sigfussons; but you ride unwarily, nonetheless.'

'Why are you so concerned with the Sigfussons?' asked Thorgeir. 'What do you know about them?'

The women replied, 'They were at Raufarfell last night, and

were planning to reach Myrdale this evening. But we were pleased to see that they were afraid of you still, for they asked when you were expected home.'

The women went on their way. Kari and Thorgeir spurred their horses.

'What do you want to do?' asked Thorgeir. 'Do you want to ride after the Sigfussons?'

'I've no objections to that,' replied Kari.

'What target should we set ourselves?' asked Thorgeir.

'I would not like to say,' replied Kari, 'for those we murder with our mouths often live longest. But I know what you have set yourself; you are planning to take on eight of them. And even that is an easier task than when you killed seven men in a gorge after lowering yourself down to them by rope. You and your kinsmen are so made that you are always eager to excel yourselves. The least I can do is to be an eye-witness for you, to tell the story afterwards. So the two of us alone shall ride after them, for I can see that your mind is already set on it.'

They rode east by the upper route, by-passing Holt, for Thorgeir did not want his brothers to be implicated in anything that might happen. Then they rode east to Myrdale, where they met a man leading a horse carrying peat-panniers.

This man said, 'There are not enough of you today, friend Thorgeir.'

'What do you mean by that?' asked Thorgeir.

'I mean that there could be good hunting here,' he replied. 'The Sigfussons have ridden past and are probably sleeping east in Kerlingardale all day, because they do not intend to go further than Hofdabrekka tonight.'

With that they parted. Kari and Thorgeir rode east on to Arnarstakk Heath, and had an uneventful journey to Kerlingardale River, which was then in spate. They rode up along the river, for they had caught sight of horses with saddles on. They rode up to them, and saw some men sleeping in a hollow, with spears stuck in the ground just above them. Kari and Thorgeir removed the spears and threw them into the river.

Then Thorgeir asked, 'Do you want to wake them first?'

'Need you ask,' replied Kari, 'when you must already have made up your mind not to attack men in their sleep and thus kill dishonourably?'

They shouted at the men, who all woke up, jumped to their feet, and reached for their weapons. Kari and Thorgeir gave them time to arm themselves before attacking.

Thorgeir Skorar-Geir then rushed at Thorkel Sigfusson. Another man ran round behind Thorgeir, but before he could land a blow, Thorgeir raised the axe 'Battle-Troll' violently with both hands. Swinging it back, he crashed the hammer down on the head of the man behind him, shattering the skull into fragments and killing him instantly; swinging the axe forward, he struck Thorkel on the shoulder and sheared off his arm.

Mord Sigfusson, Sigurd Lambason, and Lambi Sigurdarson all attacked Kari. Lambi came up on him from behind and lunged with a spear. Kari caught sight of him and leapt high with legs apart to straddle the thrust. The spear lodged in the ground, and Kari came down on it, snapping the shaft. He himself had a spear in one hand and a sword in the other; he carried no shield. He lunged right-handed at Sigurd Lambason; the spear caught him full in the chest and came out behind his shoulders. Sigurd fell dead at once. With his left hand, Kari hacked at Mord Sigfusson and struck him on the hip, slicing through both hip and backbone. Mord pitched forward on to his face, dead. Then Kari spun on his heel like a top and made for Lambi Sigurdarson, who took the only chance of saving himself by running away.

Now Thorgeir turned to face Leidolf the Strong. They struck at each other simultaneously, and Leidolf's blow was so powerful that it cut clean through the shield where it landed. Thorgeir swung two-handed with his axe; the lower horn of the blade caught Leidolf's shield and split it, and the upper horn cut through his collar-bone and dug deep into his chest. Just then Kari came up and slashed off Leidolf's leg at mid-thigh. Leidolf fell down dead at once.

Ketil of Mork said, 'Let us run to our horses. We cannot stand our ground against men of such terrible strength.'

They ran to their horses and mounted hastily.

'Do you want us to chase them?' asked Thorgeir. 'We could kill a few more yet.'

Kari replied, 'The man riding last is someone I have no wish to kill – Ketil of Mork. Our wives are sisters, and he has always been the most honourable of our enemies.'

They mounted their horses and rode home to Holt. Thorgeir sent his brothers east to Skogar, where they owned another farm, for he did not want them to be accused of truce-breaking. After that, Thorgeir kept a number of armed men around him, never fewer than thirty. There was great jubilation. People thought that Thorgeir had greatly enhanced his prestige, and Kari as well, and their expedition was often recalled, how the two of them had ridden against fifteen, killed five, and put the rest to flight.

Meanwhile, Ketil of Mork and the others rode as fast as they could all the way to Svinafell, where they reported their misfortunes. Flosi said that it was not unexpected – 'and let this be a warning to you,' he said, 'never to travel like that in future.'

Flosi was a very genial man and an excellent host, and it has been said of him that he had nearly all the qualities of a true chieftain.

He remained at Svinafell for the rest of the summer and the following winter. After Christmas, Hall of Sida and his son Kol came from the east to visit him. Flosi was delighted to see him, and they talked often about the lawsuits. Flosi commented that they had already paid dearly for them; Hall replied that the dispute had gone very much as he had predicted. Flosi asked him what he thought was the most sensible thing to do now.

'My advice,' replied Hall, 'is that you try to make a settlement with Thorgeir Skorar-Geir, if possible. But he will be very hard to persuade to any reconciliation.'

'Do you think that this would put an end to the killings?' asked Flosi.

'No,' replied Hall, 'but there will be fewer opponents to contend with if Kari is on his own. However, if you do not come to terms with Thorgeir, it will cost you your life.'

'What terms should we offer him?' asked Flosi.

'The only terms he would accept will seem to you harsh,' said Hall. 'He will agree to a settlement only on condition that he pays nothing for what he has done, but is paid one third of the compensation for Njal and the Njalssons, his due share.'

'These are hard terms,' said Flosi.

'They are not so hard as far as you are concerned,' said Hall, 'for it is not your duty to claim compensation for the Sigfussons; that is the task of their brothers, and it is Hamund the

Halt's duty to do it for his son Leidolf. You yourself can make settlement with Thorgeir now, for I shall accompany you there and Thorgeir will always give me a welcome of sorts. And none of those whose duty it is to raise actions can dare to remain on their farms in Fljotshlid if they do not share in this settlement, for it would cost them their lives, and not surprisingly, considering Thorgeir's temperament.'

The Sigfussons were sent for and this proposal was put to them. The outcome, thanks to Hall, was that they agreed to everything he suggested and were eager to make settlement.

Grani Gunnarsson and Gunnar Lambason said, 'If Kari is on his own, we can easily manage to make him no less afraid of us than we are of him.'

'You should not talk like that,' said Hall. 'Any dealings you have with Kari will cost you dearly, and you will suffer heavy losses before this is over between you.'

They discussed it no further.

147

HALL OF SIDA and his son Kol, with four others, rode west over Lomagnup Sand and Arnarstakk Heath, and did not pause until they reached Myrdale. There they asked whether Thorgeir would be at home at Holt. They were told that he was, and were asked in return where they were going.

'To Holt,' replied Hall, and was told that he was on a good mission. They stayed for a while and rested their horses. Then they mounted and rode to Solheim that evening, where they stayed the night.

Next day they rode to Holt. Thorgeir and Kari and their men were outside, and recognized Hall, who was wearing a blue cape and carrying a small axe inlaid with silver. As they came riding into the home-meadow, Thorgeir walked to meet them and helped Hall to dismount. Both Thorgeir and Kari embraced him and ushered him between them into the main room, seated him on the high-seat on the dais, and asked him for all the news.

He stayed there that night. Next morning he approached

Thorgeir on the question of a settlement and told him what terms were being offered, describing them with great eloquence and good-will.

'You must be aware,' replied Thorgeir, 'that I refused to accept any settlement with the Burners.'

'Things were different then,' said Hall. 'The blood-lust was on you then, and you have done quite a few killings since.'

'That is so,' said Thorgeir. 'But what terms do you offer Kari?'

'He will be offered honourable and fitting terms,' replied Hall, 'if he wishes to accept a settlement.'

Kari said, 'I beg of your, Thorgeir my friend, to agree to a settlement for yourself, for you will never be in a stronger position than this.'

'I would hate to forsake you by accepting a settlement,' replied Thorgeir, 'if you are not going to accept it too.'

'No,' said Kari, 'I do not want reconciliation. Though I consider that we have now avenged the Burning, to me my son is still unavenged; and that is a task I have resolved to carry out by myself, as far as I can.'

But Thorgeir still refused to accept a settlement, until Kari threatened to become his enemy unless he did so. Then Thorgeir guaranteed Flosi and his men a truce until a peace-meeting could be held, and Hall gave pledges to Thorgeir on behalf of Flosi and the Sigfussons.

Before parting, Thorgeir gave Hall a gold bracelet and a scarlet cloak, and Kari gave him a silver necklace with three gold crosses on it. Hall thanked them warmly for their gifts, and rode away in high honour. He did not pause until he reached Svinafell, where Flosi welcomed him warmly. Hall told Flosi all about his mission and his discussion with Thorgeir, and how Thorgeir had refused to accept any settlement until Kari had intervened, pleaded with him, and then threatened to become his enemy unless he did so – but that Kari himself had refused to come to terms.

'There are few men like Kari,' said Flosi. 'He is the man I would most like to resemble in character.'

Hall and the others stayed there for a while. Then at the appointed time they rode west to the peace-meeting, and went to Hofdabrekka, as had been arranged.

Thorgeir then arrived from the west, and they discussed the

settlement. Everything went just as Hall had predicted. Thorgeir insisted on a condition that Kari should be allowed to live with him whenever he chose – 'and neither side is to harm the other in my home. Also, I do not want to have to collect the compensation from you all one by one; I want you, Flosi, to be responsible to me for it and collect it from your followers yourself. I want the agreement that was made at the Althing about the Burning to be kept in every detail. And I want you, Flosi, to pay me the third share that I am entitled to.'

Flosi quickly agreed to all this. Thorgeir refused to remit the sentences of exile or district outlawry.

Then Flosi and Hall rode east. Hall said to Flosi, 'Hold faithfully to this settlement, son-in-law, the exile and the pilgrimage to Rome and the payment of compensation. If you carry out your duties manfully, you will be accounted a good man even though you stumbled into this disaster.'

Flosi gave his promise. Hall rode home to the east, and Flosi went back to Svinafell, and remained there for a while.

148

THORGEIR SKORAR-GEIR rode home from the peace-meeting. Kari asked him whether the settlement had been effected. Thorgeir said that they were now completely reconciled.

Then Kari wanted to saddle his horse and go away. Thorgeir said, 'You have no need to go away, for it was stipulated in the settlement that you should be allowed to stay here whenever you wished.'

'No, kinsman,' said Kari, 'that must not be, for if I kill someone, they will immediately accuse you of being in league with me, and I do not want that. But I should like you to take over my property and let it be assigned to you and to my wife, Helga Njal's-daughter, and my daughters. Then it can never be confiscated by my adversaries.'

Thorgeir agreed to what Kari said, and Kari's property was formally made over to him.

Then Kari left, taking two horses and his weapons and

clothes, and some valuables in gold and silver. He rode west round Seljalandsmull and then up along Markar River into Thorsmork. In that district there are three farms, all called Mork. In the middle one there lived a man called Bjorn Kadalsson, known as Bjorn the White; he was the grandson of a man called Bjalfi, who had been a slave freed by Asgerd, the mother of Njal and Holta-Thorir. Bjorn the White was married to a woman called Valgerd, the daughter of Thorbrand Asbrandsson and of Gudlaug, the sister of Hamund, the father of Gunnar of Hlidarend. Valgerd had been married off to Bjorn for the sake of his money and did not have much love for him, but they had some children together.

There was plenty of everything at their farm. Bjorn was always bragging about himself, which his wife disliked intensely. He was keen-sighted and good at running.

Kari went there to stay overnight, and the couple welcomed him with open arms. Next morning they talked, and Kari said to Bjorn, 'I should like you to let me stay here, for I think I have come to a good place, coming to you. I should also like to have you with me on my travels, for you are keen-sighted and swift-footed, and I expect that you are also full of daring.'

'I cannot find fault with my eyesight or my daring or any of my other manly qualities,' replied Bjorn. 'You have come to me because all other doors are closed to you; and at your request, Kari, I won't treat you like just anybody. I shall certainly help you in any way you ask.'

His wife overheard this and said, 'The trolls take your boasting and bragging. Don't try to fool yourself and Kari with such conceited nonsense. For my part I shall gladly give Kari food and other necessities which I know will be of use to him. But don't rely on Bjorn's manliness, Kari, for I'm afraid that he'll prove less courageous than he makes out.'

'You have often abused me,' said Bjorn, 'but I have such confidence in myself that I would never flee from anyone; and to prove it, there are few people who pick a fight with me, because no one ever dares to.'

Kari stayed there secretly for a time. Very few people knew about it; everyone now assumed that he had gone to the north to visit Gudmund the Powerful, because Bjorn, on Kari's instructions, told the neighbours that he had met Kari on the

track and that he was then on his way north through Godaland to see Gudmund the Powerful. This story spread throughout the country.

149

MEANWHILE, Flosi said to his comrades, the Burners, 'We can
no longer afford to remain inactive. We must be thinking of
going abroad and paying our compensation and fulfilling the
conditions of the settlements as honourably as possible. Let each
of us arrange a passage wherever he prefers.'

They asked him to make the arrangements.

Flosi said, 'Let us ride east to Hornafjord, where there is a
ship laid up, owned by a man from Trondheim called Eyjolf
Nose. He wants to marry, but cannot have the woman of his
choice unless he settles in Iceland. We shall buy the ship from
him. We have little money but plenty of men; the ship is a
large one and will carry us all.'

They said no more about it, but a little later they rode east
without a pause to Bjarnaness in Hornafjord. There they met
Eyjolf Nose, who had been staying there over the winter. Flosi
was given a good welcome, and stayed there overnight with his
men. Next morning Flosi offered to buy the ship from Eyjolf,
who said that he would not be unwilling to sell it if he got what
he wanted for it. Flosi asked him how he wanted to be paid.
The Easterner said he wanted payment in land, preferably
somewhere nearby, and told Flosi all about his marriage-nego-
tiations with the farmer. Flosi promised to lend him his support
in arranging the marriage, and then to buy the ship from him.
The Easterner was delighted. Flosi offered him land at Borgarhofn. Eyjolf then had a talk with the farmer, with Flosi present,
and Flosi used his influence to conclude the marriage-deal. Flosi
made over to Eyjolf the land at Borgarhofn, and accepted
ownership of the vessel. Flosi also received from Eyjolf, as part
of their bargain, twenty hundreds of cloth.

Then Flosi rode back. He was so well liked by his followers
that he could get any goods from them on loan or as a gift,

just as he wished. He rode home to Svinafell and stayed there for a time. Then he sent Kol Thorsteinsson and Gunnar Lambason east to Hornafjord; they were to stay there at the ship and get it ready, set up booths, pack the cargo, and lay in supplies.

The Sigfussons told Flosi that they were going to ride west to Fljotshlid to see to their farms and fetch their goods and anything else they needed – 'we have no need to be wary of Kari now that he is in the north.'

'I am not sure how much truth there is in these stories about Kari's movements,' said Flosi. 'Reports from much nearer at hand than these often turn out to be garbled. It is my advice that you travel in numbers, separate as seldom as possible, and be very much on your guard. And you, Ketil of Mork, should now bear in mind the dream I told you about and which you asked me to keep secret; for many of those who were summoned in that dream are now in your company.'

'A man's life can be no longer than its allotted span,' replied Ketil. 'But I know you mean well by your warning.'

They said no more about it. The Sigfussons and those who were to go with them made ready for the journey, eighteen in all. Before they left they embraced Flosi. He said that he would never again see some of those who were riding away, but they did not let that deter them and rode on their way. Flosi had asked them to fetch his goods in Medalland and convey them east, and do the same in Landbrot and the Skogar District.

They rode to Skaptrivertongue and then up into the mountains, north of Eyjafells Glacier, then down into Godaland and through the woods into Thorsmork.

Bjorn of Mork caught sight of the riders and went at once to meet them. They exchanged friendly greetings. The Sigfussons asked about Kari Solmundarson.

'I met Kari,' replied Bjorn, 'but that was a long time ago now. He rode north to Gasasand and was on his way to see Gudmund the Powerful. I got the impression that he was rather afraid of you, and felt himself quite friendless.'

'He will be more afraid of us yet,' said Grani Gunnarsson, 'as he will find out when he comes within range of us. We are not scared of him in the slightest now that he is on his own.'

Ketil of Mork told him to be quiet and stop boasting. Bjorn asked them when they would be coming back.

'We shall be staying for about a week in Fljotshlid,' they replied, and told him on what day they would be going up into the mountains on their way back. With that they parted.

The Sigfussons rode to their farms, where everyone was delighted to see them. They stayed there for a week.

Bjorn returned to the house and told Kari everything about the Sigfussons' journey and plans. Kari said that he had shown him great friendship and loyalty over this.

Bjorn replied, 'I was quite sure that if I promised anyone my protection it would make a considerable difference to him.'

His wife said, 'You can be a bad lot without necessarily being a traitor.'

Kari stayed there for the next six days.

150

KARI said to Bjorn, 'We shall now ride east over the mountains and down to Skaptrivertongue, and travel stealthily through Flosi's country, for I am planning to board ship in Alptafjord and go abroad.'

'This is a terribly dangerous journey,' said Bjorn, 'and few would have the courage to make it except you and me.'

His wife said, 'If you let Kari down, you had better realize that you will never be allowed into my bed again, and that my kinsmen will force a division of property between us.'

'You are much more likely to have to find some other grounds for divorce than that, housewife,' replied Bjorn, 'for I shall give ample evidence of my courage and exploits when it comes to fighting.'

They rode east that day into the mountains north of the glacier, never using the main track, and down to Skaptrivertongue, keeping well above all the farms on the way to Skapt River. There they led their horses into a hollow and kept close watch while remaining out of sight themselves.

Kari then said to Bjorn, 'What should we do if they ride down from the mountains at us?'

'Aren't there two courses open?' replied Bjorn. 'Either we can ride away from them to the north in the lee of the slopes and let them ride past, or else wait and see if any of them lag behind and then attack them.'

They discussed this at length, and one moment Bjorn was all for fleeing as fast as possible, and the next moment he was all for staying to deal with them. Kari found it all most entertaining.

The Sigfussons left their homes on the day they had told Bjorn they would. They arrived at Mork and knocked on the door, wanting to speak to Bjorn. His wife came to the door and greeted them. They asked at once for Bjorn; she replied that he had gone down to the Eyjafells district and east past Seljalandsmull to Holt — 'for he has money outstanding to him there.'

They believed this story, for they knew that Bjorn had money to collect in that area. They rode east into the mountains and did not pause until they reached Skaptrivertongue. They rode down along the river and rested their horses just where Kari had expected them to. Then they split up. Ketil of Mork rode east to Medalland with eight men, and the others lay down to sleep. The first thing they knew was that Kari and Bjorn were coming at them.

There was a little tongue of land projecting into the river. Kari took up position there and told Bjorn to stand behind him and not to expose himself too much, but make himself as useful as possible.

'I had never thought,' said Bjorn, 'that I would use another man as a shield, but under the circumstances you had better have your way. With my brains and dash I can still do our enemies no little damage.'

The others all jumped up and rushed at them. Modolf Ketilsson was the quickest of them, and he lunged at Kari with a spear. Kari had his shield up; the spear pierced it and stuck fast. With a wrench of the shield, Kari snapped the spear; his sword was already drawn, and now he hacked at Modolf, who struck back simultaneously. Kari's sword struck Modolf's hilt-guard, glanced off it on to the wrist and severed it, so that hand and sword fell down together. Kari's sword swept on into Modolf's side, deep between his ribs. Modolf fell, and died instantly.

Grani Gunnarsson seized a spear and hurled it at Kari. Kari

jammed his shield down into the ground so hard that it stood upright by itself, caught the spear in flight, hurled it back at Grani, and then caught hold of his shield again – all with his left hand. Grani had his shield up; the spear struck the shield and went through it, through Grani's thigh below the groin and then into the ground, pinning him down. Grani could not free himself, but his companions pulled him away and laid him in a hollow under a protective covering of shields.

A man rushed up to try and cut off Kari's leg. He managed to get to one side of him; but Bjorn struck out at him, cutting off his hand, and then dodged back behind Kari before a blow could be landed on him. Kari swept at this man with his sword and cut him in two at the waist.

Then Lambi Sigurdarson rushed at Kari and hacked at him with his sword. Kari parried it flat-shielded, and the sword did not bite. Then Kari thrust at him with his sword and caught him full in the chest. The point came out between his shoulders, and Lambi died.

Thorstein Geirleifsson rushed at Kari from the side. Kari caught sight of him, slashed at him with his sword shoulder-high, and cut him in two. A little later he killed Gunnar of Skal, a worthy farmer.

Bjorn had wounded three men who were trying to kill Kari, but at no time did he expose himself to any danger. Neither he nor Kari was wounded in the encounter, but all the survivors on the other side were injured; they jumped on to their horses and dashed out into Skapt River as fast as they could. They were so frightened that they kept clear of all farms, not daring to stop anywhere to tell what had happened.

Kari and Bjorn jeered at them as they fled. The survivors rode east to the Skogar District and did not pause until they reached Svinafell. Flosi was not at home when they arrived, and so no attempt was made from there to search for Kari and Bjorn. Everyone thought the Sigfussons' journey an ignominious one.

Kari rode to Skal and announced that he was responsible for the killings. He reported the death of Gunnar, the master of the house, and the other four men, and also Grani's wound. He suggested that Grani had better be brought indoors if he was to survive.

Bjorn said that he had not had the heart to kill him, although he richly deserved it. The bystanders replied that few men were rotting in their graves on account of Bjorn. Bjorn retorted that he was now in a position to make as many of the men of Sida rot in their graves as he chose. That would be disaster indeed, was the reply.

Then Kari and Bjorn rode away.

151

KARI asked Bjorn, 'What should we do now? I want to test how good your brains are.'

'Do you think it important that we should be particularly clever this time?' asked Bjorn.

'I do indeed,' replied Kari.

'Then it's easy to decide,' said Bjorn. 'We'll fool them all like ignorant giants. We'll pretend to be riding north into the mountains, and then as soon as the hill conceals us from them, we'll turn back and ride down along Skapt River and hide ourselves in the most convenient place while the search is at its height, if in fact they come after us.'

'That is just what we will do,' said Kari. 'It is the very thing I had in mind myself.'

'You'll find out,' said Bjorn, 'that I am no more lacking in brains than in bravery.'

They rode down along Skapt River as planned, to the point where the river divided, branching off to the east and the southeast. They turned down along the middle branch, and did not pause until they came to Medalland and reached a swamp called Kringlumire. There was lava all round it. Kari told Bjorn to look after the horses and stand guard – 'for I am very sleepy.'

Bjorn kept an eye on the horses and Kari lay down; but he was scarcely asleep before Bjorn wakened him. He had brought both horses up and they were standing nearby.

'You are certainly in need of me,' said Bjorn. 'Anyone else less brave than I would have deserted you by now, for your enemies are coming at you. You had better get ready for them.'

Kari took up position under an overhanging crag. Bjorn said, 'Where am I to stand now?'

'There are two courses open to you,' replied Kari. 'You can either stand behind me with a shield to protect yourself with, if it's of any use to you; or else mount your horse and ride away as fast as you can.'

'I certainly don't want that,' said Bjorn, 'and for several reasons. In the first place, it could be that malicious tongues might suggest that I abandoned you from cowardice, if I ride away. In the second place, I know what a catch they would think me, and two or three of them would ride after me, and I would be of no help or use to you then. So I prefer to stand by you and defend myself as long as it is granted me.'

They had not long to wait before some pack-horses were driven past the swamp. There were three men with them.

'They have not seen us,' said Kari.

'Then let them pass,' said Bjorn.

The three rode past, but then another six came riding straight towards them. They all leapt from their horses at once and rushed to the attack.

Glum Hildisson was in the lead; he lunged at Kari with a spear. Kari swivelled on his heel and Glum's spear missed and struck the rock. Bjorn saw this and at once hacked the head off Glum's spear. Kari, still off balance, struck at Glum, and his sword caught him on the thigh and sliced off the leg. Glum died instantly.

Then Vebrand and Asbrand, the sons of Thorfinn, attacked. Kari ran at Vebrand and drove his sword through him, and then hacked both legs from under Asbrand. At that moment, Kari and Bjorn received wounds.

Ketil of Mork now rushed at Kari and lunged at him with a spear. Kari jerked his leg up and the spear dug into the ground. Kari jumped on the shaft and snapped it. Then he seized hold of Ketil and held him fast. Bjorn came running up and wanted to kill him.

'Leave him alone,' said Kari. 'I am giving Ketil quarter. However often I have your life in my hands, Ketil, I shall never kill you.'

Ketil said nothing. He rode off to join the rest of his companions, and reported all this to those who had not yet heard what had happened. They told the news to the men of the district, who gathered a huge force at once and searched along all the rivers so far into the mountains that it took them three days. Then they turned back and dispersed to their homes, while Ketil and his companions rode east to Svinafell and told the news.

Flosi showed little concern, but said that he was not convinced that this would be the end of it – 'for there is no one now in all the land like Kari.'

152

MEANWHILE, Kari and Bjorn rode out to the sands. There they led their horses to a hummock overgrown with lyme-grass, and cut some of the grass to keep the horses from starving to death. Kari was so accurate in his guessing that he left there just as the others gave up the search. He rode by night up through the district to the mountains and took the same route back which they had used on their way east. They did not pause until they reached Mork.

Then Bjorn said to Kari, 'Now you must be a real friend to me when we meet my wife, for she won't believe a word I tell her. This is of vital importance to me. Repay me now for the fine support I have given you.'

'Certainly,' said Kari.

They rode up to the farm. Bjorn's wife asked them their news and then welcomed them warmly.

Bjorn said, 'Our troubles have certainly increased, woman.'

She made no reply, but smiled a little. Then she said, 'How useful did you find Bjorn?'

Kari replied, 'One's back is bare without a brother. Bjorn was extremely useful to me. He dealt with three men, and was even wounded himself. He made himself as helpful to me as he possibly could be.'

They stayed there for three days. Then they rode to Holt to see Thorgeir, and told him in private what had happened, for the news had not yet reached there. Thorgeir thanked Kari, and it was obvious that he was pleased at all this. But he also asked Kari how much he had yet to accomplish of what he had set out to do.

'I intend to kill Gunnar Lambason and Kol Thorsteinsson, if

opportunity occurs,' replied Kari. 'We shall then have killed fifteen men, counting the five that you and I killed together. And now I have a favour to ask of you.'

Thorgeir said that he would do anything he asked.

'I would like you to take care of this man,' said Kari. 'His name is Bjorn, and he was with me at these killings. Exchange his farm for him and provide him with a fully-equipped one somewhere near you here, and protect him so that no vengeance can be taken on him. This will be an easy matter for such a chieftain as you.'

'Certainly,' said Thorgeir. He provided Bjorn with a fully-equipped farm at Asolfskali and took over the farm at Mork. Thorgeir himself conveyed Bjorn's household and possessions to Asolfskali. He arranged a full settlement on Bjorn's behalf and effected a reconciliation for him with all his enemies. Thereafter Bjorn was considered much more a man than he had been before.

Kari rode away and did not pause until he came to Asgrim Ellida-Grimsson, who welcomed him most warmly. Kari told him all about the killings. Asgrim expressed his pleasure, and asked Kari what he was intending to do now. Kari said that he was planning to go abroad in pursuit of the others and wait for a chance to kill them, if he could. Asgrim said that there was no one like him for courage.

Kari stayed there for a few days. Then he rode to see Gizur the White, who welcomed him with open arms. He stayed there for a time, and then told Gizur he was going out to Eyrar. Gizur gave him a fine sword as a parting gift. Kari then rode down to Eyrar. There he arranged a passage with Kolbein the Black, an Orcadian, an old friend of his and a very brave man. He welcomed Kari with open arms and said that they would stand or fall together.

153

FLOSI and the Burners rode east to Hornafjord accompanied by nearly all his followers. They brought with them their goods and the other supplies which they were taking for the journey. They prepared the ship; Flosi stayed by it until it was ready to sail, and as soon as there was a favourable wind they put to sea. They had a long and stormy voyage, and lost their bearings completely.

One day some huge waves, three times bigger than usual, broke over the ship. Flosi said that these were breakers, and that they must be near land. There was thick fog, and now the weather worsened until it was blowing a gale. Before they knew it, they were driven ashore in the middle of the night. No lives were lost, but the ship was completely wrecked and none of the cargo could be saved. They had to go and look for shelter to keep warm.

Next morning they climbed a hill. The weather had cleared by now. Flosi asked if anyone recognized this country. There were two men who knew it and said that they were on Mainland in Orkney.

'We could have had a luckier landing,' said Flosi, 'for Helgi Njalsson, whom I killed, was one of Earl Sigurd Hlodvisson's retainers.'

They looked for a hiding-place and spread moss over themselves and lay there for a while; but very soon Flosi said, 'We must not lie here any longer and be found like this by the inhabitants.'

They stood up and discussed what to do. 'Let us give ourselves up to the earl,' said Flosi. 'We have no other choice, for our lives are in his hands anyway, if he wished to take them.'

They all left that place. Flosi warned them not to tell anyone what had happened or about their journey until he himself had told the earl. They walked on until they met some people who directed them to the earl. They went before him, and they all greeted him. The earl asked who they were. Flosi gave his name and told from what part of Iceland he came. The earl had already heard about the Burning, and he realized at once who they were. He said to Flosi, 'What can you tell me about my retainer Helgi Njalsson?'

'Only this,' replied Flosi, 'that I cut off his head.'

The earl ordered them all to be seized, and this was done. At that moment Thorstein, the son of Hall of Sida, appeared; Flosi was married to Thorstein's sister, Steinvor. Thorstein was himself one of Earl Sigurd's retainers, and when he saw Flosi being seized he went before the earl and offered all that he owned in exchange for Flosi's life. The earl was at his angriest and was obstinate for a long time, but eventually, thanks to the entreaties of Thorstein and other good men – for Thorstein had many friends, who all supported his plea – the earl agreed to accept a settlement and spared the lives of Flosi and his men.

The earl followed the custom of great rulers and let Flosi fill the place in his retinue that Helgi Njalsson had held. Thus Flosi became Earl Sigurd's retainer and soon earned himself a high place in his affections.

154*

KARI and Kolbein put to sea from Eyrar a fortnight after Flosi's departure from Hornafjord. The winds were favourable and they had a fast voyage. They landed at Fair Isle, which lies between Shetland and Orkney. Here a man called David the White received them. He told Kari everything he had heard about Flosi's travels. David was a great friend of Kari's, and Kari spent the winter with him. They got news of everything that was going on in Mainland.

Earl Sigurd invited Earl Gilli of the Hebrides, his brother-in-law, to stay with him; Gilli was married to Sigurd's sister, Hvarflod.

* Scholars agree that the Brian episode (Chapters 154–7) is based on a lost *Brian's Saga* of the late twelfth century or a lost *Earl Sigurd's Saga*. The Battle of Clontarf was fought just outside Dublin on Good Friday in 1014 (23 April). There are several Irish accounts of the battle, particularly the contemporary Annals of Ulster and the twelfth-century 'War of the Gaedhil with the Gaill' (*Cogadh Gaedhel re Gallaibh*). The battle was fought between Brian Boruma, the ageing champion who had been High-King of Ireland since 1002; and on the other hand a Norse-Irish alliance led by Sigtrygg Silk-Beard (King of Dublin) and Maelmordha, king of Leinster, the brother of Brian's divorced wife Gormflaith (Kormlod). Brian's sons were Murchad (Margad), Donnchad (Dungad) and Tadc (Tadk), and his grandson was Toirdhelbach (Kerthjalfad); only Murchad of Brian's sons took part in the battle. In the broadest outlines, the Irish sources and *Njal's Saga* agree. The lost *Brian's Saga* is also used in *Thorstein Sida-Hallsson's Saga*. *Translators' note.*

A king from Ireland, called Sigtrygg, was also there. He was the son of Olaf Kvaran. His mother was called Kormlod; she was endowed with great beauty and all those attributes which were outside her own control, but it is said that in all the characteristics for which she herself was responsible, she was utterly wicked. She had been married to a king called Brian, but now they were divorced. He was the noblest of all kings, and lived in Kincora in Ireland. His brother was Ulf Hreda, a great champion and warrior.

King Brian had a foster-son called Kerthjalfad; he was the son of King Kylfir, who had fought many battles against King Brian but eventually had fled the land and entered a monastery. When King Brian had gone south on a pilgrimage he had met King Kylfir and there had been a reconciliation; King Brian had adopted Kerthjalfad, and loved him more than his own sons. At this point in the saga, Kerthjalfad was fully grown, and was the bravest of men.

King Brian had a son called Dungad, another called Margad, and another called Tadk – he was the youngest, and we call him Tann. King Brian's elder sons were fully grown, and very brave men.

Kormlod was not the mother of King Brian's sons. She was so filled with hate against him after their divorce that she wished him dead. King Brian would always forgive men he had sentenced to outlawry, even when they committed the same offence thrice; but if they transgressed yet again, he let the law take its course. From this it can be judged what kind of a king he was.

Kormlod kept urging her son Sigtrygg to kill King Brian. For that purpose she sent him to Earl Sigurd to ask for support. King Sigtrygg arrived in Orkney before Christmas, and Earl Gilli came there at the same time, as was written earlier.

The hall was so arranged that King Sigtrygg sat on the centre high-seat with the earls on either side of him. The followers of King Sigtrygg and Earl Gilli sat on one side, and on Earl Sigurd's side sat Flosi and Thorstein Hallsson. Every seat in the hall was occupied.

King Sigtrygg and Earl Gilli wanted to hear all about the Burning and what had happened since. Gunnar Lambason was chosen to tell the story, and a chair was placed for him to sit on.

155

MEANWHILE, Kari and David the White and Kolbein arrived secretly at Mainland and landed immediately, leaving a few men to guard the ship. Kari and his comrades went straight to the earl's residence, and arrived at the hall during the feasting, at the very time that Gunnar Lambason was telling his story. Kari and the others stood outside, listening. It was Christmas Day.

King Sigtrygg asked, 'How did Skarp-Hedin bear the burning?'

'Well enough to start with,' replied Gunnar. 'But in the end he wept.'

His whole account had been extremely biased, and riddled with lies. But this was too much for Kari. He burst into the hall with his sword drawn and said:

> 'These battle-thirsty warriors
> Are boasting of Njal's burning;
> But have they yet told you
> How we forced them into flight?
> Their burning zeal
> Has been amply repaid;
> The ravens have gorged
> On a surfeit of raw flesh.'

He ran the length of the hall and struck Gunnar Lambason on the neck with such violence that his head flew off on to the table in front of the king and the earls. Earl Sigurd recognized the man who had done the killing and cried, 'Seize Kari and put him to death.'

Kari had been a member of the earl's retinue himself and was well liked by everyone; and no one stood up to carry out the earl's order.

Kari said, 'Many would say, my lord, that I have done you a service, by avenging your retainer Helgi Njalsson.'

Flosi said, 'Kari has not done this without cause. He is not in any settlement with us, and he only did what was his duty.'

Kari left the hall, and no one went in pursuit of him. He and his comrades went down to their ship. The weather was good, and they sailed south to Caithness and went ashore at Freswick to the home of a worthy man called Skeggi, where they stayed for a long time.

In the earl's hall in Orkney, the tables were scrubbed and the dead man carried out. Earl Sigurd was told that Kari and his companions had sailed off south to Scotland. King Sigtrygg said, 'That was a resolute man, to act so boldly and give no thought to his safety.'

'There is no one like Kari for courage,' replied Earl Sigurd.

Flosi now took it upon himself to tell the story of the Burning. He gave every man his proper due, and this account of it was believed.

King Sigtrygg then raised the matter of his mission to Earl Sigurd, and asked him to go to war with him against King Brian. The earl was stubborn for a long time. Finally he agreed, but only on condition that he should marry Sigtrygg's mother, Kormlod, and become king of Ireland if they defeated Brian. All his men urged him against the expedition, but without success. When they parted, Earl Sigurd had promised to take part in the expedition, and King Sigtrygg had promised him his mother and the kingdom. It was agreed that Earl Sigurd should come with all his army to Dublin on Palm Sunday.

Sigtrygg sailed south to Ireland and told his mother that the earl had joined forces with them, and told her what he himself had committed them to. She was pleased at this, but said that they would have to amass an even larger force. Sigtrygg asked where they could expect to get that.

Kormlod replied, 'There are two Vikings lying off the Isle of Man with thirty ships, and they are so formidable that no one can withstand them. They are called Ospak and Brodir. Go and meet them, and spare nothing to induce them to join you, whatever conditions they demand.'

King Sigtrygg went in search of the Vikings and found them off Man. He stated the purpose of his visit at once, but Brodir refused to have anything to do with the scheme until Sigtrygg promised him the kingdom and his mother. This was to be kept quite secret, to prevent Earl Sigurd from hearing of it. Brodir was to come to Dublin before Palm Sunday. Sigtrygg went back home and told his mother.

Then Brodir conferred with Ospak. He told Ospak all about

his talk with Sigtrygg, and asked him to join him in the war against King Brian. He said that it was of vital importance to him. Ospak said that he had no wish to fight against so good a king. They both became angry, and made a division of their forces; Ospak got ten ships, and Brodir twenty.

Ospak was a heathen, and a very shrewd man. He anchored his ships inside the Sound, while Brodir lay just outside it.

Brodir had been a Christian and had been consecrated a deacon, but he had abandoned his faith and become an apostate. Now he sacrificed to heathen spirits and was deeply skilled in magic. He wore armour that no weapon could pierce. He was tall and powerful, and his hair was so long that he tucked it under his belt; it was black.

156

ONE night a terrible clamour broke out above Brodir and his men. They all awoke and jumped up, and put on their clothes. At the same time, boiling blood rained down on them. They tried to protect themselves with their shields, but several of them were scalded. This phenomenon lasted until dawn, and one man on each ship was killed. The others slept all that day.

Next night the clamour came again, and they all jumped up once more. Their swords leapt from the sheaths, and axes and spears flew into the air and fought of their own accord. The weapons attacked the men so fiercely that they were forced to protect themselves, but several of them were wounded and one man on each ship was killed. This lasted until dawn. Then they slept again during the day.

The third night the same clamour was heard. Ravens came flying at them with beaks and talons that seemed made of iron. The ravens attacked them violently, but they defended themselves with swords and sheltered behind their shields. This lasted until dawn, and once more one man on each ship lost his life. Then the others slept again for a while.

When Brodir awoke he heaved a great sigh and ordered a boat to be lowered, saying that he wanted to see his sworn-brother Ospak. He stepped into the boat with some of his men.

When he met Ospak, he told him of all the weird events that had occurred, and asked him to explain what they could mean. Ospak refused to tell him until he was given a pledge of peace. Brodir gave his pledge, but even so Ospak put off telling him until nightfall, for Brodir would never kill at night.

Then Ospak said, 'The blood raining down on you signifies that you shall shed much blood, your own as well as other people's. The great clamour you heard signifies the rupture of the world: you shall all die soon. The weapons attacking you signify battle, and the ravens which attacked you signify the demons which you once believed in and which shall drag you down to the torments of Hell.'

Brodir was so enraged that he could not speak. He went straight back to his men and blocked the Sound with ships, fastening them to the shore with cables. He intended to kill Ospak and all his men next morning. Ospak saw their preparations, and made a vow that he would accept Christianity and join King Brian and follow him for the rest of his life. Then he made his men cover all their ships and pole them along the shore; then they severed the cables of Brodir's ships, which drifted together while the men on board slept. Ospak and his men escaped from the Sound and set sail west for Ireland, and did not pause until they reached Kincora. Ospak told King Brian everything he had learnt, received baptism from him, and committed himself to his protection. King Brian then gathered forces throughout his realm; they were all to assemble at Dublin the week before Palm Sunday.

157

EARL SIGURD HLODVISSON made ready to leave Orkney for Ireland. Flosi offered to accompany him, but the earl refused, since Flosi still had to carry out his pilgrimage to Rome. Flosi offered fifteen of his own men for the expedition, and this the earl accepted. Flosi himself went with Earl Gilli to the Hebrides.

With Earl Sigurd went Thorstein Hallsson, Hrafn the Red, and Erling of Stroma. The earl did not want a man called Harek to come with them, but promised that he would be the first to hear what happened.

Earl Sigurd arrived at Dublin with all his army on Palm Sunday. Brodir and his forces were already there. Brodir tried to learn by means of sorcery how the battle would go; the answer he got was this, that if the battle took place on Good Friday, King Brian would win the victory but lose his life, and that if the battle took place earlier, all Brian's opponents would lose their lives. Then Brodir said that they should not join battle before Friday.

On the Thursday a man on a dapple-grey horse came riding up, carrying a javelin. He talked for a long time with Brodir and Kormlod.

King Brian had already reached Dublin with all his forces. On Good Friday his army came marching out of the town, and both sides drew up in battle array. Brodir was on one flank and King Sigtrygg on the other, with Earl Sigurd in the centre.

King Brian did not wish to wield weapons on Good Friday; so a wall of shields was formed round him, and his army was drawn up in front of it. Ulf Hreda was on the flank facing Brodir, and on the other flank facing King Sigtrygg were Ospak and King Brian's sons. In the centre was Kerthjalfad, with the banners aloft before him.

The armies clashed, and there was bitter fighting. Brodir waded through the opposing ranks, felling all those in the forefront, and no weapons could wound him. Ulf Hreda turned to face him and thrust at him thrice with such violence that Brodir was knocked down each time and could scarcely regain his feet. As soon as he scrambled to his feet the third time, he fled into the woods.

Earl Sigurd had a fierce struggle with Kerthjalfad, who advanced with such vigour that he felled all those in the forefront. He burst through Earl Sigurd's ranks right up to the banner, and killed the standard-bearer. The earl ordered someone else to carry the standard, and the fighting flared up again. Kerthjalfad at once killed the new standard-bearer and all those who were near him. Earl Sigurd ordered Thorstein Hallsson to carry the standard, and Thorstein was about to take it when Amundi the White said, 'Don't take the banner, Thorstein. All those who bear it get killed.'

'Hrafn the Red,' said the earl, 'you take the standard.'

'Carry your own devil yourself,' said Hrafn.

The earl said, 'A beggar should carry his own bundle'; he ripped the flag from its staff and tucked it under his clothing.

A little later Amundi the White was killed, and then the earl himself died with a spear through him.

Ospak advanced right through the opposing flank; he was severely wounded, and both King Brian's sons were dead. But even so King Sigtrygg fled before him, and at that his whole army broke into flight.

Thorstein Hallsson stopped running while the others were fleeing, and tied up his shoe-thong. Kerthjalfad asked him why he was not running.

'Because,' said Thorstein, 'I cannot reach home tonight, for my home is out in Iceland.'

Kerthjalfad spared his life.

Hrafn the Red was chased into a river, and there he seemed to see down into the depths of Hell itself, with devils trying to drag him down. He said, 'Your dog has run twice to Rome already, Saint Peter, and would do it a third time if you allowed it.' Then the devils released him and he managed to reach the other bank of the river.

Brodir could see that King Brian's forces were pursuing the fugitives, and that there were only a few men left to man the wall of shields. He ran from the woods and burst through the wall of shields, and hacked at the king. The boy Tadk threw up an arm to protect Brian, but the sword cut off the arm and the king's head. The king's blood spilled over the stump of the boy's arm, and the wound healed at once.

Then Brodir shouted, 'Let the word go round that Brodir has felled King Brian.'

Messengers ran to tell the pursuing forces that King Brian had fallen. Ulf Hreda and Kerthjalfad turned back at once. They surrounded Brodir and his men, and smothered their weapons with tree-branches.

Brodir was taken alive. Ulf Hreda slit open his belly and unwound his intestines from his stomach by leading him round and round an oak-tree; and Brodir did not die before they had all been pulled out of him. Brodir's men were all put to death too.

King Brian's body was laid out. The head had miraculously grafted to the trunk again.

Fifteen of the Burners died in this Battle of Clontarf; there, too, fell Halldor Gudmundsson and Erling of Stroma.

On the morning of Good Friday, it happened in Caithness that a man called Dorrud went outside and saw twelve riders approach a woman's bower and disappear inside. He walked over to the bower and peered through a window; inside, he could see women with a loom set up before them. Men's heads were used in place of weights, and men's intestines for the weft and warp; a sword served as the beater, and the shuttle was an arrow. And these were the verses they were chanting:

> 'Blood rains
> From the cloudy web
> On the broad loom
> Of slaughter.
> The web of man,
> Grey as armour,
> Is now being woven;
> The Valkyries
> Will cross it
> With a crimson weft.

> 'The warp is made
> Of human entrails;
> Human heads
> Are used as weights;
> The heddle-rods
> Are blood-wet spears;
> The shafts are iron-bound,
> And arrows are the shuttles.
> With swords we will weave
> This web of battle.

> 'The Valkyries go weaving
> With drawn swords,
> Hild and Hjorthrimul,
> Sanngrid and Svipul.
> Spears will shatter,
> Shields will splinter,
> Swords will gnaw
> Like wolves through armour.

'Let us now wind
The web of war
Which the young king
Once waged.
Let us advance
And wade through the ranks,
Where friends of ours
Are exchanging blows.

Let us now wind
The web of war
And then follow
The king to battle.
Gunn and Gondul
Can see there
The blood-spattered shields
That guarded the king.

'Let us now wind
The web of war,
Where the warrior banners
Are forging forward.
Let his life
Not be taken;
Only the Valkyries
Can choose the slain.

'Lands will be ruled
By new peoples
Who once inhabited
Outlying headlands.
We pronounce a great king
Destined to die;
Now an earl
Is felled by spears.

'The men of Ireland
Will suffer a grief
That will never grow old
In the minds of men.

The web is now woven
And the battlefield reddened;
The news of disaster
Will spread through lands.

'It is horrible now
To look around,
As a blood-red cloud
Darkens the sky.
The heavens are stained
With the blood of men,
As the Valkyries
Sing their song.

'We sang well
Victory songs
For the young king;
Hail to our singing!
Let him who listens
To our Valkyrie song
Learn it well
And tell it to others.

'Let us ride our horses
Hard on bare backs,
With swords unsheathed,
Away from here.'

Then they tore the woven cloth from the loom and ripped it to pieces, each keeping the shred she held in her hands. Dorrud left the window and went home. The women mounted their horses and rode away, six to the south and six to the north.

A similar marvel was seen by Brand Gneistason in the Faroe Islands.

At Svinafell in Iceland, blood fell on to the priest's stole on Good Friday, and he had to take it off. At Thvattriver on Good Friday, the priest seemed to see an abyss of ocean beside the altar, full of terrible sights, and for a long time he was unable to sing Mass.

In Orkney, Harek thought he saw Earl Sigurd and some of his men. Harek mounted his horse and rode to meet the earl. They were observed to meet and go riding behind a hill, but they were never seen again, and not a trace of Harek was ever found.

Earl Gilli in the Hebrides dreamed that a man came to him, calling himself Herfid, and said that he had just come from Ireland. The earl asked him for news, and the man replied:

> *'I was present where men fought;*
> *Swords shrilled in Ireland.*
> *Weapons were shattered*
> *In the clash of shields.*
> *I heard that the battle was fierce;*
> *Sigurd fell in the storm of spears.*
> *Wounds bled freely.*
> *Brian fell, but conquered.'*

Flosi and Earl Gilli talked for a long time about this dream. A week later, Hrafn the Red arrived and told them everything that had happened at the Battle of Clontarf, the death of King Brian and Earl Sigurd and Brodir and all the Vikings.

'What can you tell me about my own men?' asked Flosi.

'They were all killed,' replied Hrafn, 'except your brother-in-law Thorstein Hallsson. He was spared by Kerthjalfad and is with him now. Halldor Gudmundsson was also killed there.'

Flosi told Earl Gilli that he was going away – 'for we still have a pilgrimage to Rome to carry out.'

The earl told him to do as he wished; he gave Flosi a ship and anything else they needed, as well as a load of silver. Then they sailed to Wales and stayed there for a while.

158

KARI asked Skeggi to get him a ship. Skeggi provided him with a fully-manned longship. Kari and David and Kolbein embarked and sailed south through the Minch. There they met men from the Hebrides who told them the news from Ireland, and also that Flosi and his men had gone to Wales.

When Kari heard this he told his comrades that he wanted to sail south to Wales to find them. He told anyone who would rather part company with him to do so now, for he would not conceal from anyone the fact that he felt he had not yet fully avenged his grief on the Burners. They all preferred to accompany him. They sailed south to Wales, where they put into a secluded creek.

That morning Kol Thorsteinsson went to the town to buy some silver; he had always been the most loud-mouthed of all the Burners. Kol had been keeping close company with a rich lady, and it was all but arranged that he should marry her and settle in Wales.

Kari went to the town that same morning. He arrived at the place where Kol was counting out the silver and recognized him at once. Kari rushed at him with his sword drawn and slashed at Kol's neck. Kol kept on counting, and his head said 'Ten' as it flew from his shoulders.

Kari said, 'Let Flosi know that Kari Solmundarson has killed Kol Thorsteinsson. I give notice that I am responsible for this killing.'

Then he went back to his ship and told his companions about the killing. They sailed up to Berwick, where they laid up their ship and travelled to Hvitsborg in Scotland, where they stayed with Earl Malcolm for the rest of the winter.

Flosi went to the town and had Kol's body laid out, and paid a large sum for the burial. He never uttered a word against Kari. From there Flosi sailed south across the Channel and started on his pilgrimage. He walked all the way to Rome, where he was accorded the great honour of receiving absolution at the hands of the Pope himself; he paid a large sum of money for it. Then he returned by the east route, staying in many large cities, where he presented himself before great lords and was highly honoured by them. He stayed the following winter in Norway, and was given a ship by Earl Eirik to travel to Iceland, as well as a large quantity of flour; and many others did him honour.

Then he sailed for Iceland. He landed at Hornafjord and rode home to Svinafell. He had now fulfilled all the terms of the settlement, both exile and payment of compensation.

159

KARI went back to his ship the following summer and sailed south across the English Channel, and started his pilgrimage in Normandy. He walked south and received absolution and returned to Normandy by the west route; he boarded his ship and sailed north across the Channel to Dover, in England. From there he sailed west round Wales and north through the Minch. He did not pause until he reached Freswick, in Caithness, to see Skeggi.

Kari gave Kolbein and David a cargo-boat; Kolbein sailed this ship to Norway, but David stayed behind in Fair Isle.

Kari spent the winter in Caithness. During that winter his wife Helga died in Iceland. Next summer Kari prepared to sail to Iceland. Skeggi gave him a cargo-boat. There were eighteen of them on board. They were rather late in getting away to sea, and had a long and difficult voyage. Eventually they reached Ingolfshead, but the ship was smashed to pieces, although all the crew were saved.

It was snowing furiously. His men asked Kari what they should do now. Kari replied that his plan was to go to Svinafell and put Flosi's nobility to the test. They walked to Svinafell through the snowstorm. Flosi was sitting in the main room. He recognized Kari at once and jumped up to welcome him, embraced him, and placed him on the high-seat beside him. He invited Kari to stay for the winter, and Kari accepted.

They made a full reconciliation, and Flosi gave to Kari in marriage his niece Hildigunn, the widow of Hoskuld Hvitaness-Priest.

To begin with they lived at Breidriver.

This is how men say that Flosi died: when he was an old man he went abroad to fetch himself some house-timber. He spent the winter in Norway, and next summer he was late in getting ready to sail. People warned him that his ship was not seaworthy, but Flosi replied that it was good enough for a doomed old man. He boarded the ship and sailed out to sea. Nothing was ever heard of that ship again.

Kari had four children by his first wife, Helga Njal's-daughter – Thorgerd, Ragneid, Valgerd, and Thord, the boy who was burned at Bergthorsknoll. By Hildigunn, Kari had three sons – Starkad, Thord, and Flosi, who became the father of Kolbein, one of the most outstanding men of that line.

And there I end the saga of the Burning of Njal.

GENEALOGICAL TABLES

—

THESE TABLES ARE BASED ON 'NJAL'S SAGA'
AND DO NOT ALWAYS AGREE
WITH OTHER HISTORICAL SOURCES, NOTABLY
THE 'BOOK OF SETTLEMENTS'

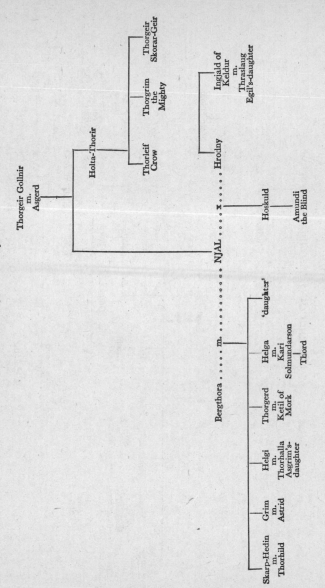

1. *The Njal Family*

2. Gunnar of Hlidarend

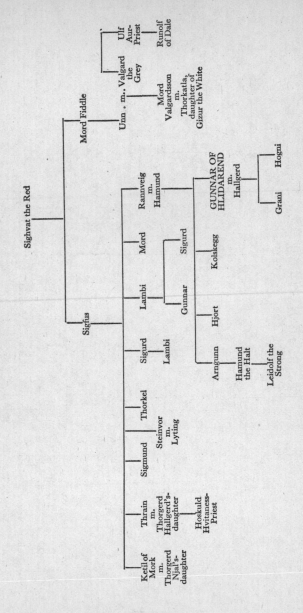

3. *Flosi Thordarson*

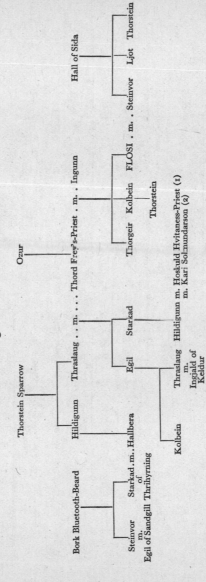

4. Gizur the White

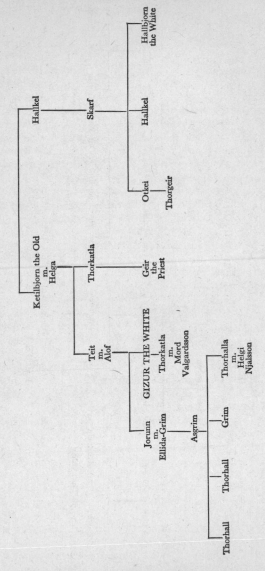

GLOSSARY OF PROPER NAMES

This Glossary of proper names is by no means a complete index to all the characters mentioned in this saga. It is intended as an aid to readers who may become confused by the intricate relationships and complex loyalties that motivate much of the action. Anyone who is *not* included may be assumed to play only an insignificant part in the saga; but some characters of rather minor importance have nevertheless been included, either because they appear at such long intervals that their previous mention may have been forgotten, or because they might be confused with others.

The numbers refer to chapters, not pages. Each entry is in the form of an indexed summary of the part played by the character concerned, and is listed under the Christian name.

—

AMUNDI THE BLIND, son of Hoskuld Njalsson, 98; kills Lyting, 106.

ARNI KOLSSON, one of the Burners: in Flosi's dream, 133; prosecuted by Asgrim Ellida-Grimsson, 141; killed at the Althing, 145.

ASGRIM ELLIDA-GRIMSSON, chieftain, of Tongue, 26; father-in-law of Helgi Njalsson, 27; supports Gizur the White against Gunnar of Hlidarend, 56; helped by Gunnar, 60; arbitrates, 66; supports the Njalssons, 112, 118–22; supports Kari after the Burning, 132, 135–7, 139–45, 152.

ASTRID OF DJUPRIVERBANK, a rich widow: marries Grim Njalsson, 25; escapes from the Burning, 129.

ATLI, a labourer, employed at Bergthorsknoll, 36; kills Kol at Hlidarend, 37; killed by Brynjolf the Unruly, 38.

BERGTHORA, wife of Njal, 20; attends Gunnar's wedding, 34; quarrels with Hallgerd, 35; sends Atli to kill Kol, 37; sends Thord Freedmansson to kill Brynjolf, 39; goads her sons to kill Sigmund, 44; goads them to kill Thrain, 91; likes Hildigunn, 97; goads her sons to kill Lyting, 98; dies with Njal in the Burning, 129.

BJARNI BRODD-HELGASON, of Hof: promises Flosi support, 134; helps Flosi bribe Eyjolf Bolverksson, 138; escapes death at the Althing, 145.

BJORN THE WHITE, of Mork: shelters Kari, 148; helps Kari take vengeance on the Burners, 149–52.

BORK STARKADARSON, one of three sons of Starkad of Thrihyrning, 57; killed by Gunnar in the Knafahills battle, 63.

BRYNJOLF THE UNRULY, kinsman of Hallgerd: kills Atli, 38; killed by Thord Freedmansson, 39.

EGIL KOLSSON, of Sandgill: brother-in-law of Starkad of Thrihyrning, 58; at the horse-fight, 59; ambushes Gunnar at Knafahills, is killed, 61–3.

EGIL THORDARSON, half-brother of Flosi, 95; father-in-law of Ingjald of Keldur, 116.

EILIF ONUNDARSON: in the confederacy against Gunnar, 75; wounded by Gunnar in the attack on Hlidarend, 77.

EINAR THVERÆING, brother of Gudmund the Powerful, supports the Njalssons, 120–2.

EIRIK, son of Earl Hakon of Norway: helps Thrain, 82; helps Grim and Helgi Njalsson, 89; succeeds his father, entertains Flosi, 158.

EYJOLF BOLVERKSSON, a lawyer, kinsman of Snorri the Priest: in Flosi's dream, 133; bribed by Flosi to defend the Burners, 138; conducts Flosi's defence, 141–4; killed by Kari in the Althing battle, 145.

FLOSI THORDARSON, chieftain, of Svinafell, leader of the Burners, son-in-law of Hall of Sida, 95; gives his niece Hildigunn in marriage to Hoskuld Hvitaness-Priest, 97; converted to Christianity, 101; learns of Hoskuld's death, is goaded by Hildigunn, goes to the Althing, 115–17; refuses a settlement, 121–3; plans the attack on the Njalssons, 124; burns Bergthorsknoll, 126–30; dreams of Lomagnup, 133; seeks support, 134; rides to the Althing, 136; bribes Eyjolf Bolverksson, 138; in court, 141–4; fights, is outlawed, 145; goes abroad, 153; returns to Iceland, 158; reconciliation with Kari, dies, 159.

GEIR THE PRIEST, chieftain, of Hlid, kinsman of Gizur the White, 46; involved by his kinsman Otkel in lawsuit again Gunnar, 49–51; prosecutes Gunnar for the killing of Otkel, 55–6; supports Mord Valgardsson against Gunnar, 66; helps Gizur prosecute Gunnar for the killing of Thorgeir Otkelsson, 73; joins the attack on Hlidarend, 75–7; makes settlement with Hogni Gunnarsson, 80.

GILLI, Earl of the Hebrides, 85; brother-in-law of Earl Sigurd of Orkney, 89; visits Sigurd, 154; host to Flosi, 157; dreams of the Battle of Clontarf, 157.

GIZUR THE WHITE, chieftain, of Mosfell, uncle of Asgrim Ellida-Grimsson, 46; involved by his kinsman Otkel in lawsuit against Gunnar, 49–51; helps prosecute Gunnar for the killing of Otkel, 55–6; father-in-law of Mord Valgardsson, 65; supports Mord against Gunnar, 66; prosecutes Gunnar for the killing of Thorgeir Otkelsson, 73; leads the attack on Hlidarend, 75–7; goes abroad, 102; brings Christianity to Iceland, 104–5; supports the Njalssons at the

HAUK EGILSSON, son of Egil Kolsson of Sandgill, 58; at the horse-fight against Gunnar, 59; killed by Gunnar in the Knafahills battle, 63.

HELGA, daughter of Njal, attends Gunnar's wedding, 34; marries Kari, 90; escapes from the Burning, 129; dies, 159.

HELGI NJALSSON, youngest son of Njal, 25; marries Thorhalla, daughter of Asgrim Ellida-Grimsson, 26–7; attends Gunnar's wedding, 34; helps kill Sigmund and Skjold, 45; supports Gunnar, 64–6; goes abroad with his brother Grim, 75, 82; saved by Kari, 83–4; escapes from Earl Hakon in Norway, 89; returns to Iceland with Kari, 90; claims compensation from Thrain, 91; helps kill Thrain in the Markar River battle, 92; attacks Lyting, 99; falls in with Mord Valgardsson, 108; helps kill Hoskuld Hvitaness-Priest, 111; seeks support at the Althing, 119; killed by Flosi at the Burning, 127–9.

HILDIGUNN, daughter of Starkad Thordarson and niece of Flosi, 95; marries Hoskuld Hvitaness-Priest, 97; finds Hoskuld dead, 112; goads Flosi to take vengeance, 116; marries Kari, 159.

HILDIGUNN THE HEALER, daughter of Starkad of Thrihyrning, 57; praises Gunnar, 58, 61, 63.

HJALTI SKEGGJASON, chieftain, of Thjorsriverdale: urges Gun-nar to make settlement after the Knafahills ambush, 66; refuses to join the attack on Gunnar, 75; blasphemes the heathen gods, goes abroad, 102; outlawed for blasphemy, brings Christianity to Iceland, 104–5; supports the Njalssons, arbitrates, 122–3; joins the hunt for the Burners, 131; searches for the bodies at Bergthors-knoll, 132; supports Kari, 137, 139–45.

HJORT HAMUNDARSON, youngest brother of Gunnar of Hlidarend, 19; killed in the Knafahills ambush, 62–3.

HOGNI GUNNARSSON, son of Gunnar of Hlidarend and Hallgerd, 59; sees apparition of his father in his burial-mound, 78; avenges his father with Skarp-Hedin's help, 79; makes settlement, marries, 80; supports Ketil of Mork, 93.

HOLMSTEIN SPAK-BERSASON, of Bersastead: supports Flosi after the Burning, 134; in the Althing battle, 145.

HOLTA-THORIR THORGEIRSSON, brother of Njal, 20; attends Gunnar's wedding, 34; father of Thorgeir Skorar-Geir, Thorleif Crow, and Thorgrim the Mighty, 20, 96.

HOSKULD DALA-KOLLSSON, of Hoskuldstead, father of Hallgerd, 1; helps his half-brother Hrut to marry Unn, 2; marries Hallgerd off to Thorvald Osvifsson, 9–10; pays compensation for Thorvald, 12; marries Hallgerd to Glum Olafsson, 13–14; pays compensation for Glum, 17; supports Hrut against Gunnar, 23–4; marries Hall-

escapes, makes settlement, 99; killed by Amundi the Blind, Hoskuld's son, 106.

MODOLF KETILSSON, one of the Burners: supports Flosi, 115; arbitrates, 122–3; joins the Burners, 124; at the Burning, 130; in Flosi's dream, 133; prosecuted at the Althing, 141; killed by Kari in the Skapt River battle, 150.

MORD FIDDLE, chieftain, of Voll, 1; betroths his daughter Unn to Hrut, 2; helps her divorce Hrut, 6–7; claims the dowry, loses to Hrut, 8; dies, 18.

MORD SIGFUSSON, fourth of the Sigfusson brothers, uncle of Gunnar: supports Flosi, 117, 124; killed by Kari in the Kerlingardale River battle, 146.

MORD VALGARDSSON, of Hof, son of Valgard the Grey and Unn, kinsman of Gunnar of Hlidarend, 25; hates Gunnar, 25, 46; attends Gunnar's wedding, 34; discovers Hallgerd's theft, 49; marries Thorkatla, daughter of Gizur the White, 65; prosecutes Gunnar, 66; plots trouble against Gunnar, 67, 70–1; joins the attack on Hlidarend, 75–7; gives Hogni Gunnarsson self-judgement, 79; opposes Christianity, 102; plots the destruction of the Njalssons and Hoskuld Hvitaness-Priest, 107; persuades the Njalssons to kill Hoskuld, takes part himself, 108–11; starts proceedings against the Njalssons, 112; pretends to join Flosi, 117, 119; joins the Njalssons, 121; supports Kari, 131; prosecutes the Burners, 135, 137, 139, 141–5.

NJAL THORGEIRSSON, of Bergthorsknoll, 20; helps Gunnar against Hrut, 21–4; discourages Gunnar from going to the Althing, 32; disapproves of Hallgerd, 33; attends Gunnar's wedding, 34; friendship with Gunnar as their wives quarrel, 35–44; gives Gunnar compensation for Sigmund, 45; helps Gunnar against Otkel, 51; gives Gunnar prophetic advice, 55; helps Gunnar in court, 56; at the horse-fight, 59; helps Gunnar in court, 64–6; saves Gunnar from attack, 69–70; helps Gunnar in court, 73–4; warns Gunnar of attack, 75; sends Skarp-Hedin to help Hogni avenge Gunnar, 78; advises his sons how to kill Thrain, 91; pays compensation for Thrain, 93; adopts Hoskuld Thrainsson, 94; seeks marriage for Hoskuld with Hildigunn, 97; founds the Fifth Court, gets chieftaincy for Hoskuld, 97; makes settlement with Hoskuld over Lyting's killing of Hoskuld Njalsson, 99; converted to Christianity, 100, 102; pays compensation for the killing of Lyting, 106; disapproves of Mord Valgardsson, 108–10; tries to make settlement over the killing of Hoskuld Hvitaness-Priest, 122; dies in the Burning, 128–30; body found, 132.

OLAF THE PEACOCK, of Hjardarholt, son of Hoskuld Dala-Kollsson, 1; attends Gunnar's wedding, 34; friendship with Gunnar, 59;

supports Gunnar against Mord Valgardsson, 66; gives Gunnar the watch-dog Sam, 70; invites Gunnar, 75.

ONUND OF TROLLWOOD, brother of Egil Kolsson of Sandgill, 58; prosecutes Gunnar, 65; joins the attack on Hlidarend, 75; kills the dog Sam, 76.

OTKEL SKARFSSON, of Kirkby, kinsman of Gizur the White: refuses Gunnar food, 47; burgled by Hallgerd, 48; refuses compensation from Gunnar, 49; prosecutes Gunnar, fails, 50–1; injures Gunnar with his spur, 53; killed by Gunnar in the Rang River battle, 54.

OZUR, uncle of Hrut, urges him to go to Norway, 2; with Hrut in Norway, 3, 5.

OZUR HROALDSSON, of Breidriver, one of the Burners: converted to Christianity, 101; arbitrates, 122; supports Flosi, 124; killed by Skarp-Hedin at the Burning, 128.

RANNVEIG, mother of Gunnar of Hlidarend, 19; criticizes Hallgerd, 36, 39, 42; sees Gunnar being killed, 77–9.

RUNOLF OF DALE, son of Ulf Aur-Priest, kinsman of Gunnar: attends Gunnar's wedding, 34; entertains Otkel before he is killed, 52–3; supports Mord Valgardsson against Gunnar, 65–6; entertains Thrain before he is killed, 92; supports Flosi, 115, 119, 121; arbitrates, 122.

SÆUNN, an old woman, foster-mother of Bergthora: prophesies the Burning, 124; dies in the Burning, 132.

SIGMUND LAMBASON, kinsman of Gunnar of Hlidarend: comes to Hlidarend, persuaded by Hallgerd to kill Thord Freedmansson, 41–2; libels the Njalssons, 44; killed by Skarp-Hedin, 45.

SIGURD HLODVISSON, Earl of Orkney: admits the Njalssons to his court, 85–6; entertains them, 89; makes Flosi a retainer, 153; agrees to help King Sigtrygg fight King Brian, 154–5; killed in the Battle of Clontarf, 157.

SIGURD LAMBASON, one of the Burners, nephew of Thrain Sigfusson; supports Flosi, 124; killed by Kari in the Kerlingardale River battle, 146.

SKAMKEL, of Lesser-Hof, friend of Otkel Skarfsson, 47; involves Otkel in trouble with Gunnar, 47–51; insults Gunnar, 53; killed by Gunnar in the Rang River battle, 54.

SKAPTI THORODDSSON, chieftain, Law-Speaker: supports Gizur the White against Gunnar, 56; institutes the Fifth Court, 97; refuses to help the Njalssons, 119; refuses to help Kari, 139; advises on law at the Althing, 142; wounded by Asgrim Ellida-Grimsson in the Althing battle, 145.

SKARP-HEDIN NJALSSON, eldest son of Njal, 25; marries Thorhild,

31; attends Gunnar's wedding, 34; kills Sigmund Lambason, Gunnar's kinsman, 45; at the horse-fight with Gunnar, 59; helps Hogni avenge Gunnar, 78–9; claims compensation from Thrain, 91; kills Thrain in the Markar River battle, 92; kills Lyting's brothers, 98–9; falls in with Mord Valgardsson, 108–10; kills his foster-brother Hoskuld Hvitaness-Priest, 111; goes to the Althing, 118; insults chieftains at the Althing, 119–20; insults Flosi, 123; dies in the Burning, 128–30.

NOTE ON THE CHRONOLOGY

Exact dating of all the events in *Njal's Saga* is impossible. There are all sorts of inconsistencies, both within the saga itself and in relation to the known historical framework of Iceland and Scandinavia.

Professor Sveinsson has shown that the chronology of the saga events was dictated by aesthetic demands, not by history. The order of event is frequently transposed (for instance, Hallgerd's first two marriages must have preceded Hrut's marriage to Unn, and we know for a fact that the institution of the Fifth Court took place some years after the conversion of Iceland to Christianity, not before it); also, some characters are introduced into the saga too early, in particular Mord Valgardsson. (Hrut could not have met Queen Gunnhild in Norway before 960, therefore Unn's second marriage, to Valgard the Grey, cannot have been much before 970; but Mord Valgardsson is busy solving the burglary at Kirkby round about 983!)

The author of *Njal's Saga*, in fact, made no real attempt to achieve consistency of historical dating, as some other saga-writers did. Year merges imperceptibly into year, decade into decade. The events as he portrays them have a busy, inexorable logic of their own, more potent than that of the calendar.

However, for the benefit of readers who may be curious to know the rough framework of the saga's fifty-five-year span, the following tentative table will be helpful. It is based on certain key dates ignores several inconsistencies, and follows the lines generally approved (with minor variations) by most scholars.

Njal born	c. 930
Hallgerd born	c. 940
Gunnar born	c. 945
Hallgerd marries Thorvald	c. 956
Hallgerd marries Glum	c. 959
Hrut goes abroad	c. 960
Hrut marries Unn	c. 962
Unn marries Valgard the Grey	c. 969
Gunnar marries Hallgerd	c. 974
Sigmund killed by Skarp-Hedin	c. 979

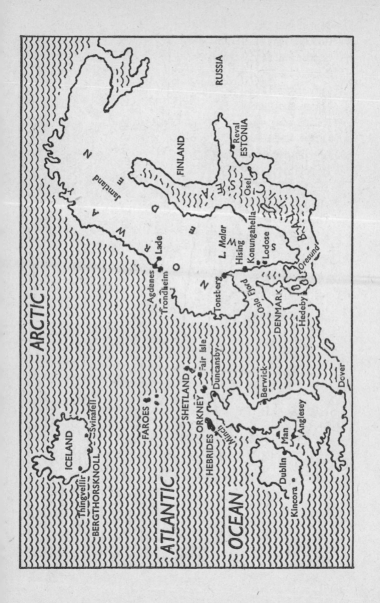

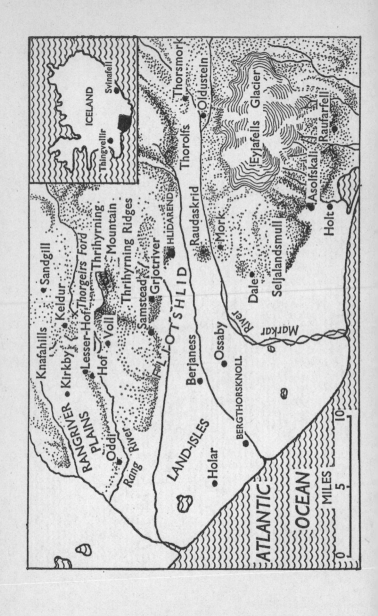

MORE ABOUT PENGUINS
AND PELICANS

Penguinews, which appears every month, contains details of all the new books issued by Penguins as they are published. From time to time it is supplemented by the *Penguin Stock List*, which is our complete list of almost 5,000 titles.

A specimen copy of *Penguinews* will be sent to you free on request. Please write to Dept EP, Penguin Books Ltd, Harmondsworth, Middlesex, for your copy.

In the U.S.A. : For a complete list of books available from Penguins in the United States write to Dept CS, Penguin Books, 625 Madison Avenue, New York, New York 10022.

In Canada : For a complete list of books available from Penguins in Canada write to Penguin Books Canada Ltd, 2801 John Street, Markham, Ontario L3R 1B4.

LAXDAELA SAGA

Translated by Magnus Magnusson
and Hermann Pálsson

Of all the great medieval Icelandic sagas, *Laxdaela Saga* (composed by an unknown author *c.* 1245) has always stirred the European imagination the most profoundly. Romantic in style, in taste and in theme, it culminates in that most enduring and timeless of human relationships in story-telling, the love triangle. Gudrun Osvif's-daughter, the imperious beauty who is forced to marry her lover's best friend, is one of the first great romantic literary heroines.

With its clerical religious learning, its courtly chivalry, its antiquarian feeling for history and its sympathy for the old heroic poetry, *Laxdaela Saga* reflects European tastes and preoccupations. But it is also intended as a national epic, giving dignity and grandeur to a young nation's past.

HRAFNKEL'S SAGA

Translated by Hermann Pálsson

All seven stories in this volume date from the thirteenth century, and exemplify the outstanding qualities of realistic fiction in medieval Iceland. Falling into two distinctive groups, three of the stories – *Hrafnkel's Saga, Thorstein the Staff-Struck*, and *Ale Hood* – are set in the pastoral society of native Iceland; the homely touch and stark realism giving the incidents a strong feeling of immediacy. The remaining four – *Hreidar the Fool, Halldor Sorrason, Audun's Story*, and *Ivar's Story* – were written without first-hand knowledge of Scandinavia, and describe the adventures of Icelandic poets and peasants at the royal courts of Norway and Denmark.

SIR GAWAIN AND THE GREEN KNIGHT
Translated by Brian Stone

Sir Gawain and the Green Knight is the masterpiece of medieval alliterative poetry. The unknown fourteenth-century author (a contemporary of Chaucer) has imbued his work with the heroic atmosphere of a saga, with the spirit of French romance, and with a Christian consciousness. It is a poem in which the virtues of a knight, Sir Gawain, triumphant in almost insuperable ordeals, are celebrated to the glory of the House of Arthur. The impact made on the reader is both magical and human, full of drama and descriptive beauty.

THE VINLAND SAGAS
THE NORSE DISCOVERY
OF AMERICA

Translated by Magnus Magnusson
and Hermann Pálsson

The two medieval Icelandic sagas translated in this volume
tell one of the most fascinating stories in the history of
exploration – the discovery of America by Norsemen, five
centuries before Christopher Columbus. In spare and
vigorous prose they record Europe's first surprised glimpse of
the eastern shores of the North American continent and the
Red Indian natives who inhabited them. The Sagas describe
how Eirik the Red founded an Icelandic colony in Greenland
and how his son, Leif the Lucky, later sailed south to explore
and if possible exploit the chance discovery by Bjarni
Herjolfsson of an unknown land.

THE PENGUIN CLASSICS

Some recent and forthcoming volumes